Slipping [illegible] ...own, the sun warm[illegible] ...upping my swollen breasts in [illegible] ..., I gently squeezed them, my nipples distending, standing proud, begging to be suckled. I liked my breasts, my nipples. I liked sucking them, having them whipped. They brought me immense pleasure.

My hands between my thighs, my fingertips tracing my swollen outer lips, running up and down my wet crack, I shuddered. My body, my temple – it was as if I'd been sleeping for a thousand years and had suddenly woken to discover my body, my cunt . . .

Also by Ray Gordon in New English Library

Arousal
House of Lust
The Uninhibited
Submission!
Haunting Lust
Depravicus
The Splits
The Degenerates
Enslaved
Girl School
Sextro
Sex Practice
Hot Sheets
Addicted

Naked Lies

Ray Gordon

nel

NEW ENGLISH LIBRARY
Hodder & Stoughton

First published in Great Britain in 1999
by Hodder and Stoughton
A division of Hodder Headline
First published in paperback in 1999
by Hodder and Stoughton

A New English Library Paperback

10 9 8 7 6 5 4 3

A CIP catalogue record is available from the British Library

ISBN 0 340 72812 4

Typeset by Hewer Ltd, Edinburgh
Printed and bound in France by
Brodard & Taupin.
Reproduced from a previously printed copy.

Hodder and Stoughton
A division of Hodder Headline
338 Euston Road
London NW1 3BH

Chapter One

I am not what I once was, nor ever again will be. Changes around me, changes in others, rippling but relentless changes in myself, were to transform me. Like a hapless butterfly in the summer sun I was to be caught, laid bare, dissected – violated beyond belief. My fragile peacock colour, my delicate femininity, my very soul abused, erased, I was to die and metamorphose into an entirely different creature.

What creature? To this day, I am unsure. Winged or in a cage, or in a cage with wings, I am ignorant as to the nature of my being. All I know is that I am a creature of great intrigue, of boundless heights and depths, of great perversity. Do I wallow in the mire? Or soar in a clear blue sky? Only time will tell.

Never would I have believed that a plot was being drawn against me. A wicked plot to rock my very core – to use me for debased sex. My naked body chained, whipped with a leather strap, my buttocks thrashed with a bamboo cane, every orifice plundered, I was to travel far beyond the boundaries of what society believes to be normal sex.

But what *is* normal sex? Is it the missionary position once weekly? The nightly entwining of naked bodies in sixty-nine? And what is love? Are sex and love so tightly bound together that they can never be detached? Since my transformation, to me the two are as alien to each other as the Earth and Mars. Before, I thought I knew love, that tender alliance expressed through sex. Now I know only sex. Cold sex, as devoid of the warmth of love as midwinter.

Do I miss love? For the sake of my soul, I would like to believe so. And what of sex – cold sex? Sadly, gloriously, this new, perverse creature cannot live without it. Will it always be so? I sometimes wonder in my chains. Again, only time will show.

Casting my mind back to more conventional days, I wonder who was more devious than who in perpetrating the plan against me. Who the wickeder? That fateful summer morning almost a year ago was only the beginning of a plan so incredible, so devious, that even now I find it difficult to comprehend. That bright, sunny, normal Monday morning when a loud knock sounded on the back door and changed me, my life, forever, will remain etched as on granite in my memory . . .

Who on earth would go round to the back of the house rather than ring the front doorbell? The dustman? I pondered, as that fateful knock sounded. Tossing the sponge into the sink as I turned on my heels from the washing-up, I dried my hands hurriedly on a tea towel. No, the dustman called on Tuesdays.

'Oh,' I smiled coyly as I opened the door to Den, our new neighbour. Wondering what he wanted as he brushed his dark hair away from his deep-set eyes, I opened the door wider. 'Er . . . how are you?' I asked. Clutching a magazine, he looked over my shoulder as if making sure I was alone.

'Couldn't be better,' he grinned, brusquely pushing past me into the kitchen.

I was taken aback. He'd only moved in a couple of months previously and had become pretty friendly with my husband Mat. I knew him only to say hallo to, perhaps mention the weather should we pass in the street. We certainly weren't on familiar enough terms for him to barge into my kitchen like that!

What did he want? I again wondered. He knew that Mat was at work, so what was he doing here? A friendly visit to get to know me, perhaps? Closing the door, I thought about offering him a cup of tea, but he didn't allow me the opportunity for such an English pleasantry.

'You're a very attractive woman,' he remarked coolly. 'A very sexy woman.' My eyes widened at his impertinent remark. So much for the friendly visit! 'You have a good body, Jane.'

'Er . . . I'm . . . I'm busy right now,' I stammered, surprised and mystified by his brash manner.

'The washing-up can wait,' he winked, glancing at the dishes piled in the sink. His eyes caught mine, his stare almost accusing. 'I have something that'll interest you far more than washing-up. Take a look at this,' he grinned, eagerly opening the magazine.

Standing beside him, I nervously hooked tendrils of my long blonde hair behind my ears. His masculine frame towering above me, I realized how good-looking he was. Wearing a crisp white shirt and tight blue jeans, he radiated an air of male prowess, strength, that I'd not known before. But what was it he wanted to show me? A holiday brochure? A car magazine?

'I don't want to see that!' I gasped, focusing my startled eyes on a familiar-looking naked girl sprawled across the centrefold, her open vagina crudely exhibited between her parted thighs.

'Don't you recognize her?' he asked surprisedly.

I paused to take stock of my whirling thoughts. 'No, of course I don't!'

'You should, Jane.' He chuckled, holding the magazine closer to my face. 'After all, it's you.'

My stomach sank as he sat on one of the four pine chairs and spread the magazine out on the table. A wicked glint in his eyes as he looked up, he scrutinized me, my pert breasts teasing my tight blouse, my long shapely legs. Noticing him staring at my thighs, I began to tremble as fear gripped me. Alone in the house, anything could happen. Alone, defenceless, vulnerable . . . But this was my neighbour! Surely he wouldn't try anything?

A chill of foreboding ran down my spine as his lustful gaze continued to rest on my thighs. I couldn't believe this was happening. Den, showing me a dirty magazine, accusing me of being the naked tart blatantly displaying all she had between her legs . . . I tried to convince myself that I was dreaming, but the horror was all too real.

'Well?' he finally smiled, dragging his lascivious gaze from my quivering thighs, caressing the model's ice-cubed nipples with his fingertip.

'Well what?' I asked shakily, my heart racing wildly.

'Admit it, Jane – it *is* you, isn't it?'

'No!' I gasped, my breathing unsteady as my anxiety rocketed.

'How old are you? Twenty-five, twenty-six? I reckon you were about eighteen when this was taken. Nice firm tits, tight cunt . . .'

'Take your filthy magazine and get out of my house!' I spat, flinging the back door open. Glimpsing the garden, at least I now had an escape route should he . . .

'It's a shame you've adopted that attitude,' he sighed. 'I really thought . . . Oh well, I'll show Mat the photograph. I don't suppose he knows that his twee little wife was once a porn queen.'

'I was *not* a porn . . .'

'You can see from a mile off that it's you, Jane. Look, the hair, the features . . . Any fool can see that it's you.'

'It is *not* me! What the hell do you think I am?'

'I don't know what you are now, but I can see what you were then.' His eyes seemed to deepen, reflecting a base inner desire as he stared hard at me. 'So, what's it to be?'

'What do you mean?'

'Do I show Mat, or . . .'

'Or what?'

'Or are you going to pose for me, the way you posed for the photographer?'

My face flushed, my hands trembling uncontrollably, I closed the door and sank into a chair opposite my unscrupulous neighbour. Mat had always been extremely suspicious and possessive – jealous in the extreme. The blatant little beauty could well have been my double. If he were to see the photograph . . . My chest tight, my stomach churning, I swallowed hard. He'd never believe me if I denied all knowledge of the lewd picture, that was for sure! Instinctively, I knew that this was the beginning of a horrendous nightmare.

Gazing at the pouting girl again, I focused on her vaginal lips, devoid of public hair, swollen in arousal. It was inconceivable! What the hell was this man trying to do to me? My heart banging hard against my chest, I rested my arms on the table and clasped my quivering hands. I had to put a stop to this nightmare, and quickly.

'It's not me!' I asserted firmly.

'Take your blouse off,' Den instructed me unashamedly, grinning as he ogled me across the table, my nipples clearly defined by the tight satin of my blouse.

'No! Look, Den . . .'

'No, Jane, *you* look! This could ruin your marriage. If Mat found out that you were nothing more than a tart, your marriage would be over.' He paused, obviously giving me time to think – time to sweat. 'Well, what's it to be?' he finally repeated.

'You can't do this! Christ, you can't force me to . . .'

'You're right, I can't *force* you to do anything. But I suggest you do as I ask or you'll find your marriage destroyed.'

Triumphantly, he flicked over the page of the magazine, displaying a photograph of the girl bending over, her bulging vaginal lips nestling between the indents at the top of her shapely thighs, perfectly symmetrical below her rounded buttocks. 'Look, I'll make it easy for you,' he smirked, as if showing me some sympathy. 'Just take your blouse and bra off.'

My trembling fingers toying with my hair, my eyes wide with fear, I stared hard at my perverse neighbour. This had been a normal Monday morning, washing up the breakfast things after Mat had left for work, my best friend, Carole, coming round later for coffee . . . And then, bang! My whole world blown into oblivion within minutes.

'If you think I'm going to . . .'

'It's up to you,' Den interrupted me. 'Either you do as I ask, or Mat sees the photographs.'

'But it's not . . .'

'Of course it's you! Stop playing games and admit it.'

Admit it? Perhaps it was best to confess, I pondered in my rising confusion. He'd go on and on, insisting that it was me, and then he'd show Mat and cause no end of trouble. Gazing through glazed eyes at the glossy photograph, a small voice echoed within me. *Own up, Jane. Own up.* Was I listening to my thoughts?

'You were quite a tart in your teens. There was Brian Johnson, you shared a flat with him. Then there was Derek, you lived with him for some time.'

'How do you know that?' I asked incredulously.

'I know more about you than you think. I'll bet Mat knows nothing of your sordid past.'

'My past is *not* sordid.'

'There was James, the black guy you screwed around with.'

'How do you know about James?'

'As I said, I know more about you than you think. Admit that it's you, Jane.'

'I was at university,' I sighed eventually, wondering at my sanity. 'There was this photographer and . . . I needed the money.'

'So you stripped off and sold your body.'

'I didn't sell my . . . It was only photographic work.'

'And I have the evidence, Jane.'

'Look, if you show Mat, he'll . . .'

'I know only too well what he'll do. Just your blouse and bra, that's all I ask.'

How on earth did he know about my past relationships? He must have met someone who had known me during my teenage years, I decided. What else did he know about me? Hopefully, not the relationship I'd enjoyed with a considerably older man. If Mat were to discover that, he'd go insane with jealousy!

My fingers playing with the top button of my blouse, I knew that Den would come back again and again. It wouldn't stop at my blouse and bra, it would go on – my skirt, stockings, panties, and then . . . And then sex. I wanted to die.

'Come on!' he coaxed me, turning back to the centrefold. 'Let's see how your tits compare. A sort of before-and-after!' he chuckled.

'Den, I . . .'

'Just your blouse and bra. It's not a lot to ask, is it?'

'Will you give me the magazine if I do it?' I murmured, astonished that I was even considering complying with his lewd demand.

'We'll see.'

'But you could come here every day and insist that I . . .'

'I said, we'll see.'

Slowly releasing the top button of my blouse, I moved my fingers down to the next, my eyes transfixed on Den as I continued my enforced undressing. Would he go once he'd seen my breasts? I wondered fearfully, strangely aware of my favourite song playing on the radio. From now on, the song would bring different memories flooding back – not, as before, sweet memories of my honeymoon but acrid hauntings of my depraved neighbour ogling my naked breasts.

Apprehension swamped me as I imagined baring my breasts, displaying my nipples. Again, I thought of Mat, his suspicious mind, what he'd say if he were to see the photographs. He'd always questioned me about other men, whether I'd fancied so-and-so at a party or fantasized about other men when we made love. He'd been going on about pornography recently, the way girls demeaned themselves – he'd never believe that the model wasn't me. As if an icy finger was running down my spine, cold fear gripped me. Did I have a choice? No, I decided I didn't. Blackmailers afford their victims no choice.

Pulling my blouse open, I slipped the garment off my shoulders, revealing my straining lace bra. Images of Mat formed in my racked mind as I placed my blouse on the table – his smiling face, his immaculately groomed brown hair. He'd be back that evening to kiss me, ask me how my day had been. What would I say? What *could* I say?

'Go on,' Den urged me, staring at the valley of my deep cleavage. 'You're nearly there.' Nearly where? I wondered. Nearly showing my breasts, my nipples? Nearly committing adultery, for God's sake!

Reaching behind my back as I supported myself on my

trembling legs, I unhooked my bra. The silk cups falling away from my firm breasts, my sensitive nipples stood erect, proud, from the darkening discs of my areolae. Remorse engulfed me as I looked down at my breast buds. What on earth was I doing? Hanging my bra over the back of the chair, I stood before my neighbour as he rose to his feet, my face flushing with embarrassment as he scrutinized my mammary spheres, my brown milk teats. A solitary tear rolled down my cheek.

'Nice, very nice!' he praised me. 'You have wonderful tits.'

'May I dress now?' I asked softly, my head hung in shame.

'No, not yet.'

'I've done as you asked!' I returned, lifting my head and tossing my hair over my shoulder defiantly. 'What more do you want?' I knew what he wanted. What all men want.

He grinned as he focused his glinting eyes on my erect nipples, obviously contemplating my question. I tried to produce more tears in the futile hope that he'd feel some compassion, but they wouldn't come. Desperately trying to find the inner strength to resist the fiend, I found only weakness.

'Your nipples are nice, long – suckable.'

'No! Don't you dare to . . .'

'Think of your marriage, Jane.'

I did think of my marriage as Den cupped my breasts in his warm hands as if weighing them, squeezing my globes, my nipples distending, pointing accusingly towards his perilously close, lecherous countenance. Living in the beautiful old country cottage my aunt had left me, I had a loving husband who worked hard in London to support our enviable lifestyle. With his-and-her BMWs, at least two holidays abroad each year, an abundance of love and a warm sex life between us, our marriage was good. After five years together, we had it all . . . yet here I was destroying all we'd built! The sensations permeating my firm breasts as Den tweaked my nipples, I winced as I thought of my sex life with Mat.

Although there was no swinging from chandeliers, no all-night sessions of burning passion and desire, we enjoyed the closeness, the warmth of love and friendship our lovemaking brought. Mat was the perfect gentleman – considerate, unselfish, never overlooking my needs. He'd take me to orgasm during foreplay, ensure that I derived satisfaction when we made love. Could I face him again after this – live with a lie? Could I live with myself, let alone Mat?

As Den sucked my milk teat into his hot mouth, his teeth gently sinking into my sensitive brown tissue, I jumped. 'No!' I squealed, pulling away. 'That's not part of the deal!'

'Deal?' he frowned, pinching and twisting my nipples painfully.

'You said . . .'

'I told you to take your blouse and bra off, I didn't say anything else. There was no *deal*, as you put it.'

'But . . .'

'Does Mat suck your nipples?'

'Piss off!' I hissed, holding my hand to my head as confusion fogged my tormented mind.

'Oh, don't be like that! Doesn't he lick your clitoris to orgasm?'

His crude words reverberating through the haze of my mind, I squeezed my eyes shut as he again engulfed my nipple in his drooling mouth. His zealous tongue snaked around my bud, teasing, tasting. Breathing in his unfamiliar aftershave, I wondered what the hell I was doing standing half-naked in my kitchen with my neighbour suckling my naked breasts. How could I allow this blatant violation of my body? Opening my eyes, looking down at his lips pressed against my startled areola, I watched in disbelief as he sucked and mouthed on my nipple.

It wouldn't end there, I knew. His hands moving down to my smooth stomach, tickling my warm flesh, he caressed my navel. His fingers descended further, pressing against the softness of my sex mound through my skirt. No, it wouldn't end there!

'That's enough!' I cried as he slipped a finger between my skirt and my stomach.

'Enough is never enough,' he murmured, my nipple slipping from his mouth as he stood upright and gazed into my eyes, his strong, warm hands clutching the gentle curves of my hips.

'Den, please!'

'Please what?'

'Please go!'

'Already? I'll tell you what, let's go through to the lounge and . . .'

'No!'

'Listen, you can have the magazine. But I want you to pose for me first, like you did for the photographer.'

I hesitated. 'If I do, you'll give me the magazine and then leave?' I asked shakily. I must have been insane!

'I promise.'

Leading him through the hall, I knew that his promise was worthless. He was a monster, an evil man, and he'd stop at nothing to have his wicked way with me. As I stood meekly in the centre of the lounge, he sat on the sofa, grinning, smirking, gazing greedily at my naked breasts. I felt dirty, demeaned.

'Why are you doing this?' I asked, aware of my wet nipples stiffening in the cool air of the lounge.

'I was unpacking a tea chest and the magazine dropped to

the floor. I thought I recognized the face and when I passed you in the street, I knew it was you.'

'So you decided to blackmail me.'

'Not blackmail, Jane. We're just having some fun. Harmless fun while Mat's at work.'

Perhaps he *would* give me the magazine after his fun, I pondered, naive though the notion was. Harmless fun while Mat was at work? Catching his gaze, I didn't think he was the sort of man to force himself upon me. My next-door neighbour . . . I couldn't envisage him raping me. After all, he'd said that he couldn't *force* me to do anything. Recalling a true-life story I'd once read in a magazine, I shuddered.

'How much do you value your marriage?' he leered.

I folded my arms across my trembling breasts. 'What sort of question is that?'

'A simple one. What lengths will you go to in order to save your marriage?'

The words fell effortlessly. 'I'll pose for you.'

'How will you pose for me?'

'I'll pose like the magazine picture.'

'Go on, then. Pose for me. Just like you did for the photographer.'

Stepping out of my white heels, I tugged my short lycra skirt down my long legs, revealing the triangular patch of red material covering my full sex lips. Succumbing to blackmail was a grave mistake, I knew as I kicked the garment aside. But I couldn't see that I had a choice. If Mat were to see the magazine . . . It was a mistake I'd make only once, I promised myself.

Den was weak, pathetic in his male weakness, I reflected as I fiddled with my suspender belt. He wasn't a blackmailer at heart – just in the vicinity of his trousers. Most likely he couldn't help himself, couldn't control his instinctual male desires. To appease the pitiful creature I'd pose for him, turn my alluring naked body this way and that – then serve him his marching orders.

There'd be nothing he could do, I reasoned, other than show Mat the magazine. But I felt that he wouldn't resort to that. He knew as well as me that, once the pussy was out of the bag, the game would be over. All the time Den had the incriminating photographs, he had a chance to gawp at my naked body. Showing my husband would only serve to wreck that chance. Somehow, I'd get my hands on the magazine and destroy it.

But was I destroying myself? I wondered as I unclipped my suspender belt and reluctantly rolled my black stockings down my legs. Wearing only my panties, a pang of guilt stabbed my conscience as I looked around the lounge. The marital home. Mat's armchair. The coffee table where he placed his glass of scotch every evening . . . I couldn't do it, I decided. Couldn't bring myself to unveil the most intimate part of my body before this virtual stranger. The room was watching me, my adultery.

'Come on, show me your cunt,' Den ordered me crudely, a hint of urgency in his dark voice as he noticed my hesitation. 'I want to see where Mat sticks his cock. Show me your juicy cunt.'

'Den, I . . .'

'Remember that I know a hell of a lot about you, your past. You lived in Shropshire until you were thirteen. You then moved to Dorset and . . .'

'How do you know all this?'

'That's my secret. Now, show me your cunt.'

The obscene word battering my swirling mind as I stood before my neighbour, my stomach somersaulting, I knew I'd gone too far to turn back. I'd crossed the bridge, transgressed the threshold of choice. Picturing the photograph in the magazine, I imagined sprawling out on the floor, my legs open, my femininity crudely displayed. Mat had never used the word *cunt*.

Just this once, the inner voice urged me as I slipped my thumbs between the tight elastic of my panties and my curvaceous hips. *Just this once*. My trimmed blonde pubes coming into view as I eased my panties down, I hung my head as shame and guilt engulfed me.

'Keep going,' Den prodded coarsely as he moved forward in his excitement on the sofa. 'That's it, pull your knickers down like a naughty little tart and show me your cunt.'

Taking a deep breath, I lowered my panties to my knees and stood upright, my pinken sex crack clearly visible beneath my sparse pubes. My scant scarlet shield dropping to my ankles, I kicked the garment aside, again imagining posing for my lecherous spectator. The degradation, the humiliation of lying on the floor with my legs wide open . . . I knew I couldn't do it.

'Very nice!' Den breathed, focusing his lustful eyes on my inner petals protruding alluringly from my moist sex valley. I winced, closing my eyes as I sensed his gaze burning into my most intimate place. Only Mat had ever seen me there since our marriage, feasted his eyes on my vaginal smile. But now? Now, as in the magazine photographs, my once-sacrosanct temple was blatantly on display, crudely exhibited. Was I a tart? I felt so.

'Stand with your feet as wide apart as you can,' Den ordered me, his prurient gaze glued to my sex slit. Trembling, I parted my feet, knowing that my secret valley was opening, my moist inner folds unfurling. Humiliated as I sensed my lubricious juices bubbling between my pussy lips, I prayed that he wouldn't take the glistening sex fluid as a sign of arousal.

'Open your cunt lips,' he instructed me with no hint of

compassion, his arousal obvious by the massive bulge in the crotch of his tight jeans. 'I want to see inside your cunt.'

'Do you know how you make me feel?' I asked shakily.

'Good?'

'Evil.'

'Then be evil!' he chuckled.

My fingers trembled as I moved my hands to my lower stomach. Then, as if suddenly waking from a dream, I realized what I was doing. 'Go on, pull your cunt lips wide apart and show me your cock hole,' he breathed as I snatched my hands to my sides. 'You don't want Mat to discover your sordid past, do you?'

Through my haze of horror I became aware of a car pulling up in the driveway. I almost fainted in my fear, my iniquity, as Den leapt up from the sofa and dashed to the window. 'Christ, it's Mat!' he cursed through gritted teeth, throwing me a parting malevolent leer before dashing from the room. I stood motionless in my horror, frozen to the spot as the back door slammed shut and my blackmailer made his escape. Mat's key turning in the front-door lock, I was impelled to look about me, at my skirt and stockings strewn across the lounge floor.

'Jane!' Mat called in his familiar homecoming tones, closing the front door.

'In here!' I returned shakily, snatching up my clothes.

'Christ, what are you doing standing in the lounge starkers?' he gasped as he entered the room to confront my naked, curvaceous body.

'I . . . I was about to take a shower when . . . What are you doing home?' I blustered, tugging my skirt up, veiling my disconcerted pussy.

'I had to go and see a client. He's local, so I thought I'd call in for coffee. Are you all right, Jane? Your face is very flushed.'

'Yes, I'm fine.'

'Why undress in the lounge?'

'I thought I heard the phone and . . .' Remembering that my bra and blouse were in the kitchen, I forced a smile. 'I'll go and put the kettle on,' I said, brushing past him.

The magazine had gone, I noticed as I hurried into the kitchen and slipped my blouse on. Den had taken the incriminating evidence, no doubt to return and have me strip naked again. From now on, I realized intuitively, the nightmare could only get worse.

As Mat appeared in the doorway, suspicion reflected in his brown eyes as he scrutinized me, I did my best to appear cool and calm. I dared not fuel his suspicion by showing tell-tale signs of the anxiety and guilt that were flooding my mind, drowning me. Forcing the picture of Den's mouth engulfing my nipple to the dark corners of my thoughts, I took a deep breath as Mat sauntered over to me.

'Why is your bra over the chair?' he asked suspiciously as I filled the kettle.

'It's to be washed. You don't mind if I wash my bra, do you?' I smiled with an air of innocence that surprised me.

'No, no, of course I don't mind.'

Mat perched himself on the edge of the table as I took two cups from the cupboard and opened a jar of Nescafé. I felt his eyes boring into me as I spooned coffee into the cups – boring into my soul. But there was no way that he could read it, I reasoned with myself. He'd never know of my illicit striptease act – that I'd showed Den my cunt. *Cunt*. I hated the word.

I'd always dressed provocatively for Mat, ensuring that he glimpsed my scanty panties as I made myself comfortable in the armchair, allowing him a peek of my nipples as my blouse fell open. But that was our secret, our private game. Not once during my marriage had I ever dreamed of displaying my naked body to another man.

Recalling my treacherous disrobing as the kettle boiled, Den's wide eyes as I'd unveiled my vaginal crack, a mixture of fear and remorse overwhelmed me. Guilt swamping me as Mat stood behind me, holding my hips and kissing my neck, a shudder ran down my spine. For five years I'd been faithful, never even dreaming about other men, let alone . . . But I'd not sullied my body, I consoled myself. Until Den's crude approach, I'd not allowed another man to touch me. Never in a million years would I have done that! As Mat slipped his hands up my skirt and cupped my naked buttocks, I jumped.

'Den!' I cried, immediately realizing my mistake.

'Den?' Mat echoed as I turned guiltily to face him.

'Den, he . . . I spoke to him earlier. He was in his front garden.'

'What did he have to say?'

'Not a lot, he just mentioned the weather. There's your coffee.'

'Thanks. Why mention his name?'

'I was only going to say that I'd seen him.'

'Oh, right. So, what have you been up to?'

Was he testing me? No, of course he wasn't! He was only making conversation, asking what I'd been up to. What *had* I been up to? My stomach sank as I imagined Mat walking into the lounge and discovering me standing naked before another man. God, what the hell had I done?

What I'd done had been immoral, wrong, and would haunt me forever, I knew. But I'd had no choice. It wasn't as if I'd stripped of my own free will, displayed my feminine intimacy out of my own lust. *Blackmailed, forced, coerced* . . . The whispered words comforted me. I was innocent in my guilt.

'I have to go up north tomorrow,' Mat said, sipping his coffee. 'I'll be away for the night, I'm afraid.'

'Away?'

'It can't be helped.'

'You've never had to stay away before.'

'There's a problem with . . . I won't bore you with the details. You'll be OK alone, won't you? I mean, it's only for one night.'

'Yes, yes, I suppose so.'

Alone? If Den were to discover that Mat was away for the night, I *wouldn't* be alone! But I didn't *have* to answer the door to Den, did I? With the house locked, the curtains drawn, I'd be safe enough while Mat was away. Again, I pictured myself naked, standing before my neighbour, displaying my intimacy. But it had only been once, and that was the way it was going to stay. I'd not succumb to my blackmailer's demands again.

'You say the phone rang?' Mat asked.

'I thought I heard it ringing when I was upstairs.'

'Why not answer it in the bedroom? Why come all the way downstairs?'

'I . . . I wanted to check the back door before I had a shower, I thought I'd left it open.'

As Mat finished his coffee and placed his cup in the sink, I caught his gaze again. He seemed different, as if he knew of my wicked indiscretion. But he couldn't know, could he? *I* was different, I decided. Different in my guilt. I pondered on the word *guilt*. Blackmailed, forced, coerced . . . I'd stripped in front of my neighbour. Whatever the reason, I'd laid myself bare to a virtual stranger. I was guilty.

'I'd better be going,' Mat smiled, kissing my cheek. 'I'll see you this evening.'

'All right. I thought we'd have steak.'

'That'll be nice. I'll pick up a bottle of red wine on the way home. About seven, OK?'

'OK.'

As Mat drove off, I became acutely aware of my bare pussy. Alone in the house, I felt vulnerable, completely defenceless. Den would hear Mat's car back out of the drive and . . . Locking the back door, I dashed into the lounge to retrieve my panties and cover my nakedness. But I couldn't find them.

'Shit!' I cursed, my mind swirling with a million thoughts. Carole would be arriving for coffee soon and I hadn't even done the washing-up. But dirty plates were the least of my worries. Dirty tricks, more likely! My panic rising, I returned to the kitchen and checked the back door again. It was locked – I was safe, secure. I had to calm down and relax.

Tossing my bra into the washing machine, I looked about me feverishly. There was no evidence of my disgusting disrobing, no tell-tale signs – only dreadful images of my exhibitionism careering through my tortured mind. Carole would never know, Mat would never know – my sordid secret was safe. But where were my panties?

Taking a deep breath to compose myself, I stood at the sink to finish the washing-up, desperately trying to push the morning's events to the back of my mind. As the phone rang, I dropped a glass, nearly jumping out of my skin as it smashed loudly in the sink.

'God, I'm a nervous wreck!' I breathed, dashing into the hall and lifting the receiver.

'Jane, it's me.' Den's voice was dark, menacing. 'I see Mat's gone.'

'Yes, but he'll be back in about ten minutes.'

'No, he won't. I've been thinking, why don't you come round and see me?'

'No! Mat will be back soon and I have a friend coming round for coffee.'

'OK, there's no rush. I'm only next door, so we'll have plenty of opportunities to . . .'

'You took the magazine. You said that you'd . . .'

'For safe keeping, Jane. I mean, we don't want Mat to see it, do we? We don't want him discovering your sordid past.'

'You told me you'd give me the magazine.'

'I have your panties here. They smell nice, a fresh, girlie aroma.'

'Den, I'm warning you . . .'

'And they're beautifully stained!'

'Den, if you . . . There's the doorbell, it'll be my friend.'

'I'll ring you later, my horny little sexpot.'

'No!'

Shakily replacing the receiver, I opened the front door, forcing a smile as I invited Carole in. 'Are you OK?' she asked, immediately realizing that something was wrong as she stepped into the hall.

'Yes, of course!' I laughed. A nervous laugh.

'You look very flushed.'

'I'm fine. Come through and I'll put the kettle on.'

I tried to compose myself as she made herself comfortable at the kitchen table. I was showing signs of anxiety, guilt, and I didn't want her asking any searching questions. But it was obvious that something was badly amiss. My face burning, my hands trembling, I was far from my usual jovial self. Twinkling in the light, the glass shards winked at me from the sink as I filled the kettle.

'I've not been feeling too well,' I finally offered in way of an explanation.

'I thought you looked off-colour. Have you got a temperature?'

'Just a tummy bug, I think. So, how are things with you?'

'Fine. John's up for promotion again, which is good.'

'Do you reckon he'll get it?'

'Yes, I think he . . .'

'Have you ever been unfaithful?' I thought aloud, wishing I hadn't.

'Unfaithful? Why do you ask?'

'I . . . I heard something on the radio about infidelity,' I lied. 'It was quite interesting.'

'No, I haven't. There was a friend of John's who fancied me, but that was a long time ago. Nothing happened, of course. Have you?'

'Have I what?'

'Been unfaithful.'

'Er . . . No, no, of course I haven't!'

Had I? Intercourse was the criterion I'd always held to define unfaithfulness, infidelity. Since marrying Mat, I'd not had intercourse with another man. I'd never allowed another man to touch me. Den had looked – but not touched. I hadn't been unfaithful – had I?

Passing Carole a cup of coffee, I scrutinized her. In her early twenties, with long black glossy hair, she was extremely attractive. Would *she* have stripped before her lewd neighbour? I wondered, eyeing her firm breasts swelling her tight blouse. In the same situation, would she have complied with her blackmailer's demands? Probably not. Definitely not!

'Have you ever done anything you regret?' I pursued, turning the radio off and sitting opposite her.

She frowned, cocking her head to one side. 'How do you mean?'

'Well, anything you'd rather John didn't know about.'

'No, I don't think so. What are you getting at?'

'Oh, I don't know. I've been thinking, that's all.'

'What's happened, Jane? There's something wrong, I can tell.'

'A tummy bug, like I said, that's all.'

'No, it's not that.'

'I was just thinking back to my teens when . . . I suppose we all did things in our teens that we'd rather not remember.'

'When I was sixteen, there was this boy . . .' Carole hesitated, letting out a giggle as she obviously recalled something wicked. 'Well, as you said, we've all done things we'd rather not remember.'

'It's funny, isn't it? I mean, the things life throws at you out of the blue . . .'

'Are you OK with Mat?'

'Yes, never better.'

OK with Mat? Yes, I decided, I was OK with my husband. What had happened earlier that morning would never happen again, I promised myself for the umpteenth time. No matter what Den threatened or did, never would I demean myself like that again. Never would I display my naked body to another man, no matter what the consequences.

Carole didn't stay as long as usual. Making some feeble excuse, she finished her coffee and stood up. She was suspicious, I knew – but suspicious about what? Again, I told myself that no one could possibly know what I'd done, and no one would ever discover my sordid secret.

'I'd better dash,' Carole smiled, moving towards the kitchen door. 'I have a lot to do today.'

'Yes, all right. I'll see you tomorrow.'

'I'll ring you.'

When she'd gone, I flopped onto the sofa in the lounge, contemplating my day. I'd go into town, buy something to cheer myself up. Some new clothes, I decided, recalling a burgundy velvet dress I'd seen in Boyd's window. I'd wear it for Mat that evening – appease my guilt by dressing nicely for my man.

But the vivid images of Den wouldn't leave my mind.

However much I tried to push all thoughts of him away, he was still there, scrutinizing my curvaceous body, his dark eyes devouring my feminine intimacy. Lifting my skirt, I parted my thighs, examining my vaginal crack, my pink, petalled flora.

Like a reflection, I saw Den in the soft, glistening folds. He'd seen me there, fed his hungry, lustful eyes on my intimacy, my most secret place. Pulling my sex lips wide apart I gazed at my clitoris, imagining Mat licking me there, transporting me to orgasm. Can clocks turn back?

'Damn!' I cursed, tugging my skirt down as the phone rang. Leaping up and grabbing the receiver, I prayed that it wasn't Den again. It could be anyone, I rationalized, pressing the receiver to my ear. My mother, a friend . . . anyone.

'Hi,' Den whispered huskily. 'It's me again.'

'Den . . .'

'I noticed your friend leave so I thought I'd give you a ring.'

'What for?'

'To have a chat, of course. I've been looking through my mags and I've found two more with your photographs in. There's Miss December and Miss July – both *very* naughty, I must say!'

'What do you want?' I asked, knowing full well what he wanted!

'What do I want? I want to look at you, Jane. I want to see your lovely cunt, your beautiful tits.'

'Well, you can't!'

'But I can. You don't seem to understand that I have the incriminating evidence of your more colourful days. I'm holding your marriage in the balance.'

'No, you're not! Look, I don't care if you show Mat. He won't believe . . .'

'Are you going to gamble your marriage on a whim?'

'It's not a whim.'

'Don't forget that I have your panties. How will you explain to your husband that I have your stained panties?'

'You can't prove that they're mine.'

'True, but he'll be somewhat suspicious, won't he? I mean, the photographs, your dirty knickers . . . You'd be taking quite a risk.'

'If you think you can come round here whenever you want and . . .'

'I don't *think*, Jane – I *know*. OK, this is the deal. I'll keep your filthy secret, but you'll do everything I ask in return.'

'Never!'

'Think about it, Jane – think very, very carefully.'

'I don't have to think about it!'

Slamming the phone down, I wondered what to do as I ambled into the kitchen. I should have denied all knowledge of the bloody pictures, just laughed it off. But it was too late for that now, I knew as I sat at the table, my head slumped in my hands. I'd as good as committed adultery. I'd stripped before my neighbour, exposed my intimate sex flesh . . . It was too late to turn back now.

Agonizing on what to do for the best as I walked aimlessly through the hall, I noticed an envelope on the doormat. Den? I pondered tremulously, tearing it open. Unfolding the sheet of paper, I was shocked to read the cruel words. *You filthy tart*. Surely Den wouldn't bother to send me a note like that? But who else knew what I'd done? No one could possibly know, I decided. A wave of emotional devastation hitting me, I thought I would drown in my river of tears.

Chapter Two

Mat had packed his case and left by eight the following morning. Alone in my bed, with my turbulent thoughts, I pictured Den. He would have heard Mat's car back out of the drive, his cue to call on his victim and make his lewd demands. But I wouldn't answer the door, I decided. He could knock and knock, ring and ring until his perverse penis and sperm-heavy testicles jangled – but I wouldn't succumb.

I'd not left the house since Den's visit the previous morning. Feeling vulnerable, I hadn't even driven into town to buy the velvet dress. I'd thought Den might be watching my every move, might follow me and . . . Realizing that I was becoming paranoid, I leaped out of bed.

Trying to plan my day, I wandered into the bathroom and took a shower. A quiet day, I decided – housework, reading . . . Massaging the soap into my fleshy sex folds, again, images of standing naked in the lounge before my vile neighbour filled my mind. It was like a recurring dream, a nightmare that wouldn't go away. But yesterday was gone – dead. Although the incredible events were real enough, I vowed never again to succumb to Den.

Refreshed from my shower, I wandered downstairs in my dressing gown and filled the kettle. The kitchen seemed different somehow, probably because I'd stood in that very room with my naked breasts displayed to Den and allowed him to suck my nipples into his treacherous mouth. The lounge had seemed different the night before. Mat sitting in his chair with his scotch, me on the sofa, I'd recalled Den there, gazing at my naked body, my pussy. I had felt guilty in the extreme. But it would soon become a distant memory, I consoled myself. What had happened was history, never to be repeated. Does time heal?

The phone rang as I poured the coffee, but I ignored it. He wouldn't get to me, no matter how persistent he was. I wouldn't answer the phone or open the door. I'd stay in the house, safe and secure behind locked doors. The nightmare was over.

I mooched back and forth from the kitchen to the lounge, making more coffee, watching TV. Chat shows, phone-ins . . . everyone had their problems, it seemed. Should *I* phone in? Ten o'clock passed, eleven . . . I felt hemmed in. The summer sun was hot, beckoning – I wanted to spend time in the garden, relax on the patio in my bikini. But *he* was next door – lurking, spying, waiting.

'This is ridiculous!' I finally breathed, flinging the back door open. 'I'll not be a prisoner in my own home!' Walking across the lawn, the sun warming me through my dressing gown, I turned and glanced up at Den's house. All looked quiet and peaceful. Perhaps he was out? I pondered. He worked from home as a financial consultant, but he might have gone out to see a client.

Wandering down to the end of the garden, I stood beneath the old apple tree, gazing at the lush grass. As Mat wasn't coming home that night I wondered whether to go out for a drink with Carole. I had to get out of the house for a while, had to escape my surroundings. I'd ring her later and suggest it.

Although feeling a little easier, I locked the back door as I wandered into the house to dress. The day was already becoming very hot and I'd have preferred to have left it open. But there was no point in inviting trouble.

Climbing the stairs, I slipped my gown off, tossing it over the banister as I crossed the landing to my bedroom. Perhaps I'd take a trip into town and buy the dress, I mused, standing before the full-length mirror and scrutinizing my naked body. Coffee at the shop in the High Street, a browse around the bookshop, and then . . .

'Very nice!' Den grinned, leaning in the doorway.

I screamed, adrenalin pumping through my veins as I turned to face him. 'You bastard!' I yelled.

'That's a nice greeting, I must say!'

'What the hell are you doing in my bedroom? You nearly gave me a bloody heart attack!'

'I noticed you down the garden so I thought I'd slip in through the back door you'd left open and wait for you.'

Instinctively covering my breasts with my folded arms, I stared at him in horror. Even my own bedroom was no sanctuary from his prying eyes! How dared he sneak into my boudoir and gawp at me! I was stunned at the audacity. Trembling, I wondered at his next move in the escalating nightmare, what he'd demand of me. But he just stood there, watching me, no doubt enjoying every minute of my plight.

'I lied,' I said at length. For some incomprehensible reason, I imagined his penis inside me, thrusting deep into my vagina, sperming inside me. My mind was leaving me. 'It's not me in the photographs, I was joking.'

'I don't think Mat will look upon your confession as a joke.'

'It's your word against mine. You can't prove . . .'

'I had a small tape recorder in my pocket, Jane. Your confession, the university, the photographer . . . It's all on tape.'

'I lied.'

'You can't change your story now!' he laughed. 'How will you explain to Mat that you were lying? By the way, I went to see a friend of mine last night. He's an amateur photographer, so I got him to take some shots of the magazines. I have some really nice glossy prints of you now.'

'Den, this is silly,' I smiled, forcing a laugh as I grabbed a towel from the bed and held it in front of my naked body. 'Look, I *was* joking about the magazine. I suppose I just wanted to see how far you'd go, that was all. It was only a joke.'

'Stripping off and showing me your cunt . . . I don't suppose Mat would think it a joke.'

'It's not me in that bloody magazine! Agreed, the likeness is pretty good, but it's not me.'

'I know, we'll let Mat listen to your confession and look at the magazine. He can decide whether you were lying or joking.'

'No, no, don't do that! Look, you had your fun yesterday, we both had our little joke, so let's . . .'

'Turn round, Jane. I want you to stand with your feet apart and bend over.'

'No!'

'I want to see your cunt lips bulging between your sexy thighs.'

A strange feeling welled inside me. Fear, anticipation, expectation . . . Arousal? Whatever it was, I didn't understand it. An icy chill ran down my spine as I imagined my naked body bent over, my legs straight, my hands on the floor, my vaginal lips parted between my open thighs – Den's gleaming eyes transfixed there.

Another unfamiliar feeling gripped me as the towel fell away from my firm breasts, revealing my alert nipples. What was it? Did the danger excite me? My stomach somersaulted, churning as I stared at my blackmailer. This had all been a grave mistake, I reflected. Why hadn't I denied the photographs, put it down to an uncanny resemblance and left it at that? If only I'd known that he was recording me, my stupid confession.

'This turns you on, doesn't it?' he smirked.

'No!'

'It does, Jane. The thought of showing me your cunt turns you on.'

'You turn me off! And what was the point in sending me that stupid note?'

'What note?'

'The note saying . . .'

'I haven't sent you any notes.'

Covering my breasts, my full melons, with the towel, I tried to compose myself. I was sure Den hadn't sent the note. He was getting what he wanted, so why would he bother? The situation was ridiculous, horrendous. Here I was, standing naked behind a towel in my bedroom with my neighbour demanding to see my pussy! How the hell had I ever got myself into this mess?

'Come on, Jane,' he persisted. 'Show me your juicy cunt.'

'Den, please!' I cried. But there was no compassion, no sympathy reflected in the dark pools of his eyes.

'It's entirely up to you. Show me your cunt – or I'll show Mat the photographs and let him hear the tape recording.'

Dropping the towel to the floor, I stood before him, allowing him to scrutinize my naked body, my curves, my hillocks. My heart missing a beat as he ordered me to lie on the bed, I didn't know what to do. I was trapped – trapped in my own bedroom with my perverse blackmailer. What choice did I have? *None at all*, my whispering thoughts told me.

Perched on the edge of the summery counterpane, I

reclined tentatively, closing my legs as I sensed his gaze between my thighs. My mind torn, I didn't know whether to flee the house and put an end to the degradation or remain lying on the bed of perfidy, of humiliation, that was of my own making. I felt crude, dirty – treacherous.

'You have a nice cunt,' he praised me. 'A long slit, full, fleshy lips. A *very* nice cunt. Are you juiced up?'

My eyes closed, I imagined the view he had of my swollen vaginal lips, my sex crack. My juices trickling from my hot duct as I involuntarily parted my trembling thighs, I suddenly wondered what I was doing. I didn't want Mat seeing the photographs or listening to the tape, but how far would I be prepared to go to save my marriage . . . or to destroy it?

Hearing movements, I shuddered. I thought Den was going to touch me. Sitting bolt upright, I gazed at him wide-eyed, my face flushing as I noticed the bulge in his tight jeans – his penis bulge. This was a dangerous game, I knew as I grabbed the towel and shielded my naked body again. But it was no game!

'I'd like you to stand with your back to me and bend over,' he instructed as if telling me to put the kettle on.

'Den, I . . .'

'Do it, Jane! Do it, or Mat will see the magazines and hear your confession.'

There was aggression in his voice, anger. I felt frightened. The master and the slave, the blackmailer and the victim. Never in my wildest dreams had I imagined that I'd find myself in such a degrading situation. What choice was there? Dropping the towel once more to the floor, I turned and stood with my feet wide apart. Tentatively leaning over, I knew my vaginal lips were on display, nestling between my parted thighs, crudely exposed. Further I bent, until my hands rested on the floor and I was looking up at my smug blackmailer between my long legs.

'A very nice cunt,' he murmured appreciatively, dropping to his knees.

'You can only look,' I quavered as he moved closer to my most private place. 'Touch but not look,' I murmured in my muddlement.

'Touch but not look?' he chuckled.

'I mean . . .'

'God, you're wet,' he gasped. 'Very wet!'

Why was I doing this? I wondered, trying to block out my shame by squeezing my eyes shut. Just like the photograph in the magazine, I'd crudely exposed my vaginal lips, my inner sex folds. There could be no turning back now. My wanton behaviour, the disgusting adulterous act I'd performed, could never be erased.

As my debased neighbour's finger started speculatively stroking my wet sex valley, I grabbed the towel again and leaped up. 'No!' I screamed, swinging round to face him. 'No!'

'Come on, Jane. Bend over again and let me . . .'

'No, never!'

'In that case, I'll just have to show Mat . . .'

'I don't care what you do, I'm not going to . . .'

'I think *Mat* will care what you did all those years ago.'

'It's not me in that bloody magazine! I only said it was because I was afraid.'

'Afraid?'

'I thought you were going to . . . Mat's the suspicious type, deadly jealous – if he saw that picture, he'd believe it was me.'

'But it *is* you, Jane! You said so yourself.'

'It's not! Christ, why don't you believe me?'

'First you deny it, then you say you did it for the money, now you deny it again. It's you, there's no doubt about it.'

'All right, show Mat, see if I bloody care!'

I sank sobbing with relief onto the bed as Den coolly left the room. I had to admit he was right. First I'd denied the tart was me, then I'd confessed to it, then . . . No matter what I said now, he firmly believed it *was* me, and that was that. After hearing my so-called confession, Mat would believe the worst, I knew only too well! I had to put a stop to the farce, confront Mat, tell him about Den, his blackmailing – and hope for the best.

Wandering into the hall, I looked for my dressing gown. I recalled leaving it over the banister, but it had gone. Suddenly realizing that Den had taken it to build up his evidence against me, the severity of my predicament hit me.

How could I ever explain why my gown was in Den's house – or my panties, come to that? Returning to the bedroom, I looked about me, wondering what else he'd stolen. He'd never steal my fidelity. Opening my dressing table drawer, I gasped, immediately realizing that he'd been rummaging through my underwear while I'd been in the garden. All my suspender belts had gone.

This had gone too far, I decided as I flung my clothes on. I had to confront Den, come to some arrangement or other with him. But there was only *one* arrangement he'd agree to! Grabbing the receiver as the phone rang, I decided to talk to him, try and make him see sense.

'Oh, Carole!' I gasped, relieved to hear her voice.

'Are you OK, Jane? What's the matter?'

'Everything!'

I didn't know where to begin my incredible story, but I knew that I had to tell my best friend. What she'd think, I had no idea, but I desperately needed to confide in her. A problem shared? A secret shared is no longer a secret.

'I undressed in front of my neighbour,' I blurted out.

'What?'

'I undressed in front of him. And I . . . I lay on my bed, naked.'

'Are you feeling all right?'

'No, I'm not. Listen, he came here yesterday morning with a dirty magazine. The girl in the centrefold . . . He thought it was me and blackmailed me. He said that he'd show Mat unless I . . .'

'*Is* it you?'

'Whether it is or not doesn't matter, the point is that he *thinks* it's me.'

'I don't understand, how can he blackmail you if it isn't you?'

'Mat will believe it's me, you know what he's like.'

'If it's not you, then . . .'

'He had a tape recorder in his pocket. I didn't want him causing trouble so I admitted that it was me and . . .'

'It's all right, calm down. Tell me what happened, exactly.'

'I stripped off in the lounge. Later, he came into my bedroom and . . . and made me bend over. I was naked and . . .'

'Jane, the only thing you can do is tell Mat.'

'No, I can't do that. Mat's so suspicious, possessive, that he'd . . .'

'Unless you do something, it'll go on and on, get worse and . . .'

'I know that!' I snapped. 'I'm sorry, Carole, I didn't mean to yell at you. Mat's been increasingly suspicious lately. He keeps on about other men, whether I fancy them or not. And he's got a thing about pornography, about the girls and . . .'

'Look, I'll come round and we'll talk about it.'

'OK.'

'Give me half an hour.'

'I'll be here.'

Replacing the receiver, I drifted downstairs, pleased that I'd told Carole, and yet wishing I hadn't. Now two people knew about the magazine! The nightmare was worsening by the minute. Pacing the lounge floor, my head spinning, I felt that I was becoming neurotic. Again, I wished I'd put a stop to the ridiculous situation before it had got out of hand. But it was too late now. Checking my watch, I decided to go and see Den and try to explain, to reason with him.

My heart was in my mouth as I rang on his doorbell, imagining him dragging me inside and . . . And what? I felt as if I was going crazy as I waited for him to answer. I *was* going crazy! My life in ruins, my marriage on the line . . . What the hell was going on?

'Ah, I thought you might pay me a visit,' Den smiled, displaying a perfect row of white teeth as he opened the door. 'You'd better step inside.'

'That's what the spider said to the fly,' I murmured pensively as I walked into his hall, into his lair.

'Step into my parlour!' he chuckled.

'I'm here to talk, Den, not to . . .'

'I know why you're here. Come into the lounge.'

Following him as he closed the front door, I felt my stomach sink. Another grave mistake, I knew, as I entered the lounge to confront several framed prints of the lewd magazine photographs adorning the walls. Noticing one of my suspender belts strewn over the back of an armchair, I realized that he'd become obsessed with me.

'You need help,' I remarked as he waved at the sofa, indicating for me to sit down. *I* was the one who needed help!

'I don't need any help,' he laughed. 'I'm more than capable of . . .'

'You're besotted, obsessed.'

'Obsessed?'

'The photographs, my suspender belt, my panties . . . Where's my dressing gown?'

'It's safe enough. It smells of your body, Jane – a sexy smell.'

'You're a pervert.'

'Am I?'

'There's no other word for it.'

'I'm glad you came round because I want to look at your cunt again.'

'That's *not* what I'm here for!' I returned, my hands trembling. What *was* I there for?

'I've decided to show Mat the photographs and give him a copy of the tape.'

'Why?'

'Because things aren't going according to plan. You keep resisting, arguing with me and . . .'

'I did as you asked.'

'I was only touching you, stroking your cunt, and you yelled at me. No, I don't like the way things are working out, so I'll show Mat.'

I should have known that there could never be a limit – that he'd push me further, make ever more demands of me. He was debased, deviant – desperate. To even contemplate being able to reason with such a man was ludicrous. There was no reasoning. In my crass stupidity, I was now standing in his lounge, defenceless, vulnerable, once again at his mercy. The spider and the fly.

'I have a friend coming round, I'd better get back,' I said, moving cautiously towards the door.

'I'd like to watch Mat fucking you.'

'You're pathetic!'

'When did he last push his cock into your tight cunt and spunk up you?'

'I'm going, Den. There's no point in . . .'

'The photographs, tape, your dressing gown, suspender belts, panties . . . I wouldn't like to be in your shoes when Mat sees that dirty little package!'

I was lost, defeated. Den's hold over me was increasing by the day. What to do? Either I had to put an end to the horror there and then or . . . do as he asked and live the rest of my life lying to Mat. But I couldn't enjoy a happy marriage and have a perverted relationship on the side. If Mat were to discover the evidence of my debauchery, my marriage would be over. There again, if I offered my body to Den, what sort of marriage would I have left? Either way, I was a loser.

'Strip off and I'll give you the tape,' Den leered.

'No, I . . .'

'Don't you want the tape?'

'Yes, of course I do!'

'Then strip off.'

Twice before I'd allowed Den to see me naked and, this time, for some reason, the thought wasn't so bad. But he'd touch me, and I didn't want that. Touching, seeking, violating. It was one thing looking, another touching – the difference between adultery and . . . And what?

I stripped quickly, almost automatically, tossing my clothes onto the sofa and standing naked before him. Carole would arrive soon, I thought in my nudity. I had to get this over with as quickly as possible and go home.

Gazing at me, his dark eyes focused on my pussy, scrutinizing me there. Was this all he wanted? Did he want only to look at me, to admire my naked body? I was a fool to wonder what he wanted!

'Pull your cunt lips apart,' he ordered me crudely. I did as he asked, my fingers seemingly moving without conscious effort, stretching my outer voluptuous sex-pads wide apart, exposing my once-secret inner flesh to his widening eyes. Guilt enveloped me as I held my humiliating pose, but I had no choice. I was only displaying my naked body, my inner sex folds, I tried to console myself. All women were the same the world over – there was nothing unique about me. *Nakedness is chaste*, the inner voice whispered. But this wasn't!

'You're wet,' Den grinned, kneeling before me and examining my sexual centre. 'I'm going to push my finger into your cunt.'

'No!' I protested, releasing my outer lips, veiling the entrance to my vagina.

'Do you want the tape or not?'

'Yes, but . . .'

'But what?'

It was only his finger, I reflected numbly. First his finger would enter me, and then his . . . I glanced at the mantelpiece clock and thought of Carole. My mind riddled with confusion, I decided to allow Den to commit the degrading act. Once he'd had his way, I'd be free to go home with the tape. The tape? The notion was crazy! I knew he wouldn't hand the tape over in a million years. *Just one finger*, the inner voice urged me. *Just one finger in the pie!*

'All right,' I sighed lamely, closing my eyes as I hung my head. 'Just your finger.' He glided into my vagina with ease, massaging my soft inner flesh, inducing my sex milk to flow. Did I feel arousal? Bewildered, befuddled, I didn't know what I felt as he trespassed deeper into my sex duct, my sanctum.

This was one step further, one step nearer to . . . His hot breath warming my vaginal lips, his wet tongue licking my gaping sex valley, I shuddered. Pulling my outer lips up and apart, he licked the sensitive tip of my exposed clitoris, sending electrifying sensations through my quivering pelvis. The lapping sounds of lust haunting me, I tried to scream, to speak, to tell him to stop, but the words wouldn't come. Paralysed with guilt, with confusion, with latent lust, I couldn't move, couldn't pull away from my predator as he sucked my clitoris into his hot mouth.

Breathing deeply, I was shocked as my sex nub swelled and pulsated in response to his sweeping tongue, his caressing tongue. How could I allow another man to perform such an intimate act, to lick between my vaginal lips? Mat . . . Poor Mat! But he'd never know of his wife's whorish behaviour! He'd never discover the sordid truth.

'God!' I breathed involuntarily as my clitoris pulsated and my vagina tightened around his pistoning finger. The birth of my orgasm stirring within my quivering womb, I knew I was going to come. Though I desperately tried to hold back, to deny the incredible sensations permeating my trembling body, my climax suddenly welled, erupting within my solid clitoris as he repeatedly licked me there.

My legs sagging, I clung to his head as he sustained my wonderful orgasmic apex. My body trembled with pleasure while my mind swirled with guilt as he thrust a second finger into my drenched vagina, stretching my sensitive inner flesh. His saliva and my pussy juice mingled, running in rivers down my inner thighs as waves of pure sexual ecstasy rolled though my shuddering body, I had never experienced an orgasm of such power and duration.

The intense pulses surging through my reeling body, he thrust a third finger into my tightening vagina, adding to my adulterous pleasure. Barely able to stand as he licked and fingered me, I gripped his head harder, grinding my open vulva into his face, maintaining my mind-blowing climax. My knees bent, my thighs parted, I thought I was going to pass out as my clitoris swelled and throbbed and my vagina bubbled and spurted out its creamy thanksgiving. *Mat!* What was I doing to Mat?

At last, the incredible sensations finally began to subside and I looked down at Den, his dark mop of hair, his lapping tongue, wondering at my adulterous act. *Adultery.* The word battered my racked mind, torturing me as Den told me what a nice cunt I had. *Cunt.* A crude word, befitting a crude woman like me.

As Den slipped his fingers out of my dripping vagina and stood before me, I averted my eyes. Embarrassed, shamed, I couldn't look him in the face. Grabbing my skirt and panties, I just wanted to go home, to put the lewd act behind me and forget it. But, pulling my panties up to conceal my adulterous cunt, I knew I could never forget. Never in a million years could I forget my adultery.

'You're not going, are you?' Den asked, his jeans bulging.

'Yes,' I replied, my vaginal juices soaking my panties.

'I haven't fucked you yet.'

'You're not going to.'

'But I thought you wanted the tape?'

'I've allowed you to . . . Just give me the bloody tape and let me get out of here!' I snapped, buttoning my blouse.

'No fuck, no tape,' he grinned wickedly.

Drifting dreamlike down the hall to the front door, I knew he'd have a hold on me forever. The hot sun warmed me as I emerged from the relative coolness of his house and I took a deep breath before walking the few yards home. The marital home, I mused sadly as I opened the front door. The broken marital home.

To my horror, another envelope was lying on the mat. Tearing it open, I cringed. ' "Now douche your cunt",' I read aloud. It wasn't from Den, I was sure. But who else knew what I'd done? Had someone been spying through the window? No one knew. *Someone knows.*

Screwing the letter up, I tossed it into the kitchen bin. My mind reeling, I couldn't face Carole and decided to pretend that I was out. After my illicit orgasm, my wanton adultery, I couldn't face myself, let alone Carole! But I *had* to face myself, to face up to reality. There was no point in dwelling on the obscene act I'd allowed Den to perform on my naked body. I had to move on. But, in my heart of hearts, I knew that wasn't possible.

My mind swirling with a thousand thoughts as I wandered into the lounge and flopped onto the sofa, I became aware of my drenched panties. A stark reminder of my infidelity, I reflected. But there would be stark reminders daily. Living next door to my partner in adultery, I would never be able to forget my sex crime. Would cruel notes arrive daily?

My cunt had been eternally violated, my marriage vows shattered. 'Cunt,' I breathed, in awe of the powerful expletive. The crude word had never passed my lips before, not even in anger. But now? 'Cunt,' I murmured again, strangely mesmerized by the term.

Leaping to my feet as the doorbell rang, I dashed out of the room and hid in the kitchen. Was I hiding from Carole, or from myself? I wondered as the bell rang out again. I couldn't hide from myself, from reality. As Carole persisted, I realized with horror that my hand was up my skirt, toying with my sex lips through my wet panties – playing with my cunt.

'God!' I whispered, wondering what on earth I was doing as I pulled my hand away from my soaked knickers. My clitoris swelling, my vaginal muscles contracted as images of Den fingering and licking me buffeted my mind. It seemed that the forbidden carnal experience had transformed me – I was sexually aware as never before. Was the change permanent? I wondered, allowing my hand to slip up my skirt again, my fingers yanking my wet panties aside to explore my yearning inner lips. Had the illicit experience roused a sleeping passion?

As Carole had obviously given up, I pulled my saturated panties off and tossed them onto the kitchen table. I needed to come again, I knew, as my clitoris throbbed expectantly. I'd not masturbated since my teens, but now I craved the relief of orgasm so much that I couldn't resist the temptation to massage my pleasure bud and satisfy my urgent desire.

In the lounge, I sat in Mat's armchair and pulled my short skirt up over my stomach. I was wet, very wet, I observed, parting my outer lips and scrutinizing my blushing sex flesh, my vaginal entrance. Hanging my legs over the arms of the chair, my cunt opening wide, I focused on my yawning vulva.

Never before had I examined myself there, my clitoris snugly canopied beneath the exquisite fusion of soft labia, the wet flesh surrounding my sex portal. Painfully stretching my outer sex pads, I gazed at the intricate folds of my inner lips, the glistening flesh forming a cone around my open hole.

Massaging my erect rosebud, breathing deeply as the wonderful sensations permeated my contracting womb, I reclined in the chair. Never in my life had I needed to come so much. Was it the thought of Den fingering and licking me to orgasm that had caused my libido to soar? I didn't know what it was as my flowering bud threatened to burst beneath my vibrating fingertips.

Something within me had stirred, roused like a sleeping monster deep within my subconscious. Whatever had happened to me, I felt alive with sex, exhilarated, as waves of ecstasy emanated from my clitoris and rolled through my trembling body. My cunt had been rudely stimulated, shaken – roused from its customary inertia.

My head lolling to one side as I masturbated, my glazed gaze caught the fruit bowl on the nearby coffee table.

Grabbing a large banana, my vagina aching, rhythmically contracting, I ripped the peel from the fruit and pressed the end against the wet flesh surrounding my open hole. I'd never slipped anything into my cunt before, not even a finger: my teenage masturbation had been entirely a matter of clitoral stimulation. For a rational moment I hesitated, wondering at my wanton behaviour.

My hand trembling as my arousal mounted, I was finally driven to plunge the fruit deep into my tight sex duct, gasping as my hot cunt tightened. The fruit phallus cooling my inner flesh, I closed my eyes, revelling in the wonderful sensations. Imagining a solid penis inside me, I thrust the banana in and out of my drenched pussy as I massaged my nub with my free hand, the incredible sensations driving me wild as I arched my back and whimpered in my rising pleasure.

My lust juices running down between my buttocks, trickling over my secret anal portal, I increased my rhythm, pistoning the banana in and out of my burning cunt as I vigorously massaged my pulsating clitoris. My climax nearing, I felt my sensitive nipples stiffen and I pictured Den sucking my areolae into his hot mouth, gently nibbling my erect breast buds.

My unscrupulous neighbour had turned my life upside down – held my marriage to ransom with his obscene blackmailing. At least I'd discovered my sexuality! I thought gratifyingly as my vagina embraced the pistoning banana, sending electrifying tingles marauding through my trembling frame. But at what price?

Again, I promised myself never to allow Den to ogle my naked body, let alone finger my cunt, lick my clitoris and take me to orgasm. What I'd done was vulgar, deceitful and degrading in the extreme. Faith had been broken, my marriage vows tossed on the wind of lust, my body defiled.

It was a terrible price to pay for relearning the fine art of masturbation, rediscovering my sexuality.

But the bill was settled, I'd paid, and could now relax and enjoy the appetizing spread before me. Whatever happened now, I had my cunt, my clitoris, to bring me pleasure. Whether in my bed or in the lounge, I could masturbate, could bring out wondrous orgasms. I didn't need Den . . . Did I need Mat?

As my orgasm welled, my breathing heavy, my vagina pulping the pistoning banana, I cried out in my insurmountable pleasure. My clitoris solid, transmitting electrifying pulses of sex deep into my contracting womb, I felt as if I was possessed by carnality itself. A deep sense of wickedness gripped me, crushing my mind as my climax peaked.

My entire body quivering, my aroused nipples aching as my orgasm rolled on, images of Den watching me masturbate loomed in my mind. Lurking outside, spying through the window as I thrust the banana in and out of my beautiful cunt, his penis erect, I pictured him watching my most intimate act.

Did I *want* him to watch me masturbate? The notion excited me, yet frightened me. My thoughts were drifting way off course. As my climax began to subside, the last waves of orgasm rippling through my sated body, I wondered what I was becoming. Bending over and showing Den my vaginal lips, my legs over the arms of the chair, a banana stuffed up my cunt as I frigged . . . Into what kind of creature was I metamorphosing? On what foreign course was I set?

I remembered Jane, the faithful, innocent, loving wife. Where was she? Was she locked inside my mind, screaming for freedom? Or forever banished? Slowing my clitoral massaging, my vaginal thrusting, I sighed as warmth and serenity bathed me. Wherever Jane was, whoever I'd become, it didn't matter as I lay with my legs spread, my abused cunt burning. Was it too late to turn back, to rediscover the old me? As I scooped the pulped phallus from my inflamed vagina, I knew there was still time to turn back – if I wanted to.

Licking my slippery pussy juice from the steaming banana, I took a bite, savouring the hot fruit. Taking another nibble of the delicacy as I gently massaged my clitoris, my carnal senses tingled with gratification. Mashed banana and cream! I'd do this again and again, I promised myself. Thrust a banana in and out of my beautiful cunt, take myself to an explosion of cream and then relish the wicked concoction.

Licking my lips as I swallowed the last of the delicacy, I rose to my feet, my skirt dropping over my drenched vulval flesh as I swayed on my sagging legs. Not only had I committed adultery but, for the first time since meeting Mat, I'd masturbated! I didn't know what I felt as I wandered light-headedly into the kitchen. I didn't recognize the emotions welling inside me.

My ultra-sensitive nipples aching for attention, I slipped my blouse off and unclipped my bra. Looking down, admiring my milk teats, I realized that I'd never derived pleasure from my firm breasts. Even in my early teens when I'd masturbated, when my young breasts were unpastured hillocks, I'd not touched my nipples. Running my fingertips round my areolae, my milk buds painfully hard, I gasped as the sensations rippled through my mammary spheres. Another discovery, another awakening.

Aware of my vaginal juice trickling down my inner thighs, I wondered again what had happened to me. Slipping into my blouse, my nipples caressed by the smooth silk as I moved, I tried to push all thoughts of sex to the back of my mind. I couldn't spend all my time masturbating, toying with my breast buds: I had to do something constructive. Although only early afternoon, I started feeling apprehensive about spending the evening alone in the house. Why did Mat have to go away?

I dared not ring Carole and suggest we go out for a drink. I couldn't face her questions, bring myself to talk about Den. I'd spend the evening watching television, I decided – the doors locked, the curtains drawn, I'd sip wine and relax. I'd also begin a diary, record my thoughts and feelings, events and experiences – keeping it well hidden from Mat, of course! No, perhaps I wouldn't keep a record of my adultery.

Wandering into the garden, I became less worried about Den as I sat on the soft grass, the green blades tickling my alert red sex lips. I'd enjoy the summer, sunbathe in my bikini, not become a prisoner in my own home. But instinctively, I knew that he was there as I looked up at his house out of the corner of my eye. He *was* there, at an upstairs window, lurking, gazing at me. Initially, panic gripped me and I turned on my heels to run into the house and lock the door. But then, strangely, I didn't mind him watching me.

I knew that he wouldn't show the photographs to Mat – to do so would ruin any further chance he might have of fingering and licking me. He wouldn't be fool enough to destroy his hold over me. *His hold over me?* Suddenly, it dawned on me that it was *me* who had the hold over *him*. It was my body he wanted. Insanely, I decided to tease him, to allow my blouse to fall open, to expose my nipples. Was arousal the whiplash?

Perhaps I was subconsciously getting my own back for what he'd done. I'd have nothing to gain by flaunting my breasts, but the thought of arousing him and then slipping into the house before he could get at me delighted me.

Reclining on the grass, stretching my limbs out languorously, I had an even more wicked idea.

Allowing my legs to part, displaying my well-juiced vaginal crack, I watched him through my eyelashes. My stomach somersaulting, I parted my thighs further, exposing my naked femininity in all its glory. The game was more than dangerous now: it was lethal! But I couldn't help myself as I brought my knees up, allowing them to fall apart and show off my beautiful cunt. Cunt, vulva, vagina, pussy, love slit . . .

In my confusion, I tried to understand why displaying my vaginal crack to my blackmailer sent a thrill through me. Deliberately leading him on like that, dangling a platinum carrot before him, was perilous. But the sense of power was exhilarating! I'd turned the situation round. For the time being, at least, I was in control. Displaying my beguiling feminine wares, *I* was the omnipotent one.

As he disappeared from view, I leaped to my feet and dashed into the house, locking the door behind me. He'd taken the bait and would come running, threatening me with his precious magazines and tape. In the safety of the kitchen I stood motionless, breathing deeply as I waited for a knock on the back door or the phone to ring.

I waited for what seemed like hours. Nothing happened. Where was he? What was he doing? I wished I'd not teased him like that – I couldn't afford to play spurious games. He was bound to realize that I'd exposed my sexual epicentre deliberately, and to take it as a come-on. I'd been a complete fool!

An ominous-looking package was lying on the front doormat as I ventured through the hallway. It was addressed to Mat, and I immediately sensed trouble. Ripping open the brown paper, I was horrified to discover one of my lacy red suspender belts – stained and freshly wet with sperm. I didn't allow myself to imagine how Mat would have reacted had he opened the dirty packet. There'd have been no positive proof that the garment was mine but, with his suspicious mind, he'd have put two and two together and come up with me.

I froze as the doorbell rang. After a minute, a loud knock sounded on the back door. It was Den, trying to get at me, my body. The adulterous act I'd committed in his house, my blatant exhibitionism in the garden . . . I'd teased him, played with him, roused the monster in him. And now it was after me!

Chapter Three

I spent the rest of the day hiding in the lounge with the curtains drawn, not even daring to venture into the kitchen to prepare a meal. Den had been out there, waiting, lurking in the dark like a monster, and it was only when I climbed the stairs to my bedroom and locked the door that I felt a little safer.

Sleep had cruelly evaded me for much of the night. I had heard movements downstairs, but had been too afraid to investigate. Was the house creaking as the rafters cooled from the heat of the day? Or was it Den? Was he in the house, looking for me, hunting for my naked body? Finally putting it down to my imagination, I somehow managed to get to sleep. But I dreamed terrible dreams.

Through the velvety curtains of my dreams, I saw myself standing naked before Den in the lounge, my hands tethered behind my back. My feet wide apart, my secret valley gaping, he was thrusting something in and out of my vagina. It was long, huge, and it stretched my pussy lips wide apart, plunging in to the hilt. As he violated my vaginal sheath, lustfully straining erect penises drifted around me, moving close to my face, threatening to enter my mouth. Suddenly, the purple phalluses exploded in orgasm, showering me with sperm, splattering my cheeks, my mouth, until I was drowning in a sea of perverted sex.

I woke with a start to a new morning, wondering what the day would bring. Mat would be home that evening, but the thought worried me. If Den dropped another package through the letter box and Mat happened to open it . . . I'd played with fire, and was sure to be burned.

I shouldn't have gone to Den's house, let alone allowed him to finger and lick me to orgasm. I shouldn't have allowed him to suck my nipples, lick my sex valley, and I shouldn't have played dangerous games in the garden. Mistakes had been made, to be followed inevitably by dire consequences.

Making coffee, I pondered on the recent events. It had been like a game to me, teasing Den, giving him the come-on and then hiding in the house. Masturbating as I'd pictured him watching me had been exciting, enhancing the heavenly sensations. But now the game had turned sinister.

I still had a chance to turn the clock back, though, I decided. No matter what I'd done, there was no proof . . . No proof? Den's bloody tape recording was all the proof he needed! Once Mat heard my so-called confession, all hell would be let loose!

Sitting at the kitchen table sipping my coffee and munching toast, I became aware of my clitoris calling for attention – swelling and throbbing within my sex valley. My vaginal juices wetting my panties, something within me had definitely been roused. But what? Was I a latent nymphomaniac? Masturbating with the banana and then savouring the hot fruit had stimulated me no end. But was I really a nymphomaniac?

As the front doorbell rang, I froze. It could have been the postman or the milkman, but I knew instinctively that it was Den. 'Jane!' he called through the letterbox. 'Jane, I know you're in there!' My hands trembling, spilling coffee as I deposited my cup on the table, I didn't know what to do. 'Jane!' he persisted, his deep voice menacing. 'I've put something through the letterbox. Take a look at it!'

Tentatively walking through the hall, I picked up a photograph from the doormat. Stretched out on the grass with my skirt up over my stomach, my open pussy blatantly displayed, the picture was clear evidence of my obscene exhibitionism. I felt sick as Den coolly informed me that there were several copies. My heart thumping against my chest, I didn't know what to say as he insisted that I let him in.

'Come on, Jane!' he wheedled as I gazed glassy-eyed at the photograph. 'Either you let me in, or Mat gets a copy of the picture!'

'All right, all right!' I finally conceded, reluctantly opening thc door.

'That's more like it,' he grinned, stepping into the hall, his dark eyes locked to mine. 'So, what do you think of the picture?'

'I think it's me relaxing quite innocently in the garden.'

'What, with your cunt deliberately on show?'

'I forgot to put my panties on. All this proves is that you're a pervert.'

'It proves that you were showing me your cunt, Jane. When Mat sees . . .'

'When Mat sees it, he'll probably punch you in the face.'

'I think not,' he smirked, sauntering through the hall to the lounge. Meekly following him, I wondered at his next move. 'How many women sunbathe like that?'

'Me, for starters.'

'How many women have posed for men's mags, left their panties, their suspender belts and their dressing gown in their neighbours' houses?'

'I . . .'

'There's one other thing, Jane.' He chuckled evilly as he stared at me. 'I have the most wonderful photograph of you standing naked in my lounge with my fingers up your tight cunt.'

'You can't have!' I returned.

'Can't I?'

'There was no camera!'

'Oh, yes, there was. A hidden camera, operated by . . .'

'I don't believe you.'

'I don't care whether you believe me or not, the fact is that I have several shots of you with my fingers up your wet cunt.'

Shaking uncontrollably, I leaned on the back of the armchair to steady myself as I felt my legs crumple. Den was capable of any treachery, I knew – I had no reason to disbelieve that he'd taken vile photographs of me. Nausea embraced me and my head spun as I imagined Mat discovering my wanton adultery. Mistakes are inevitably followed by dire consequences, I reflected as Den stood grinning triumphantly at me. Who was sending me the notes?

'OK, take your panties off,' he instructed me as he removed his leather belt. Obediently, I slipped my hands up my skirt and pulled my panties down, trying to conceal the stained crotch as I kicked my shoes off. 'Now lift your skirt right up and bend over the back of the armchair,' he ordered me as I stepped out of my panties.

'Den,' I began, realizing that he was going to do far more than lick and finger me.

'Do it, Jane! From now on, I am the master and you the slave – remember that!'

The master and the slave? He was right! I was nothing more than a slave to him, an object to be used, belittled, humiliated . . . I gazed in horror at the leather belt, knowing full well what he intended to do with it. 'Do it, Jane!' he repeated angrily. 'I will not tolerate disobedience!'

Raising my skirt, I leaned over the back of the armchair, exposing my naked buttocks, my vaginal lips swelling between my thighs. Moving behind me, cracking the belt like a whip, he chuckled as I pressed my face into the cushion and whimpered incoherent words of fear. Stroking my tensed buttocks, running his fingers up and down my bottom crease, his chuckle became a wicked laugh.

'Have you ever been thrashed?' he leered menacingly.

'No, I haven't,' I whispered, trembling at the thought. I didn't have to do this, I didn't have to endure a thrashing, but . . . *You might enjoy it.*

'You have a nice bum, you'd look good in a gymslip.'

'Den . . . Den, please . . .' I stammered.

The leather belt cracking loudly across my taut buttocks, my rounded bum melons, my body jolted violently. As I tried to stand upright, the belt struck me again, the stinging pain permeating my bottom as I collapsed over the back of the chair. My mind racked with guilt and humiliation, I imagined Mat walking into the room, the horror on his face as he confronted the debased spectacle. How had I ever got myself into this situation? I wondered dazedly as the belt seared my bottom again. My buttocks burning as the thrashing continued, I cried out, begging for mercy. But my pleas were met only with wicked laughter.

'Please!' I sobbed, my buttocks on fire as the belt lashed me again and again. 'Den, please!'

'This is what you get for being a naughty young schoolgirl!' he cried in his devilry, bringing the belt down with a deafening crack.

There was no point in pleading with the monster. All I could do was squeeze my eyes shut and endure the pain, which became more bearable as the demented leather numbed my stinging buttocks. I found myself counting the lashes . . . thirteen, fourteen, fifteen, sixteen . . . On and on the gruelling thrashing continued until the pain melted into a deep burning heat.

My vaginal juice seeping between my swollen sex lips, trickling down my inner thighs, I imagined the view my abuser had of my most intimate place. Even Mat had never seen me in such a degrading position. Our lovemaking had never involved crudity such as this. Would Mat like to thrash me?

Imagining Mat alighting on my bottom weals as Den finally halted the thrashing, I was sure that my marriage was doomed. There'd be no way I could explain the tape and photographs, let alone the blatant evidence of a recent buttock-thrashing.

'Kneel before your master, bitch!' Den ordered me cruelly, grabbing my arm and yanking me up from the chair like a rag doll.

'No, Den!' I protested, eyeing his solid penis jutting from his jeans.

'Worship my cock, or you'll have another thrashing! Kneel before me, your master, and kiss my cock!'

'Den . . .'

'Jane, think about Mat, what he'd say if . . . I'm not playing games! Beg to suck my cock and drink my spunk.'

'No!'

'Beg, or I'll thrash you again.'

'Please . . . please let me suck your cock and drink your spunk,' I recited demurely.

Kneeling before him, I gazed at his solid penis through the curtain of matted blonde hair cascading over my flushed face. I focused on his purple glans, his sperm slit, as he pulled his foreskin back. Kiss it? Or endure another thrashing? Whether or not I kissed his rigid penis, I guessed I'd be in line for another beating. There again, if I masturbated him, quenched his thirst for orgasm, he'd probably leave. I was naive beyond belief!

My lips pursed, I leaned forward and kissed his silky knob. Gasping, he pressed his glans to my mouth, obviously craving far more than a kiss. I pulled back. I couldn't bring myself to take another man into my mouth, no matter what the consequences! Looking up, my tearful eyes caught his: they glinted dangerously as he raised the belt above his head. I knew I had no option.

Opening my mouth, I took his glans inside and sucked. A thousand thoughts cascaded through my mind. Where was Mat? What was he doing? What on earth was I doing? First my mouth, and then my . . . As Dcn clutched my head, driving his marauding knob to the back of my throat, his thick black pubic thatch tickling my face, I knew he was about to come.

'Christ, that's good!' he gasped, withdrawing his cock and driving into me again, using my mouth as he would my vagina, crudely fucking me there. My buttocks burning, my mind brimming with remorse, I had no choice other than to allow him to use me to satisfy his base desires. 'Coming!' he finally cried, thrusting his bulbous knob down to my tonsils.

His salty sperm jetting, bathing my tongue, filling my cheeks as he mouth-fucked me, I swallowed hard. Now I was a fully-fledged adulteress, a perverted tart, a wanton whore . . . But I'd had a choice, hadn't I? I hadn't *had* to commit the vile and degrading act. The inner whisper consoled me. *You had no choice.*

As Den's penis twitched, his treacherous sperm baptizing my throat, I again thought of Mat. My innocent husband was working hard for our future while I was on my knees before another man, destroying that work. My neighbour fucking my mouth, spunking down my throat . . . There was no future now.

'God, I needed that!' Den breathed, slipping his wet penis out of my jismed mouth. 'Lick me clean, whore! Lick the spunk from my cock!' Meekly, I did as he asked. I'd committed the profane act – there seemed little point in protesting now.

As I lapped up the spilled sperm from his veined shaft, from his glistening purple knob, he let out little gasps of pleasure. I felt his come running down my chin and recalled sucking Mat to orgasm. I was the best, an expert, he'd praised me as I'd swallowed his love fruit. I *was* good, expertly licking and sucking my husband to ecstasy but now . . . Never again could I suck Mat's penis. Never.

But, in my confusion, I told myself that a penis was a penis. There was no love, no warmth, only the indifferent coupling – flesh to flesh. What did it matter whether I'd sucked another man to orgasm or not? A cock was a cock, after all. It had been only a physical act, nothing more.

'You're bloody good,' Den grinned as he looked down at me. 'You give a good blow job.' The crude term battered my mind, hurting me. As he tugged his jeans down, I wondered what he'd demand of me next, what crude act he'd instruct his slave to commit. His heavy balls jiggling into view, his cock restiffening, I again tried to convince myself that this was purely a physical act involving no feeling or emotion.

'Suck me off again,' he murmured, pulling his foreskin back. I took him into my mouth, his knob swelling, his shaft becoming solid again as I sucked. Rolling my tongue over his silky glans, my lips stretched tautly around his broad shaft, I closed my eyes. My cunt would be next, I knew, as I imagined him driving into me, my body jolting as he fucked me.

Was being fucked by another man simply a physical coupling? I tormented myself. Flesh to flesh – ashes to ashes. How would I feel after I'd been fucked? How would I feel when Den had gone, knowing that I'd sucked his knob and swallowed his sperm? How did I feel, being used for crude sex? At that time I didn't know how I felt. If I had emotions, they were alien to me.

'Lick my knob,' he breathed, pulling back until my wet lips enveloped just his ballooning glans. 'Go on, lick it.' The taste of sperm lingering in my mouth, I snaked my tongue round his purple globe, wondering whether he'd ever be satisfied. 'Play with my balls,' he instructed me. Obediently, I cupped his balls in the palm of my hand, gently squeezing them as I moved my head back and forth, repeatedly taking his phallus deep into my mouth.

He took longer to come this time, giving me more time to think about the lewd act I was performing. His balls in one hand, his solid shaft in the other, his swollen knob gliding over my wet tongue, I felt my clitoris swell and pulsate. My cunt squeezed, quivered, wetting. Even though this was only a physical coupling, my arousal instinctively rose. It wasn't that I was deriving pleasure from sucking my neighbour's cock, I told myself. Just a natural response to the crude act.

Did I want to come? I wondered as the mouth-fucking continued. Did I want Den to lick and finger me to orgasm? My cunt juicing, contracting, my erect nipples caressing the inside of my silk blouse, I became horrifically aware of my soaring arousal. Was it the latent nymphomaniac in me, stirring, waking? I didn't know. I'd thought I would have been numb, an emotional wasteland. But the treacherous union was stimulating me incredibly.

As Den groaned in his pleasure, I became acutely aware of a desperate longing for his sperm. The prohibited act, the danger, the notion of master and slave, excited me, sent a thrill running through my quivering pelvis. Again, I imagined his cock driving deep into my hot vagina, fucking me, spunking inside me – cervix-spunking. It didn't seem to matter what I did now, I couldn't have fallen any further into the murky pool of wanton adultery. I'd traversed all boundaries, crossed the divide. I might as well be hanged for a sheep as for a lamb.

'Coming!' Den cried for the second time, his sperm jetting from his orgasming knob, bathing my snaking tongue. I didn't swallow this time. In a dreamlike state, I savoured his salty offering as my mouth filled and overflowed. On and on his sperm pumped from his throbbing knob, oozing between my wet lips and his solid shaft to run down my chin.

I was sure that he wouldn't be able to fuck me now and spunk up my drenched cunt. I didn't want him there, in my cunt, and yet . . . Again, in my confusion, I didn't know *what* I wanted. As he drained his swinging balls, he clutched my head, gently rocking his hips as the last of his sperm oozed from his sex slit. My cunt was wet, hot, contracting – I didn't want him there.

'God, you're something else!' he gasped, finally slipping his cock out of my mouth as I swallowed hard. Licking my lips, I sat back on my heels and wiped the sperm from my chin as he tugged his jeans up. Was that it? I pondered. Twice he'd come in my mouth, he'd thrashed me, used, abused and humiliated me. Was that it?

'Now what?' I whispered, my face flushing as I looked up at him through my matted hair. *My master*.

'Now it's your turn to come,' he directed.

'No, I . . .'

'You're going to come like you've never come before,' Den grinned, lying on the floor on his back. 'Come and kneel over my face with your juicy cunt pressed against my mouth.'

My vaginal muscles tightened as I pictured myself in the lewd position. How could I behave like this? I wondered as I lifted my skirt and knelt with my knees astride his head, my dripping vaginal crack gaping above his mouth. What was possessing me to act like a wanton whore? Blackmail – or arousal? I shuddered as I felt his hot breath against my most intimate flesh.

'You're sopping wet!' he chuckled, grabbing my hips and pulling me down. 'Christ, your cunt juice is pouring out!' My sex lips meeting his mouth, his tongue driving into my hot vaginal sheath, I gasped as the beautiful sensations coursed through my pelvis. Gazing down at his dark hair as he lapped up my flowing juices, I covered his head with my skirt, trying to blot out his view of the adulteress. But I couldn't erase the magical sensations, couldn't deny the immense pleasure his sweeping tongue was bringing me. The walls watched me, spying on my adultery. Would they tell?

Desperately trying not to cry out as he mouthed and licked my erect clitoris, I tossed my head back as the sensations built and permeated my contracting womb. Surge after surge of pre-orgasmic pleasure emanating from my pulsating clitoris, wave after wave of pure sexual ecstasy rolled through me. I couldn't begin to comprehend the immense pleasure, the fantastic sensations gripping my quivering body as my juices of lust flowed from my hot sex sheath. Although I tried to hold my orgasm back, to relish the beautiful pulses of sex erupting within my clitoris, the explosion inevitably came. My mouth open, gasping, my eyes rolling, I sank into a pool of exquisite sexual pleasure as my climax seized me.

Rocking my hips, my inflamed sex valley gliding over Den's mouth, his sweeping tongue, I sustained my multiple orgasm. As if in a dream, I was completely oblivious to my surroundings as the intensity of my climax became almost unbearable. Never had I experienced such a heavenly, almost spiritual state of consciousness, such complete and utter fulfilment of both body and mind.

My head lolling forward, I lifted my skirt and gazed at Den, my outer lips enveloping his wet mouth as he sucked out my orgasm. My juices bubbling within my vaginal sheath, streaming over his face, my cunt rhythmically contracting, I thought I'd die as the wondrous sensations peaked again, casting me into a swirling sea of sexual utopia. Waves of pleasure crashing over me, drowning me, my burning cunt became the centre of my trembling body, the epitome of my very being.

At last, my orgasm began to wane, leaving me quivering in its wake, trembling uncontrollably as my juices decanted and my clitoris subsided. Falling to one side, my dripping cunt vacating Den's sated mouth, I lay sprawled out on the floor, a trembling heap of limbs as I drifted gently down from my sexual heaven.

'How was it?' he asked as he climbed to his feet and wiped my orgasmic juices from his mouth. *How was it? Wonderful, heavenly, exquisite . . . Perverted, adulterous, profane . . .* 'You'd like me to fuck your tight cunt now, wouldn't you?' he grinned, towering over my sated body. 'You'd like my stiff cock spunking up your tight cunt.'

His crude words careered through the wreckage of my marriage strewn around my mind. Images of Mat welled from the rubble, his accusing eyes gazing at me, his face scowling. A voice emanated from the destruction, a familiar goading voice. *Let him take you. Fuck your cunt.* Were my thoughts speaking to me?

'Well? Do you want me to spunk up your wet cunt?'

'No!' I screamed above the goading. 'No!'

He turned and left the room, the back door slamming shut as he returned to his own house, satisfied, fulfilled. I lay there, unable to move as my breathing slowed and the stark reality of my wanton act seeped into my mind. I felt my juices oozing from my hot cunt, trickling down between my stinging buttocks. I tasted the sperm lingering on my lips, recalling his penis fucking my mouth. I was the ultimate adulteress.

My fingers pulling and twisting my drenched inner lips, I sat bolt upright as I heard a noise. Had it come from the kitchen? Had Den returned to fuck me? Dragging my weak body up, I stood on my quivering legs and tugged my skirt down. As a rustling sound drifted into the room from the hall, I froze. Still dazed from my incredible orgasm, I listened to the deafening silence. Was my pained mind playing tricks on me?

'I'm imagining things,' I murmured, tentatively walking to the door and peering into the hall. Creeping into the kitchen, I noticed that the back door was wide open. I hadn't imagined hearing Den slam it shut. The catch couldn't have caught properly, I surmised, conveniently, obliquely.

Closing and locking the door, I took a deep breath, again wondering at my lewd behaviour, my wanton act of infidelity. What was done was done, I reflected, my trembling hand grabbing the kettle. I didn't actually want coffee but it was something to do, a distraction for my torrid thoughts. I didn't know what I really wanted. A shower to wash away the guilt? Fresh clothes to stifle the odour of adulterous sex?

'Hi, Jane!' Mat was smiling as he appeared in the kitchen doorway.

'Mat!' I cried, more out of fright than fear of him discovering what I'd done. 'Christ, you made me jump!'

'Sorry, I didn't mean to sneak up on you. Are you OK? You look awfully . . .'

'Why shouldn't I be OK?' I snapped, my guilt rising as I felt my vaginal juices coursing down my inner thighs like rivers of cream.

'You look flushed.'

'I've been exercising,' I replied stupidly, my chest tightening with anxiety as I imagined him catching me kneeling over Den's face, crying out in orgasm.

'I rang last night, but there was no reply.'

'I went to bed early.'

'I rang at six, at seven, at . . .'

'In that case, the phone must have been out of order. How was your trip?'

As he told me about his journey, the hotel, the meeting, I wondered what tell-tale signs I'd left in the lounge. Had Den taken his leather belt? Was the carpet stained? Were my panties still on the floor? Mat's words drifted past me, floating to the ceiling as I sidled from the room. I couldn't listen to Mat – my only concern was for Den, my wet panties, evidence of the thrashing, the mouth-fucking, the pussy-eating. In the lounge, I grabbed my forlorn panties and looked about me. The armchair was in the centre of the room, the cushion wet with my tears.

'Are you sure you're OK?' Mat persisted as he joined me. 'You look terribly guilty.'

'Guilty?' I echoed, pushing the chair back and adjusting the cushion. 'Why should I look guilty?'

'I don't know, you tell me.'

'I'm not guilty of anything, don't be so silly!' I trilled, my stinging buttocks cruelly reminding me of the thrashing.

'What are you doing with your knickers?'

'I . . . I'm about to do the washing,' I smiled, suddenly recalling the photograph Den had dropped through the letterbox.

Where had I left the incriminating evidence? I wondered fearfully. On the hall table? In the lounge? Trying not to panic, my eyes embraced the room, unable to remember. Mat was watching me, suspicion in his eyes as he surveyed my dishevelled hair. But he couldn't have known what I'd done. Den had left by the back door, and I'd been in the kitchen when Mat had arrived. No way could he know of my treachery. Unless the walls had told him.

'Your hair's a right mess!' he laughed. 'What on earth have you been up to?'

'I told you, I've been exercising.'

'You look as if you've just finished a marathon.'

'I *feel* as if I've just finished a marathon! Are you going to work or . . .'

'Yes, I have to go in for the rest of the day. There are reports to complete and a mountain of paperwork to wade through. By the way, I thought we might invite Den round for a meal this evening.'

I felt my heart leap into my mouth. I couldn't sit at the table with Den and Mat! I had to come up with an excuse, and quickly! As Mat helped himself to a banana from the fruit bowel, my stomach sank. I watched him eating the fruit, recalling my wanton masturbation session, savouring the hot, sticky phallus . . . The nightmare was escalating!

'Not tonight, Mat,' I finally replied.

'Why not?'

'Well, I . . .'

'Den's OK. He's a nice chap, you should get to know him.'

'I do know him.' *Intimately!*

'No, I mean, get to know him properly. He *is* our neighbour, after all.'

'I really don't feel like entertaining, Mat.'

'I'll tell you what, I'll do the cooking. How's that sound?'

It sounded dreadful, but worse, where was the bloody photograph? I couldn't take much more mental harassment. I had to come up with an excuse for not having Den to dinner. But the priority was to find that obscene portrait of me before Mat did. The hurt would kill him.

'It's not the cooking,' I proffered, searching the room. 'It's just that I . . . I want us to have an evening together, Mat. You were away all last night and . . .'

'To be honest, I wanted Den's advice on some financial matters. Having him round for dinner would give me the opportunity to talk to him.'

'I suppose so,' I finally conceded, realizing that there was no way out of it.

'Great. Well, I'd better get going. I'll be home around six.'

'OK, I'll see you later.'

'I'll pop into Den's and tell him.'

'All right, I'll see you this evening.'

As Mat left, I held my hand to my head in anguish. I felt as if I was imprisoned between the two men – Mat on one side and Den on the other. How could I play the smiling hostess and sit at the same table as my husband and my blackmailer? But I'd do it, I decided. I'd play my role to perfection and not allow Den to get to me. He'd quietly threaten and tease, I knew, but I'd not allow him to rile or upset me.

I felt that things were changing as I searched for the photograph. Strangely, I seemed to be rising above the situation, almost delighting in the illicit sex and the danger. I was changing, changing so much that I found myself actually looking forward to the evening. Den would try and embarrass me, but I'd play him at his own game and humiliate him. I might even wear my short skirt without panties and flash my cunt at him when Mat wasn't looking. God, what was I thinking? Was I going insane?

I searched everywhere for the elusive photograph, without success. Reckoning that Den had taken it, my stomach somersaulted as I observed the bananas in the fruit bowel. My cunt wetter than ever, aching for attention, I inhaled deeply. This was no time for masturbation! Somehow, I had to turn my thoughts away from sex.

I busied myself throughout the day, laying the table in the dining room, taking a shower and dressing in a very short skirt and a loose blouse for the evening. A powerful sense of wickedness gripped me as I practised sitting in the armchair with my skirt up and my thighs slightly parted. My vaginal crack displayed, I was innocent in my innocence.

I was going to be in control that evening. With my knickerless cunt, I was going to call the shots. Den would obviously have made his plans, but he'd have the shock of his life when I flashed my pussy slit at him at every opportunity. He'd become confused, wondering who was supposed to be blackmailing whom, why I was deliberately placing my marriage on the line by taking such risks with Mat around. Elation, as well as arousal, gripped me.

With the time nearing six, I was ready. I'd thought Den would arrive before Mat, just to tease me, but I was wrong. Mat turned up early, somewhat over-excited about the evening, although I didn't know why. I finally concluded that he was looking forward to some neighbourly financial enlightenment. *I* was looking forward to some neighbourly erotic excitement.

Mat praised me, my efforts in the dining room and the way I'd dressed. Of course, he had no idea that I wasn't wearing any knickers! I'd not bothered to wear a bra, either. Leaning forward slightly when Mat wasn't looking, my blouse falling open, my elongated nipples were clearly visible. I felt horny as never before. My cunt wetting, my vaginal juice creaming my inner thighs, I needed to come.

I might even pounce on Mat when Den had gone, squat over his face and bring myself off, I decided. Strangely, the thought of having sex with Mat after Den didn't worry me any more. I'd thought that I'd not be able to face him after my adultery, let alone have sex with him, but now . . . Now, *I* was in control!

Den made his appearance at half-past six, wielding a bunch of flowers. He grinned at me, licking his lips and rubbing his crotch as Mat poured the wine. He was a bastard, but I had plans to bring him down! My hands trembling, a thrill running down my spine, I decided to bring up the subject of relationships as we relaxed in the lounge before dinner.

'You're not married, are you, Den?' I asked, smiling sweetly.

'No, the idea never appealed to me,' he replied, obviously wondering at the nature of my game.

'Don't you have a lady friend?'

'No, I . . . There is one young lady who I . . . Well, you know how it is. Our relationship is purely sexual. She needs me and I need her.'

'Purely sexual?' I echoed, parting my thighs and displaying my crack to Den as Mat switched the hi-fi on.

'Er . . . Yes, I . . .'

'Is she local?'

'She lives nearby.'

'Unattached?'

'She . . . Yes, she is. So, what do you do for a living?'

'I don't work,' I purred, delighting in the cat-and-mouse game as he leaned forward, focusing on my excited pussy as I parted my thighs further.

'So, what do you do all day?'

'I keep myself busy.'

'Jane keeps the garden nice,' Mat broke in. 'She's a dab hand.'

'Yes, I can see that!' Den smiled as I closed my legs. 'Your garden looks really nice.'

'I'll check the food,' Mat said, leaving the room.

Reclining with my thighs wide apart, my buttocks over the edge of the chair, I blatantly showed Den all I had between my legs. He frowned, gazing at me, my gaping sex slit, obviously wondering why I was taking such a risk. He didn't understand me, my game. I didn't understand myself!

'What are you trying to do?' he finally asked softly.

'Trying to do?' I echoed, licking my lips provocatively.

'You're a fool, behaving like this with Mat around.'

'Behaving like what?'

'You know damn well what I mean.'

'I'm sorry, Den, I have no idea what you're talking about.'

As Mat opened the door, I sat upright hurriedly and closed my legs. Although Den had more than enough on me to ruin my marriage, I felt that he had nothing on me now. There was no way he'd wreck any chance he had of getting his hands up my skirt, his fingers up my juicy cunt! Although he had the evidence of my debauchery, I was sure that he'd no longer blackmail me.

Den tried to rile me during the meal, but I wasn't having any of it. Laughing at his witty comments and giving him as good as he gave me, there was no way he was going to win. It wasn't until Mat left the room again and Den pulled a photograph from his jacket pocket that I realized that I'd assumed a false position of power. Propping the picture up against the Liebfraumilch, he grinned.

'You see, I do have photographs of you standing naked in my lounge with my fingers up your wet cunt,' he whispered triumphantly. I stared in horror at the incriminating picture. My face clearly visible, Den's fingers deep inside my sex sheath, it was obvious that I was enjoying every minute of his intimate attentions. If Mat were to see it, he'd surely kill me!

I'd been a fool to believe that I could win against Den. He was a ruthless blackmailer who'd stop at nothing to have his evil way with me. Fear flooded through me, washing away all my newly acquired sense of power. My face flushing, burning as Mat returned, I didn't know what to do. Grabbing the photograph, Den slipped it into his pocket, grinning victoriously at me as Mat sat down.

I was doomed, I knew, as the men chatted about money, stocks and shares. My marriage, my life . . . Everything was doomed! Although I still reckoned that Den wouldn't reveal the dreadful truth, he had me exactly where he wanted me. That ridiculous magazine photograph meant nothing now. My dressing gown, suspender belts, panties, the tape . . . Den had all he needed in the form of one lousy photograph to bring me crashing down!

'Do you know what I forgot to get?' Mat asked me.

'No, what's that?'

'Cigars. I meant to pick some up on my way home.'

'It doesn't matter,' I smiled. 'I'm sure Den won't mind going without.'

'I'll go and get some, it'll only take a few minutes.'

'No, don't bother, Mat,' I blurted out, knowing what Den would do the minute we were alone.

'It's no bother. You both have a chat, I won't be long.'

My stomach churned as Mat left the room and Den grinned at me. I heard the front door slam shut. I was alone with my blackmailer. Yet again, I'd played the complete fool. He knew that I wasn't wearing panties, that my pussy was naked, easy prey. What had happened to my plans? I wondered as he stood up and moved around the table. What the hell had happened to my plans of revenge, of power?

'Suck me, bitch!' he ordered me, hauling his erect penis

out through the unzipped fly of his tight jeans as he stood by my chair. 'Come on, whore, suck me off!'

'Den, Mat will only be . . .'

'He'll be long enough.'

'But . . .'

'Suck me off, or I'll show him the photograph! Ask me to fuck your mouth and spunk over your tongue.'

'Den, for Christ's sake!'

'Beg me to fuck your mouth and spunk over your tongue! I mean it, I'm not playing games, making false threats.'

'Please . . . please fuck my mouth and spunk over my tongue,' I finally breathed.

As he pulled his foreskin back, I looked around the room. The curtains were drawn, no one could see in, my dirty secret would be safe. But how often would this happen? I wondered, focusing on his veined shaft, his swollen glans. How often would he demand that I suck him to orgasm? My mouth had become a lustmouth, a second cunt.

'You'd better hurry up, bitch!' he growled, pushing his penis closer to my face. Opening my mouth as he yanked his foreskin right back, I engulfed his silky knob and gently sucked. The sooner it was over, the better, I reflected as he began to breathe deeply. The sooner I'd swallowed his sperm, quelled his libido, the better.

'You're bloody good at this,' he whispered, holding my head and slowly rocking his hips, his purple knob sliding back and forth over my tongue. 'That's it, whore! Suck me, lick me until I spunk down your throat!' Closing my eyes as he drove his knob to the back of my throat, I prayed for him to come quickly. 'Ah, yes!' he gasped, his penis twitching. 'God, that's good! Do this for me every day, and your sordid little secret will be safe.'

Every day? I mused bewilderedly, moving my hand up and down his wet shaft to bring out his sperm before Mat returned. He definitely had me exactly where he wanted me. I was nothing more than his sex slave! 'Do it properly, bitch!' he admonished me. 'Use your tongue properly!'

Snaking my tantalizing tongue round his swollen knob, I again prayed for him to come. If Mat walked in . . . God, all hell would be let loose! Ridiculous thoughts battered my mind as he rocked his hips faster, fucking my mouth. We could move house, go to a different area far away from Den. Perhaps I could get a job, work all day in the safe surroundings of an office. I didn't know what the answer was.

'Coming!' Den cried as his purple knob swelled. His sperm gushing, flooding my mouth, I swallowed again and again. 'Wank me!' he ordered me. 'Do it properly, bitch!' Wanking his solid shaft, sucking his orgasming knob, I drank his treacherous sperm, draining his balls, quelling his libido. I was nothing more than an object, an object with a hot, wet mouth to fuck as and when the notion took his fancy.

His flow finally stemming, I swallowed for the last time. Again, he'd fucked my mouth, baptized my throat with his blasphemous lust juice. Again, I'd succumbed to my evil blackmailer. Slipping his spent penis out of my mouth as Mat called out from the hall, he coolly zipped his jeans back up and seated himself. Frantically licking my lips, wiping my mouth on a serviette, my face flushed as Mat breezed in.

'Cigars!' he announced triumphantly, passing one to Den. 'I wasn't too long, was I?'

'No, your timing was perfect!' Den grinned. 'We've had a nice chat, haven't we, Jane?'

'Yes, a nice chat,' I echoed softly, the taste of sperm lingering on my tongue. 'I . . . I think I'll go up to bed. I'm not feeling too well.'

'Oh, I am sorry,' Mat frowned. 'I hope it's nothing you've eaten.'

'Maybe it's something you drank,' Den winked, flashing me a salacious grin.

'Maybe. I'll see you later, Mat. Goodnight, Den.'

Climbing the stairs, tears staining my cheeks, I knew that I had to put an end to the relentless ruination of my marriage – my life. But how? Short of running away, there was nothing I could do. Stripping off and climbing beneath the summery quilt, my mind reeling as male laughter drifted up the stairs, I cried myself to sleep and dreamed my dreams of Den's penis spunking in my mouth – my cunt-mouth.

Chapter Four

I woke to yet another day – a day of potential fear, blackmail and, no doubt, crude sex. I needed to think, to plan the end of the nightmare. I couldn't go on like this, living in constant fear, jumping every time the phone rang or someone knocked on the door, I told myself.

Leaving Mat sleeping, I slipped out of bed and stood before the full-length mirror. Turning my naked body, I surveyed the weals fanning out across my buttocks, wondering whether Mat had seen this evidence of the thrashing as he'd climbed into bed. Obviously not, I decided, or he'd have said something, questioned me all night long, hurled accusations at me.

Naked, as I no longer owned a dressing gown, I wandered downstairs to the kitchen and filled the kettle. It was only six-thirty but the summer sun was already up, warming the garden, opening the pink petals of the flowers. My own pink sex petals had opened to Den's tongue, but not to his penis. I vowed never to take his penis into my cunt – never! *Cunt*. I chided myself for the vulgarity.

Opening the back door, I recalled sitting at the dining-room table with Den's cock in my mouth, his sperm gushing over my tongue. I imagined that I could still taste his jism. Thank God Mat hadn't pestered me for sex when he'd eventually come to bed, I reflected, wandering out onto the patio, the light and warmth of the sun charging my naked body.

Sitting on a chair, I knew that Den wouldn't be up and about yet. I was safe in the garden – for a while, at least. I had time alone, time to think. Contemplating my firm breasts, I wondered whether Den would ever suck my nipples again. Could I halt the degradation, the humiliation? What plan could I come up with to put an end to the nightmare?

Looking up at his house, I contemplated breaking in and retrieving the evidence. But even if I managed to get in, I'd never find the photographs and the tape. Den wasn't stupid, they were bound to be well hidden. He had me exactly where he wanted me, I again reflected. Living next door to him, I was permanently available for crude sex, always there to service him. I felt hunted, like a fugitive – caged, like an animal.

Unconsciously parting my thighs and toying with my wet inner lips as I relaxed beneath the warming sun, my mind drifted. Sex reared its ugly head – its beautiful head! My arousal soaring as my clitoris stiffened, I closed my eyes, unwittingly rubbing between my swelling sex lips, massaging my secret button. The exquisite sensations built quickly, reaching every nerve ending, tightening every muscle, consuming me. My naked body trembling, I opened my eyes, suddenly aware that I was masturbating in the garden.

'God!' I breathed, leaping to my feet. 'I can't keep doing this!' Wandering down the garden, I tried to clear my head, to push all thoughts of masturbation and orgasm to the back of my mind. I was becoming sex-crazed, my insatiable clitoris leading me astray, down the seductive path to complete and utter depravity. But, as much as I tried, I couldn't deny my soaring arousal, my desperate yearning for orgasm. The spirit of sex had touched me.

At the end of the garden, the grass soft beneath my naked

feet, I looked about me. I wasn't consciously aware of what I was looking for until I'd found it. Driven into a flower border, the garden hoe beckoned me, its green plastic handle at forty-five degrees, inviting my cunt. Standing with my feet wide apart, the rounded end of the handle only inches from my swollen vaginal lips, I suddenly wondered what had come over me.

'No,' I protested weakly, turning to walk away. I couldn't commit the degrading act. But the notion intrigued me, beckoned me, and I turned back, the long green phallus attracting me like a magnet. Crude thoughts whispered in my head. *Bury the handle in your cunt and fuck yourself to orgasm.* I was weak, my arousal strong. I knew I'd lose the battle, though I tried desperately to resist. 'God, no!' I sighed lamely again as my cunt spasmed, my clitoris pulsated and my lust juices bubbled down my inner thighs.

Positioning the end of the handle between my ballooning outer lips, I manoeuvred my hips, aligning the shaft with my sex duct. Taking a look around the garden to make sure that I really was alone, I moved forward, the plastic handle entering my tight cunt. The shaft was bigger, longer and broader than any penis, the filling sensation heavenly. My inner flesh stretching, opening to accommodate the massive phallus, I gasped as my clitoris swelled and throbbed.

Parting my feet further, I rocked my hips, the shaft driving in and out of my cunt, fucking me, taking me to frightening heights of arousal. Tweaking my erect nipple, I massaged the solid nub of my exposed clitoris with my other hand, bringing out beautiful pre-orgasmic sensations. I desperately needed to come, to quell my incredible libido, to find the peace and tranquillity that only orgasm brings. A nymphomaniac? The word haunted me.

Massaging my clitoris faster, I swung my hips vigorously back and forth, abusing my naked body, fucking my beautiful cunt in my sexual frenzy. Gasping, I leaned back, my burning sexual centre projected, taking the handle deep into my gripping pussy as my climax approached. 'God, yes!' I cried as my clitoris swelled and erupted in orgasm. 'Oh, oh, God!'

Unconscious of my surroundings, I fucked myself faster, massaging my clitoris with a vengeance, crying out as my climax repeatedly peaked. My naked body shuddering, my lust juices coursing down the green handle, I rocked my hips faster, ramming my cervix. In my sexual delirium, I lost control, the handle slipping out of my cunt and sliding down between my buttocks.

'Ah!' I cried, propelling my hips forward before I'd realized what had happened, the cunny-wet handle suddenly driving deep into my bottom-hole. 'Ah, no!' Slowly moving back, the shaft slipping out of my private duct, the sensations drove me wild. Never had I woken the sleeping nerve endings there, derived pleasure from my bottom.

'Jesus,' I whispered as I tentatively moved forward, the shaft penetrating my bottom again, opening me, sending electrifying sensations deep into my quivering pelvis. Massaging my clitoris again, the shaft embedded deep within my secret hole, I took myself to another shuddering orgasm.

Whimpering as my anal sphincter muscles gripped the invading shaft, I swayed back and forth, fucking my own tight bottom-hole with the hoe handle. Never had I known that such beautiful sensations existed, not realized the pleasure derivable from my secret sheath: I contemplated using two shafts, fucking both my holes simultaneously. My whole body trembling, vibrant with sex, I thought I'd die as my incredible climax rode on. My heart racing, my breathing heavy, I almost crumpled to the ground as my rectal duct tightened again, squeezing the thrusting shaft.

Hearing Mat calling me, I stood still, only my fingers

moving between my yawning cunt lips, gently massaging the last waves of my climax from my appreciative nub. 'Jane, where are you?' he called as I moved back, the handle slowly gliding out of my inflamed bottom-hole, leaving me quivering uncontrollably. Birds fluttered about the old apple tree. Had they watched me?

Staggering towards the house, I scooped my sticky vaginal cream out of my sex crack and sucked my fingers. Wiping my inner thighs, I smiled innocently as Mat appeared in the doorway and asked me what I was doing in the garden without my clothes on. My pussy juice tasted nice, a comforting taste. I wanted to lick my own cunt.

'What are you doing out here naked?' he asked again.

'Watching the birds,' I replied nonchalantly, sitting on a patio chair and crossing my legs, concealing not only my swollen pussy lips, my gaping cunt, but my weal-lined buttocks. 'And sunbathing.'

'You've never done that before,' he remarked, his brown eyes frowning as suspicion obviously got the better of him.

'Yes, I have. I often sunbathe naked while you're at work.'

'You've never told me.'

'You've never asked. The kettle's boiled, if you'd like to make the coffee.'

'Oh, right.'

'What time did Den go last night?'

'Around one o'clock. We finished off the wine, smoked cigars and had a pretty good night. It's a shame you weren't feeling well. Are you OK now?'

'Yes, I'm fine,' I smiled.

'Good. I'll go and make the coffee. Unfortunately, I have an early start today.'

As Mat chinked the cups and rattled the teaspoon, I parted my thighs and gazed down at my swollen, irrigated labia. The garden hoe would become an intimate friend, I mused, recalling the incredible sensations deep within my bloated bottom. I'd slip down the garden every day and . . . Remembering Den's words as he'd fucked my mouth, I shuddered. *Do this for me every day, and your sordid little secret will be safe.*

Again, I imagined that I could still taste his sperm on my tongue. I pictured his solid penis driving in and out of my mouth, my lips rolling along his glistening shaft, his sperm bathing my tongue, jetting to the back of my throat. A bolt of fear hit me as Mat sauntered into the garden with the coffee. There was no escaping Den and his insatiable penis, no safe haven – not even my bedroom.

'Den's window overlooks the garden,' Mat said with a hint of petulance as he placed my coffee on the table. 'You shouldn't be out here without anything on.'

'I'm sure he's seen a naked woman before,' I quipped.

'Don't you mind?'

'He won't be looking out of his window at this time of the morning, Mat.'

'But you said that you often sunbathe naked while I'm at work.'

'I'm sure Den has better things to do than stare out of the window at me.'

'Yes, but . . .'

'What's the matter, are you jealous?'

'No, of course I'm not. It's just that . . . Oh well, it's up to you. I'd better go and get ready.'

It was odd that he'd not insisted that I dress, conceal my naked femininity. With his suspicious mind, his possessiveness, I'd have thought that he'd have ordered me into the house rather than leave me naked on the patio. And he'd not made a great fuss about my sunbathing naked while he was at work. Perhaps he'd changed? No, *I'd* changed!

Recalling the photograph Den had of me, I decided that it *would* be worth sneaking into his house in an attempt to retrieve the evidence. No matter how well hidden, given time I was sure that I'd find it – and the tape. He'd said something to Mat over the meal about seeing a client in London in the morning. My cue to break into his house?

Contemplating the idea as the sun rose higher in the sky, I tweaked my nipples, the beautiful sensations permeating my pert breasts. Never had my milk teats been so sensitive, so responsive, and I cupped the fullness of my breasts as I raised them in my hands and gently sucked each brown protrusion in turn. My clitoris swelled, my cunt ached, and I knew that I needed to come again.

Repeatedly sucking on each milk teat, my areolae darkening, I gently bit my succulent nipples. Picturing Den's stiff penis, sperm jetting from his bulbous glans, I realized that I'd not had sex with Mat for some time. What would it be like now, sucking Mat to orgasm? How would he compare as he came? How would his sperm taste after Den's? A cock was a cock.

'It's seven-thirty, I'll see you this evening,' Mat smiled as he stepped onto the patio, making me jump. 'You'd better cover yourself up before Den . . .'

'I'll put my bikini on after I've had my coffee,' I smiled.

'Right, I'll see you later.'

It was time to retreat into the house before Den started roaming, hunting me like an animal, I decided. Wandering into the kitchen and locking the back door, I went into the lounge and looked out of the window. Den's ageing BMW was still in his drive. I had time to dress and have breakfast before I retrieved the photographs and tape from his house. If my mission was successful, he'd no longer have anything on me. And he could go to hell!

After a refreshing shower and a breakfast of scrambled

eggs on toast, I looked out of the lounge window again. Den's car had gone! My hands trembling, I slipped out of the front door and crept up his path. At last I had an opportunity to end the nightmare! Although the chances of breaking in were pretty remote, at least I had to try.

Creeping around the back of his house, I noticed that the dining room window was partially open. Looking around the garden, I knew I was alone, but I still felt afraid. If Den caught me in his house . . . But he'd gone, and Mat had gone, so I had no need to worry. Climbing through the window, my breathing heavy, my heart racing, I stood in the dining room, wondering where to begin the search.

Stealing through the hall, I slipped into the lounge. The photographs still adorned the walls, my dressing gown over the back of an armchair. *So far so good*, I thought positively, wondering where the other photos were. About to open a bureau, I froze as I heard a key in the front-door lock. My heart pounding wildly, I looked frantically about me as the door opened and closed.

Diving behind the sofa, I held my breath as Den breezed in. What the hell had he come back for? I wondered anxiously as he moved about the room. He must have forgotten something. Hopefully, he'd get whatever it was and leave. My body shaking, my palms wet with fear, I knew I wouldn't be able to play dead indefinitely.

As he sat down and punched the buttons on the telephone, I realized with horror that he might spend half an hour chatting, or even longer. 'Hi, it's Den,' he chirped as I tried to make myself more comfortable. 'Not bad, bearing up under the strain. Listen, the photographs are ready. Yes, a dozen showing her naked, and it's pretty obvious by the expression on her face that she's enjoying a massive orgasm! No, I was careful to duck every time I pressed the camera remote. You can see everything, believe me! No, they're not here, they're with my photographer friend. Yes, I'll be taking some more today. Don't you worry about that, I've got so much on her now that she'll have no bloody choice. OK, I'll see you later. Bye.'

Wondering who he'd been talking to as he left the room, I breathed a sigh of relief as I heard the front door slam shut. There was no point in stripping the walls now that he had another dozen shots of me. Besides, he'd know that I'd been into his house, and I didn't want that.

Creeping through the hall, I made my escape through the dining-room window, wondering when he planned to take more photographs of me. He was right – he had so much on me now that I wouldn't have any choice. I'd be forced to pose for him, even though it would consolidate his evidence of my debauchery.

The phone was ringing as I stepped into the hall of my own house and closed the door, but I didn't answer it. My mind reeling, I was in no mood to chat to anyone. Relaxing on the sofa in the lounge, I wondered what to do, now that my plan had failed. This was my life, I reflected. How on earth had someone gained complete control over me? I felt a slave in every sense of the word. I dared not leave the house for fear of Den following me. My body as good as belonged to him.

Carole had been right – the only way out of the mess would have been to tell Mat everything. But it was too late for that now. I found myself contemplating divorce. It was a terrible thought, but it would certainly solve my horrendous problems. I finally decided to ignore Den and accept the consequences, whatever they were. I couldn't live two lives, the respectable married woman and the covert sex slave. It just wasn't possible.

The phone rang several times during my hour or so of contemplation, but I ignored it. What Carole must have thought of me, I had no idea. I should have contacted her and explained . . . But explained what? I'd told her that I'd bent over and showed my neighbour my cunt. There was nothing to explain.

'Ah, there you are!' Den grinned as he breezed into the lounge, clutching his Pentax.

'How . . . how did you get in?' I stammered, my heart racing as I leaped to my feet.

'The front door was open.'

'It wasn't!'

'How do you think I got in, then? I didn't walk through the wall!'

'Get out of here!'

'That's not very nice, Jane. I've come here to masturbate you, to bring you pleasure.'

'I'm not going to be blackmailed any more. I've had enough, Den.'

'I have another photograph for you to look at. The lighting's not too good but you can see quite clearly.'

Grinning triumphantly, he pulled the picture from his jacket pocket and passed it to me. I gazed in horror at the obscene image of me chomping on Den's meaty penis at the dining-room table. More incriminating evidence! More food for blackmail! How on earth had he managed it? Where had the camera been? By the angle of the shot, it must have been on the windowsill, the lens peeping through the gap in the curtains.

'Pretty good, isn't it?' he leered.

'Den, how . . .'

'You can keep it, I have plenty more. As you can see, I have my camera so . . .'

'No! No, you're not taking any more of me!' I broke in, a bolt of fear hitting me as I imagined Mat gazing at the obscene banquet.

'I thought you might say that so I've made contingency plans.'

'If you show Mat, you'll be in as much trouble as me.'

'I'll say that you kept begging me for sex, that you came to my house and stripped off, that you insisted that I allow you to suck me off while Mat went to get the cigars. That's it, I had to take photographs, threaten to show him the evidence so you'd stop pestering me.'

'He'll never believe you!'

'I'll tell him that you pushed your panties and suspender belts through my letter box, that you threatened to tell him that we were having an affair.'

'That's ridiculous, he'll never believe . . .'

'I'll tell him that you have dozens of men coming here for sex. Anyway, the contingency plans . . . I've posted a couple of photos to Mat's office.'

'What?'

'They should get there tomorrow morning.'

'But . . .'

'Don't worry, they're not of you. I cut them out of a magazine and wrote discreet captions like *I've seen your wife posing like this.*'

'Why on earth . . .'

'It's just a taste of what *could* happen, Jane. You know what Mat's like, he'll become highly suspicious and question you about it. Of course, you'll talk your way out of it, put it down to some idiot trying to cause trouble, but if he then received the real thing . . . So, let's start by having you strip naked.'

On and on Den would come at me, like the breakers rolling towards the shore, one after another, never-ending – perpetual. Sex ruled my life, Den ruled my life – possessed me. I might as well have been possessed by the devil himself for all the difference it would have made! Perhaps he *was* the devil?

Again ordering me to strip as he placed his camera on the coffee table, he moved an armchair into the centre of the room. How was I to pose for him? Sprawled naked over the chair? Reclining with my legs wide apart, my cunt crudely exhibited?

Unbuttoning my blouse, I became resigned to the fact that I was Den's sex slave. A mixture of fear and arousal gripped me as I slipped my blouse over my shoulders and tossed it onto the sofa. Having no choice other than to surrender, to yield to his crude demands, to my horror the thought tightened my cunt, my juices flowing from my sex sheath.

'Hurry up!' he chuckled as I released my bra, revealing my firm breasts, my erect nipples. Looking down at my milk teats, I recalled taking them into my mouth, the beautiful sensations as I'd sucked the sensitive brown protrusions. I wanted to suck them again. Did I want Den to bite my breast buds?

Stripping before my blackmailer had almost become a way of life, I reflected. It was expected of me, and I automatically complied. Stepping out of my shoes, I dropped my skirt and tugged my wet panties down, again wondering whether Den was going to suckle my breast buds. There was a longing within my nipples that cried out for satisfaction. What did my heart long for?

As I stood there naked, I wondered where it would all end, if it would ever end. Nothing lasts, I reflected. The end would come, but how and when? Would Mat eventually discover my wanton ways? Would we move house? Inevitably, the end *had* to come one day, and in one way or another.

Instructing me to sit in the chair, Den moved towards the door. It was as if I was anaesthetized, hypnotized, as I obediently sat down. I was a lust robot, a sex machine. I remained motionless as he left the room and returned with two lengths of rope. I didn't even try to stop him when he pulled me forward, positioning my buttocks over the edge of the cushion with my thighs wide apart.

Tying one end of the rope to my right foot, he ran it round the back of the chair and secured my left foot. My knees bent, my feet pulled either side of the chair, my naked body was vulnerable to his every perverted whim, and I knew that the time had come for him to fuck me. The final act of degradation, the ultimate act of adultery.

Placing my hands by the side of the chair, he ran the rope behind the chair and secured my wrists. My femininity crudely stripped, my naked body tethered, defenceless, I wondered what he was going to do first. Would he start by fucking me? Or would he lick me to orgasm? My thighs wide apart, my cunt gaping, he grinned as he grabbed his camera.

'You can come in now!' he chortled unexpectedly. My heart leaped into my mouth as I faced the door to see a naked teenaged girl drift into the room, silent, almost angelic. 'There she is!' Den grinned, pointing at me. 'Tied up and ready for you. OK, let's have some really good lesbian poses.'

Her long black hair cascading over her firm breasts, the dark angel licked her lips provocatively as she stood before me, scrutinizing my naked body. Lowering my eyes, I focused on her fleshy vaginal lips, shaved, devoid of pubic hair. Her inner labia peeping out from her sex crack, I wondered whether I'd be forced to lick her there, lick her clitoris to orgasm as Den captured my debauched act on film. Who was she? I wondered as she gazed hungrily at my gaping cunt. A friend? A prostitute? It didn't matter who she was. An unknown girl, a passing angel of sex.

My eyes wide with apprehension, my heart racing as she knelt on the floor between my thighs, I could say nothing.

My mind grew numbed as the words of protest stuck in my throat. As I felt her warm breath on my inner thighs, her long tresses tickling my sensitive sex crack, I struggled to free myself, pulling hopelessly on the ropes. Den clicked the camera as she moved up and licked my lower stomach, cleansed and wet my smooth skin. I screamed inside as she kissed and sucked on each vaginal lip – for what, I don't know.

'She has a beautiful cunt,' the girl breathed crudely, licking the full length of my gaping sex valley. Her pink tongue was wet, hot, and I shuddered as I gazed in disbelief at her pretty face, lesbian passion reflected in her dark eyes. A young girl licking my cunt? I couldn't believe what was happening to me, and I wondered what else Den had in store for me.

'God, she tastes good,' the girl sighed, parting my outer lips with her slender fingers and exposing my swollen clitoris to her sweeping tongue. I focused on my taut vaginal flesh, her tongue licking me, tasting me. What did lesbians do to each other? Would she finger me?

Closing my eyes as Den clicked the camera, I felt the girl's tongue move down my open crack and sweep in circles around my vaginal entrance. Suddenly, her pink mouth-snake entered my sex hole, exploring inside me, licking my wet inner flesh. I'd known that Den would use me for his own sexual gratification, but to force me to endure lesbian sex? I'd misjudged him, underestimated his decadence beyond all comprehension!

As the young lesbian's fingers penetrated my vagina, massaging me, stretching me wide open, I shuddered. I felt humiliated, degraded in the extreme as she sucked my stiffening clitoris into her hot mouth. The most private part of my body blatantly on show, abused by a naked girl as the camera shutter clicked, I knew that I'd sunk to the bottom of the murky pool of depravity. In my naivety, I was sure that I could sink no further. Surely there could be nothing more perverted than having a lesbian finger and lick me?

My clitoris responding to her feminine tonguing and sucking, I tried to convince myself that a tongue was a tongue, a finger a finger, male or female. But her perfume wafted up my nostrils, the smell of her hair, her female scent. There was no getting away from the fact that my clitoris was responding to the sexual stimulation of another woman.

My sex juices flowing in torrents, she slipped her wet fingers out of my tightening vaginal sheath and stood up, her dark eyes locked to mine. As she knelt on the arms of the chair, her shaved vaginal lips gaping, only inches from my face, my mouth, I focused on the globules of opaque liquid clinging to her distended inner petals. I couldn't perform the lesbian act, I knew, as she moved forward, the heady scent of her cunt filling my nostrils.

'Lick her,' Den instructed me as he knelt on the floor beside the chair, focusing the camera on my flushed face. 'Lick her cunt, bitch!' He was angry, male, cruel and hard – she was soft, smooth in her femininity. Pressing her yawning sex crack against my mouth, her warm cream wetting me, she gasped as I tentatively pushed my tongue out and tasted her there. Her juices trickled down my chin, bathing me, dribbling.

Pulling her fleshy lips apart, she exposed her erect clitoris, her pearl, to my sweeping tongue, her naked body quivering as I repeatedly lapped at her sex button. Savouring the taste of another woman's vaginal juices, I closed my eyes, my frightening appetite for lesbian sex spiralling as I discovered another side to me.

'Tongue my cunt!' the young girl breathed, swivelling her

hips and aligning her open sex hole with my mouth. I felt my own juices of arousal seeping from my vagina, running down between my buttocks and wetting my anal entrance as I slipped my tongue deep into her hot pussy. Her cream tasted beautiful, feminine, sexy – her inner flesh hot, smooth and soft. I drank from her young sex duct, lapping up her flowing juices, savouring her sticky honeydew as she stretched her pussy lips wide apart, opening her love hole to my thirsty mouth. In my arousal and confusion, I began to wonder whether or not I'd be able to enjoy a penis after my lesbian experience. Was I now bisexual?

I wasn't aware of Den kneeling between my parted thighs until he rudely rammed his penis deep into my tight cunt. Gasping through a mouthful of wet vaginal flesh as he withdrew and thrust into me again, my tethered body jolting, I wondered at my emotions. My naked body tied with rope, a young lesbian about to come in my mouth, a man's cock about to spunk inside my cunt . . . I was awash with sex.

I felt alive with arousal but, at the same time, riddled with guilt. My body trembling as my own orgasm neared, my pulsating clitoris massaged by Den's pistoning cock, the girl's sex nodule throbbing beneath my snaking tongue, never had I known the pleasure obtainable from perverted sex. Far removed from making love with Mat, I was wallowing in the most crude three-way coupling I could imagine.

My husband at work while I lapped at a young girl's vaginal folds, my face drenched with her juices of lust, my cunt bloated by a huge penis, I pondered on my marriage. I'd thought I'd found eternal love with Mat, but now? I'd desecrated my marriage vows, destroyed the sanctity of my partnership, cast my soul into the eternal fires of hell.

'God, you've got a tight cunt!' Den cried as his penis swelled and throbbed inside me, breaking my reverie.

'And she has the most wonderful mouth!' the young lesbian gasped. 'Oh, I'm . . . I'm coming!'

Her clitoris swelling and pulsating, her cunt milk flowing in torrents, she shuddered as she cried out in her coming. My own mind-blowing climax erupted simultaneously with Den's. His cock ramming deep into my hot vaginal sheath, his sperm jetting, bathing my cervix, I experienced an orgasm of an intensity and duration that I hadn't known was possible.

On and on the waves of pure sexual ecstasy rolled through my sated body, shaking me to the core, gripping my very being. I could feel Den's sperm, filling me, oozing from my inflamed vagina and coursing down between my buttocks as I sucked on the girl's pulsating nub, sustaining her incredible orgasm. We were locked in lust, our genitals throbbing in orgasm, our bodies trembling as we gave and received pleasure.

My climax finally waning as Den stilled his thrusting cock, I gently licked the girl's clitoris, bringing out the last ripples of her orgasm as she gasped her appreciation. As she swivelled her hips, aligning her open love hole with my thirsty mouth, I sucked out her juices, drinking the heady wine from her exhausted young body. Never had I known the immense pleasure to be elicited from another girl's cunt, and I sucked and drank until I'd drained her burning sex sheath.

'That's enough,' she finally whimpered as she clambered off the chair and Den slipped his deflated penis out of my drenched vagina.

'You'd better clean her up,' Den chuckled as she knelt between my parted thighs. 'Lick my spunk out of her cunt and then I'll fuck her mouth.'

As the girl licked and sucked, her mouth pressed hard against my open vaginal entrance, swallowing the cocktail of sperm and my copious pussy juice, Den grabbed the Pentax and took several more shots of the young lesbian. *And then I'll fuck her mouth.* The crude words resounding through my tormented mind, I watched the nameless girl drinking from my hot cunt, wondering when my abusers would allow me my freedom.

My blonde pubic hairs matted with sperm and sex milk, my vagina inflamed, my clitoris throbbing, I gasped as I sensed the beginning of another orgasm welling in my contracting womb. To my horror, the very thought of a girl's tongue delving deep into my cunt had sent my arousal soaring, and I almost begged her to lick my insatiable sex nodule.

'That's enough,' Den finally instructed the young beauty. But it wasn't enough – I wanted more. Casting his eyes around the room as if looking for something, he moved to the mantelpiece. 'This is ideal,' he grinned, brandishing the camera and passing her a long candle. 'Stick it up her cunt and I'll take some real firecrackers.'

As the girl slipped the waxen shaft deep into my drenched vagina, I thought of the garden hoe, the incredible sensations as its handle had slipped into my private sanctuary, my bottom-hole. If Mat found out what I'd been up to, the abuse, the crude lesbian sex, he'd disown me, send me packing. But I knew that I couldn't turn back now. Even if Den were to leave me alone, stop his blackmail threats, my sexual appetite was now voracious. I could never be the same loving, demure plain Jane again – I'd masturbate, fuck myself with bananas and the hoe handle, suck and bite on my own nipples . . . What had I become? Who had I become? In the distance, the inner voice whispered. *I am not what I once was.*

'Right, now you take a few shots of me fucking her mouth,' Den instructed, kneeling on the arms of the chair as the girl moved aside. His solid penis protruding from his trousers, he yanked his foreskin back and pressed his purple plum against my lips. 'Suck me off, whore!' he ordered me as his accomplice focused the camera on my face, on his huge organ.

I took him into my mouth, savouring the mingled taste of his sperm and my vaginal fluid as he pushed his knob to the back of my throat. Withdrawing, he drove into me again, my lips rolling along his wet shaft as he crudely fucked my mouth. 'I'll spunk over her face!' he gasped. 'Make sure you get her beautiful pearls in frame!'

Quickening his rhythm, sliding his knob in and out of my mouth, I imagined the photographs of his sperm jetting, splattering my mouth, my face. With all the evidence he now had of my debauchery he'd be able to force me to do anything. Whether he demanded sex in the middle of the night or the middle of the day, I'd have to go running to him with my knickers down. If his lesbian friend wanted me licking between her legs, sucking her clitoris to orgasm, I'd have no choice.

'I'm going to tell Mat,' I blurted out as he slipped his penis out of my mouth and ran his hand up and down his swollen shaft, wanking his cock to orgasm. His spunk suddenly jetted from his bulbous glans, splattering my face, running down my chin. 'I'm going to tell him everything.'

'Keep wanking!' the girl cried, taking shot after shot. 'Spunk over her lips!'

Driving his penis back into my mouth as the last of his sperm dribbled from his knob, the camera shutter clicking, I sucked and drank for what I prayed would be the last time. Never again would I allow him to use me like this, I vowed. I had to put an end to the degradation, no matter how high my arousal soared. I didn't want a lesbian licking my cunt, and I didn't want to lick a lesbian's cunt. I wanted Mat.

'OK,' Den finally breathed, turning to the girl as he slipped his cock out of my spermed mouth and zipped up his trousers. 'Get dressed and wait for me at my place. I'll finish off here and then pay you.'

So the girl *was* a prostitute, I mused as she drifted out of the room. Was I prostituting myself? I wondered. Giving my naked body in return for Den's silence was as good as prostituting myself, even though I'd had no choice. But I had a choice now. Even if it meant losing Mat, I would fall no further into the depths of depravity, the turbid pool of perverted sex.

'I might as well leave you tied up,' Den chuckled in his wickedness as he placed the wet candle on the mantelpiece. 'Mat will have quite a shock when he gets home and sees you like that!'

'Do what you like, it's over,' I murmured, his sperm running down my flushed face.

'Over? Don't be silly!'

'I'm telling you, it's over.'

'In that case, I *will* leave you tied up. And I'll make sure Mat gets a copy of every photograph, and a copy of the tape.'

'Go to hell!'

'Have it your way.'

As he left, I tried to untie the rope, my fingers just able to reach the knot by my wrist. I had to free myself and have a shower, wash away the sperm and cunt milk before Mat returned. Wondering when Den would show Mat the photographs, I finally managed to loosen the rope and free my hand. Untying my feet, I hauled my aching body out of the chair, trying to think what to say to Mat in way of an explanation for my immoral behaviour. There was nothing

I could say, I knew, as I pushed the chair back into place. There were no words to save my marriage.

As I was about to grab my clothes, Mat appeared in the doorway and frowned at me. 'Jane, what *are* you up to?' he asked accusingly as I discreetly kicked the ropes beneath the sofa.

'Mat . . . Mat, I . . .' I stammered, my body trembling as he focused on my glistening, matted pubic thatch. Raising his eyes, he scrutinized my guilty face.

'What's that on your face?' he demanded. 'I think you'd better tell me what's been going on here.'

'I've been exercising,' I replied stupidly, wiping the sperm from my cheeks, my chin. 'I was just about to take a shower.'

'Exercising? What sort of exercises require you to be naked?'

'As I said, I was about to take a shower. What are you doing here, anyway?'

'I'm on my way to see a client. Jane, what *have* you been doing?'

'I've already told you, Mat!' I laughed.

'Why is your face wet?'

'It's cream, face cream.'

'And why are you so wet down there?' he asked, lowering his eyes to my sopping muff.

'I'm hot, that's why I was about to take a shower. Why all these questions, Mat? Anyone would think that you suspected me of committing adultery, the way you're going on.'

'Have you?'

'Of course not!' I giggled. 'As you can see, I'm alone. Besides, you know I wouldn't do such a thing.'

'Do I? Look, we'll talk about this later. I don't believe you've been exercising.'

'Well, I'm sorry, but I can't prove it!' I returned with a hint of anger.

'The other day I came home and found you naked in here, this morning you were naked in the garden, and now . . . I'll be back later, and I want some answers, Jane.'

As he flounced from the room, the front door slamming shut, I flopped onto the sofa. Answers? I had no answers, other than the truth. At least he hadn't seen the weals across my buttocks. And thank God he hadn't arrived ten minutes earlier! I had to think, write my script and rehearse my lines – my lies. The taste of girl juice lingered, reminding me, teasing me.

Chapter Five

The evening came all too quickly. I wasn't prepared, had not rehearsed my lines – I had no lines. When Mat began firing questions at me, all I could do was repeat myself, ramble on inanely about exercising – but he wouldn't let go. Again and again he demanded to know why I'd been naked in the lounge, why my face had been wet, why I had looked as if I'd been dragged through a hedge backwards.

I was beginning to feel exasperated. Why shouldn't I have been exercising? Why was the notion unbelievable? In the privacy of my own home, what was so strange about my being naked? Realizing that he was getting nowhere, Mat finally changed his line of questioning.

'Are you seeing someone else?' he asked forthrightly.

'Of course I'm not,' I smiled innocently as he poured his scotch and deposited himself in his armchair – the cunt-wet armchair. 'Whatever makes you think that?'

'When I called in earlier, I noticed that you were red down there. Your pussy was sore, inflamed.'

'I'd been . . .'

'Been what?'

It was pretty obvious that exercising wouldn't inflame my pussy lips. Not normal exercising, anyway! As he repeated his question, I didn't know what to say, what lies to tell. For some reason, I felt like telling him the truth, telling him that Den had screwed me as I'd licked a teenaged girl to orgasm. Fortunately, I wasn't that stupid.

'I masturbated,' I finally confessed.

'Masturbated?'

'You've heard of masturbation, surely?'

'Of course I have, but . . .'

'I felt randy and, as we've not had sex for a while, I masturbated.'

'I don't believe you, Jane.'

'Mat, I'd hardly admit to masturbating if it wasn't true!'

'You've never done that before.'

'How do you know?'

'Well . . .'

'For all you know, I might masturbate several times a day.'

'There's another thing . . .' He paused, taking something out of his jacket pocket. 'These arrived at my office this morning. They've been torn out of a magazine. Read the captions.'

Taking the crumpled pages, I surveyed the naked models displaying their open cunts. ' "I've seen your wife posing like this",' I murmured, my heart thumping. 'Someone's having a laugh!' I forced a giggle. 'No one's seen me like that, not even you!'

'It's odd that I find you naked, wet and sore the day these arrive in the post.'

'Mat, I wasn't going to tell you but . . .' A lie came to mind. 'Someone sent me a picture of a naked man with a similar caption about you.'

'Where is it?'

'I threw it away. It was obviously sent by someone trying to cause trouble.'

'Who on earth would want to do that?'

'A crank, I would imagine. It's best to ignore it, forget about it.'

Sipping his scotch, Mat watched me as I sat in the

armchair opposite him. He couldn't argue now that I'd admitted I'd masturbated and had received a magazine picture, but I knew he was still suspicious. The idea suddenly occurring to me that I could turn the situation round, I donned a frown.

'There was a phone call earlier,' I began, watching for his reaction. 'A woman asked for you.'

'Who was it?'

'She wouldn't say. I heard another woman in the background. She was laughing, saying something about his wife.'

'Whose wife?'

'Your wife, obviously. I should be asking *you* whether you're seeing someone else.'

'Don't be silly!' he laughed, moving uneasily in his chair.

'Why's it silly? The magazine cutting, the phone call . . . And you stayed away the other night.'

'I was on business, you know that.'

'Look, let's change the subject, Mat. We won't get anywhere if we're suspicious about each other. Agreed?'

'Agreed. Oh, by the way, Den's coming over.'

'What for?'

'He was in his front garden when I came home. He wants to talk to me about something-finance, more than likely.'

'When will he be here?'

'He didn't say a time.'

My heart sank, my head spinning at the sound of his name. I'd successfully explained away my sore pussy, I'd got over the problem of the magazine pages, and now this! Den, Den, Den. Den coming round for a meal, coming round to screw me, coming round to see Mat . . . I couldn't escape the bloody man! Did he intend to bring the photographs and the tape? I wondered. Was he going to show the evidence of my whoring to Mat? I felt despondent, annoyed, and again I wondered how on earth I'd got myself into this situation.

As Mat went out into the garden, I wondered whether to ring Carole and suggest that I go round for coffee. I needed to talk to someone, to get out of the house for a while – to get away from Den. I'd have to contact her at some stage, explain things to her – but not yet. I had enough on my plate as it was, I decided, making a mental note to call her later.

What did Den really want to see Mat about? If he *did* show him the photographs he'd never be able to have sex with me again, or blackmail me. No, he wouldn't reveal the sordid truth, I was sure. There again, he might . . . My mind was swirling, my head aching, my whispering thoughts confusing me. My chest tight with anxiety, I wandered out into the garden to find Mat. I had to come across as cool and calm, not riddled with guilt and anxiety.

'It's a lovely evening,' I smiled, walking across the lawn to join him.

'I love the summer,' he remarked. 'How about a barbecue?'

'I was going to prepare a salad.'

'No, let's have a barbecue. As Den's coming round, he might as well eat with us.'

'Can't we have an evening alone together, Mat?' I sighed.

'I don't suppose he'll stay for the whole evening. I'll light the barbecue and then invite him to join us.'

As Mat wandered towards the house, I gazed at the garden hoe, recalling the anal abuse, the beautiful base sensations. My cunt spasmed, my clitoris swelling as I ran my fingers over the round end of the plastic handle. I needed to come, but there was no time. I'd masturbate later, lock myself in the bathroom and massage my insatiable clitoris to a wonderful orgasm.

Turning, I watched Mat fiddling with the barbecue,

dreading the thought of Den joining us. Couldn't he leave me alone for a while? Constantly, he was infiltrating my life, hanging around, lurking, spying, waiting for an opportunity to abuse me. My clitoris swelled, my knickers wetting as I recalled him fucking me. I had to stop thinking about Den, and about sex.

'It's hot, I think I'll go and put my bikini on,' I called, meandering across the lawn towards Mat.

'OK. Right, the fire's going, I'll go and give Den a shout.'

I didn't know why I'd decided to wear my bikini. Perhaps, subconsciously, I wanted to tease Den. Did I want to tease myself? I wondered as I climbed the stairs. Whatever the reason, I'd wear my skimpy bikini, show off my curvaceous young body. My swollen pussy lips would bulge the glossy lycra running between my thighs. Would the tight material outline my sex crack? The thought sent a quiver up my spine.

'He's on his way,' Mat announced as I finally stepped out onto the patio. 'He's bringing a friend along.'

'A friend?' I echoed.

'Lisa, a girlfriend. There's more than enough food to go round.'

'Yes, but . . .'

'A foursome, it's better that way.'

'Yes, I suppose it is,' I sighed.

A girlfriend? If that was the case, he wouldn't be able to touch me the minute Mat turned his back. A foursome? Two penises, two cunts . . . A lascivious quiver ran up my spine as my thoughts whispered, goading me.

'Hi, Jane!' Den interrupted my rude reverie as he walked around the side of the house. 'This is Lisa, a friend of mine.' I stared in horror at the dark angel, the young lesbian, an obscene tableau of me licking her to orgasm flashing before me. As she sat next to me, her pretty face grinning as she eyed my breasts ballooning my bikini top, I felt claustrophobic. I couldn't escape – there was nowhere to run, nowhere to hide. Remembering Den's massive penis in my vulnerable mouth, I wanted the ground to open up and swallow me.

Lisa's long black hair shining in the sunlight, cascading over her shoulders, her blouse open, partly revealing her pert, rounded breasts, I recalled her kneeling on the arms of the chair, her shaved vulval lips pressed against my open mouth. Her sex flesh had been warm, her juices exotic as I'd pushed my tongue deep into the estuary of her hot vagina. What was I thinking?

'I'll get the wine from the fridge,' Mat obliged, leaving me alone with my abusers, my thoughts of lesbian sex.

'There's nothing like a barbecue,' Den smiled, sitting the other side of me, trapping me. 'So, how did you enjoy our little sex session?'

'Shut up!' I spat.

'*I* enjoyed it!' Lisa giggled. 'You have a lovely cunt, Jane.'

'For Christ's sake, both of you shut up!'

'Chilled wine!' Mat grinned, stepping out of the back door. 'Or would you prefer a beer, Den?'

'No, wine's OK.'

'I'll get the glasses,' I said, making my escape.

Lisa followed me into the kitchen, running her hands over my naked hips as I reached up and opened the cupboard. 'Stop it!' I whispered through gritted teeth. 'My husband will see!'

'Put your hand up my skirt,' she smiled. 'I'm not wearing any panties.'

'No!'

'Den has the photographs in his pocket, and the tape. Unless you finger me, he'll show your husband.'

Her back to the window, she pulled her blouse to one

side, exposing her full breast topped with its erectile nipple. I had an overwhelming desire to suck on her milk teat, to gently nibble her beautiful budling. Squeezing her breast. her breast, her nipple lengthening as her globe ballooned, protruding alluringly from her darkening areola, she moved closer to me.

'Suck me,' she whispered, her dark eyes sparkling, reflecting a sensuality I'd never observed in a girl before. Bending, I opened my mouth and sucked on her inviting breast bud, gently biting, nibbling as she gasped in her arousal. I felt my vagina tighten, my juices flowing as I mouthed and sucked. Was I a lesbian? I again wondered.

'Finger my cunt,' she breathed. 'Make me come.' Her nipple slipping out of my mouth as I stood upright, I watched Mat through the window. He was busy with the barbecue, unaware of my lesbian act as I tentatively slipped my hand up Lisa's skirt, stroking her hairless sex hillocks. My clitoris stirring, I wondered what I was doing as I pushed a finger between her soft petals and drove it deep into her hot cunt.

As she licked her full red lips, her eyes closed, I realized how attractive she was, and I wondered what it would be like to kiss her. I was drawn to her, moving forward as I fingered her, massaged her sweet inner flesh. Our lips close, I stopped short of kissing her.

'My clitty,' she whispered, opening her dark eyes and smiling at me. 'Rub my clitty.' Slipping my wet finger out of her tight vagina, I moved up her wet sex valley and massaged her solid clitoris. Her eyes rolling, her breathing unsteady, she squeezed my breasts, pinching my nipples through my bikini. 'Don't stop,' she murmured, her body trembling as I massaged her sex button faster. 'God, I'm going to come.'

Shuddering as I masturbated her, she let out long, low

moans of pleasure as her orgasm erupted. Laughter came from the garden as I sustained her climax, and I looked out of the window at Mat and Den. How could I masturbate a young lesbian in the kitchen with my husband just outside the back door? I must have been mad!

'God, don't stop!' Lisa cried rather too loudly as her orgasm rolled on. Her clitoris pulsating beneath my wet fingertips as I massaged her, she leaned on the worktop to steady her quivering body. Gasping, whimpering, her face flushed, her head thrown back as I sustained her climax, she flung her arms around me as her ecstasy rode on.

'Jane, where are the glasses?' Mat called impatiently.

'Hang on!' I replied shakily, retrieving my wet hand and moving away from the dark-haired girl. I sucked my sticky fingers, savouring her exotic pussy juice. I wanted to push my tongue into her young cunt.

'That was nice,' Lisa gasped, her cheeks crimson, her eyes glazed. 'You can bring me off again later.'

'No!' I returned, taking the glasses from the cupboard. 'I'm not going to . . .'

'I'll bring *you* off later. You'd like that, wouldn't you, Jane?'

'Lisa, for Christ's sake – my husband's outside!'

'Would you like me to kiss you?'

Leaving the kitchen, my stomach somersaulting, my clitoris painfully erect, I placed the glasses on the patio table and sat down. I couldn't even enjoy a barbecue in my own garden: the situation was ludicrous. I wasn't going to be intimidated. No matter what threats they threw at me, I wasn't going to be blackmailed any longer.

But Lisa had woken something within me, stirred a deep longing, and I again wondered whether I was a latent lesbian. I gazed at her succulent, pouting lips as she sat down, imagining kissing her, driving my tongue deep into her pretty mouth. My cunt wetting my bikini, I had to stop thinking about sex!

Sipping wine, I kept quiet as Mat cooked the food. Den and Lisa kept looking at me, grinning, eyeing my breasts, the ballooning material of my bikini running between my legs, hugging my aching cunt. Several times, Den took a small photograph out of his shirt pocket, flashing the evidence at me when Mat wasn't looking. Lisa giggled, sitting opposite me and parting her thighs, exposing her shaved vaginal lips. Her cunt seemed to smile at me, beckoning me. I ignored the evil pair as best I could, averting my eyes when Lisa opened her legs, looking the other way every time Den showed me another crude shot.

'The food will be ready soon,' Mat announced, prodding a sizzling steak with a fork. 'I'm just going up to put my shorts on, I won't be a minute.' My heart leaped as he disappeared into the house, leaving me alone, vulnerable, with my tormentors. As Den abruptly stood up, I knew what was going to happen. I knew he'd demand that I suck him to orgasm and drink his sperm.

'What's it to be?' he grinned evilly, towering above me and unzipping his trousers. 'Your mouth or your cunt?' I stared at his erect penis as he pulled his foreskin back, exposing his purple glans, his sperm-slit. 'Well?' he taunted, moving closer to me, wanking his solid shaft.

'Neither,' I replied, turning my head away.

'We haven't got much time, Jane. I suggest you make up your mind before it's too late.'

'I'm not going to be forced to suck you off every time . . .'

'The minutes are ticking away.'

'I don't care!'

'All right, have it your own way. It's a shame to have to ruin the barbecue by showing Mat the . . .'

'Shut up, Den!'

'He means it,' Lisa broke in.

'Why don't *you* suck him off?' I returned.

'Time's running out,' Den goaded me, wanking his penis faster. 'Open your mouth, Jane.'

As he moved forward, his huge cock close to my face, I parted my lips and sucked his glans into my mouth. I'd failed, but I'd had no choice. I knew that I'd never be free as he clutched my head and gasped. Rolling my tongue around his twitching knob, I thought it might be just as well if Mat appeared to catch me in the adulterous act. It would put an end to the blackmailing – it would put an end to everything!

'Coming!' Den breathed, his knob swelling, his jism jetting into my mouth as Lisa knelt beside him, eagerly watching the crude coupling. Sucking out his seed, I swallowed, imagining Mat catching me, his expression, what he'd say. 'Keep sucking, bitch!' Den ordered me as he drove his knob to the back of my throat. Pulling away as I heard Mat nearing the kitchen, I watched as Lisa wanked Den, the last of his sperm splattering my face, baptizing my cleavage. Hurriedly zipping up his trousers as Mat walked through the kitchen, Den sat down with Lisa.

'That's better,' Mat said, showing off his shorts as he emerged from the house. 'It's far too hot for trousers.' Den grinned, smirking as he watched me wipe his sperm from my face, my cleavage. 'Right, the food's ready. Who's hungry?' Mat asked.

'I'm hungry,' Den replied. 'How about you, Jane? I'll bet you could do with something hot to eat.'

'I'm going to the loo,' I said, rising to my feet.

'I'll come with you,' Lisa smiled, eagerly following me.

Climbing the stairs with the young lesbian in tow, I decided to slip into the bathroom and lock the door before she could get at me. The taste of Den's sperm lingering in my mouth, the last thing I wanted was to drink her cunny juice. Successfully closing and locking the door before she could get into the bathroom, I stood by the window, wondering at my predicament as she tapped on the door, offering to kiss me, to masturbate me.

Ignoring her, I took a flannel from the basin and cleaned my face, my cleavage. Pulling my bikini bottom down, I wiped my vaginal crack, the flannel soaking up my sex juices as I listened to Den and Mat laughing and joking in the garden below the window.

'You'll have to come round more often,' Mat said, much to my annoyance.

'There's nothing I'd like more!' Den chuckled.

'Bring Lisa, too.'

'Bring me where?' she asked, obviously having given up on getting her hands on my body, her tongue up my cunt, and gone back down to the garden.

'Mat was just saying that we should come here more often.'

'Mmm, good idea.'

Was she a prostitute? I wondered, tugging my bikini bottom back up. Surely, Den wouldn't pay her to accompany him on social visits? Whatever she was, I didn't want her coming round as and when she felt like it. It suddenly occurred to me that she might wheedle her way in, become friendly with Mat, and he'd invite her round during the day to keep me company. I hated her, I hated everyone. Did I hate myself?

I wandered downstairs to the lounge. There was no rush to join the others in the garden, no rush to have Den and Lisa ogle my body. I felt alone, lost, as I plonked myself on the sofa. Laughter emanating from the garden as the wine flowed, I felt isolated, cast adrift. What did I really want from life? I wondered, gazing around the room, the candle, on the mantelpiece catching my eye. What did life want from me?

'What are you doing in here?' Mat asked as he appeared in the doorway. 'Aren't you going to come and eat?'

'I'm not hungry,' I replied sulkily, gazing at his shorts, images of Den's cock sperming in my mouth looming in my mind.

'Jane, you can't sit moping in here when we have guests.'

'Is *that* what you call them?'

'What do you mean?'

'Nothing. I'll be out in a minute.'

Two people blackmailing me, I mused as Mat returned to the garden. Den and Lisa both had a hold over me. They both wanted to use my naked body for perverted sex. What could I do? How could I halt the escalating nightmare? First Den, then Lisa, then . . . Who else would join the list of abusers? Would Den bring his male friends round to fuck me? Who'd sent the notes?

Laughter came from the garden again as I paced the lounge floor. This was my own house, but I felt that I had to hide. I couldn't even walk out into the garden and enjoy the hot summer evening. I might as well pack my things and leave, I found myself thinking. Escape from the prison, the claustrophobia, the crude sex.

'Come on, Jane!' Mat said with a hint of anger as he put his head round the door. 'I don't know what they'll think of you if you hide in here all evening.'

'I'm not hiding,' I lied.

'What are you doing, then?'

'Thinking.'

'Den and I are going down to the off-licence, so you'll have to entertain Lisa.'

'I don't want to entertain . . .'

'Shall we go?' Den interrupted, joining Mat in the doorway.

'Yes, Jane's going to join Lisa in the garden.'

'Don't be long, Mat,' I sighed.
'Ten minutes, OK?'
'OK.'

As it turned out, I didn't have to join Lisa in the garden. She joined me in the lounge the minute the front door had closed. Standing before me as I sat on the sofa, her feet wide apart, her hands on her hips, she licked her lips, grinning at me, her dark eyes sparkling. I gazed at the slight swell of her skirt following the contour of her sex mound and pictured her shaved pussy. Did she want me to masturbate her again, lick and finger her to orgasm?

'Why did you do it?' she asked softly, kneeling down and placing her hands on my knees.

'Do what?'

'Allow Den to blackmail you.'

'I didn't allow him!' I returned as she ran her hands up my inner thighs, forcing my legs wide apart.

'It wasn't you in that magazine, so why did you say it was?'

'My husband's a very suspicious man, he'd have believed it was me. Why are *you* doing what you're doing?'

'What do you mean?'

'Why are you in league with Den? Why are you blackmailing me?'

'That's my business. Take your bikini bottom off.'

'No.'

'When Den gets back, he'll ask me how I am. If I say I'm thirsty, he'll know that you wouldn't cooperate and he'll expose you. If I say I've had too much to drink, then . . .'

'So I allow you to sexually abuse me and . . .'

'Not sexually abuse you, bring you pleasure. Allow me to make you come.'

'I don't want to come.'

'But *I* want you to come, Jane. Take your bikini bottom off and open your legs as wide as you can.'

Again, I had no choice. I had to submit to the young lesbian's demands, allow her to lick me, to suck my clitoris to orgasm. Did I want to kiss her? I didn't know what I wanted. A quiver of expectancy ran up my spine as I imagined her cunny-wet tongue delving into my mouth.

Slipping my bikini bottom off, I reclined on the sofa with my thighs wide apart, my cunt blatantly on offer to the sex-crazed girl. Wasting no time, she peeled my pussy lips apart and buried her head between my thighs, her eager tongue sweeping up my moist valley, running over my clitoris. My eyes closed, I thought of everything and anything other than the lewd act I was allowing the girl to perform, desperately trying to deny the immense pleasure she was bringing me.

'Like it?' she asked, driving three fingers deep into my wet vaginal sheath.

'No,' I breathed, I lied.

Parting my outer lips further, the dark angel of sex continued licking my clitoris, stiffening my sex nodule as her fingers pistoned and twisted deep inside my drenched cunt. Her long hair tickling my naked stomach, her saliva wetting my most intimate sex flesh, I felt my clitoris swell and pulsate in response to her snaking tongue. I was going to come, I knew. Although I tried to hold back, the beautiful sensations quickly built within my trembling womb, spreading like fire through my pelvis.

'Let it come, Jane,' she breathed, obviously aware of my intense state of arousal. 'Be a good girl and come in my mouth.' A thousand thoughts rolled through my mind – Mat, my marriage, lesbianism, adultery, the marital home . . . But I'd crossed the threshold of no return, there was no way I could halt my orgasm now. 'Come in my mouth,' I heard the husky female voice repeat, as if from far away. I parted my thighs as wide as I could and clutched her head in my hands, grinding my open cunt into her gobbling mouth.

'Oh, God!' I breathed involuntarily as my orgasm erupted within my solid clitoris. 'God, I'm there!' Her saliva and my vaginal juices streaming down between my buttocks, I pulled on her head, drowning her, suffocating her as my body shook violently. Her fingers ramming deep into my cunt, my clitoris pulsating within her hot mouth, she sustained my amazing climax, hurling me into a state of semi-consciousness as the electrifying sensations rolled through my sated body.

My head tossing from side to side, my eyes rolling, I clung to her head, swivelling my hips, my gaping sex valley forced into her wet mouth as she sucked out my climax. Again and again powerful shock waves of orgasm exploded from my throbbing clitoris, rippling through my quivering body, reaching every nerve ending, tightening every muscle. I thought I'd die as my pleasure peaked and I cried out my appreciation.

'Don't stop!' I screamed as the angel of sex expertly fingered my cunt and sucked on my clitoris as only another woman knows how. 'God, don't stop!' On and on the staggering sensations rocked my quivering body, taking me to almost paralysing heights of sexual pleasure. My cunt milk pouring from my bloated vagina, my clitoris aching with pleasure, I wondered how much more I could endure as a massive orgasmic peak lurched through my abused body. My breast heaving, my face burning as my inflamed cunt gripped her thrusting fingers, I gasped as another wave of pure sexual ecstasy crashed through me.

Was I a lesbian? I again wondered, opening my eyes and gazing at my outer lips enveloping her pretty mouth as my orgasm finally began to subside. Was the feminine softness of a girl's mouth pressed against my sex flesh what I really wanted? Her tongue circling the base of my clitoris, she slowed her fingering, skilfully bringing out the last pulses of orgasm. *As only another woman knows how*, I reflected again as her fingertips massaged my G-spot.

'Did you enjoy that?' she whispered, looking up at my flushed face as I finally released her head.

'Yes,' I murmured through my sexual haze. 'Yes, yes.'

'You have a nice cunt, Jane. Would you like me to suck out your sex milk?'

'Yes, yes,' I babbled involuntarily, my head lolling to one side, my body trembling in the aftermath of my lesbian-induced climax.

'You'd like me to lick your cunt out, wouldn't you?'

'Yes, yes.'

As she slipped her fingers out of my drenched vagina, her tongue entering me, licking deep inside my hot cunt, my exhausted body shuddered, my mind swirled with a thousand thoughts. Den and Mat would soon return. Lisa would whisper to Den, tell him that she'd licked and fingered me to orgasm, Mat would notice my sex-flushed face, the damp patch on my bikini as my lust juices drained . . .

'There, I've licked you clean,' the devil's daughter soothed as male voices drifted into my dazed mind. 'They're back, so you'd better put your bikini back on,' she whispered, rising to her feet. My hands trembling, my body still shaking, I grabbed my bikini bottom. Dragging the garment up my quivering legs, I lifted my buttocks off the sofa and veiled my inflamed cunt, concealing the hot evidence of my lesbian encounter.

'Oh, there you are,' Mat smiled as he popped his head round the door.

'We've been having a chat,' Lisa told him, tossing her ebony tresses over her shoulder.

'Are you going to join us in the garden?'

'Yes, we'll be right with you.'

Taking my hand as Mat left the room, Lisa pulled me to my feet and brushed my damp blonde hair away from my face. I found myself gazing at her, an unfamiliar longing welling in my heart. She was very pretty, extremely attractive, and I wasn't sure what I wanted. I didn't understand the alien thoughts tormenting my racked mind.

Following her into the garden, I sat on a sunchair, wondering at the lewd act, the lesbian sex, my incredible orgasm. Since Den had cut me loose from the secure moorings of fidelity, I'd meandered a long way down the river, drifted far away from the realms of normality. Where would the flow take me? I wondered. What lay in wait beyond the estuary, on the cruel sea?

'Did you enjoy Lisa's company?' Den asked sarcastically, breaking my train of thought as the girl wandered over to the barbecue to join Mat.

'Yes, very much,' I smiled. 'We had a chat about certain things.'

'Certain things?'

'About you, among other things.'

'Me? What did she say about me?'

I felt a plan hatching – a plan to set Lisa and Den against each other. If I told him that she'd said this about him, and told her that he'd said that about her, the trouble would begin to brew. Suddenly I detected a glimmer of light at the end of the tunnel of doom.

'She told me one or two very interesting things,' I finally replied.

'Such as?'

'I'm not repeating anything said in confidence, you'll have to ask her. Mind you, I very much doubt that she'll tell you.'

'What are you up to?'

'I'm not up to anything.'

As he mooched over to the barbecue, his dark eyes frowning, Lisa made her way towards me. Den said something to Mat, and they both laughed as Lisa sat beside me. But I felt that, before too long, I'd be wiping the smile off Den's face.

'Den was just saying that you . . .' I began, watching for her reaction.

'Saying that I what?' she asked.

'I'd better not repeat it.'

'What did he say?'

'Nothing. I'm going up to change, it's turning chilly.'

'What did he say, Jane?'

'It was said in confidence so . . . I'm going to change.'

Making my way upstairs, I felt that I'd started a ball rolling and nothing would stop it. If it began to slow down, I'd give it another shove, sending it spinning on its way again. The bedroom door locked, I quickly changed into my skirt and blouse, sure that Den and Lisa would be asking each other what had been said behind their backs. Now was the time to leave them to stew for a while, I reflected as I bounded downstairs.

'Mat, Carole just rang,' I called from the back door. 'She wants me to go over and give her a hand with something.'

'What, *now*?'

'Yes, it can't be helped, I'm afraid. I won't be long.'

'But Jane . . .'

'I won't be long.'

Hurriedly making my escape, I left the house and walked down the leafy avenue. As I quickened my pace, relieved to be free, my thoughts whispered to me, told me to turn back. I stopped, watching an old lady cycle by as I contemplated creeping back into the house. But what would I gain? I wondered. Den and Lisa wouldn't say anything worth hearing in front of Mat.

Deciding to go for a long walk, I headed for the recreation ground. The evening sun warming me, an overwhelming sense of freedom enveloped me and I quickened my step. For the first time in days I felt good, alive, and I determined to escape Den and his accomplice for good. A holiday might be an idea, I mused. A couple of weeks on a Greek island would recharge me, give me the strength to carry on. Yes, I definitely needed a break.

Returning home a couple of hours later, I slipped my key into the front-door lock and crept into the house, praying that the evil pair had gone. Another note lay on the mat, and my heart sank as I opened it. ' "Filthy whore!" ' I breathed, screwing the paper up. It wasn't Lisa – she'd not been on the scene when the other notes had arrived. Den? I pondered again. No, there'd be no point.

Stealing into the kitchen, I dropped the note into the bin, wondering what I was doing with Mat. Did he really need me? Did I really need him? Our relationship, the so-called marital home, the notes – what was it all about?

Looking out of the window, I saw Mat sitting alone on the patio. The terrible duo had gone, thank God! I stood there gazing at him for several minutes, wishing that I could turn the clock back. If only Den hadn't moved in next door, if only I'd denied the magazine photographs, if only . . . It was no good looking back, I knew. What was done was done. The clocks of life can't be turned back.

'Hi,' I smiled, stepping out of the house.

'Jane, where have you been?' he asked, almost angrily.

'Sorry, I was longer than I thought I'd be.'

'Den and Lisa left about ten minutes ago, it's a shame you missed them.'

'Never mind, no doubt we'll be seeing them again.'

'We will. Den's invited us to dinner tomorrow evening.'

'Aren't we overdoing this Den thing?' I sighed despondently.

'What do you mean?'

'It's Den this, Den that . . . He came here to dinner, the barbecue, and now we're going to his place for a meal. We'll never have an evening alone together at this rate.'

'Don't you like him?'

'It's not that, it's just that we're never alone, Mat.'

'There'll be plenty of evenings . . .'

As he dashed into the house to answer the phone, I wandered down the garden. I'd not go to Den's the following evening, I decided. I'd feign a stomach ache or something. I couldn't face another evening of perverted sex. Standing beneath the old apple tree, I pondered on my life. Den ruled me, and Lisa, but it was still my life. If I didn't want to go to his place for dinner, I wouldn't. If I didn't want him coming to our house, then he wouldn't. I wasn't going to be bamboozled by Den and Lisa – or by Mat.

The sun sinking, dusk bathing the garden, I decided to go to bed. I'd endured yet another day of humiliation, degradation, blackmail. But worse were my thoughts, my persistent thoughts of lesbian sex, of Lisa. As I wandered across the lawn to the house, I pondered on Carole, what it would be like to suck her clitoris to orgasm. My inner desires were becoming disquieting. Feeling that my mind would explode, I knew I had to escape the nightmare.

'Who rang?' I asked Mat, walking wearily into the kitchen.

'Dave, from down the road. He's decided to sell his computer and wondered whether I was interested.'

'Are you?'

'I could do with another computer, I'll go and have a look – if it's OK with you.'

'Yes, of course. I'm going up to bed, anyway.'

'All right, I'll see you later.'

'Don't wake me up, will you?'

'No, I won't.'

As Mat left, I filled the kettle to make some tea. At least he wouldn't want sex, I thought thankfully, taking a cup from the cupboard. The last thing I wanted after a day of crude sex was Mat fucking me! Jumping as the phone rang, I knew instinctively who it was. Rushing into the hall, I grabbed the receiver, ready to tell Den to go to hell.

'Is Mat there?' Den asked.

'He's in the lounge,' I lied.

'Jane, go out into the garden and stand by the fence between our houses.'

'What for?'

'I've drilled a hole in the fence, I want to come in your mouth.'

'Den, I am *not* going to . . .'

'In that case, I'll post a couple of photographs to Mat's office.'

'Haven't you used and abused me enough today?'

'Be by the fence in two minutes, or you'll be sorry.'

'Den . . .'

He'd hung up, obviously knowing that I had no choice other than to suck him off yet again. Morning, noon and night I was at his beck and call. He wasn't concerned in the slightest that I'd said that Mat was in the lounge. There really was no escaping the bloody man!

Wandering outside, I rounded the corner of the house, just able to make out Den's penis sticking through a hole in the high fence in the gathering dark of the night. Kneeling, I wasted no time, sucking his bulbous plum into my mouth, desperate to get the vile act over with and climb the stairs to the safety of my bed.

'Mmm, that's good!' Den gasped. 'Give me a bloody good blow job, bitch!' Moving my head back and forth, repeatedly taking his swollen knob to the back of my throat, I wondered how many times I'd be forced to kneel at the fence and swallow his sperm. How many times did he need to come each day? Four? Five? Six?

'You like my knob spunking down your throat, don't you?' he breathed. Ignoring his crudity, I mouthed and sucked on his glans, praying for him to come quickly. I was tired, physically and mentally exhausted, and all I wanted was my bed. 'Mouth-fuck me, whore!' he cried in his growing excitement, his shaft twitching, his knob swelling dangerously.

His sperm gushing, bathing my tongue, filling my cheeks, I sucked and drank from his orgasming cock, draining his balls yet again. I felt dirty, crude, as his jism dribbled from my mouth and ran down my chin. *Whore.* The word haunted me, resounded through the wreckage of my mind. Did I want Lisa's clitoris in my mouth, or Den's cock? Confusion reigned as I sucked out the last of his salty sperm and clambered to my feet.

Ignoring Den as he asked me if sucking him off had wetted my cunt, I hurried back into the house. I hated myself for failing yet again, for succumbing to my blackmailer's crude demands. Locking the back door, I ran upstairs, the taste of sperm lingering on my tongue. *Never again*, I promised myself as I cleaned my teeth, washing away the reminder of my lewd act.

In bed, I pulled the quilt over my head, hiding from the cruel world. But I knew I couldn't hide from myself. I'd run away from Den, from Lisa . . . From Mat? As sleep began to engulf me, I thought again about a holiday on a Greek island. The sun, the beach . . . I wanted to dream about an idyllic holiday, not crude sex. Images of Lisa's open cunt loomed in my mind. I couldn't choose my dreams, but I could choose my way of life.

Chapter Six

Mat seemed different during breakfast. He was quieter than usual, watching me over the top of his newspaper as I sipped my coffee. He didn't even mention the computer he'd been to look at the night before. Trying to appear normal, not noticing his strange mood, I busied myself, making toast and chatting about the weather.

'How come you never wear a dressing gown now?' he asked suddenly, folding the paper.

'I prefer to dress before coming downstairs,' I replied.

'Or come down naked. You always used to wear your gown in the mornings.'

'I don't any more.'

'Several things seem to have changed recently. No dressing gown, this exercising business, you naked whenever I come home . . .'

'I'm *not* always naked when you come home!' I giggled. 'A couple of times I was naked, that was all.'

'You were in a strange mood last night. Sitting alone in the lounge when we had guests, and then going out.'

'I had to see Carole, it couldn't be helped.'

'You seem different, Jane.'

'I don't know why you think that, I'm still the old me.'

'Well, I'd better be going. Don't forget we're going to Den's this evening.'

'How *could* I forget?'

'What do you mean?'

'Nothing. I'll see you this evening.'

Watching Mat's Audi disappear up the road, I decided to ring Carole. She'd offered to come round and talk, and I was feeling increasingly guilty for not answering the door to her. She deserved an explanation. Did I have an explanation?

'I'm sorry I've not been in touch,' I said sorrowfully as she answered the phone.

'What's been happening?' she asked. 'I came round and you weren't in, and I've phoned several times.'

'I had to go out. Look, why don't you come round for coffee this morning?'

'All right, in an hour or so. What's been happening with your neighbour?'

'I'll tell you when I see you.'

'OK. You won't go out again, will you?'

'No, I'll be here.'

Wondering whether or not to tell Carole the truth, I thought it best to play things by ear. I wanted to tell her everything – Den, Lisa, the crude sex, the notes . . . She was my best friend, and that's what friends were for. There again, what would she think of me if I told her about the garden hoe?

Gazing out of the kitchen window at the scandalous tool concerned, I felt my vagina tighten, my clitoris swell. Could I . . . ? No, I couldn't repeat the beautifully vile act now, but I desperately needed to come. I thought of Lisa, her tongue, her baby-smooth cunt lips, her long, succulent nipples.

What was I becoming? What *had* I become? I felt so lost, alone, confused. Talking to Carole wouldn't help, I reflected. She'd try to persuade me to tell Mat about Den, insist that he'd understand if he really loved me. Had she ever had lesbian sex? I wondered. Did she masturbate, rub her clitoris to orgasm?

My arousal soared as I waited for her to arrive. I had to come, to masturbate and relieve my mounting sexual tension. Pulling my wet panties off, I slipped my hand up my short skirt and toyed with my sensitive inner lips, pulling and twisting my pink petals. I was wet, very wet. My clitoris swollen, I desperately needed an orgasm.

Had I time to masturbate before Carole arrived? Time or not, I *had* to bring myself off. In the lounge, I sat down, placing my legs over the arms of the chair and tugging my skirt up over my stomach. Parting my thighs further, my vaginal crack wide open, I slipped a finger deep into my hot sex duct, caressing my inner flesh, inducing my creamy pussy milk to flow.

Massaging my clitoris with my free hand, I closed my eyes, quivering as the beautiful sensations mounted, gently rippling through my body. I was becoming addicted to orgasm, craving the immense satisfaction and pleasure masturbation brought. The very act of slipping my panties down, opening my legs, just thinking about masturbating, triggered powerful sexual feelings.

I was developing a strong affiliation with my cunt, almost an obsession, a fascination. My clitoris had become the epitome of my body, the essence of my very being. I could feel an almost spiritual energy flowing through my pulsating pleasure nodule as I masturbated, an uncanny sexual energy I'd never known before. My breasts swollen, my nipples ached for my caress, yearned for the wet heat of my mouth. My body longed for my love.

Unbuttoning my blouse, cupping a firm breast in my hand, I lowered my head, took my sensitive nipple into my mouth and gently sucked. Resuming my clitoral massaging, my vaginal fingering, I bit on my nipple, the wonderful sensations permeating my full breasts, running through my quivering womb. My whole body was alive with sex, my thighs twitching, my stomach rising and falling, my mind drifting on a cloud of carnal ecstasy. Faster I massaged my pulsating sex button, fingered my wet cunt, my orgasm building within my contracting womb as my erect nipple slipped out of my mouth. I wanted Lisa's mouth there, sucking my brown bud, milking me.

Gasping, my eyes rolling, my head tossing from side to side, I shuddered as my orgasm came, erupting within my throbbing clitoris. My vagina lovingly gripping my pistoning fingers, I pictured Lisa licking and fingering me, the images adding to the beautiful waves of pure sexual ecstasy, intensifying my climax. I longed for her shaved cunt pressed against my mouth, my tongue lapping up her orgasmic cream. I imagined my tongue delving deep into her hot sex hole, licking her, fucking her.

As my orgasm rolled on, I moved my buttocks forward, my legs opening wider, almost at right angles to my trembling body, my cunt slit gaping. I desperately wanted Lisa between my thighs, masturbating me, drinking from my hot duct, fingering me. Did I want Den fucking me? I wondered as my climax finally began to wane. Did I want him sperming in my mouth? Did I want Mat?

Slowing my masturbating rhythm, my mind drifting down from paradise, I caught sight of the candle on the mantelpiece. My vaginal juices running down between my parted buttocks, lubricating my anal portal, I wondered whether to slip the wax shaft deep into my bottom and masturbate again. I felt dirty, wicked, crude. I craved perverted sex and looked frantically around the room for something long and wide to slip into my spasming vagina.

Eyeing the brass doorknob, I clambered to my feet and crossed the room. Pulling my skirt up as I stood by the door, I manoeuvred my hips, slipping the brass knob between my swollen pussy lips. It was very big and I wasn't sure whether my cunt would stretch to accommodate the cold phallus. I was thinking like a perverted nymphomaniac, behaving like a wanton whore, but I couldn't help myself. Bouncing up and down, the knob forcing my inner labia wide apart, massaging my wet sex valley, I wondered whether Carole had ever committed such an obscene act.

Suddenly, the rounded knob slipped into my vaginal duct, filling me, cooling my hot inner flesh. 'God, what am I doing?' I breathed as I gyrated my hips, the brass knob stretching me wide open, massaging deep inside my cunt. Leaning back, slowly rocking my hips, I shuddered as the beautiful stretching sensations sent a quiver up my spine. I'd found yet another phallus to use every day, yet another friend to comfort my insatiable cunt. Did Carole fuck doorknobs?

My finger between my buttocks, tentatively toying with the sensitive brown tissue surrounding my anal duct, I'd become truly sex-crazed. I was discovering new sensations, new crude acts to appease my craving for debased sex. My finger driving deep into my tight arsehole, waking the secret nerve endings there, bringing me incredible sensations of perverted sex, I rocked my hips faster, fucking myself with the solid doorknob. I imagined Carole bottom-fingering herself.

As my drenched vagina tightened, gripping the knob, my second orgasm erupted, taking me to amazing heights of sexual pleasure as I thrust my finger in and out of my hot anus. My lust for debauched sex was rocketing, and I wondered to what heights of self abuse I'd fly, to what depths of sexual depravity I'd sink. A banana, the candle, the garden hoe, the doorknob . . . What else would I force deep into my cunt and fuck myself with?

'God!' I cried, clinging to the door as my legs crumpled beneath me. 'God, it's beautiful!' Rocking my hips faster, the doorknob driving in and out of my aching pussy, I finally fell back, the hot phallus slipping out of my inflamed vagina as I staggered across the room. Pulling my finger out of my tight rectal sheath, I flopped onto the sofa, trembling, gasping, whimpering as I drifted down from my sexual heaven.

Did other women behave as I had while their husbands were at work? I wondered. I recalled my schooldays, looking around the class at the other girls, wondering whether they masturbated in their beds at night as I did. I'd always thought that only I committed the dirty act, that the other girls never rubbed their clitties to paradise. I couldn't imagine any of my friends masturbating, let alone fucking a doorknob.

The doorbell ringing, I brushed my damp locks away from my burning face and scanned the room. There was no evidence of my debauchery, no signs of my incredible self-abuse. Staggering to my feet, yanking my skirt down, I teetered through the hall and opened the door to Carole, smiling sweetly as she stepped inside.

'Are you OK?' she asked concernedly.

'Yes, I'm fine.'

'You're very flushed, and you're sweating. You haven't got a temperature, have you?'

'I've been exercising,' I parroted as she followed me to the kitchen. 'I'm on a keep-fit thing at the moment.'

Seating herself at the table, her suspicious gaze fell to my discarded cunny-wet panties. Picking them from the floor, I casually tossed them into the washing machine and filled the kettle. My cunt milk coursing down my inner thighs, my hands still trembling, I wondered whether she'd guessed what I'd been doing. Did she finger-fuck her bottom?

'Do you masturbate?' I asked, immediately wishing I hadn't.

'That's a funny question!' she laughed. 'Do *you*?'

'Yes,' I replied coolly, spooning coffee into the cups. 'I read somewhere that most women masturbate.'

'I used to, in my teens, but not now. I have John, so I don't need to.'

'I have Mat, but I still masturbate.'

'This is an odd subject to be discussing when you're being blackmailed. Tell me about this neighbour of yours, what he's been up to.'

'It's OK now,' I lied. 'He's . . . he's moved away.'

'That must be a relief.'

'It is! I've put it all behind me now, moved on.'

'There's still something troubling you, Jane, I can tell. There's something different about you.'

'Have you ever . . . Have you ever had a lesbian relationship?'

'A lesbian relationship? What's all this about? What are you driving at?'

'An article I read – it said that a lot of women experiment with their own sex at some time or other.'

'Well, at school . . . I went to a boarding school and . . . Can't we talk about something else?'

'Go on, I'm interested.'

'Jane, I really don't want to talk about masturbation and lesbian relationships.'

'Sorry, it's just that I found the article interesting.'

'How's Mat? I saw him leaving as I arrived. Has he got a day off?'

'No, no, he left over an hour ago. Are you sure it was him?'

'Yes, he didn't see me, but it was him all right.'

Passing Carole her coffee, I wondered whether Mat had forgotten something and . . . It suddenly occurred to me that he might have seen me in the lounge. Lost in my sexual haze, I wouldn't have heard him come in. Had he watched me? How long had he been there, spying on me during my most private moments? If he had seen me, at least he'd now believe that I masturbated. But the thought of him watching horrified me.

What if Den and Lisa had been in the lounge, fucking me, abusing me? I'd have to put the latch up on the front-door lock the next time I masturbated. The last thing I wanted was Mat barging in and discovering me naked, fucking myself with a banana! And if he were to see me with the garden hoe stuffed up my bottom!

'John's just booked for us to go to Portugal for a couple of weeks,' Carole said, obviously trying to lighten the conversation.

'That'll be great. I'm thinking about going to Greece,' I replied. 'A week or two on a Greek island would be heavenly.'

'We all need to get away at times.'

'Tell me about it! I just want to get away from Den.'

'Den?' she echoed.

'Er . . . I mean . . .' I stammered, wondering how to explain. 'He's a friend of Mat's. They work in the same office and he calls round most evenings.'

'Tell Mat that you don't want him coming round.'

'It's usually about work, so . . . Anyway, how's John's promotion going?'

'We're still waiting to hear. It's a real nail-biting time, I can tell you! Shall we sit in the garden? It's a lovely day.'

Turning and looking out of the window, I wondered whether Den was at home. If we sat in the garden, he might spy on us, take photographs and . . . Realizing that I was becoming paranoid, I opened the back door and stepped outside.

'You're right,' I said as Carole joined me on the patio. 'It is a lovely day.'

'The garden's looking nice,' she remarked, wandering across the lawn with her coffee. 'I see you've been hoeing.'

'Yes, I . . . It keeps the weeds down.'

My vagina spasmed as I joined Carole and contemplated the hoe, the rounded end of the green handle. My sex juices still oozing from my vaginal opening, irrigating my inner thighs, I felt an urgent need to masturbate again. I really was becoming addicted to orgasm, and I wondered whether to nip up to the bathroom to appease myself. As I was about to tell Carole that I was going up to the loo, Den sauntered into the garden.

'Hi!' he called, walking across the lawn towards us. 'Nice day.'

'Oh, er . . .' I began, my hands trembling as he approached. 'Er . . . Carole, this is . . . This is Dave, he lives down the road.'

'Pleased to meet you,' Carole smiled, shaking his hand.

'Mat's out, I'm afraid,' I said, glaring at the audacious bastard.

'I camc to see you but, as you have company . . .'

'It's OK, I was about to go,' Carole broke in. 'I have things to do.'

'In that case, I'll stay.'

'No, Carole. You . . . you don't have to go,' I said shakily. I didn't want to be mouth-fucked. 'Stay and . . .'

'I have to go into town to pick up one or two things, and I must call into the bank. I'll see myself out.'

'But . . .'

'I'll give you a ring.'

As she disappeared into the house, I turned and faced Den. He grinned triumphantly as he reached out and squeezed my breast through my blouse, commenting on my full melons, my succulent nipples. The situation had become absurd, I thought angrily. I couldn't even enjoy a coffee and a chat with my best friend without Den spoiling things! Seething with rage as he slipped his hand up my skirt and cupped my wet vaginal lips, I stepped back.

'How you have the gall to wander into my garden when I'm with a friend, I really don't know!' I spat.

'What do you think about the hole in the fence?' he asked cheekily. 'It's rather ingenious, isn't it?'

'It's disgusting!'

'I'll let you into a little secret, Jane.'

'What secret?'

He chuckled, obviously delighting in keeping me in suspense. 'It wasn't me you sucked off last night,' he finally laughed.

'What?' I gasped.

'A friend of mine called to see me. He stuck his dick through the hole and you sucked him off, swallowed his spunk.'

My heart sank as I recalled the anonymous knob in my mouth, the sperm gushing, sacrilegiously baptizing my tonsils. In the dark, I'd not noticed that it was a different penis. After all, a cock is a cock. Even in daylight, I'd probably not have known the difference. I felt like a prostitute, sucking a stranger to orgasm for payment. Although my remuneration was Den's silence rather than cash, it was still payment for sex.

'I nearly exploded with laughter when he spunked in your mouth!' Den sniggered. 'The great thing about it was that I charged him ten pounds for the pleasure!'

'I've never met anyone as vile and despicable as you!' I hissed through gritted teeth. 'This is the last straw! As from now, you can forget the whole bloody thing!'

'Oh dear. I really don't think Mat will be too pleased to discover . . .'

'Let me tell you something,' I smiled sweetly. 'I've been having an affair for the last three years. One week from now, I'll be living in a beautiful house in the Cotswolds with another man.'

'You're bluffing.'

'Am I? I wasn't going to tell Mat that I'm leaving him until the last minute. The only reason I allowed you to blackmail me was because I didn't want you rocking the boat, ruining my plans.'

'I don't believe you, Jane.'

'I really don't care whether you believe me or not. Of course, you can cause me problems by telling Mat, showing him the photographs and playing him the tape. It will mess my plans up because the house won't be ready until next week, but I can easily stay with a friend in the meantime.'

'There's no way you've been having an affair, Jane. You'd never have allowed me to blackmail you if you were leaving Mat.'

'As I said, I really don't care what you believe.'

'Your confession isn't the only thing I have on tape. I have you saying that you'll pose for me, like the magazine picture. And I recorded you begging to suck my cock and drink my spunk. You then begged me to fuck your mouth and spunk over your tongue. When you were in the lounge with Lisa, the recorder was beneath the sofa. It's a good recording, Lisa telling you to let it come, to be a good girl and come in her mouth. And judging by your own euphoric utterances, it was a pretty good orgasm.'

'As I said, I don't care.'

' "Don't stop! God, don't stop!" The whole lot is on tape. Lisa saying that you have a nice cunt and asking you whether you'd like her to suck out your milk, you pleading "Yes, yes!" '

He had far more on me than I'd ever imagined! I'd

thought my affair trick would have made him back off, but now? What he had on tape was the ultimate proof of not only my adultery but also the perverted lesbian sex I'd had with Lisa. Den, it seemed, had finally won.

'OK, into the house and strip off,' he grinned, leading the way across the lawn. 'I'll really put you through your paces this time!'

'I told you!' I screamed. 'It's over!'

'Unless you do as you're told, you'll be sorry!'

As he disappeared into the house, I wondered despairingly what to do. If I surrendered yet again, the blackmailing, the sexual abuse, would never end. But if I dug my heels in . . . As usual, I knew that I had no choice. He had complete domination over me, ruled my very life.

Dragging myself into the house, my heart thumping hard against my chest, I knew instinctively that I was going to have to endure the most vile and sordid sex yet. I couldn't face another session of sexual corruption, sexual abuse. But my body no longer belonged to me. It was Den's property, to do what he wanted with, when he wanted.

'One week from today, I won't be here,' I asserted in a last-ditch attempt to be rid of him as I walked into the lounge. He was pulling lengths of rope from his jacket pockets, ignoring me, obviously not believing one word of my story. 'You'll have no one to use and abuse.'

'Why submit, then?' he finally asked, running the ropes through his hands.

'I didn't say that I was going to submit.'

'Take your clothes off and lean over the back of the armchair,' he ordered me, taking it for granted that I was indeed going to submit as he pulled the chair into the centre of the room.

My cunt aching, my clitoris solid, I wondered again why I'd become so hungry for sex. The thought of Den tying me to the chair, abusing me, sent a quiver up my spine, but I had to stop him exploiting me every day. My body wasn't a commodity, an object to be used purely to satisfy his debased desires.

'Come on, Jane,' he said irritably. 'I haven't got all day.'

'I'm only doing this because I don't want my plans ruined,' I breathed, unbuttoning my blouse and slipping my shoes off. 'I don't want to have to leave a week early. I'm only doing this because . . .'

'You're doing this because you have no choice. You know as well as I do that you're not leaving Mat.'

Slipping my blouse over my shoulders, my naked breasts displayed to my blackmailer, I tugged my skirt down, revealing my knickerless pussy. He was right. He knew it and I knew it – I had no choice. Leaning over the back of the chair, my head resting on the cushion, my feet wide apart, I allowed him to tie my wrists and ankles, securing me in the demeaning position.

'I'm just going to get a couple of things from my house,' he smiled, leaving the room. *A couple of things?* I pondered fearfully. How had I fallen prey to the beast again? Why had I been so naive? He'd mentioned the tape recorder before – I should have known that he was taping me when he asked me to beg to suck his cock and swallow his sperm. I'd have to submit to my master now, surrender to his every command. If only I'd . . .

Hindsight was no good, I mused. There was no point in looking back, and as for the future . . . I could see no light at the end of the tunnel of doom. My plan to set Den and Lisa against each other hadn't worked. But it wasn't too late to give the pernicious ball another shove, to keep it rolling, I reflected optimistically. It was my only chance, futile though it was.

'OK!' Den chuckled as he returned and placed something

on the floor behind me. 'Take a look at this.' Brushing my hair away from my face with the end of a long, thin bamboo cane, he grinned. 'Naughty girls need to be caned,' he declared, an evil glint in his eyes. 'You've been extremely disobedient so you'll have to be thrashed. But first, I'll blindfold you.'

'Why do that?' I asked shakily.

'You'll see.'

Wrapping a folded handkerchief around my head, he tied the ends. In the dark, I felt alone, lost, even more defenceless. Why did he have to do this? I wondered. What was the point? In his devilment, I imagined him committing an act so vile, so obscene, that he didn't want me turning my head and looking at him. Where was the dark angel of sex, the devil's daughter?

'Lisa came to see me earlier,' I imparted, wondering what on earth I was planning.

'What, this morning?'

'Yes, just after Mat left for work.'

'She didn't tell me that . . .'

'Why should she tell you? Anyway, I don't suppose she's seen you since.'

'She would have told me, Jane. You're lying.'

'Why would I lie? Why would I say that Lisa came round if she hadn't? I'd have nothing to gain, would I?'

'Did she want sex?'

'She came round for a coffee and a chat. Unlike you, she doesn't want debased sex all the time. I think we might become good friends.'

'I'll thrash the truth out of you!' he stormed.

'I've *told* you the truth!'

The first stinging lash of the cane across my tensed buttocks jolting my naked body, I wished I'd never mentioned Lisa. Again, the thin bamboo landed squarely across my quivering bottom-melons with a deafening crack, and I yelped. The marks from the last thrashing hadn't faded, yet, and now fresh weals would fan out across my taut buttocks. Mat was bound to notice and . . .

'Lisa didn't come here, did she?' he asked angrily, thrashing me again. I had to endure the gruelling punishment, I couldn't admit to lying. 'She didn't, did she?' he demanded to know again as the cane struck my stinging bottom. 'Tell me you're lying, bitch!'

On and on he thrashed me, the excruciating pain finally numbing my burning buttocks. But I was determined that he'd never get the truth out of me. He obviously didn't like the idea of Lisa visiting me without his consent. He'd ask her about it and she'd deny it, but the ball was rolling again. He'd begin to doubt her, begin to wonder what her game was – and there'd be no end of trouble.

'Tell me you're lying, whore!' he stormed again, the cane swatting my burning arse orbs for the umpteenth time. As he continued the merciless thrashing, I remained silent, my whimperings hushed. I was determined to win this round in my quest to set the evil pair against each other. The cane landed across my buttocks with one deafening crack after another, but I bit my lip, not even letting out a yelp as he thrashed me harder.

'Right, as that doesn't seem to be working, we'll try something else,' he muttered, dropping the cane to the floor. Smearing something cold and greasy between my burning buttocks, over my sensitive anal entrance, I thought he was going to commit the ultimate violation on my tethered body and fuck my bottom.

'This should be fun!' he laughed, pressing something cold and hard against my tightly closed anal rose. 'Let's see if your arse is big enough to take a bloody great cucumber!'

'No!' I screamed in my darkness as the thin end of the

fruit slipped past my sphincter muscles and penetrated my tight duct. 'Christ, no!'

'Tell me you're lying about Lisa, or it'll be "Christ, yes!" '

'I wasn't lying! She told me not to tell you that she'd been to see me!'

'Lying bitch!'

'No!'

As he forced the cucumber deep into my tight rectum, my inner flesh stretching to capacity, I knew that, even if I admitted to lying, he'd continue with the plunder of my most private hole. I couldn't believe what he was doing to me, the depths of depravity he'd sunk to. Where had my gentle femininity gone? My bottom-hole aching, I was sure that he'd force his penis up me next, sperm in my bowels. I cried inside.

'No!' I screamed again as the cucumber glided deeper into my inflamed anal sheath. Ignoring my pleas, he twisted the shaft, repeatedly pulling it out and driving it into me again. My pelvis bloated, my naked body jolting as the huge green shaft thrust in and out of my bottom, I felt that I was going to split open.

Finally slipping the huge phallus out of my aching bottom-hole, he unzipped his trousers. My cunt lips swollen, parted, my vaginal entrance lay crudely open, inviting his erect penis. Another fucking, I mused numbly as he slipped his knob deep into my cunt, his shaft stretching me. How many more times would he fuck me?

'No!' I screamed as his shaft glided out of my vagina to press against my inflamed bottom-hole. 'Den, no!' Suddenly he drove into me, his huge cock forcing open my rectal duct, his balls pressing against my wet cunny lips as he completely impaled me. Gasping, he withdrew his shaft and drove into me again, my body quivering as the sensations of corrupt sex permeated me. I couldn't believe the debasement, the obscene violation. No one had ever fucked my bottom!

'Take it out!' I cried as he grabbed my hips, ramming his penis deep into my bowels. 'God, take it out!'

'Never!' he chuckled. 'I've been dreaming of fucking your beautiful arsehole!'

'You're vile!'

'And you're tight and hot!'

My inflamed brown ring gripping his thrusting shaft, his knob massaging my rectal tube, I felt my clitoris swell in response to the animalistic abuse of my tethered body. Never had I dreamed that a man's cock forcefully fucking my bottom-hole would turn me on like this. Never had I believed that I'd experience anal sex.

'I'm going to spunk up your arse!' he chuckled, ramming his swollen knob deep into my bowels. 'You enjoy a good arse fucking, don't you?' My eyes squeezed shut, I bit my lip, trying to deny the immense pleasure rolling through my quivering body. Only a whore would derive pleasure from such a debased act, only a common slut, a tart . . . What was I? I wondered through my sexual haze, the birth of a climax rousing within my contracting womb. Was I the devil's daughter?

'Here it comes, bitch!' he gasped, ramming into me with a vengeance. I felt his sperm gushing, jetting deep into my bowels, lubricating the shameful coupling. His swinging balls slapping my swollen pussy lips, my anal duct almost riven, repeatedly stretched to capacity, I whimpered as my climax tried to erupt within my neglected clitoris.

I desperately needed fingers massaging between my drenched cunt lips, rubbing my throbbing sex nodule, bringing out my orgasm, and I imagined Lisa masturbating me as Den fucked my bottom. My vile thoughts rising from the bottom of a deep pool of depravity, the depths of immorality, I was shocked. What lurked within the dark shadows of my mind? I wondered. Evil monsters, sex fiends . . . Was I evil?

Panting as his climax faded, Den slowed his pistoning cock, the last of his sperm oozing from his knob. I could feel his male cream lubricating his glans, lessening the friction of my hot rectal walls as he slowly withdrew from my bumhole and entered me, withdrew and entered. Was he satisfied now? Would he release me and allow me to rest after the thrashing, the anal abuse?

Sliding his shaft out of my inflamed bottom sheath, he checked the blindfold, ensuring that I couldn't see. What was his plan? What evil act was he going to commit next? He was moving about behind me, fiddling with something. Was I to endure the cucumber again?

As he yanked my buttocks apart, I could feel his lust juice inside me, bathing me, oozing from my open anal portal and running down between my cunt lips. Imagining Lisa licking between my thighs, lapping up the spilled orgasmic cream, I shuddered. I needed to come, to experience a massive orgasm to relieve my sexual tension, and I prayed for Den to slip his hand between my wet thighs and bring me off.

'Right, now for another arse-fucking!' he laughed. 'My cock's ever-ready to fuck you, always stiff and hard!'

'Please, not again!' I protested as I felt the eager knob pressing against my tender brown ring. 'Den, I can't take it again!'

'Of course you can! That's what your arsehole is for, a damned good fucking.'

His knob gliding deep into my sperm-filled rectal tube, I grimaced, wondering at his unquenchable thirst for debauched sex, his insatiable penis. Could I endure anal sex twice every day? Could I suffer a thrashing every day? How would I feel the next time Mat made love to me? When Mat entered my vagina, I'd recall the anal fucking, the thrashing. A deep sense of debasement engulfed me.

'God, you're bloody hot and tight!' Den cried. 'I'm going to spunk up your arse again!' His shaft swelling, opening me, he began to gasp as his orgasm approached. My clitoris still sadly neglected, I desperately needed to come, but the beast's pleasure was obviously more important than mine. As he grunted, my bottom bucking, I felt the sperm jetting into me again, my bowels brimming with male cream as his shaft slid in and out of my sore anal sheath.

Slowing his thrusting, his balls drained, he finally stilled his cock, his knob still deep within the burning heat of my bowels. My pelvic cavity bloated, my anal canal inflamed, my brown ring taut around the base of his huge cock, I waited for him to withdraw and allow me to rest.

'Two loads of spunk!' he chuckled. I lifted my head, my heart racing as I realized that he was kneeling on the floor at the front of the chair.

'Who . . .' I began as the penis within my anal duct twitched.

'A friend of mine,' Den sniggered. 'You've had your sweet arse fucked by two different cocks.'

'You bastard!' I screamed as the mystery penis slipped out of my sore bottom-hole. 'You bastard!'

'You sucked the sperm out of another man's cock through the hole in the fence last night, and now you've had your arse fucked by two men!'

'That's it!' I cried as the lounge door closed and his accomplice made his escape. 'Never again will I . . .'

'You don't have a choice, slave!' Den laughed, slipping the blindfold off my head.

Releasing the ropes, he helped me to stand up. *Now what?*

I wondered as he gathered up his instruments of abuse, the cane and a jar of Vaseline. Was I to kneel either side of his head with my cunt pressed against his open mouth? The notion swelled my clitoris, sent an electrifying tingle through my quivering womb.

'I'll be back later to take some more photographs,' he grinned, stuffing the ropes into his jacket pocket as he moved to the door.

'You're not taking any more!' I hissed.

'I'll see you later.'

Surveying the room as he left by the back door, I gazed at the cucumber lying on the floor, unable to believe that he'd managed to force the massive shaft deep into my bottom-hole. Picking the fruit up, I pushed the chair back into place, looking for any other evidence of sexual abuse. Apart from my clothes strewn across the floor, the only testimony was my weal-lined buttocks.

My bottom aching, two men's sperm oozing from my inflamed brown hole and trickling down my legs, I decided to take a shower. How many more men would he bring round? I wouldn't open the door when he returned with his camera: I'd had more than enough for one day! As I was about to gather my clothes up, I glanced idly out of the window – and froze. Mat was standing by his car, talking to Den. What the hell was he doing home?

My heart pounding, my hands trembling, I knew I had to get upstairs to the bathroom before my husband came in. The last thing I needed was him catching me naked in the lounge again. Kicking the cucumber beneath the sofa, I scanned the room again for incriminating evidence before making my getaway.

'Not again!' Mat gasped as he appeared in the doorway. 'Christ, Jane, what on earth . . .'

'Oh, hi,' I smiled weakly. 'I was just about to take a shower.'

'What have you been up to? And don't tell me that you've been exercising!'

'Up to? I've been gardening, exercising, and now I'm about to . . .'

'I've just been talking to Den,' Mat broke in angrily as I tugged my skirt up, concealing my crimson buttocks, my dripping cunt, the sperm oozing from my bottom-hole.

'What did he say?' I endeavoured to ask innocently.

'He said that you're going to live in the Cotswolds with another man.'

'What?' I laughed, buttoning my blouse. 'Live in the . . .'

'You told him that you're leaving me next week.'

'I told him . . . He's mad, I never said anything of the sort!'

'Don't lie to me.'

'I'm not lying! Mat, in all honesty, if I was going to leave you, do you think I'd tell Den?'

'Don't deny it, Jane.'

'I *do* deny it! What the hell is he trying to do?'

'What do you mean?'

'I mean, why is Den trying to cause trouble between us by lying? Leave you for another man? Live in the Cotswolds? Good God, he's off his head!'

'Are you sure you've said nothing about the Cotswolds or . . .'

'Mat, I don't even know where the Cotswolds are! Wait a minute . . . This all fits into place. The magazine pages, Den lying about me leaving you . . . He's trying to break us up.'

'Why would he want to do that?'

'How the hell do I know? Another thing, that woman who asked for you – I reckon it was Lisa. Den must have put her up to it.'

As Mat poured himself a scotch, I realized how well things were going my way. If Mat believed that Den was trying to cause problems, trying to split us up, I might be able to put an end to the whole affair. This was the perfect excuse not to go to Den's for a meal that evening, or ever have him visit us.

'There's no way I'm going to his place tonight,' I said firmly. 'Or any other night, for that matter.'

'We can't just not turn up,' he sighed.

'You'll have to go and tell him that we're not coming. And don't invite him here again, I want nothing to do with him. Leaving you to live in the Cotswolds? For Christ's sake!'

'I'll go and tell him now. I really don't understand any of this.'

'Neither do I, and I don't want to! I don't ever want him here again.'

As Mat left, I gathered my knickers and shoes and headed for the bathroom. No more Den and Lisa at our barbecues, no more Den coming round to dinner . . . Den was annoyed because I'd said that Lisa had visited me, now Mat was suspicious of Den. Things were beginning to look up!

Chapter Seven

Mat and I spent the weekend together, sunbathing in the garden, enjoying meals, watching TV . . . With no sign of Den and Lisa, and no more notes, I was beginning to put the nightmare behind me. But I didn't kid myself. I was sure that Den hadn't given up, although I didn't let the thought spoil my brief sojourn with normality.

Mat attempted to make love to me a couple of times, but I managed to avoid it. I wasn't going to let the terrible state of my thrashed buttocks come between us! Images of two men's penises fucking my bottom, shooting sperm into my bowels – I didn't know whether I'd ever be able to make love with Mat again. The debased episode with Den and the unknown man haunting me, I needed time before even contemplating sharing my body with my husband.

I was relieved that Den didn't phone or hammer on the door the minute Mat had left for work on Monday. Perhaps he *had* given up? I ruminated as I busied myself in the kitchen. Perhaps, knowing that the barbecues and dinner parties were over, he wouldn't bother me again. Naivety seemed to be a sad trait of mine!

I soon realized as I finished washing up the breakfast things that one thing hadn't changed. My insatiable yearning for orgasm was visibly still intact. My juices of desire wetting my panties, my vagina aching, my clitoris swollen, whatever deep-seated desires had lain fallow in the shadows of my mind had now been successfully harvested.

Although I desperately fought the urge to masturbate, I finally lost the battle as I was preparing vegetables to make a curry. Taking a long, thick carrot from the worktop, contemplating slipping it deep into my vagina, I felt my clitoris throb in anticipation. I had to stop doing this, I reflected as I slipped my wet panties down – I had to turn my thoughts away from sex.

Bending my knees, my thighs wide apart, I slipped the thick end of the carrot between my bloated vaginal lips and gently pushed it into my sex hole. The orange shaft glided into my drenched pussy with ease, stretching me, filling me. Pulling my panties up, the tight crotch holding the carrot in place, I walked about the house. With every step I took, the massaging sensations were heavenly. It was like having a solid penis in my cunt, fucking me as I went on my way.

Picking a package up from the front doormat as I drifted through the hall, I tore it open. It was a video tape with my name written on the label, and I immediately realized that it was from Den. *Now* what evidence had he got? I pondered, hurrying into the lounge and ramming the tape into the machine.

The screen flashed, and then a clear picture of the cucumber being forced into my bottom-hole appeared. Gazing at the sheer size of the green shaft, my stretched brown tissue gripping the fruit as it drove deep into my bowels, I realized that Den's perverted friend must have been operating the camera.

I shuddered as the scene changed to Den's huge penis fucking my bottom-hole, thrusting deep into my bloated rectal duct. The camera panning in, a close-up of his solid cock driving in and out of my most secret hole filled the screen. I couldn't believe what I was seeing – my buttocks held wide apart, my brown anal tissue distended around the huge organ, my naked body abused beyond belief.

The tape was obviously a copy, I surmised. Den would have kept the original as more evidence of my debauchery. As I watched the debased fucking, a shot of my face momentarily came into view. Although I was blindfolded, the shot was clear proof of my identity. My stomach sank. The obscene photographs had been bad enough, but a video? God only knew what Mat would do if he were to see it!

I sat on the floor for five minutes watching the vile scene, the anal abuse. The carrot massaging my vagina as I finally ejected the tape and stood up, I again wondered what I'd become. Lesbian sex, anal sex, oral sex, a cucumber driven into my bowels, a carrot in my vagina, the garden hoe . . . I'd plummeted so deep into a pit of depravity that I couldn't climb out. The vile acts Den had forced me to endure had changed me forever.

Slipping the tape beneath the sofa as the phone rang, I knew it was Den. He'd obviously given me time to view the video before ringing with his threats and lewd demands. I wasn't going to answer it, but it rang and rang until it was driving me mad.

'What the hell do you want?' I stormed as I finally grabbed the receiver.

'That's a nice greeting, I must say!' Den chuckled. 'By the way, I liked your little trick.'

'What trick?'

'Telling Mat that I was making up stories about you leaving him. Yes, a good trick – but not good enough. So, what do you think of your debut as a porn star?'

'I think you're vile!'

'I have several copies of the tape and, unless you shape up, Mat will . . .'

'I am *not* going to shape up!'

'Jane, you really must start thinking about your future, and I don't only mean with Mat.'

'What are you talking about?'

'I'm sure your mother would be horrified if she were to see her fruity daughter.'

'My mother?' I gasped uncomprehendingly.

'Yes, your mother. So, are you going to play the game or not?'

Hanging up, I imagined my poor mother watching the video, her reaction to my wanton behaviour. The ropes not once coming into shot, she'd believe that I'd been a willing participant to the debauchery, thc blindfold being a titillation added to my debased pleasure. Den had got me into a compromising situation I'd never have believed possible.

Pacing the lounge floor, I tried to think, to clear my mind and come up with an answer to my horrendous predicament. Even if I ran away, found a flat somewhere, he'd send Mat and my mother copies of the tapes. Never again would I be able to face Mat, let alone my family. There was only one answer – comply with Den's every obscene instruction, open my legs to him and his perverted friends on demand.

Ignoring the renewed ringing of the phone, I gazed out of the window at the weeds in the front garden. Like Den, they wouldn't go away, constantly reappearing no matter what I did to get rid of them. Weedkiller, poison . . . There was one way of dealing with Den. What on earth was I thinking?

As Den walked up the path, I dashed out of the room and hid in the kitchen. The front doorbell ringing, I stood motionless, praying that he'd think that I'd gone out. 'Jane, let me in!' he called through the letter box. I couldn't take much more of this. The bell ringing, my blackmailer shouting through the letter box . . . It was driving me insane!

'Piss off!' I finally yelled, dashing into the hall. 'Bloody well piss off!'

'Who's in a bad mood, then?'

'Piss off and leave me alone!'

Returning to the kitchen, I sat at the table. All I could do was wait for him to give up. I knew that I'd have to endure more perverted sex at some stage, but I wasn't going to be at his beck and call. It occurred to me that even if I had to give in to his demands I might still be able to do a deal with him – set times and days rather than have him turn up as and when the lusting cock-monster in his trousers dictated.

The more I thought about it, the more the idea appealed to me. Properly planned, perhaps I *could* lead a double life. Enjoy evenings and weekends with Mat, and endure Den now and then during the weekdays. But there'd have to be conditions. No strangers, only Den. Lisa? I didn't know what I thought about Lisa.

'I do wish you'd answer the bell,' Den leered, appearing in the doorway.

'How the hell did you get in?' I gasped, leaping to my feet, suddenly aware that the carrot was still inside my cunt.

'I used a credit card. Shall we have some coffee?'

'No, we bloody well won't!'

'In that case, let's get straight down to some perverted sex.'

'Den, I . . .'

'You have no choice.'

'Yes, I know that. Look, I want to talk to you.'

'What about?'

'A deal.'

'I don't make deals with my sex slave.'

'No, listen. I'll agree to . . . to your demands, allow you to have sex with me, but only at certain times. I thought we could set aside certain days and . . .'

'What if I feel like fucking your mouth, and it's the wrong day? No, I don't want to make any deals.'

'I'll have to know when you want me . . .'

'I'll tell you when I want you. I'll tell you when, where,

and how I want you. Anyway, why try to make deals when you're going to the Cotswolds this week?'

'Because I . . .'

'Because you're not going, that's why. By the way, Lisa told me that she didn't come here for coffee.'

'She'd hardly admit it. She didn't want you to know so . . .'

'You really must stop lying, Jane. The Cotswolds, Lisa coming here . . . It's all a pack of lies.'

'I'll tell you something that isn't a lie.'

'What?'

'I *am* having an affair, and I *do* intend to leave Mat.'

'Rubbish.'

'It's true. As yet, I don't know when I'm leaving, but I'm definitely leaving.'

'Why tell me?'

'Because you'll tell Mat and, when the day comes, it won't be such a shock for him.'

'We're wasting time. Take your clothes off.'

'I can't, I'm expecting my brother to arrive any time now.'

'You're lying again.'

'I'm not, he phoned earlier.'

'In that case, we haven't got much time. Kneel on the floor.'

Again, he was going to fuck my mouth, force me to swallow his sperm. As I fell to my knees, he pulled his penis out, his shaft solid in arousal, his purple knob swollen. At least I'd not have to endure an hour or more of perverted sex in the lounge, I reflected as I sucked his silky glans into my mouth. This would only take a few minutes and then I'd be free – for a while, at least.

'Use your tongue, bitch!' he gasped as he rocked his hips back and forth, fucking my wet mouth. 'Ah, ah! God, that's it!' As he clung to my head, his broad shaft stretching my lips, I felt my vagina gripping the carrot. I needed to come. I'd fuck the brass doorknob when Den had gone, fuck the knob and massage my clitoris to a massive orgasm. Would I be able to slip the knob into my anal duct? I wondered. The dreadful thought swelled my clitoris.

'I'll be back later to fuck your arsehole!' Den breathed, ramming his knob deep into my bloated mouth. 'Fuck your arsehole and spunk in your bowels!' As his salty sperm jetted from his slit, dousing my tongue, filling my cheeks, I imagined three men using me, fucking all my orifices. The ultimate degradation . . . Ultimate sexual bliss?

Gobbling and sucking on Den's cock, swallowing the last of his sperm, I tried to push the terrible thought of three men having me simultaneously out of my mind. One penis driving deep into my bloated bottom-hole, another fucking my tight cunt, a third sperming in my thirsty mouth . . . Images of three men fucking me wouldn't leave my mind.

'I needed that!' Den gasped, finally slipping his spent organ out of my spermed mouth. 'Lick my cock, lick it all over, whore!'

'Den, my brother . . .'

'Lick the spunk from my cock, slave!'

My tongue repeatedly running up his wet shaft, over his bulbous glans, I cleansed him until he ordered me to stop. Standing before him as he zipped his jeans, licking the sperm from my lips, it was as much as I could do to stop myself from asking him to slip his hand up my skirt and bring me off. My clitoris solid, my cunt drenched, rhythmically gripping the carrot, I pondered on lying over the table, my thighs wide, and asking him to lick me to orgasm.

'I'll see you later,' he said menacingly, walking into the hall. 'I'll be back to fuck your arsehole.' Trembling, desperate to come, I waited until I'd heard the front door close before dashing up to the bathroom. Grabbing a jar of Vaseline, my heart fluttering, I bounded downstairs to the lounge and closed the door.

My craving for orgasm reaching frightening heights, I hurriedly stripped, tossing my clothes across the room in my urgency to abuse my naked body. Smearing Vaseline between my buttocks, over the brass door knob, I stood with my back to the door.

Leaning forward, manoeuvring my hips, I eased the cold knob between my buttocks. Would it go in? I wondered. The massive cucumber had slipped into my anal duct, so why not the door knob? Swivelling my hips, aligning the brass phallus with my secret entrance, I gasped as my rectal canal suddenly sucked the knob deep inside.

'God!' I breathed, my bloated anal tube sending electrifying sensations deep into my pelvis. 'God, what am I doing?' My vaginal muscles taut around the carrot, my rectum stretched to capacity, I couldn't believe my degenerate behaviour.

Den had roused my nipples from their sleep state, and I'd sucked and nibbled them. He'd woken my taste buds, and now I craved sperm. He'd rudely brought my bottom to life with the cucumber and his cock, and now I was sustaining that awakening. What next? I wondered as I wiggled my hips, the door knob massaging my secret inner flesh, tantalizing the nerve endings there. What would he rouse next?

My graceful femininity had faded into oblivion, I reflected through my mounting carnal paroxysm. The sensual mounds and valleys of my naked body, once veiled with silk and lace, were now indecently bared, brazenly traded as wares. I'd wandered through the door that led to crude and perverted sex, and it had closed firmly behind me. I could never turn back. Never again would my life be the same.

Pistoning the carrot in and out of my tightening cunt, I

massaged my clitoris with my fingertips, bringing out the most incredible sensations I'd ever experienced. The doorknob brought me pain as I rocked my hips and shuddered with the inconceivable pleasure. But the pain somehow aroused me, my inflamed anal canal tightening with pleasure around the plundering brass phallus. My sphincter muscles aching, stretched to capacity, I was deriving immense gratification from my discomfort.

Suddenly, my orgasm erupted, exploding within my pulsating clitoris, transmitting waves of pure sexual bliss through my quivering frame. My two holes bloated, I massaged my clitoris faster, sustaining my climax as my legs sagged. My entire body bathed in orgasm, I lost myself in my sexual frenzy, abusing my femininity in the name of lust. Never again would I make love, I knew. In my ever-deepening depravity, I now knew only how to fuck.

Shame engulfed me as my climax waned, my clitoris sending out the last ripples of sex, my cunt aching, my bottom inflamed. Shame, remorse, guilt . . . I'd abused my naked body beyond belief, derived debased pleasure from my wanton immorality, my most wicked and sinful act. But it was my secret, I consoled myself as I tentatively moved forward, the doorknob relinquishing my ravished anal sheath with an obscene sucking sound. Only the devil and I knew to what depths of depravity I'd fallen.

Staggering across the room, I lay full length on the sofa, quivering, trembling uncontrollably as my cunt tightened rhythmically around the carrot. My clitoris still swollen, as if begging for my massaging fingertips, I tried to slow my breathing, recover from my fantastic climax. Closing my eyes, I knew that I couldn't masturbate again. I needed rest.

Waking from obscene dreams, I hauled my naked body up with a start. The reality was worse than the fantasy, I realized fearfully, my wakeful eyes taking in the sticky doorknob. My bottom-hole aching, I recalled my corrupt act, my brown anal tissue stretched tautly around the cold phallus. What would I do next? I wondered as I climbed the stairs to the bathroom, the carrot massaging my vaginal walls. What perverted and debased act would I commit next? The pit of depravity was bottomless!

After a shower, I dressed and returned to the kitchen to finish making the curry. The carrot still bloating my pussy, inducing my lust cream to flow, I pulled my wet panties aside and slipped the hot phallus out of my sex sheath. In my wickedness, I sliced the dripping carrot and tossed it into the saucepan. *Nice and spicy!* I laughed inwardly, wondering whether to marinate all the vegetables in my well-juiced cunt before tossing them into the pot. 'Pussy-juice curry!' I giggled. But my horrendous situation was far from funny.

The curry simmering, I pondered on Den's words. *I'll be back to fuck your arsehole.* I recalled the recent events, the hole in the fence, the leather belt, the bamboo cane, the candle, the cucumber . . . He'd even used a credit card to get into my house. Now he could slip in as and when he wanted to use and abuse me, my naked body.

I knew that it was only a matter of time before Mat walked in and discovered the awful truth – Den and Lisa using my naked body for perverted sex. If only Den had agreed to set days and times. I was forever at his beck and call! By the law of averages, the day would come when Mat discovered Den coming in my cunt and Lisa coming in my mouth. The end of an era. The end of a marriage.

Wandering aimlessly around the house, I discovered another note on the doormat. *Dirty little wet cunt.* The crude words battered my mind, but I was determined not to allow whoever it was to rile me. I'd be strong and . . . but I had no strength.

Screwing the note up, I realized how mundane my life was. With Mat earning good money, we'd decided that I should stay at home and do the gardening and cooking. I'd been quite happy with the situation – but now? What was I? I wondered. A housewife? A home maker? I was a whore – a home breaker.

Before I'd met Mat, I'd worked in publishing, hoping to carve out a good career for myself. After we married, I gave up work to build a home. But all I'd become was the gardener, the cook, the cleaner, the hostess . . . All I'd done was support Mat, allow him the time and space to build his career. Perhaps I would be better off out of it? I pondered as the phone rang.

'Hallo,' I said softly, ready to hang up on Den.

'Jane, it's Lisa.'

'Lisa? Er . . . What do you want?' I asked surprisedly.

'You told Den that I'd been round for coffee.'

'Yes, I said that because . . .'

'I'd like to come round.'

'What, just you?'

'Yes.'

'Why?'

'Well, because . . . I'd like to see you, that's all.'

'See what, my cunt?'

'Not necessarily.'

'Where are you?'

'In a phone box, not far from your place.'

'All right, come round. If Den's with you, I won't answer the door.'

'No, no, I'll be alone. Give me ten minutes.'

'OK, I'll be here.'

What did she want? Sex? Did I want sex with her? My mind was so muddled that I honestly didn't know *what* I wanted! But I might be able to glean some information, where she'd met Den, how she'd become involved, whether or not she was a prostitute . . . I might even discover what his long-term plans were – as if I didn't already know!

When the front doorbell rang, my heart leaped. I knew it was a grave mistake. Peeping through the letterbox, I could see that she was alone, but Den might have noticed her arrive. Letting her in, I closed the door and put the latch up, locking out the world. Credit card or key, no one would be able to get in. I was safe – wasn't I?

She stood in the hall gazing at me, her long black hair cascading over her big dark eyes. My stomach somersaulting, my clitoris throbbing, my vaginal muscles tightening, I led her into the lounge and invited her to sit down. The dark angel of sex.

There was no point in arguing, spitting questions at her, not if I was to gain her allegiance. I had to come across as amicable, pleased to see her. Through the mist of my tormented mind, the swirling images of the young girl's shaved cunt, her wet tongue, I tried to forget about sex and compose myself.

'I'll put the kettle on in a minute,' I smiled, eyeing her deep cleavage revealed by her partially open blouse.

'I've been thinking,' she said pensively, her short skirt riding up her shapely thighs as she reclined on the sofa. Was she wearing panties?

'Thinking about what?' I asked, standing with my back to the mantelpiece.

'This business with Den and everything . . .'

'What about it?'

'You didn't really want me at your barbecue, did you?'

'That's a stupid question!' I returned. 'My husband was in the garden, and I was in the kitchen fingering . . . I didn't want Den there, either.'

'I enjoyed the barbecue, the time with you.'

'I didn't enjoy my time with a prostitute. How do you know Den? How did you get involved with him?'

'We met at a party. I'm not a prostitute, it's just that I'm very short of money.'

'Having sex in return for money is prostitution.'

'Jane, I . . . I shouldn't have come here.'

'Why not?'

'I don't know. I had everything planned, what I was going to say and . . . and now I don't know what to say.'

'Coffee or wine?'

'Wine, please.'

'Don't go away, I'll be back in a minute.'

Taking the Reisling from the fridge, I knew that she felt something for me, something more than sex. I felt something for her, but I wasn't sure what. Was it her soft, warm femininity, her teenage curves and crevices that excited me? Or did I prefer the male, with his strength, power and granite penis? What did I really want? A penis penetrating me, fucking me, jolting my naked body, sperming into my orifices? A female tongue licking between my sex folds, taking me to orgasm as only a woman knows how? I wanted both.

Taking two glasses from the cupboard, I returned to the lounge to find Lisa relaxing on the sofa, naked. So she *had* come round for sex. She was a bitch, in league with Den, forcing me to masturbate her, finger her cunt, lick her clitoris . . . What had she planned with Den this time? Would he arrive and join in the enforced sex? The latch was up, but Lisa would threaten me, blackmail me – and I'd have to let the bastard in.

'So that's your game,' I said, placing the wine and glasses on the coffee table.

'I'm not playing games,' she demurred, her eyes sparkling, reflecting her lesbian desires.

'What *are* you doing, then?'

'I want you.'

'You want my cunt, you mean?'

'Yes, no, I mean . . .'

'When's Den arriving?'

'He's not.'

'Don't lie to me, Lisa. This has all been planned, hasn't it?'

'No, it hasn't! I came here because . . . because I wanted to be with you.'

'I know your games.'

'I don't play games with those I love.'

Love? Was she capable of loving someone? Was *I* capable? Scrutinizing her naked body, the fullness of her young breasts, her pouting, hairless pussy lips nestling between her parted thighs, I wondered yet again at my emotions. The sex I'd had with Lisa in the past had been enforced, I'd had no choice, but now? Now I had every choice, and the thought sent a bolt of terror through me. If I said no, I might regret it forever. If I agreed to have sex with her . . .

'Are you a lesbian?' I asked stupidly.

'Yes, I am. Are you?'

'No, I . . . I don't know. Look, Lisa, I need time to think. I've been blackmailed, used and abused by you and Den, forced to endure anal sex . . .'

'Den did that?'

'Yes, he did. I'm not in the right mind to know how or what I feel. I don't even know how I feel about my husband, let alone anyone else – let alone you. I've been living my life like a dream – a nightmare. There's nothing left. Whatever I had has been taken away from me.'

'Come and sit with me,' she smiled, parting her thighs further, displaying her teenage cunt.

Her face was partially veiled by her curtain of shining

black hair, her dark eyes reflecting an angelic innocence, but she was far from innocent. She'd been capable of using blackmail to have sex with me – she was no angel! Was I an angel? Was I innocent? Mat was the only innocent one in my life. Working like a dog to secure the best for us – our future – only he was innocent.

'I'm not a prostitute,' Lisa said again as I sat next to her. 'I know what I did was wrong, but I needed the money.'

'You had no qualms about sticking a candle up me while he took photographs. No qualms about blackmailing me.'

'It might have appeared that I didn't have qualms, but I did – and I now feel remorse.'

'Remorse? You're only here for sex, Lisa.'

'No, I'm not.'

'Why are you naked, then? Don't tell me that you were hot so you took your clothes off.'

'No, that's not why I did it. I . . . I *do* want sex with you, I can't deny it. But I want more than sex.'

'I don't know that I have anything other than sex to offer. The sexual abuse I've been forced to endure has changed me.'

'Have you no love?'

'Love is indefinable. I thought I'd found love with Mat, but now . . .'

As she slipped her hand up my skirt and pressed her fingertips into the softness of my bulging panties, I turned my head to face her. My heart pounding as she ran her fingers up and down my wet panties, massaging my sex crack, I closed my eyes. This was a battle I couldn't win, I knew, as she pulled my panties to one side and slipped her finger between my swollen love lips, driving it deep into my drenched vagina. Was it a battle I wanted to win?

'You make me feel good,' she breathed. 'Do I make you feel good?'

'I . . . I don't know,' I lied as she slipped her wet finger out of my vagina and massaged my erect clitoris.

'Is that nice?'

'Yes, yes, it is.'

As she pressed her lips to mine, kissing me with a passion I'd never know before, I reciprocated. Opening my mouth, our tongues meeting, entwining, our saliva mingling, I slipped my hand between her parted thighs and massaged her clitoris. There was no blackmail now, no coercing. Just mutual participation of our own accord in our masturbating. Our loving?

Our mouths locked, our tongues entwined, we caressed each other's clitorises, giving and receiving immense sexual pleasure – lesbian pleasure. I knew I'd won her over as our lips parted and she began her gasping. She was mine now, not Den's. I'd persuade her to have nothing more to do with him, to visit me alone for rampant sessions of sex. One small victory, I reflected as my clitoris swelled and pulsated beneath her soft, vibrating fingertips. What had I become?

'Upstairs,' I said shakily. 'In my bed.' She leaped to her feet, her pretty face flushed, her nipples fully erect. Following me as I unbuttoned my blouse, I showed her into my bedroom and closed the door, locking it for added security. As I slipped out of my skirt, she pulled the quilt back and leaped into the bed like an excited schoolgirl.

I'd make her come again and again, I decided, slipping in beside her. I'd have her begging me for sex, and promising to cut all ties with Den. She'd become a slave to me, at my beck and call. As she dived beneath the quilt, positioning her young pussy over my face and burying her head between my thighs, I contemplated using her as a double agent. If I could discover something about Den, his past, where his family were, *I* might be able to blackmail *him*. Knowledge is power. The tables were soon to turn, I was sure.

Her beautiful pussy hovering above my gasping mouth, I pulled her down, pressing my face against the wet warmth of her open girlhood. She was drenched, her cunt milk decanting, pouring into my thirsty mouth as I licked and sucked on her hot flesh. Pushing her tongue deep into my aching pussy, licking inside me as my tongue entered her love hole, we shuddered in our lesbian coupling.

Her hands beneath my rounded buttocks, her fingers snaked between my thighs, parting my pussy lips, opening my hole wide to her darting tongue. I reciprocated, stretching her hairless, fleshy cushions wide apart, exposing her dripping vaginal walls to my inquisitive tongue. Her juices flowed into my mouth, over my face, running down my temples to my ears. In my sexual delirium, I drank from her vagina, savouring the aphrodisiacal product of her arousal.

We licked and mouthed until our clitorises swelled, urgently demanding the release of orgasm. We both sucked each other's sex buttons into our cunny-wet mouths, our tongues flicking, darting, seeking, caressing our pulsating protrusions. We were both near to the ultimate ecstasy, I knew, as we trembled violently, gasping and licking in our sexual frenzy. The ultimate ecstasy of lesbian sex.

Our bodies becoming rigid, our clitorises swollen, ripe in lust, we came in unison. Sucking, licking, our limbs entwined, we brought out each other's shuddering orgasms. On and on the waves of pure sexual bliss crashed through our quivering bodies until I thought I'd pass out from the sheer pleasure.

Never had I known such an exquisite entwining of naked bodies, such immense pleasure. Tongues licking, clitorises pulsating in climax, female to female, we sustained our illicit orgasms until we were drained, exhausted, depleted in our comings. Resting the weight of her trembling naked body upon mine, she sucked on my nub, our tongues encircling our clitorises until the last ripples of girl-pleasure had faded.

'That was nice,' she breathed, her face flushed and wet as she lay beside me. The phone rang as we kissed, our pussy-wet tongues meeting. On and on it rang, like the sound of a distant bell drifting across the meadow from a country church, ignored, forgotten. I wanted to be in a meadow with Lisa, the sun bathing our naked bodies as we buried our heads between each other's thighs.

Had I found something with Lisa? I wondered as she sucked my erect nipple into her hot mouth. Was this merely sex, lesbian sex, or was there a deeper bonding? I thought of Mat as I lay in the marital bed with a young, naked girl attending my breasts. Would the lesbian scene turn him on? Would he like to fuck Lisa's shorn pussy? The phone stopped ringing.

'I'd better be going,' she finally breathed, my nipple slipping out of her wet mouth as she propped herself up on her elbow and brushed her dark hair away from her wet face.

'What will you tell Den?' I asked.

'I won't tell him anything.'

'But he'll ask you to come here with him to blackmail and abuse me.'

'I'll say no. I don't want anything to do with Den now that I have you.'

As she climbed out of the bed, the sun streaming in through the window behind her, silhouetting her naked body, I again realized how beautiful she was. As she turned, I gazed at the profile of her pert breasts. Well rounded, her young nipples pointing north, she was exquisite in her youth. Had I found love with a young girl? I wondered as I slipped out of the bed. I didn't know what I'd found.

'Will you give me your phone number?' I asked as I followed her downstairs.

'Yes,' she replied, her buttocks wiggling as she walked into the lounge and grabbed her clothes.

'Why have you shaved?'

'Because I prefer it that way.'

'Would you prefer me shaved?'

'Yes, that would be nice,' she smiled, her voice soft, husky, as she gazed at my swollen love lips, my drenched crack. 'Den was going to make you shave.'

'What else does he plan to do?'

'I don't know. The arrangement is that he'll phone when he needs me.'

'There was another man here with Den. Do you know his name?'

'Another man? No, he's not told me anything about that.'

Watching as she dressed, I was sure that she wasn't lying. But she'd been in league with Den, she must have known about the unknown man. They'd have chatted, laughed about the situation. Den must have told her. I'd have to be careful, play it by ear until I was sure that I had her allegiance.

Giving me her phone number as she finished dressing, she kissed my lips, her tongue delving deep into my mouth as she pulled my naked body close to hers. Our lips finally parting, she smiled and left wordlessly. There were no words. We both knew what we wanted. Did I really know? The front door closing, I stood alone in the lounge, my nakedness arousing me. No, I didn't know what I wanted.

The phone rang again as I wandered into the kitchen and turned the cooker off, the smell of curry filling my nostrils. Den, Mat, Carole . . . Whoever it was, I didn't want to speak to them. I didn't want to speak to anyone for a while. My mind confused, guilt swamping me, I wondered what

I'd done. Full-blown lesbian sex? Only Mat and I had ever made love in our bed. I'd never have dreamed that I'd lie there naked in lust with another, let alone with a slip of a girl!

Still naked, I made ham sandwiches for my lunch, the lesbian act I'd committed heavy in my mind. I again thought of Mat, our relationship, our future. What did the future hold for us? Did I have a future with Lisa? *Blackmail.* The word buffeted my racked mind, hurting me. I still had to deal with Den, put a stop to his continual threats. But how?

I wandered around the house naked for the rest of the day, ignoring the bells, the phone, the door. Den knocked on the back door, hammered on the front, called through the letterbox . . . The latch up, the curtains drawn, I ignored his threats, his crude demands.

The time nearing six, I decided to go out for a walk. I didn't want to face Mat, not yet. Dressed in my turquoise miniskirt and white blouse, I left the house. My pussy naked, the evening air cooling my inflamed love lips, I smiled to myself as I floated down the lane, a new spring in my step. Was I in love?

As I saw Mat's car approaching, I slipped into a driveway and hid behind a bush. I didn't want to have to explain what I was doing, where I was going. He drove by, oblivious to the fact that his wife was there behind a bush, knickerless and braless, her cunt sticky with another girl's saliva.

'The bed!' I breathed in horror, remembering that I'd left the quilt pulled back, the sheets crumpled and cunny-stained. Mat would look for me, walk into the bedroom and discover what he'd believe to be the evidence of recent sex. I'd tell him that I'd slept, that I'd felt unwell and gone to bed. More lies, more deceit . . . Was I in love with a teenage girl?

Chapter Eight

Mat's car was in the driveway when I returned. Opening the front door, I felt elated that I had Lisa on my side. As a double agent she'd give me information about Den, discover who the mysterious man was who'd fucked my bottom and, hopefully, help me put an end to the whole sorry mess once and for all.

Calling out a greeting to Mat, I was surprised when there was no answer. Stepping out of the kitchen door in search of him, I stood by the fence and listened as I heard voices and the chinking of glasses coming from Den's garden.

'One of the funniest things was when she sucked you off through the hole in the fence!' Den laughed. 'And when we both fucked her arsehole in the lounge!'

The unknown beast was obviously with Den, enjoying a chat and a drink in the garden. I couldn't see through the fence to discover his identity. The best I could do was listen to the vile duo's banter, their crude jokes about me, the way they'd abused my naked body, in the hope of some enlightenment.

'I'm surprised she didn't hear you in the hall when I was fucking her and she was licking Lisa's cunt out,' Den chortled. I couldn't believe that his friend had been there, watching.

'She's had more spunk pumped into her in the last week or so than during her whole life!'

My heart nearly stopped as I recognized the voice. Mat!

Den's partner in vile crime was my husband! I was stunned. My head spinning, awash with confusion, I could barely stand on my crumpling legs as the shocking truth sank in. I must be wrong, I tried to convince myself. Mat would never . . .

'We've really got her where we want her,' Den crowed. 'I never thought she'd fall for the magazine trick.'

'I was pretty sure she would,' Mat chuckled. 'She would have been terrified if I'd confronted her with the magazine. She knows how suspicious I am, and I really laid it on before you showed her the mag. For several days I went on about other men and how disgusting I thought pornography was. She'd have done anything to . . .'

'She *has* done anything!' Den chortled.

'Watching her suck you off when she'd thought I'd gone out for cigars was such a turn-on, I almost wanked in the hall! And the thrashing you gave her was brilliant! The next time she's tied up and blindfolded, I'll give her a bloody good spanking.'

'What d'you reckon about her pubes, then? Do I get her to shave or not?'

'Yes, do it! She'll have a hell of a time explaining why she's shaved her cunt,' Mat sniggered. 'I'd love to see her dressed in a gymslip and white ankle socks!'

'Have some more wine. We're doing well, we deserve to celebrate.'

Staggering across the patio, I wandered into the kitchen and slumped at the table. Mat, of all people! My husband had been in on the blackmail, the perverted sex, from day one! I was cold with shock, shivering as I thought of Mat hiding in the house, watching me sucking Den's cock, licking Lisa's clitoris to orgasm. Now I knew where Den had got his information from about my background, my past relationships.

Lisa must have known that Mat was in on the wicked scheme. Den would have told her that my husband knew what was going on. She'd lied to me, the bitch! Yet again, she'd used me for lesbian sex. But what had happened to Mat? I'd thought we were happily married, working to build our future. Why had he treated me as nothing more than a common whore? In league with Den, he'd fucked my bottom, come in my mouth, watched me endure a thrashing . . .

My heart racing, my body shaking violently, I left the house and wandered aimlessly down the street. Had Mat sent me the cruel notes? I wondered. Why would he bother? No, there had to be someone else, someone who'd been watching, spying.

I felt that I was dreaming and that I'd wake up to find Mat sleeping beside me. But the horror was real enough. I'd been used and abused, tricked and blackmailed – by my husband! The lies, the deception . . . I couldn't begin to comprehend what had happened. I didn't know whether to laugh or cry, I felt no emotion – just numbness.

Sitting on a bench in the recreation ground, I held my head in my hands, trying to find some logic, some explanation for the way my husband had treated me. I hated Mat, I hated Den – I hated myself. The way Mat had questioned my nakedness when he'd known exactly what I'd been forced to endure! The times he'd said he was going out for cigars, going upstairs to change into his shorts, going to see about a computer . . . He'd delighted in my plight. It was only in my seething hatred that I realized how much I'd loved Mat. But now? My husband was a first-rate bastard! No, a devil!

At least the whole ugly episode was over, I reflected. I'd tell Den where to go and there'd be nothing he could do about it. His threats held no water now, they were futile.

The perverse games were finally over. What I'd do, what I'd say to Mat, I had no idea. I wouldn't confront him, not yet. I needed time to think about my future. What future?

Lifting my head, I looked around, wondering where to go. I couldn't go home, not yet – I couldn't face Mat. I wasn't sure whether I could ever face the bastard again, but I knew that I'd have to. At some stage, I'd have to confront him, tell him that I was leaving him. But why should *I* leave? I reasoned in my rising anger. *I* hadn't been the perpetrator of the vile and wicked plan. *I* was the innocent victim.

'No, I won't leave!' I breathed through gritted teeth as I walked home. 'I'll not let the bastards win!' I had to be clever, turn the tables . . . I'd say nothing, act as if I knew nothing about Mat's lies, his evil ways. I'd do my utmost to appear normal, calm, cool.

As I closed the front door, Mat emerged from the kitchen, his tanned face smiling.

'Ah, you're back. Where have you been?'

'It's such a lovely evening I went for a walk,' I smiled, seething inwardly with hatred and anger. Had he seen the bed, the sex-stained sheets? 'What have you been up to?'

'I've been talking to Den. Look, I know you don't like him, but I need his advice. Is it OK with you if he comes over for an hour or so?'

'Why don't you go to his place?' I asked, walking into the kitchen and filling the kettle for a semblance of normality.

'Because all my papers are here, it would be difficult.'

He was obviously planning another session of sexual abuse. No doubt he'd pretend to have to go out for ten minutes and Den would force me to suck him to orgasm. Mat would be hiding, watching another man fuck his wife's mouth. He was perverse in the extreme. Deriving satisfaction from watching me being sexually abused by another man, he was evil.

'I don't mind if he comes over,' I finally conceded.

'Good, I'll go and tell him. I really do need to sort this out as soon as possible. We'll sit in the dining room, so as not to get in your way.'

'OK,' I smiled as he stepped into the garden and went off to find his perverted accomplice.

I had to think, to come up with a plan. Mat would say that he had to go out and Den would come at me with his threats . . . Should I play the game? I pondered. Should I suck the beast off, knowing that Mat was watching? I could make out that I was really enjoying it, beg for Den to sperm down my throat. No, I wanted to ruin their fun, spoil their games.

I'd tell Den to go to hell. He'd talk to Mat and they'd try to come up with a plan, hatch new ways to blackmail me. Images of my mother racked my mind. If Den sent her a copy of the video tape . . . I'd cross that bridge when I came to it.

'Hi, Jane!' Den beamed as he followed Mat through the back door. 'How are you keeping?'

'I'm fine,' I replied sweetly. 'I'm just making coffee. Would you like some?'

'Thanks.'

'Damn!' Mat cursed, holding his hand to his head. 'Damn and blast!'

'What's the matter?' I asked, knowing full well that he was about to announce his timely departure.

'I forgot to post some important letters. They're in the car, I'd better walk down to the postbox now. Er . . . You two have a coffee and I'll be back shortly.'

As Mat left the kitchen and closed the front door, Den grinned at me. The bastard was obviously hiding in the hall, spying through the crack in the kitchen door that he'd deliberately left ajar. But I was about to thwart the decadent duo's wicked game, destroy their fun!

'There's time for me to fuck your pretty mouth,' Den grinned, eagerly dragging his erect penis out of his jeans. 'Kneel down and suck me off, bitch!'

'I'd don't feel like sucking you off!' I returned.

'You'll suck out my spunk or . . .'

'It's over, Den. I'm not going to be blackmailed anymore.'

'Don't start all that nonsense again. When Mat sees the video tape, he'll . . .'

'I don't care what he does, I'm not your slave any more.'

He zipped his jeans, frowning as he realized that I really did mean it this time. After several more futile threats, he looked pathetic, confused, his dark eyes staring hard at me. He didn't know what to do, what to say, as I poured the coffee and sat at the table. Standing next to me, he pulled his penis out again, offering his bulbous glans to my mouth as I turned to face him.

'Put it away!' I stormed.

'You'll suck me to orgasm, Jane, otherwise . . .'

'Den, please get it into your thick skull – it's over!'

'But Mat . . .'

'But Mat nothing. I don't care any more, I've had enough.'

The front door slamming shut, Den slipped his penis into his jeans. Mat had hardly had time to go to the postbox! But, realizing that the game might well be over, he obviously didn't think of that as he walked anxiously into the kitchen.

'Den, let's go through to the dining room,' he suggested, his brown eyes mirroring more than a hint of confusion.

'Er . . . Yes, right.'

'You were quick!' I teased. 'You couldn't have gone to the postbox and back that quickly.'

'Er . . . No, I . . . I forgot that I'd posted the letters earlier.'

'Panic over, then. I'll be in the garden if you need me,' I smiled innocently, taking my coffee and wandering out onto the patio.

Once they'd gone into the dining room, I slipped back into the house and loitered in the hall. Den was saying that he'd done his best and Mat was cursing me. They were behaving like schoolboys who'd just lost their football over the fence. Blaming each other, I thought it was going to end up in an almighty row.

'Let's calm down,' Mat finally said. 'We've still got the video tape. There's no way she'll want her mother seeing it, so . . .'

'I'm not so sure,' Den broke in pensively. 'As you heard, she seemed pretty adamant.'

'I wonder why she's not worried any more? Do you reckon she *has* got someone else?'

'Maybe.'

'If she plans to leave me, then . . . No, there's still the tape and her mother. It's been going so well, and now this! What the hell are we going to do, Den?'

'Shit, I don't know!'

'I know, I'll show her one of the photographs, the one with her on the lawn flashing her fanny, perhaps. I'll say that it was posted to me, at my office.'

'What good will that do?'

'It'll be a taster, Den. Believing that you've sent me that photo, she'll be fearful of you sending me the others – and the video tape.'

'It might work,' Den sighed.

'It *will* work! She'll realize that you mean business. If you threaten to send the photographs and the tape to her mother, she'll have no choice other than to allow you to fuck her.'

The crafty bastards were sunk, thrashing about in the waves of the cruel sea, trying to cling to the wreckage of their evil plan. My hand up my short skirt, toying with my outer lips, I recalled the perverted sex I'd been forced to endure, wondering what I'd do now that it was all over. Lisa? I pondered. I'd enjoyed sex with her, but it had been wrong – I wasn't a lesbian. Or was I? I still didn't know what I was or what I wanted.

'Tomorrow morning's plan is out of the bloody window,' Mat sighed despondently. 'I've arranged to have a couple of hours off and . . .'

'Look, I'll try the mother angle. I'll go and tell her that you're on the phone and I'm in the garden to give you some privacy. I'll tell her that I'll send a copy of the tape to her mother unless she plays the game and sucks me off.'

'All right. Tell her that I'll be on the phone for some time, business or something.'

'OK.'

Dashing out onto the patio, I sat down and waited for Den to join me. Mat would no doubt be spying out of the dining-room window, hoping to get his perverted kicks from watching Den fucking my mouth. But he was in for a great disappointment! A plan formulating in my mind as my would-be blackmailer emerged from the house, I grinned amiably at him.

'Finished already?' I asked.

'No, Mat's on the phone. He'll be some time – time enough for me to come in your mouth.'

'Den, I've told you . . .'

'Then I'll send a copy of the video tape to your mother. I'll post it first thing in the morning.'

'And I'll phone her and tell her not to open it. I'll say that it's a present for Mat and I had to have it sent to her place in case he saw it. I'll drive over and pick it up.'

'In that case, I'll drive to her house and drop all the photographs and the tape through her letterbox, no envelopes or packaging.'

'You are clever,' I smiled. 'But not clever enough.'

'We're wasting time, Jane,' he whispered angrily, taking his erect penis out of his jeans yet again. 'Come on, bitch – suck it!'

Rising to my feet, I wandered down the garden, leaving Den with his cock straining erect from his jeans, his face frowning. I glimpsed Mat at the dining-room window as I turned and pretended to look at a flower border. The pair of them had failed miserably! I reflected. But if my poor mother were to see the evidence . . . I hadn't won yet, I knew only too well.

I became aware of another battle raging – my insatiable clitoris calling for intimate attention. The sight of Den's purple knob, the thought of his sperm bathing my tongue, had turned me on frighteningly. With horror, I realized that even if I put an end to the perverted sex I'd be cutting off my nose to spite my face.

The only partner I'd be left with was Mat, and I didn't want him. I'd have no one to satisfy my progressively increasing thirst for sex. There was Lisa, of course, but . . . No, I didn't want a lesbian relationship. I had to resist, to deny my craving for her fresh young body, her beautiful cunt. Besides, she was a lying bitch!

Wondering what plans Den and Mat had made for the morning, I smiled sweetly as Den wandered across the lawn and stood fidgeting beside me. 'I'll drive over to your mother's now,' he threatened. 'I can be there in an hour or so.'

'Den, listen to me. I'll have sex with you as and when you want it, but . . .'

'There are no buts. It's all or nothing.'

'Listen! As I told you, I'm leaving Mat for another man. I don't care whether you believe me or not, I'm leaving him. We'll have sex, but not when Mat's around.'

'He's on the phone, so you have time to suck . . .'

'No, not when he's around. Tomorrow morning, I'll ring him at work. If he's there, then I'll be sure to have at least an hour alone with you. It takes him a good hour to drive home, so . . .'

'But . . .'

'Take it or leave it, Den.'

'OK,' he sighed. 'Let me know when you've phoned him.'

'Go back into the house and I'll join you shortly.'

Now what would the evil pair come up with? I wondered as Den mooched across the lawn with his hands in his pockets. Would he tell Mat about my offer? Surely Mat got his kicks from watching another man sexually abuse me? How would he react, knowing that I was having sex while he was at work? A voyeur is only a voyeur when spying, watching others fucking. If Mat was never around he couldn't use the hole in the fence or fuck my bottom while I was blindfolded. No doubt they'd come up with some plan or other but, for the time being, I felt that I was winning.

Returning to the house, I crept into the kitchen, listening intently as they chatted in the dining room. Mat was still cursing and complaining while Den was coming up with one crazy plan after another. Again wondering why Mat had treated me like this, why he'd wanted to watch me enduring perverted sex with another man, I thought about Lisa.

Had *she* had sex with Mat? A tart like that would undoubtedly enjoy any man's cock up her cunt, and the way Mat had behaved, he'd have had no qualms about fucking her. Perhaps Den had come up with the same idea as me, I mused. Perhaps he'd sent her round to see me because she was *his* double agent. But she'd seemed genuine enough when we'd been in bed together – genuinely loving and lusting. My thoughts were muddled. She was no more innocent than Den or Mat!

Picturing the girl's alluring cunt, I pondered on shaving my pubic hairs, removing my downy cunny fleece. Mat would believe that Den had forced me to do it. I'd say that I'd done it because I preferred it that way, hairless, smooth, naked – like Lisa. I might even mark my breasts, spank my milky mammary spheres with a thin cane and Mat would believe that Den had done it. Den would deny it and Mat would become suspicious.

I'd feed Lisa false information, tell her that Den had forced me to endure anal sex with six men. I'd say that I'd had three men at once, in my mouth, my bum and my cunt – and discover whether her allegiance was true or false. If she really was the lying bitch I believed her to be, my claims of dreadful sexual abuse would get back to Mat.

But, whatever I did or didn't plan to do, the thought of Mat treating me in the despicable way he had wouldn't leave my mind. In pursuing his perverse sexual gratification, he'd put me through a living hell. He'd never shown signs of perversity in the past, never talked about anal sex, bondage, buttock whipping . . . When had he changed? I wondered. What had changed him?

When Den finally left I ventured into the lounge to find Mat pouring himself a large scotch. As he sprawled in his armchair, I sank onto the sofa, wondering what to say. He smiled at me, but there was confusion in his eyes. What would *he* say? What devilish plans had the evil pair conjured?

'Had a good day?' he ventured.

'Not bad. Oh, I forgot to tell you, Lisa phoned earlier.'

'She phoned here?' He frowned, leaning forward in his chair.

'Yes, she's coming over for coffee tomorrow morning.'

'Coffee? But . . .'

'But what? I thought it was rather nice of her to ring me. We'll spend some time together, get to know each other.'

'Is Den coming with her?'

'Den? Why would he want to come with her?'

'I just thought . . . As they're friends, I thought he might come with her.'

'No, Lisa's coming on her own. We're going to have a chat, you know, woman to woman – girl talk.'

'Does he know?'

'I have no idea. What is it, Mat? What's the matter?'

'Nothing, nothing. Er . . . I'm just nipping over to Den's. I forgot to ask him something.'

'OK. Well, I think I'll go up to bed. I could do with an early night.'

'Right, I'll see you later.'

Grinning as he scrambled from the room, I was sure that I was now way out in front, winning point after point. Knowledge is power, I reflected. Now I knew who my adversaries were, I could fight them. Was Lisa an adversary or an ally? I didn't know, but I'd soon find out. I debated whether to ring her, feed her some false information and see where it popped up. But no, not yet, I decided.

Grabbing the ringing phone, I was surprised to hear her. 'It's funny that you should phone, I was just thinking about ringing *you*,' I chuckled.

'Den's just phoned me,' she said. Her voice was cold, hard, accusing. 'Did you tell him that I'm coming round for coffee tomorrow morning?'

'You're not, are you?'

'No, but did you say that I was?'

'Why would I say that? Why would I say that you're coming round if you're not?'

'I don't know. He went apeshit, started yelling at me.'

'Why? I don't understand.'

'I suppose, after all that's happened, he doesn't like the idea of me seeing you without him.'

'I don't know what he's playing at now, but I can assure you that I've said nothing to him about you, Lisa. I haven't even seen him, let alone talked to him.'

'What about your husband? Did you say anything to him? He might have mentioned it to Den.'

'I haven't talked to Mat about you. Lisa, are you sure that you don't know who Den's friend is, the man he brought round here?'

'No, I don't know him. I wonder why Den thinks that I'm going to see you tomorrow?'

'He's up to his tricks again. I wouldn't trust him, Lisa. The best thing is to ignore him.'

'Yes, I suppose you're right. Oh, there's the doorbell. I'll . . . I'll call you tomorrow.'

'That'll be nice, I'll look forward to it.'

'OK, bye.'

The ball was rolling faster, picking up momentum. Mat had told Den, Den had rung Lisa . . . I was almost beginning to enjoy the fun and games, but the terrible things Mat had done to me weighed heavy on my mind. I'd never forget, let alone forgive. But I had to keep my wits about me, not dwell on the past. Look forward, plan ahead.

As Mat breezed into the room, I looked up, smiling sweetly. 'You were quick. Did you see Den?' I asked.

'Yes, I did,' he replied pensively. 'Jane, Den's just told me that he's going out with Lisa tomorrow morning so I don't see how she can be coming to see you.'

'That's odd. Why would she say that she's . . . Oh, perhaps she's coming here, and then going next door to Den.'

'No, they're going out early, for the day.'

'How strange. Perhaps she forgot?'

'She'd hardly forget that she'd arranged to go out with Den for the day.'

'No, I suppose not.'

'Has she been to see you before?'

'Yes, she came round before the weekend, I forgot to mention it to you.'

'You forgot? I would have thought that . . .'

'She wasn't here for long. We had coffee and a chat, and then she left. You seem worried. Do you have a problem with her coming to see me?'

'No, no, of course not. It's just that . . .'

'I'm hoping that we'll become good friends. I like her very much, we get on well together. Anyway, I'm going up to bed.'

'OK, I'll be up later.'

Knowing that he'd ring Den the minute I'd gone, I left the door ajar and lurked on the stairs. The evil bastards didn't know what the hell was going on! My little game was causing them real problems. And I'd cause them more problems before the night was out, I decided. Confuse them and set them against each other.

I was right. Like a bat out of hell Mat grabbed the phone and began rabbiting to Den. 'She said that Lisa came round before the weekend,' he whined. 'Why would she lie? Yes, I realize that someone's lying, Den. It must be Lisa – Jane would hardly say that the girl's coming round tomorrow if she wasn't. I don't know, I really don't. Look, as I've got a couple of hours off tomorrow, I'll come round to your place and we'll see what happens. Yes, I'll park the car round the corner. OK, about eight.'

Scuttling up the stairs to bed, a grin on my face, I was pleased with the way things were going. I'd lost Mat, I knew, but . . . But what? *Divorce*. The terrible word haunted me, tortured me. My marriage would soon be over. But I had Lisa, didn't I?

Mat left at eight the following morning. I gave him several minutes before creeping downstairs and spying out of the lounge window. Having parked his car somewhere out of sight, he stole up Den's path, looking this way and that to make sure that the coast was clear. He was like a thief in the night, stupid, pathetic, and I hated him. But what to do? I wondered. Lisa wasn't going to turn up, so perhaps I should go out. They'd follow me, but I'd lose them and . . .

'Christ!' I breathed, suddenly realizing that this was my husband I was playing games with. What the hell had happened to our relationship? He was using and abusing me, lying to me, I was lying to him, planning to lose him when he followed me . . . And to top it all, I'd taken Lisa into the marital bed! But Mat had started the whole thing, I reflected. I was innocent.

Remembering that I'd told Den I'd ring Mat's office to see whether he was there, I thought it best to stick to the plan. It would look suspicious if I didn't phone, and I didn't want suspicion surrounding me. Mat's secretary would confirm my call, and he'd not know that I'd rumbled him. I checked my watch – eight-fifteen. I'd have to give it an hour or so before phoning.

Perhaps it was best to stay in the house, I mused. Walking down the street and losing Den and Mat would serve no purpose at all. I didn't know what to do. Pacing the lounge floor, my mind swirling with a thousand thoughts, I was about to have breakfast when the phone rang.

'Jane, it's Den,' the bastard drawled as I lifted the receiver. 'I see Mat's gone to work.'

'Yes, I'm going to ring him in an hour or so to make sure he's there and then . . .'

'I want your cunt now. Ring his mobile number.'

'No, I want to make sure that he's at the office before . . . Oh, there's the doorbell,' I lied.

'Who is it?'

'It's none of your business. I'll call you later.'

Hanging up, I knew that Mat would have been listening to his accomplice's crude demands, rather than spying out of his window. The pathetic pair would be wondering who my mysterious visitor was, but they'd never find out. Putting myself in their shoes, I tried to work out what I'd do. If Mat went to get his car and came home, pretending that he'd forgotten something . . . I was right. Within ten minutes the predictable prat had pulled up in the drive. Leaping upstairs, I locked myself in the bathroom and turned the shower on.

'Jane, are you in there?' he called, tapping on the door in his desperation to discover the identity of my phantom visitor.

'I'm having a shower!' I yelled back. 'What are you doing home?'

'Can I come in? I want to talk to you.'

'You'll have to wait, Mat!'

I made him wait for ten minutes before emerging with a towel wrapped around me, my hair sopping wet. He was standing on the landing, his brown eyes frowning. He was lost on a sea of suspicion, floundering, trying desperately to discover what I was up to.

'What are you doing here?' I asked as he sidled into the bathroom, obviously looking for Lisa or a male lover.

'I forgot something,' he said lamely, following me into the bedroom.

He searched the house as I dressed, making out that he couldn't find his credit card. Brushing my hair as I entered the kitchen, I saw him wandering around the garden. He was obviously perplexed as he returned to the house, wondering who on earth my visitor was, and where they were hiding.

'You're going to be very late,' I remarked.

'It's OK, I phoned in. Has anyone been to see you this morning?'

'No, why?'

'I just wondered.'

'Lisa's coming round later, as I told you last night.'

'She's going out with Den!' he sighed.

'Mat, she rang me twenty minutes ago, she's coming round at eleven.'

'I don't understand. Den was adamant that . . .'

'It doesn't matter, there's nothing *to* understand. If she doesn't turn up, that's fine, if she does, then . . . I don't know why you're making such a big thing about Lisa.'

'I'm not, it's just that it seems odd.'

'*You* seem odd, Mat. You were going on about Lisa last night, and now you're harping on about her this morning! All she's doing is coming round for a chat. Perhaps she's changed her mind about going out with Den. What does it matter, anyway? Besides, it's really none of our business. Hadn't you better go to work?'

'There's no rush. I'll make some coffee. Would you like some?'

'No, I'm going to sit in the sun to dry my hair.'

Contemplating matters while sitting on a patio chair, I still had no idea what my long-term plans were. I'd play my games for a while, confuse the rats to the point where they thought they were going insane. But then what? I'd have mysterious visitors and phone calls, feed Den and Lisa false information and cause mayhem. But long-term?

Mat was deliberately hanging around, sitting in the kitchen drinking coffee, almost visibly trying to work out what I could have done with my visitor. And Den would be pacing the floor, wondering what the hell was going on. All I had to do was relax beneath the summer sun. I had all day – there was no rush.

'Aren't you going into the office?' I asked as Mat finally emerged peevishly from the house.

'Are you trying to get rid of me?'

'No, of course I'm not!' I chuckled.

'I'll be going soon.'

'Are you OK, Mat? You seem like a cat on hot bricks. What are you waiting for?'

'Nothing, nothing. I've got a lot on my mind, that's all.'

'Something's wrong, I know. You're always coming home during the day. There was a time when I never saw you between eight in the morning and seven at night, and now you're always calling in.'

'I have some local clients.'

'Look at you now, hanging around as if you have the day off. Is everything OK at the office?'

'Yes, everything's fine.'

'What's this thing you've got with Den?'

'What do you mean?'

'You're either going to see him, or he comes here to see you. What's going on?'

'Nothing's going on!' he laughed. 'Den's been helping me with some financial matters, that's all. Well, I suppose I'd better make a move. I'll see you this evening.'

As he left reluctantly, I knew that I'd won yet another round. But how many rounds were there? What was the ultimate goal? I was winning a game that had no prize. What was the point in playing? There was no point, but I had no other choice, I decided. If I confronted Mat, the marriage would be over. There again, if I kept quiet, the marriage was over!

Retreating into the house, I closed and locked the back door and rang Lisa. I wanted to find out where she lived. It was one thing making out that she was coming to see me, but if I were to tell Mat that I'd been to see her it would really upset the hornets' nest! I had to discover her address to substantiate my lies.

'Oh, Jane,' she said, a hint of anger in her voice.

'How are you?' I asked, installing myself on the sofa.

'Den's just phoned again. He wants to know why I'm going to see you at eleven o'clock this morning.'

'Not again! You're not coming here at eleven, or any other time today.'

'I know that, but he insists that you told him . . .'

'Look, we need to talk. You'd better not come here because Den might see you. How about me coming round to your place? I can come now if . . .'

'No, I'll be out until twelve.'

'Oh, I see. Look, give me your address and I might call round this afternoon.'

'OK. D'you know the electrical shop in the High Street?'

'Yes, I do.'

'It's the flat above the shop, thirty-seven A.'

'Right. I'll ring before I come round, just to make sure you're in.'

'I should be in all afternoon.'

'OK, see you later.'

I had no intention of visiting Lisa but, knowing her address, I could tell Mat that I'd done so and he'd tell Den. My plan was somewhat precarious, but it would serve to fire suspicion. Lisa would deny that I'd been to see her, Den would accuse her of lying, Mat would wonder whether I was telling the truth . . . A precarious plan, but the best I could come up with.

After breakfast, I mooched about the house wondering

what to do. My clitoris stirred for the first time that day, and I pondered on masturbation. What with Mat home for the weekend, and the horrendous things I'd discovered, I'd not had an orgasm since Friday.

I rang Mat's office, hoping that he'd arrived. If I was going to enjoy the brass doorknob, I didn't want him prowling about, lurking, spying. 'He's on the other line,' his secretary announced. My vagina tightening, wetting, I hung up and slipped my drenched panties off. Rivers of cunt milk flowed down my thighs, meandering, seeking.

'Ah, I see you're preparing for me!' Den chuckled, leaning in the doorway.

'How the . . . Get out!' I screamed.

'What about our deal? Mat's at work, you've taken your knickers off, I'm ready and waiting, so . . .'

'Get out!'

'Who came to see you this morning?'

'It's none of your business.'

'Jane, I have your mother's address. The evidence is in my car and I'm about to drive over to her house.'

'The man I'm leaving Mat for . . . He came to see me, if you must know.'

'I saw Mat come back. I'm surprised he didn't catch you with your knickers down.'

'As Mat came in the front door, my lover went out of the back and slipped round the side of the house. Mat didn't see him.'

'Right, you've had your fun, played your games, spread your lies about Lisa – and now you're going to do exactly as I say.'

'I told you, it's over.'

'Right, I'll be at your mother's within the hour.'

My mother! That was the only hold he had on me and it was a hold so tight that I couldn't wriggle out of it. At least

Mat was at the office – whatever I did with Den, I knew that he wouldn't be watching. Den would tell him, of course, but I'd confuse the issue by saying that I'd been to see Carole and then Lisa – that I'd been out all day. Den would insist that I was lying and Mat wouldn't know who or what to believe.

'There's no need to go to my mother's,' I finally sighed, realizing that I was more than ever Den's slave. 'What do you want me to do?'

'That's more like it!' he beamed triumphantly. 'Before we start, admit that you've been lying about Lisa.'

'I haven't been lying. She came here before the weekend, and she was coming here this morning. She phoned just before you arrived and cancelled.'

'I don't believe you.'

'I can't help that, Den.'

'When are you supposed to be seeing her again?'

'I was going to her place this afternoon, but I don't know whether I'll have the time.'

'You don't know where she lives.'

'Above the electrical shop in the high street. I've been there before.'

'Describe her flat.'

'No, why should I? I don't have to prove anything to you, or anyone else, for that matter.'

'Jane, I'm warning you . . .'

He broke off as the phone rang. Lifting the receiver, I was relieved to hear Carole's voice. Perhaps I had a chance to get rid of Den, I mused, a plan beginning to take shape as Carole enquired how I was.

'Yes, the coast's clear,' I said softly, huskily. 'No, Mat searched the house but found nothing.' Twigging that I had some kind of problem, Carole allowed me to ramble on uninterrupted. 'Oh, I'd love to!' I trilled as Den sat on the sofa, lapping it up. 'He's gone to work so we'll have plenty of time together. Five minutes? That's great. Yes, I'll look forward to it. You know I do, silly. Yes, very much. All right, bye.'

Replacing the receiver, I grabbed my panties from the floor and tugged them up my sticky legs. Den rose to his feet, his expression pained as I donned a victorious grin.

'Who was that?' he finally asked.

'My friend, the one I'm leaving Mat for,' I replied excitedly.

'He's coming here now?'

'Five minutes.'

'You should have put him off. You'll regret this.'

'I couldn't put him off. He's in his car, calling on his mobile, just five minutes away. He's been waiting until Mat was out of the way.'

'I'll be back later to . . .'

'Give me at least two hours and then . . .'

'And then you'll do everything I ask.'

'Yes, all right. I don't want my mother to know about . . . I'm leaving Mat and I don't want my plans disrupted. I'll do whatever you want.'

'I'm glad you've seen sense at long last. I'll be back in two hours.'

Two hours. I had time to think, to plan. As the front door closed, I realized that I should have put the latch up to keep Den out. I never learned from my mistakes. What would the bastard do now? I pondered. Would he ring Mat to tell him that he was back in business? Or would he keep his sordid secret and only visit me for sex when Mat was working? What would Mat do if he thought that the fun and games were over? Whatever happened, what would *I* do?

Chapter Nine

Like a restless animal I roamed the house, trying to work out what to do about my mother, what to say should she lay eyes on the incriminating evidence. There'd be nothing to say, no explanation. Our relationship would be ruined.

As I paced the lounge floor, a thought suddenly rose from the rubble of my wrecked mind. Putting myself in Den's shoes, I realized that he wouldn't send my mother the video tape and photographs. It was pretty obvious that she'd go berserk and not only confront me but tell Mat of my debauched ways. That would be that – marriage over.

Neither Mat nor Den would have anything to gain by revealing the truth to my mother. I was sure that Mat's motive wasn't to end the marriage. He just wanted to get his perverted kicks by watching me being sexually abused, by fucking my bottom-hole while I was bound and blindfolded, by having me suck him to orgasm through the hole in the fence.

At last I was in a position to put an end to the perverted sex. But, in my continuing confusion, I didn't know what I wanted. On the one hand I could enjoy my body to the full, indulge in rampant sex sessions with both Den and Lisa . . . But what sort of marriage would I have if I allowed the games to continue? A marriage based on lies, deceit and adultery. On the other hand, I could leave Mat, set up home in a flat somewhere. Having lived in a nice house with a beautiful garden, I wasn't sure that I could survive in a flat.

Besides, this was *my* house. Should I throw Mat out? No, he'd never leave.

Was I a nymphomaniac? I wondered for the umpteenth time as I recalled Lisa in my bed, her glorious nakedness covering mine. Whatever I was, the time was rapidly approaching for me to make my mind up. But, for now, I thought it best to play it by ear rather than come to any rash decision.

The latch up, I didn't answer the door to Den. He rattled and shouted through the letterbox, hammered on the back door in his desperation to get to my naked body, but I ignored him. I desperately needed sex, orgasm, and I wondered what to do as my clitoris swelled and pulsated between my ballooning love lips. Cut off my nose to spite my face? I'd cut off the sex to spite Mat and Den and left myself out in the cold. I didn't like dilemmas.

By lunchtime, I was aching to come. My panties drenched, my clitoris painfully swollen, I needed more than masturbation. I needed a partner. When Den phoned with his threats, demanding that I give him my body, I tried to resist. But I needed him, his cock, his sperm – there was no way I could deny it. Finally, I gave in.

He came round clutching a Tesco's carrier bag, his face beaming triumphantly as he closed the front door and followed me into the lounge. Knowledge was power, I reflected – but my insatiable clitoris was more powerful than anything. It wasn't Den who ruled my life now but my incessant yearning for debased sex.

'This is going to be good,' he murmured, rummaging in the bag as I slipped my blouse off. 'The fuck of all fucks.' Releasing my bra, my nipples stiffening as the silk cups fell away from my swollen breasts, I felt that the battle was over. I knew that I was going to give myself completely. There was no point in resisting, in fighting any more.

'Right,' Den smirked as I tugged my skirt and panties down, revealing my dripping sex crack. 'First, we'll stiffen your nipples.' Standing before me, he clipped clothes pegs onto my milk teats, the pain permeating my firm breasts as he stood back and grinned. Biting my lip as I looked down at my abused teats, the pain intense as the pegs bit into my sensitive brown protrusions, I knew that this was only the beginning of a session of sex so perverted that it would remain etched in my memory forever.

At least Mat was at work, I reflected thankfully as Den forced me to get on the floor on all fours. 'Your cunt looks good from behind,' he leered as he delved into the innocuous-looking bag again. *My cunt.* That one special part of my body that men desired, fought for, paid for – killed for.

'OK, bitch, walkies time.' Strapping a leather dog collar around my neck, he pulled on the chain, yanking my head up. He was treating me like an animal now, not simply as a sex slave. My naked body was purely an object to be used and abused, my cunt nothing more than a hot, wet hole to be fucked. My nipples pinched agonizingly by the clothes pegs, my head pilloried by the chain, I'd been plunged into the darkest depths of degradation, humiliation. I had entered my domain.

'Walkies!' he chuckled, pulling on the chain. I crawled across the carpet, my pinched nipples aching, my naked buttocks projecting, my cunny lips crudely displayed. What did he intend to do with me? I wondered fearfully as he grabbed his bag of tricks and led me through the hall into the kitchen. Opening the back door, he made me crawl down the garden like an animal.

The sun warmed my naked body as he led me to the old apple tree. Soft beneath my hands, my knees, the grass comforted me. I noticed the daisies, looking at me. *Chains.*

Daisy chains. My childhood a sepia photograph, my only chains now were my sex bonds. The garden hoe lay nearby.

I felt different now that I knew who was involved in the wicked plan. Although a slave to Den, and effectively also to Mat, I had grown to enjoy the perverted sex, the games. I was an angel of sex. My naked body my temple, sought after by men and women, I was a sex goddess.

'Right, now the fun starts!' Den laughed, yanking my head up and securing the end of the chain to a branch. The sun filtered through the leaves above me, flickering like stars. I liked sunbathing naked, feeling the warmth permeating my firm breasts, my nipples, my secret places. Now I felt the sun bathing the fullness of my buttocks once more. Was I to be thrashed?

Taking two metal stakes and a hammer from the bag, my master drove them into the ground. Tying my ankles to the stakes with lengths of rope, my feet wide apart, a bolt of arousal coursed through my vulnerable frame. The cane or the leather belt? I speculated. Was he going to drive his organ deep into my bottom-hole and sperm in my bowels?

My head held high by the chain, my feet tethered, I couldn't escape the demeaning, the provocative position. As my master blindfolded me, I speculated on what fate might be in store. Was I to be licked to orgasm, my clitoris caressed by his sweeping tongue as he fingered my cunt? Mat was at work, I reasoned in my darkness. So why blindfold me?

Hearing male voices, a cold chill ran up my spine as I realized that I was to be crudely taken by more than one man. How many were there? Would they take turns to fuck me, to spunk me? One after the other using my cunt to satisfy their lust, their perverse desires? Arousal gripped me.

'Right on cue!' Den laughed, slapping my naked buttocks with the palm of his hand. 'OK, who's going up her cunt?'

'I'll take her fanny,' a man replied eagerly. His voice was smooth, dark. Was his cock big?

'And I'll have her arsehole,' another rejoined.

'That just leaves her mouth,' Den chortled.

Someone slid beneath my naked body, his solid penis stabbing between my gaping vaginal lips as he lay on his back. Fingers yanked my fleshy folds apart, opening my vaginal mouth, exposing my most intimate sex flesh. Suddenly, the anonymous stud penetrated me, his huge shaft stretching me open, filling me to capacity. My buttocks yanked apart, a tongue licked my once-secret valley, wetting my anal portal. I shuddered as the man beneath me slid his penis out of my cunt and then drove into me again, battering my cervix. *The goddess of sex.*

The tongue left my anal rose and a solid knob pressed against my delicate brown ring, trying to enter me there. 'No!' I screamed as the glans pushed past my defeated sphincter muscles and drove into the dank heat of my rectal duct. My screams were futile, I knew, as the thick shaft glided deep into my bowels. My holes dilated by two erect organs, I thought I'd split open as the crude double fucking began. Never had I endured such a corrupt act, and I wondered at my femininity. I had no claim to femininity now, I was nothing more than a wanton whore, an obscene tart. I trembled in my pleasure.

'Open your mouth, bitch!' Den ordered me as he knelt before my sweating face. I complied, taking the third penis into my quivering body, imagining my plunderers all coming at once, filling my abused orifices with their gushing jism. There were new sensations as the penises within my bloated holes frictioned, the solid knobs massaging each other through the thin membrane separating my ducts.

I wanted to cry, but there were no tears. I tried to deny the pleasure the three phalluses were bringing me, but the beautiful sensations wouldn't grant me denial. In the dark of my blindfold I felt pubic hairs tickling my nose as Den drove his weapon to the back of my throat. I breathed in his sex-scent. It was stronger in the dark.

My naked body rocking with the triple fucking, my clitoris forced from its pink bonnet, erect in arousal, I knew I was going to come as never before. I couldn't hold back, the sensations building in my trembling womb invading my bloated pelvis, reaching out to every nerve ending. My holes sore and inflamed as the plundering organs seemed to swell to an incredible size, I knew my triple sperming was imminent. I'd dreamed of three cocks fucking me, and now, in all its perverse, its beautiful reality, my dream was seeing the light of day.

Let go, let go! My thoughts whispered as a tide of milk surged from the estuary of my bursting vagina. I felt as if I was floating on the outrushing of breath from my abusers' gasping mouths, drifting in my darkness. I wanted Lisa, her smooth, hairless cunt pressed against my mouth, my tongue deep within her creamy love hole. I didn't want Lisa.

'God!' Den cried, towering above me, his knob swelling within the wet heat of my mouth. The brown tissue of my bottom-hole gripping one of the other intruding shafts, my cunt burning, inflamed, my clitoris exploded in orgasm as the men gasped in their coming. My tongue drowning in sperm, my holes brimming with male ejaculate, I shuddered in my own massive climax.

Swinging balls smacking between my open thighs, my vaginal throat gulping spunk, my anal tube fervently sucking in male milk, I swallowed the cream geysering from Den's orgasming knob. I was alive with crude sex, revelling in my debauchery, wallowing in the baseness of the obscene act. The man riding my bottom slapped my buttocks, the stinging pain only enhancing my immense pleasure. Responding to the surges of orgasm coursing through my chained body, my pinched nipples sent electrifying tingles of sex through my swelling breasts.

I thought I'd die from pleasure as my climax peaked, gripping me in its luxurious glove, shaking me to the very core of my being. I was flying, flying like a bird on the wing high above the clouds of consciousness to a heaven of pure sexual bliss. Was this the real me? I wondered in the delirium of my sexual haze. Was I really a confirmed nymphomaniacal tart? I could come to no other conclusion. I was wicked, vile in my sordid vileness.

'Ah, ah! Spunking up her arse!' the man behind me gasped as his sperm continued to jet into my bowels.

'And her cunt!' the one beneath my tethered body rejoined as he thrust his cock into my sopping cavern.

Impaled on three apoplectic penises, my naked body rocking back and forth, my own orgasm peaked again, sending shock waves of crude pleasure through my quivering flesh. How much more could I take? I wondered, the cocks within my lust holes finding their rhythm, thrusting in unison. My three orifices fucked, spunked, my climax gripping me, I imagined Lisa licking my clitoris, her long black hair tickling my inner thighs, my stomach. Now I wanted her.

At last, my orgasm began to subside and the spent cocks withdrew, leaving their sated orifices. I swallowed Den's sperm, savouring the residue from my lips as my body shuddered in the waning of my climax. What now? I wondered apprehensively, excitedly, as the men moved about. I wanted another triple fucking.

A chink of daylight appeared before my dazed eyes. My blindfold had slipped during the debauchery. Turning my head to one side, through my peephole I glimpsed four pairs of shoes. Four? Instantly recognizing Mat's black brogues, my stomach somersaulted as I realized that he'd been watching the crude fucking. What were his thoughts as he'd watched two penises fucking the intimate holes between my thighs and buttocks? What sort of man would watch his wife being crudely abused by three other men? *An evil bastard.*

Like a thief in the night, the thought of Mat witnessing my enforced debauchery sent a bolt of arousal through my tethered body. Chained like an animal, fucked and spunked by strangers while my husband watched, I quivered as my excitement soared. Sperm oozing from my lust ducts, running in rivulets down my trembling thighs, I had never known such stimulation. I wanted to come again, to have three men fuck me again while my husband watched.

Mat's feet moved behind me. The other men moved and my buttocks were parted, crudely yanked apart to expose my sperm-wet anal inlet. It was Mat, I knew, as a bulbous glans pressed against my anal rose, my anal mouth. He was going to fuck me there while his accomplices watched.

Driving his cock deep into my bowels, he grabbed my hips and withdrew. Again, he propelled his shaft deep into my secret tube, stretching me wide open, stimulating my inner flesh. His balls slapping my dripping vaginal lips, he increased his fucking rhythm, my body rocking back and forth as he pistoned my private channel.

A solid knob brushed against my mouth as I gasped with pleasure. It was wet – sperm-wet and cunny-wet. The cock that had fucked my cunt, spunked my cervix, now wanted to fuck my mouth. Parting my lips wide I sucked the swollen glans into my hot mouth and ran my tongue over its silky-smooth cylinder. Two men – my husband fucking my bottom and a stranger fucking my mouth. I was drifting on a cloud of lust.

Never had I known that such depths of depravity existed,

such sexual ecstasy. Desires emerged from the deep canyons of my mind, unknown desires. Never had I dreamed that I'd derive such satisfaction from my husband's abuse. I hated him as he rudely fucked my bottom. I hated myself. I love-hated him. What was he? A monster, a fiend, a sexual pervert . . . What was I?

'Really give it to the bitch!' Den urged as a hand slapped my buttocks. 'Give her the arse-spunking of her life!' As Mat fucked my bottom, I sucked on the throbbing organ within my mouth, savouring the heady cocktail of vaginal juice and sperm. I wanted him to come in time with Mat, for my holes to receive their communion in unison. I craved crude sex in all its crudity.

Mat stifled his groans as his sperm gushed from his in-driving knob and jetted into my inflamed anal tube. The swollen glans in my mouth exploded in orgasm, the issuing jism bathing my tongue, filling my cheeks. Fingers delved between my saturated cunny lips, locating my yearning bud, massaging me to a massive orgasm as my body was pumped full of male come. I was discovering my sexual heaven, my inner paradise.

My entire body shaking uncontrollably, my earth-shattering climax threatened to eliminate me. The crude double fucking, my audience, my wicked husband – all combined to transport me to hitherto unknown heights of sexual gratification. On and on the spasming knobs spermed, pumping, gushing, jetting. I was full, brimming with male cream, rivers of semen streaming from my perverse pleasure holes.

At last, the flows ceased and the restless cocks stilled themselves within their sopping roosts. Trembling as my own orgasm diminished into soft ripples of pleasure, I wondered how I could ever face Mat again. How could *he* face *me*? In his depravity, his wickedness, how could he ever kiss me and make love to me as before?

'OK,' Den murmured as the knob within my mouth withdrew, dribbling spunk down my chin. 'Now for the cane.' The cane? Who was to administer the thrashing? I wondered as Mat slipped his deflating shaft out of my brimming anal canal. I heard movements behind me, muffled movements. There were no words, only silence. My blindfold was checked, adjusted, the chink of light disappearing, leaving me again within my darkness.

The first crack of the cane landing squarely across my taut buttocks, I yelped like a dog – a bitch chained by its collar. It was Mat, I knew, as the cane struck me again, the stinging pain heating my full bottom globes. On and on the gruelling thrashing continued as I wiggled and whimpered in my torturous pleasure, my arousal soaring ever higher.

Would the men, my masters, take it in turns to thrash me, their sex slave? Would they fuck me again after my punishment? I wanted Lisa. Did I want Carole? My bottom orbs burned, the fire scorching deep into my quivering flesh. Did I want to cane Carole? I wanted to lick her to orgasm, but she wouldn't allow me. I might force her, tie her over the back of the armchair and pull her knickers down. Lesbian-rape her.

'Harder!' someone cried excitedly as my naked body rocked with the merciless beating. I thought the cane might snap in two as the thrashing increased, my buttocks numbing as the fire burned within my tensed flesh. Was Mat taking out his anger? Was he venting a deep-seated hatred for me, or just satisfying his craving for perverted sex?

'I'm ready for her arsehole,' someone intoned rudely. The thrashing stopped, the cane was discarded as movements sounded behind my trembling body. My arsehole was to be fucked and spermed again. Could I take it? Could I endure another anal fucking? The choice wasn't mine, my body wasn't mine. It belonged to my masters.

'No,' I protested meekly as a bulbous knob greeted my

wet anal ring, pressing against the sensitive tissue surrounding my once-secret portal. My buttocks receiving several hard slaps, my conquered spirit was driven out of me as subservience ruled. The huge silky glans slipped past my tight ring, driving into the wet heat of my anal duct, opening me. I gasped, the taste of sperm lingering on my tongue, my pinched nipples burning as my breasts swung and heaved.

Another man, another cock fucking my arsehole. *Arsehole*. The word was crude, dirty. Three different penises had fucked my arsehole, spunked in my bowels. I was awash with sperm, brimming with male ejaculate. Could I take any more? My arsehole would overflow, rivers of depraved cream would flood my thighs as I arose – if I were ever again allowed to ascend as a human being.

Grabbing my hips, my unseen master began his anal abuse, his huge cock gliding in and out of my arsehole, massaging the inner walls of my dank sanctum. I rocked back and forth, my head held proud by the dog chain, my feet savagely spread by my tight ropes of bondage. My body no longer mine, I'd given myself completely. Now my very soul belonged to Lucifer.

'Coming!' the man cried as he rammed his knob deep into my steaming bowels. 'Christ, she's a tight-arsed bitch!' I felt his sperm pumping into my rectal duct, spurting from his pulsating organ as he rudely fucked my arsehole. Demeaned, shamed, degraded beyond belief, I shuddered as my clitoris swelled and throbbed, desperate for fingers, a tongue – Lisa's tongue.

As he gasped in his anal sperming, his heavy balls spanking the inflamed love lips of my vagina, fingers delved into my cunt. Opening me, stretching my drenched sex duct, three, four fingers thrust into me. My clitoris still sadly neglected, I wanted to rub myself there, to masturbate and bring out my orgasm. But my pleasure counted for nothing.

'Christ, that was good!' my anal abuser breathed as his weapon slid out of my arsehole. The fingers still intruded, massaging deep inside my cunt as I whimpered in my desperation for orgasm. I felt sperm flowing from my open bottom-hole, trickling down to lubricate the pistoning fingers. Never had I had so much sperm pumped into my body, endured such a fucking.

'OK, now *I*'ll fuck her arse!' Den laughed as I heard him settle on the grass behind me. I couldn't take another cock sperming in my bowels and I tried to protest, to beg for compassion, but the words wouldn't leave my mind. I screamed inside, silent screams of anguish, of hatred for myself, for what I'd become. Love and hatred are one.

My breasts swinging with the violent fucking, fingers thrusting in and out of my tight cunt, I cried a river of tears as my naked body brought satisfaction to yet another man. Again and again he drove his penis into my inflamed arsehole, using and abusing me, treating me like a rag doll. I prayed for him to come, to loose his spunk and withdraw from my aching rectal sheath.

But on and on he rode me like a horse, caning my buttocks as he galloped across a rolling heath of sex towards his orgasm. The cane struck me again and again as he shafted my anal canal and the unseen fingers fucked my cunt. Adding to the abuse, someone squeezed my breasts, my mammary globes ballooning, the torturous clothes pegs tightening around my aching nipples.

At last he came, his sperm gushing into my overflowing rectal tube, spurting from my stretched portal and coursing down my thighs. The more he pistoned my channel, the more sperm jetted from my distended hole, bubbling, spraying, splattering my buttocks. He grunted and groaned, clinging to my bucking hips as he drained his swinging balls.

The fingers driving deeper into my cunt, I screamed as the

man's fist slipped into my vaginal cavern, my love lips stretched tautly around his wrist. My pelvic cavity bloated, I grimaced as the fist clenched, distending my vaginal cave until I thought I'd split open. My anal duct compressing, crushing the indriving penis, I screamed again with fear and immense pleasure.

'She needs another spanking!' someone laughed as I was crudely ridden and whipped. Another spanking? No, I knew that I'd pass out with the pain and pleasure! I couldn't take another thrashing, another cock – I was exhausted, done, finished. As the cock slipped out of my aching arsehole and the fist withdrew from my bloated cunt, the wet sucking sounds of sex resounding through my mind, I prayed for mercy. Had Mat no compassion? Had he not an ounce of love for his abused wife? He didn't know what love was.

The men talked and joked for a few minutes before leaving. In my darkness, I heard them walking silently across the soft grass, leaving only Den – my ruler. As he unhooked the chain from the tree branch and released my ankles, I rolled onto my side, pulling my blindfold off as sperm flowed in torrents from my inflamed sex holes.

'Quite a fucking!' he chuckled, the sun behind him, his silhouette towering high above me. As my eyes adjusted to the light, I looked up at the tree, the outspread branches, the foliage. An anchor for the chain, it had witnessed my debauchery. Never would the tree allow me to forget.

Hauling my shaking body up, I sat on the grass and removed the clothes pegs from my distended nipples. Examining my red teats, the sperm bubbling from my anal portal, oozing from my aching cunt, I wondered when Den would go, leaving me with my abused body, my shattered mind.

My legs trembling, I didn't attempt to stand as he grabbed the Tesco's bag and collected up his instruments of sexual abuse. Unclipping the dog collar, I tossed it onto the grass. The chain lay like a snake, coiled, ready to pounce. Would it turn into a staff?

Leaning with my back against the tree, I closed my eyes, ignoring Den's lewd comments as he grabbed the collar and finally walked across the lawn to make his escape. There was no escape for me, nowhere to run, nowhere to hide. I couldn't hide from my mind, my racked and tormented mind.

Opening my eyes beneath the shade of the tree, I focused on the daisies. They were watching me, knew my secrets. Mat knew my secrets. But I had no secrets now. The world knew of my immorality, my adultery, my vileness. My secure moorings gone, I'd sailed down the river, floated out of the estuary and was now adrift on a sea of uncertainty. Would a passing ship rescue me?

I slept beneath the tree for an hour, maybe more. I dreamed dreams, dreams of crude sex – dreams of Lisa. Naked, my holes drained, my thighs sticky, I finally woke and looked about me. What time was it? The time didn't matter, there was no time. Staggering to my feet, I clung to the gnarled tree trunk to steady my aching body. After the debauchery the garden lay quiet again, as in a photograph. The hoe watched me.

'God!' I breathed, lurching across the lawn to the house. 'God, what have I done?' Had God been watching me? I wondered as I almost fell into the kitchen and leaned on the table. What would Saint Peter say when I arrived at the gates of heaven? At school I'd learned that I wouldn't go to heaven unless I was a good girl. No one had mentioned where I'd go if I was a bad girl. No one mentioned Satan's kingdom. What would Satan say when I arrived at the gates of hell?

Staggering through the hall, I saw yet another envelope on the doormat. Screwing it up, I tossed it into the bin and dragged myself upstairs. Taking a shower, I washed away the sperm, my lust juices, the evidence of my debauchery. The hot water stung my crimson buttocks and again I wondered what sort of man Mat was. He'd thrashed me, fucked my arsehole. I hated the word. I hated Mat. Taking the shower nozzle from the wall, I pressed it between my buttocks, my burning anal ring making a seal as the water gushed into my bowels.

'Oh, God!' I whimpered as the filling sensation sent shudders of ecstasy through my naked body. My bowels brimming, I moved the nozzle aside, the hot water and sperm gushing from my sore aperture, streaming down my legs. Parting my fleshy pussy lips, I pressed the nozzle against my vaginal entrance, filling my inflamed sex cavern with water, shuddering as my pelvis bloated.

'God!' I cried again as my trembling hand dropped the nozzle, my inflated cunt gushing, a waterfall cascading down my inner thighs. My clitoris swollen as my cleansed holes drained, I needed to come yet again, but I was too exhausted to masturbate. I needed Lisa – she'd masturbate me, lovingly lick my clitoris to orgasm with her wet tongue.

Trying to clear my mind of all thoughts of sex, I finally emerged from the shower and dried my naked body. My nipples hurting like hell, I decided not to wear a bra. My buttocks stinging, my vaginal lips inflamed, I forsook my knickers, too. I enjoyed being naked – naked beneath the veil. Lisa was always naked beneath her skirt. Her cunt was naked too, devoid of black curls. I'd shave my cunt, but not yet.

What was left of the afternoon passed quietly. There were no sounds of canes thrashing buttocks, no outrushings of breath, no squelching sounds of lust. I sat in the garden beneath the sun, gazing at the apple tree. My thoughts drifted, rising, floating like pieces of charred paper soaring up from a bonfire. They were going nowhere, meaningless.

'Hi,' Carole called as she rounded the side of the house. Her blue skirt was short, revealing her shapely thighs. Her blouse loose, her sumptuous breasts desired freedom. 'I've been ringing the bell.'

'Sorry, I was dreaming,' I smiled, rising to my feet. 'I didn't hear.'

'I'm not staying, I was just passing. Sunbathing again?' she giggled. 'It's all right for some.'

'All right?'

'Having Mat to earn the money while you live a life of leisure.'

'It's the same for you, isn't it?'

'Yes, I suppose it is. We're lucky, aren't we?'

Lucky? Was I lucky to have Mat? Hardly! Would Carole think herself lucky in my position? I imagined Carole naked, her legs spread, her thighs wide, her cunt crack gaping. I wanted to lick her to orgasm. What was wrong with me? I felt wickedness rising from the dungeons of my mind as she sat on a patio chair. I wanted to show her my cunt. *No, I mustn't!*

Sitting opposite her, my hands trembling, I parted my thighs slightly. 'How are things?' I asked, not really wanting to know as my juices bubbled between my pussy lips. The sun behind her, she was a silhouette – surreal.

'Things are fine. Jane, I've come to talk to you about . . .' She hesitated, her eyes frowning.

'About what?'

'When I rang you . . . you were in trouble, weren't you?'

'There was someone in the room with me, I couldn't talk.'

'You did enough talking!'

'I . . . I had to make someone believe that . . . It doesn't matter, it's all OK now.'

'I think there are things that you want to tell me. You've changed, you're not your old self.'

'Secrets aren't secrets when shared.'

'Friends are there to share secrets with, Jane.'

'My secrets can't be shared. Too many people know as it is. Let's change the subject.'

Parting my thighs further, I reclined in the chair, closing my eyes to the bright sun. Was she looking up my skirt, gazing at my full vaginal lips, my sex crack? I imagined she was, and I allowed my thighs to open a little wider. I didn't know what I was trying to do, why I was displaying my most intimate place to my best friend. Perhaps, in the sexual mist swirling through my confused mind, I wanted her to drop to her knees and lick my sex crack, suck my clitoris to orgasm.

'You've been letting the garden go,' she said. 'It's about time you got that hoe into action, look at the weeds.'

'I know,' I replied dreamily, the sun warming my face. Could she see my cunt? I parted my thighs even further. 'I must use the hoe more often.'

'Jane, are you OK?'

'The sun's making me a little sleepy.'

'You shouldn't sit like that without . . . without your panties on.'

'Like what?'

'With your legs apart, I can see all you've got.'

'Oh, sorry!' I giggled, sitting upright and pressing my thighs together. 'I didn't put my panties on after my shower. To be honest, I don't wear anything beneath my skirt in the summer.'

'You should be more careful, if you do that in public, you'll . . .'

'It's OK, I don't sit like that in public. It was the sun, I was almost falling asleep.'

'Are you sure you don't want to talk about the phone call?'

'Positive.'

'Well, I'd better go. It's five o'clock. John will be home soon, expecting to eat.'

'Five? God, I'd better think about the evening meal, too.'

'I'll ring you tomorrow.'

'Yes, we'll meet in town for coffee.'

'OK, see you.'

Watching her walk around the side of the house, I wondered what she'd thought about my cunt. Had she wanted to touch me there? No, probably not. I shouldn't have allowed her to see. At least she'd thought I'd displayed my vaginal lips in innocence. She didn't know the whore I really was, or of my lesbian desires.

Taking the matured curry from the fridge, I recalled the carrot massaging my inner vaginal flesh, gently fucking me as I'd moved about. Mat wouldn't know where the carrot had been as he enjoyed his meal. I felt wicked – I wanted to retaliate, to get my own back for all he'd put me through. Had *he* sent the notes?

'Why should I cook for him?' I wondered aloud, placing the bowl back in the fridge. He didn't deserve anything, I reflected. The bastard could make his own meals in future. I was about to go for a walk when I heard a key in the front door. Mat was home from work early – if he'd been to work after fucking my arsehole!

'Hi!' he smiled as he breezed into the kitchen. 'Had a good day?'

'Not bad, and you?'

'Busy, busy. What's to eat?'

'Nothing, I haven't had time to cook.'

'Why's that?'

'Lisa came round, she's only just left.'

'Lisa?'

'Yes, we sat in the garden and the time just flew. There's curry in the fridge, if you want to warm it up.'

'What did she want?'

'What do you mean, *what did she want*?'

'Why did she come round?'

'To see *me*, of course. Mat, I do wish you'd tell me what your problem is with Lisa. Every time I mention her name you start questioning me and acting funny.'

'There's no problem with her.'

'Good, because we're thinking about having a holiday together.'

'A holiday?'

'Yes, Greece for a week or . . .'

'Jane, I don't want you going off on holiday with Lisa.'

'Why ever not? You invited Den and Lisa to our barbecue and, now I've become friendly with her, you don't want me to have anything to do with her.'

'It's not that, Jane.'

'Then what is it? If I tell you that Carole's coming round for coffee, you don't flinch an eyelid, but if I mention Lisa . . .'

'Coffee's one thing, but going abroad?'

'A Greek island, just for a week. You'll be OK, won't you?'

'Yes, of course, but . . . Oh, I don't know. I was talking to Den earlier, he said that you'd had a visitor, a man.'

'A man? When was this?'

'This morning, he saw a man come here.'

'No one's been to the house today, apart from Lisa. It sounds as if he's up to his old tricks again.'

'Old tricks?'

'Trying to stir things. I don't know why you're so friendly with him, he's nothing but trouble.'

'But he saw a man arrive and come into our house.'

'It must have been a ghost because I didn't see anyone. Are you going to have curry or not?'

'No, I'll have something later.'

'Well, I'm going out for a walk. It's a nice evening and Lisa said she'd go to the recreation ground. I said I'd meet her there.'

'But I've only just got in.'

'I won't be long. When I get back, we'll have the evening together.'

Leaving him standing in the kitchen like a lost sheep, I slipped out of the front door and walked down the street. I knew he'd follow me and I quickened my pace, the evening air cooling my vaginal lips, my love lips. My nipples still swollen, caressed by my silk blouse as my breasts bobbed up and down, I felt an urgent desire for orgasm welling in my womb. But I had more important things to do. I wished I *was* meeting Lisa.

The game was silly, futile, but Mat was becoming more suspicious about my mysterious lover and probably thought I was going to meet him. There was a wood at the far side of the recreation ground and I decided to slip into the trees and hide.

As I hurried across the street and walked across the grass towards the woods, I turned my head. Mat was some distance behind. He'd be thinking about men, male lovers, clandestine meetings, illicit sex – adultery. My stomach somersaulted as I followed a small path into the woods. I felt excited, elated.

Squatting behind a thick clump of bushes, my drenched labia ballooning between the backs of my thighs, I silently waited. What I was going to do, I had no idea. Mat would look for me and eventually give up and go home. Then what?

Twigs cracked underfoot, leaves rustled and I held my breath. I could just see him through the thick foliage, searching for me. What did he expect to find? Me on my back, my legs open, my secret lover fucking me? He'd question me when I got home. I'd lie to him, tell him that I'd met Lisa and we'd walked through the woods, talking and enjoying the summer evening. He'd think that I'd sucked her clitoris to orgasm.

I watched him finally give up his search and leave the woods. Relieved, I emerged from my hide and followed the path, contemplating, thinking. Deeper I wandered into the thicket, the path becoming narrower, finally disappearing. Birds fluttering, singing, tree branches towering above me, closing in, I wanted to lose myself in the woods – in my thoughts. Emerging into a clearing, I lay on the downy grass and rested my aching body.

My skirt up over my stomach, my thighs wide, I couldn't help myself as I slipped three fingers into my drenched cunt and massaged my clitoris to a beautiful orgasm. The trees covering me, concealing my wickedness, I gasped in my carnal delight. Another climax gripped me, shook my very soul as I masturbated. My hands finally falling by my sides, I fell asleep, satisfied for the time being. The trees watched over me.

Chapter Ten

Waking to find myself engulfed in darkness, canopied by the trees from the cool night air, I clambered to my feet and inched my way back to the path. I had no idea what the time was, how long I'd slept after an exhausting day of crude sex, but time didn't matter. The later it was the better, I mused, following the path as the moon peeped at me from behind a cloud. Mat would be worried, his mind conjuring lurid scenes of me with my lover, scenes of rampant sex.

All the lights were on in the house, the front door ajar, and as I slipped into the hall I wondered whether he'd called the police. Glancing at my watch as I passed the lounge, I heard him talking on the phone and stopped to listen.

'No, she's still not back,' he was whining. My inner thighs were sticky, cunt-milk sticky. 'Well, you've phoned Lisa twice so we know that she didn't go to meet her. Den, are you sure someone came to see Jane this morning? Yes, I know you said that a man phoned while you were here, but did you actually see him arrive? No, I realize you can't spend all day looking out of the window. OK, all we can do is wait. Yes, I'll let you know. Bye.'

Taking a deep breath, I ventured into the lounge, my mind brimming with ideas, plans, lies – my vagina brimming with my lubricious lust milk. Mat turned and looked at me, his brown eyes frowning, accusing, as I flopped onto the sofa in my innocence. I wanted to finger myself and come.

'Sorry I've been so long,' I smiled sweetly.

'Long? Jane, do you know what time it is? Where the hell have you been?'

'Lisa wasn't there so I walked to her flat. We got talking and . . . Well, time flies when you're having fun.'

'Den rang Lisa and . . .'

'Yes, he rang twice while I was there. He's a strange one – she reckoned that he was making sure she was at home. Goodness knows why.'

'Why didn't she tell him that you were with her?'

'Why should she tell Den that I was there? It's none of his business.'

'I've been out of my mind with worry. I wish you'd phoned and said where you were.'

'I rang twice but it was engaged. Did you have any curry?'

'No, no, I didn't. So, where did you go when you left here?'

'I went to the recreation ground looking for Lisa. I took a walk through the woods and finally decided to go to her flat. The woods are lovely in the evening.'

'Yes, I'm sure they are. I've been really worried about you, Jane.'

Worried about me? That was a laugh! Watching as I was chained, fucked by several men and thrashed . . . The only thing Mat was worried about was losing me, putting an end to his perverted games. But I'd given the ball another shove, it was rolling fast. My lies to Den about a visitor, my lies about going to see Lisa . . . The ball really was gathering momentum.

As Mat left the room to make coffee, I couldn't help but grin. He was confused, lost in his confusion. He'd thought he'd had it all worked out so well. The magazine, the photographs, audio tape, video tape . . . His plans couldn't have gone much further off course. But it was all very sad, I reflected. I'd thought we'd been so happy together, but now? Now we were miles apart, lying, cheating, deceiving. Did I want to turn the clock back? I wondered. My sexuality woken, did I want to return to the monogamous days of lovemaking with Mat? Clocks of life only go forward.

My life upside down, my marriage in ruins, I couldn't capture my feelings – they ran away from me, like autumn leaves tossed on the wind. I had no concrete plans, no goal or aims. I couldn't live with uncertainty any more, I decided. I had to take control of my life.

'Coffee,' Mat said uneasily, placing two steaming mugs on the table. I sneaked a look at the slight bulge in his trousers and imagined him fucking my bottom-hole. 'Jane, this thing you say I have about Lisa . . . I'll be honest with you. She's a lesbian.'

'Yes, I know that!' I giggled.

'You know?'

'Of course, it stands out a mile.'

'Has she ever . . . Well, you know, made a pass at you?'

'No, of course not. She likes me very much, and I like her. We've found a sort of affiliation together.'

'What, sexual?'

'No, don't be silly! She already has a girlfriend, I've met her.'

'I didn't know that.'

'You wouldn't, would you? Mat, you said you'd be honest with me. Now I have to be honest with you.'

'What do you mean?'

'I'm not sure about us any more. Day by day, it's getting harder to stay with you.'

'Why, what's happened?'

'All sorts of things have happened. My latent feelings and desires have been woken.'

'Latent feelings and desires?'

'I can't explain, I can't find the words. It occurred to me as I walked through the woods that we haven't made love for a while.'

'Yes, but . . .'

'It takes a lot for me to say this – I don't miss it. I thought I'd found eternal love with you, I'd thought we were as one.'

'We are, Jane. I don't understand what's happened. Is it Lisa?'

'No, of course it's not Lisa! You wouldn't understand in a million years because I don't understand it myself – I can't explain it. I've changed, things have happened that have changed me.'

'Are you leaving me, is that what you're trying to say?'

'Let's not be hasty, let's give it time, Mat.'

Pouring himself a larger than usual scotch, he was obviously now in two minds about his perverted games, regretting all he'd done, all he'd put me through. It was only a guess, but I reckoned that he'd now tell Den to leave me alone, to put an end to the blackmail, the sordid sex sessions. His game had backfired on him and I was emerging as the winner. Was there really a winner?

'I don't understand this,' he sighed, gulping down his drink. 'Things have been great between us, and now you're talking about splitting up.'

'Not splitting up, just giving it time. Look, I'm going up to bed, let's sleep on it and see how we feel in the morning.'

'I know how I feel – I love you, Jane.'

'Yes, I know. Just give me time, Mat. I need time to think.'

Pausing halfway up the stairs to listen to Mat's predictable call to his partner in perversity, I felt a deep sadness in my heart. I hadn't wanted this but Mat had driven me to it, exorcised my love for him. I knew he'd do his best to hang on to me as I heard him whinging on the phone. He'd be sweet and kind from now on – but it was too late.

'We went too far, too soon,' he whined to Den. 'Let things calm down for a while and then we'll start on her again.' Climbing the stairs to bed, I felt sad, confused – lost. It was a no-win situation. At last, the tables had turned. Mat and Den had lost, but I, too, had nothing.

Crawling beneath my quilt, I lay naked in the marital bed, recalling Lisa loving me, licking me to orgasm. Her firm thighs parted, her hairless pussy open, my tongue lapping between her love lips, delving into her juicy sex hole . . . Did I have Lisa? Did I want Lisa?

Mat brought me tea in bed the following morning. Did he think that a cup of tea would change things? I wondered as I schemed my schemes. Propped up on my pillow as he washed and dressed, my plans emerged from the swirling mist of my mind – crystal clear. I'd cane my breasts, shave my pubic hair off, and he'd believe that Den was still blackmailing me. If Mat thought that Den was sexually abusing me while he was at work, I'd cause no end of trouble between the evil pair.

When Mat had gone I finished my tea and ambled into the bathroom. Running my fingertips over my downy pubic curls, I took Mat's razor and shaving foam from the shelf and sat on the edge of the bath. The cooling foam stimulated me as I massaged between my thighs, my clitoris becoming erect, my love lips swelling. Lathering my vulval flesh, I wondered whether Lisa would like my naked cunt. Yes, I decided that she would.

The razor poised over my sex mound, I hesitated. I'd never before dreamed of shaving, not even the mere thought ever having crossed my mind. Was it a mistake? I'd made so many mistakes that one more wouldn't make any difference! Besides, my curls would soon grow back, reveiling rather than revealing my love slit.

Dragging the razor over my mound, the blade leaving milk-white skin in its wake, I decided to walk out of the bedroom naked as Mat was coming upstairs. I'd gasp, feigning embarrassment as I quickly covered myself. He'd notice straight away, of course, and question me. I'd tell him that I'd read about shaving, that I preferred it that way. And he'd go running to Den with his accusations. I felt wicked.

Dragging the razor over my outer love lips, my sex mound, I stripped away my pubic curls. Stretching my vulval flesh, I removed every hair, dragging the sharp blade over my swollen lips until I was smooth and soft. Finally taking a flannel from the basin, I wiped away the foam and blonde curls, cleansing my cunt. It was too late now for a change of heart – or cunt! – I reflected, gazing down at my youthful vaginal lips, my unveiled crack.

Standing before the long mirror, I gazed excitedly at the reflection of my schoolgirlish cunt, my thoughts drifting back to pre-pubescent days when I would masturbate in my bed at night, massaging incredible orgasms from between my firm, hairless sex lips.

Stimulated by the nostalgia, and by my sleek new image, I took a plastic shampoo bottle from the shelf and eased the end between my ballooning outer labia. The bottle was almost three inches in diameter – could I drive it deep into my cunt? I wondered. My feet wide apart, my knees bent, I watched apprehensively in the mirror as the bottle slipped into my drenched duct, my outer lips stretched tautly around the improvised phallus.

'God!' I gasped as the shaft entered me, the end coming to rest against the soft hardness of my cervix. Releasing the bottle, I projected my hips forward, the mirror reflecting my vaginal abuse. My hairless love lips now rounded, forming a perfect circle around the phallus, I squeezed my vaginal muscles. The bottle gliding slowly out of my cunt, I pushed it back and squeezed my muscles again. It was an arousing sight, the wet phallus emerging below my erect clitoris, my pearl. I needed to come, but not yet, I decided. I would allow my libido to reach desperate heights before enjoying the exquisite release of orgasm.

Pulling the bottle out, my swollen cunt lips closing, concealing my sex entrance, I placed my new-found phallus on the shelf and grabbed my clothes. Slipping into my blouse and skirt, I went downstairs and opened the back door. The sun was hotter than ever and I decided to spend some time in the garden. Den wouldn't bother me, I was sure. He'd wait to hear from Mat before making a move. Even the threat of sending my mother the tape was futile now that Mat believed I might leave him. No one could touch me.

The air cooling my hairless love lips as I wandered down the garden, I was more aware of my sex centre than ever before. I wanted a tongue licking my smooth hillocks, lapping between my fleshy cushions, caressing my erect clitoris. I might ring Lisa and invite her round, I thought as I sat beneath the old apple tree. The blades of grass tickling my vaginal lips, I felt my clitoris swell and pulsate. Did I want the collar and chain? Did I want the cane?

The hoe looked at me, beckoned me as I unbuttoned my blouse and slipped it over my shoulders. Tugging my skirt down, I lay on the grass with my limbs spread, the sun filtering through the foliage above me, warming my naked body. I lay there for a couple of hours, relaxing, contemplating my life, where it was taking me. Where did I *want* it to take me?

'Jane!' Lisa called as she skipped across the lawn. 'I must say, you look very . . . Oh, you've shaved!' she beamed, towering above me.

'Lisa, I . . . It's nice to see you,' I smiled, sitting up and shielding my eyes from the sun. 'What are you doing here?'

'I came to see you, silly!' she grinned, plonking herself on the grass next to me. 'You should be careful sunbathing naked. Anyone could walk round the side of your house and see you.'

'Yes, we need a gate.'

'Why did you shave?'

'Because . . . because when I saw your . . . I prefer it that way.'

'God, you look beautiful! I'd like to . . . Jane, Den phoned me this morning. I thought I'd better come and talk to you about it.'

'What did he want?'

'He said that you spent yesterday evening at my place.'

'Did he? I wonder why?'

'I was hoping you'd be able to tell me.'

'I have no idea why he says things to people about me, where I'm supposed to have been or what I'm supposed to have done. He's mad.'

'He reckons your husband told him that you'd been to my place.'

'I went for a walk in the recreation ground, Mat knows that. Den's obviously lying, but I can't think why.'

'Something's going on, Jane.'

'You're telling me! I've been blackmailed, used and abused . . .'

'No, apart from that. Anyway, you know that I'm no longer involved in Den's games.'

'But you are, Lisa. If he's ringing you saying that I've been to see you and that you've been here for coffee, then you *are* involved.'

'Yes, I see your point. But involved in what? I don't know what's going on, why Den's saying these things.'

'Neither do I! Mat said that Den's been telling him things about me, that I'm running off with some man or other.'

'Are you?'

'No, of course I'm not. Apparently, Den said that I was going to live in the Cotswolds with another man. God only knows where he got that idea from.'

'It's not part of his blackmail tricks, is it?'

'I don't see how it can be. I mean, what would he have to gain from it?'

'I don't know. Maybe it's all leading up to something.'

'I want to know who the man was that Den brought round here.'

'He's said nothing to me about another man. It was just the two of us using . . . I wish I'd never got involved with him.'

'We wouldn't have met, would we?'

'That's true. Why don't you lie back and show me your new look?'

'Den's up to something,' I murmured, reclining and spreading my legs wide. 'He's trying to cause trouble.'

'Let's not talk about Den.'

As Lisa's fingertip ran up and down my open sex valley, I released a little sigh of pleasure. Stroking my protruding inner folds, she rested her head on my stomach, her long hair tickling my sun-warmed skin. I believed her now – she didn't know that Mat was in on Den's wicked plan. She could have been lying, but I preferred to believe her.

Lifting her head, she licked around my navel, her tongue delving into the small indentation, sending quivers of excitement through my pelvis. *As only a woman knows how*, I reflected, as her wet tongue moved over the slight swell of my stomach to my hairless sex mound. Teasing the top of my crack, snaking into my moist valley, licking the protective hood of my clitoris, she slipped a finger between my ballooning love lips and drove it deep into my sopping vaginal sheath.

'God,' I murmured as she twisted and bent her finger, the sensations running through my tightening vagina driving me wild. Her tongue caressing the sensitive tip of my clitoris, I arched my back, digging my fingernails into the soft grass as the beautiful sensations built. Desperate for orgasm, I parted my thighs as wide as I could as she slipped a second finger into my tight cunt and stretched me open.

The bud of my sex slit solid beneath her sweeping tongue, she parted my love lips, exposing my intimacy in its full glory. 'You taste nice,' she purred as her tongue delved between my pussy cushions, lapping the stretched flesh around the gentle pistoning of her fingers. She moved up my slit again, sucking my clitoris into her pretty mouth, bringing out my pleasure.

'I want to come,' I breathed, my sex button pulsating in the beginnings of orgasm. 'Lick me faster, I want to come!' Her hot mouth sucking, her tongue sweeping over my clitoris, she fingered me fervently, propelling me expertly towards my climax. 'God, yes!' I gasped as my body bucked and shook violently. 'Don't stop!'

My sex milk spewing from my burning vagina, streaming down the valley between my buttocks, I tossed my head back, my eyes squeezed shut as my orgasm erupted. It was as if I were dreaming, drifting within my psyche as the waves of sexual ecstasy rolled through me. I let go completely as my orgasm peaked, gave myself in my entirety – surrendered my very being.

As my climax began to subside, she slowed her vaginal fingering, her tongue sweeping gently over the sensitive nub of my pulsating clitoris. Slipping her fingers out of my drenched sex duct, she moved down my yawning valley, her tongue entering me, licking inside my hot vagina. Drinking from my open hole, her tongue tantalizing my inner flesh, she cleansed me, sucking and swallowing until she'd drained my open pussy.

'Nice?' she smiled as she sat up and gazed at my sex-flushed face.

'God, yes!' I breathed, her fingertip tracing circles over my wet outer lips.

'I like your shaved cunt. It's smooth, soft, fresh like a young girl's.'

'You are naughty!' I giggled.

'You can talk! I am pleased, after all, that I got involved with Den. As you said, we'd never have met otherwise.'

'I'm pleased that you came round, Lisa,' I sighed as my clitoris swelled in response to her caressing fingertip.

'So am I. Look, I'd better go.'

'Already?'

'Yes, I have things to do. I'll ring you, shall I?'

'Yes, please do. I'd like to see you again. I mean, regularly.'

'You will,' she smiled, leaning over my glistening body and sucking each nipple in turn. 'You will.'

As she scuttled off across the lawn, I closed my eyes and relaxed. I felt satisfied, calm, serene as never before. But I'd wanted Lisa's cunt pressed to my mouth, my tongue fucking her open hole . . . There'd be other times, I consoled myself as I toyed with my wet inner lips. Did I need Mat now that I had Lisa? Lisa or not, I didn't need the evil bastard! But I hadn't finished with him yet. I had more games to play.

Finally climbing to my feet, I wandered into the house and locked the back door. I was in a scheming mood, a mood to draw up plans against Den and Mat. My shaved pussy was a good start, I reflected, stroking my baby-soft love lips. I could hardly wait for Mat to discover my devilry.

He'd instantly think that Den had been round and threatened me, abused me – fucked me. Trouble was brewing!

After lunch, I killed time by going for a walk. The evening seemed an age away as I wandered the streets, the cool breeze playing on my shorn pussy. But there was no rush to inadvertently expose my nakedness to Mat, I reflected as I strode across the recreation ground towards the trees. I had all the time in the world.

Again, I pondered on my breasts, what Mat would think if he were to notice weals fanning out across the taut, pale skin of my mammary globes. I could make out that I was naked in the garden, the branches of the apple tree whipping my breasts as I tripped and fell over. He wouldn't believe me, of course, and would go rushing round to Den's house with his accusations.

Under cover of the trees, I took a long twig from the ground and opened my blouse. Gazing at my braless melons, I knew it would hurt, but I had to do it – to whip my breasts and leave tell-tale weals across my milk-white skin. Every day I'd allow Mat to see further signs of sexual abuse – whippings, sperm-matted hair, spunk-stained skin, inflamed cunt lips . . . Every day I'd cause trouble.

Raising the long twig, I began by teasing the taut skin above my areolae. The rough twig leaving no marks, I struck each breast harder, the stinging sensation causing me to gasp and wince. My nipples responding, becoming hard and elongated, my areolae darkening in my arousal, I whipped my breasts more severely.

'Ouch!' I cried as I forced myself to lash each globe as hard as I could, the thin pink weals already beginning to appear across my milky flesh. Inadvertently striking my nipples, I gasped as the strange sensation of pain and pleasure permeated my swollen breasts. Was this another awakening? I wondered, flailing each nipple in turn, my cunt wetting, my clitoris stirring as the pain increased.

Slipping my blouse off, I tossed it to the ground in my abandonment and stood by a large bush, my mind brimming with lewd ideas. Grabbing a branch level with my pert tits, I bent it back and released it. Swishing through the air, it struck me, the rough leaves whipping my stinging breasts. 'God!' I cried, bending the branch back as far as I could and releasing it again, the leaves slapping across my swollen globes, lashing my sore nipples.

My arousal soaring, I whipped my breasts until my pale flesh glowed a fire-red and my nipples became painfully erect. My cunt milk streaming down my inner thighs, I desperately needed to masturbate, to quell my sexual tension, but there was no doorknob, no hoe – nothing to push deep into my yearning cunt. I'd have to go home and appease my insatiable vagina, my swollen clitoris. I'd fuck the hoe handle, slip the doorknob into my bottom-hole and masturbate as never before. But my tits weren't nearly crimson enough yet.

Whipping my breasts again and again, birds fluttering from the trees as I cried out in my pain and pleasure, I forced myself to endure the beautiful self-inflicted abuse. What would Carole think of me? I wondered in my masochism. Would she disown me? But it didn't matter. Mat was the important one. When he saw my breasts he'd become confused, angry, guilty, jealous.

Finally halting the self-abuse, I gazed at my scarlet mammary globes. 'Perfect,' I murmured, eyeing the ugly weals fanning out across my swollen spheres. Mat was in for a high-voltage shock! Slipping into my blouse and leaving the wood, I hurried home, rivers of sex milk coursing down my inner thighs as I thought about masturbating, fucking the garden hoe. I wanted Lisa. No, I wanted a penis, three penises fucking my orifices, spunking deep into my naked body. The cane? Yes, I desperately craved the cane, a buttock thrashing. I wanted crude sex in all its crudity.

Dashing into the house, my breasts stinging like hell, I froze as I heard Mat's car pull up in the drive. Panic-stricken, I knew I shouldn't have shaved my pussy or thrashed my breasts. Fleeing upstairs to the bathroom, I locked the door, wondering what to do. I had to go ahead with my plan now, I had no choice. I was innocent. An innocent victim of blackmail.

Slipping out of my skirt and blouse as the front door opened and closed, I wandered across the landing to my bedroom. Hearing my movements, Mat climbed the stairs. This was it – the next act in the tragic play.

'Jane!' he gasped as he appeared in the doorway and gazed in disbelief at my glowing breasts, my hairless cunt. 'What the hell . . .'

'Mat, I . . . I fell over in the garden,' I stammered, feigning guilt as best I could. 'The branches of the apple tree caught me as I fell and . . .'

'What have you done to your . . . Jane, why have you shaved?'

'I read about it. A lot of women shave and I . . . I thought I'd try it.'

'Christ, you look like . . . Why shave? It's not like you to do that.'

'As I said, I read about it. Don't you like me like this?'

'Whether I like it or not doesn't . . . The *tree* did that to your tits?'

'Yes, I tripped and fell.'

'I can't believe that the tree . . . You look as if you've been whipped.'

'Of course I haven't been whipped! I was naked, and I tripped over the hoe and fell.'

'You'd better rub some cream into the weals. God, I've never seen anything like it.'

'I'm a bit sore but I'll be all right. What are you doing here, anyway? It's only half past three.'

'I was passing. Er . . . I'm just popping over to Den's with some papers.'

'OK, I'll be down in a minute.'

My plan was working admirably, I reflected as I hurriedly dressed and bounded downstairs. There wasn't a great deal Mat could say. In his mind, I'd been forced to shave my cunt and have my breasts whipped. Again, I was innocent. Slipping round the side of the house, I hovered by the fence and listened to Mat as he stood on Den's doorstep hurling his accusations. The ball wasn't just rolling now – it was hurtling full-pelt!

'I haven't even seen her,' Den protested.

'It seems odd to me that we were talking about shaving her fanny, and now . . .'

'Mat, I haven't touched her.'

'Do you honestly expect me to believe that? Christ, I was trying to calm things down, woo her back, but now? Couldn't you have waited, as we'd planned?'

'I *was* waiting, for Christ's sake!'

'Yes, it looks like it! Keep away from her, Den. Just give me a little more time and then we'll start again, blackmail her and have our fun.'

'Mat, I repeat, I haven't touched her. I don't know what's happened to her, but it had nothing to do with me.'

'She said she fell over, but I can't believe that. She reckons that she shaved her fanny because she'd read about it, but she'd never do a thing like that. It's just not like her.'

'You have to remember that she's changing, Mat. All we've put her through, she's changed.'

'Look, I'd better get back. I'll see you this evening.'

'All right. But you must believe me – I haven't laid eyes on her.'

'OK, I'll see you later.'

Dashing back into the house, I waited in the kitchen for Mat to return. *Now what?* I wondered, pouring myself a glass of orange juice. My plan had worked admirably, but to what end? Causing friction between Mat and Den wouldn't really achieve anything.

'Jane, have you been coming on to Den?' Mat asked as he stood in the doorway.

'Coming on to Den? What do you mean?'

'He said that you've been flaunting yourself, deliberately wandering around the garden naked.'

'I've been sunbathing naked, but not flaunting myself.'

'Do you fancy Den?'

'Fancy Den? You must be joking! Of all the men in the world . . .'

'I don't want you wandering around with no clothes on, Jane. It's not right.'

'I'll sunbathe naked as and when I wish. If he's going to spy on me, that's his problem, not mine. I'll not be dictated to by anyone.'

'But Jane . . . Look, he thinks you're giving him the come-on.'

'He's mad.'

'What have you been up to today?'

'Up to? I sat in the garden with Lisa, I went for a walk . . . What's this all about, Mat?'

'It's about you. Shaving your fanny, your tits looking as if they've been whipped . . .'

'Now you're being ridiculous! My tits look as if they've been whipped! Can you imagine me doing *that*? Do you think I'd abuse my body like that?'

'I don't know. What the hell was that cow Lisa doing here?'

'She's not a cow, she's a very good friend of mine.'

'I wish you'd never met her. Has Den been round today?'

'Hadn't you better get back to work?'

'Yes, in a minute.'

Mat was wallowing in regret. His plan had gone so very wrong, leaving him jealous, guilty, and almost paranoid. Again, I wondered why he'd put me through hell, used and abused me, derived pleasure from watching other men fuck me. What had triggered the idea? Why had he changed from a loving husband to a sex fiend? And how did he have the audacity to virtually accuse me of defiling my own naked body when he knew only too well that Den would have done it? Given half the chance, he would have done it!

A new plan formulating in my mind, I finished my drink and wandered out onto the patio. If I told Mat that Den had been round, had had coffee with me, had sat in the garden with me . . . The idea was good but, again, I had no goal. All I'd do would be to cause more trouble. There again, if Mat thought I was having something with Den, he might leave me. If he believed that I was willingly having sex with Den . . . Did I want him to leave me? Yes.

'Has Den been round?' Mat asked again as he joined me in the garden.

'Yes, we had coffee together earlier,' I lied, my stomach somersaulting as Mat's eyes filled with jealousy and anger.

'Coffee together?' he echoed.

'He came round the back looking for you. I said that you were at work and he stayed for coffee and a chat.'

'He didn't mention it to me.'

'Mat, why should people tell others everything they do? Why should Lisa tell Den that I was at her place when he phoned her? Why should I have to account for my every move?'

'You don't have to. I just thought it odd that Den didn't mention it to me. Was he here for long?'

'We sat in the garden talking for an hour or so. You said that I should get to know him, so what's the problem?'

'Nothing, nothing.'

As he mooched across the lawn with his hands in his pockets, I tried to imagine life without him. I wouldn't be lonely, I had Lisa for company – and sex. Life without Mat would be a life of freedom, doing what I wanted, as and when I wanted. But I'd miss the crude sex. I was *already* missing the crude sex!

Another crazy plan formulating in my wayward mind, I slipped into the house and rang Den. I must have been insane, but inspired by a lethal combination of my thirst for perverted sex and revenge, I had conceived the wickedest of plans. Although Mat had told Den to back off for a while, I knew Den would not be able to resist my naked body, a chance for crude sex. A devilish grin furled my lips as he answered the phone.

'Den, it's Jane,' I said softly.

'Jane? Oh, er . . .'

'I haven't seen you for a while.'

'No, I . . .'

'Listen, about the tapes and photographs. I don't want my mother . . . Can we come to some arrangement or other?'

'Yes, yes, of course we can!' he replied excitedly. 'What did you have in mind?'

'You're the blackmailer, I'd have thought that you'd tell me.'

'Yes, that's right. How's your lover?'

'He's fine. I . . . I can't leave Mat, the house isn't ready yet.'

'Not the Cotswolds again?'

'I'm not saying. When I've gone, I won't care what you do. But, as I have to stay here for the time being, I don't want any trouble.'

'I'm pleased that you've seen sense at last.'

'Mat's here at the moment. He'll be going soon so . . .'

'I want to have a word with him about . . . about business. I'll come round and see him.'

'All right. But no more threats, Den. I'll do anything you want, just don't go sending anything to my mother.'

'OK, I'll be round in a minute.'

'Mat's down the garden.'

'Right.'

Hiding in the kitchen, I watched Den stride down the garden and join Mat by the apple tree. Was he going to tell Mat that I'd phoned? I pondered. Was he going to tell him to hide in the house and watch as he thrashed and fucked me? Or was he going to keep his secret, use and abuse me when Mat was at work? How would Mat feel if the crude sex resumed? There were too many unanswered questions, too many pieces missing from the jigsaw puzzle to reveal the picture. All I could do was play it by ear.

When Den had gone, Mat returned to the house, suspicion firing his eyes. 'Den said that he didn't have coffee with you,' he said accusingly.

'He . . . God, the man's mad! He was here for at least an hour. Why lie about it?'

'I reckon he fancies you, he doesn't want me to know that he's been here. I can't think of any other reason.'

'Perhaps you're right, but he's not made a move, not hinted, even.'

'It's best that you don't see him when I'm not here, Jane.'

'That won't be easy, he works from home and I'm here all the time.'

'Look, I'd better get going. Try and keep out of his way, OK?'

'Well, I'll try, but . . .'

'And don't walk around the garden in the altogether. Especially now that you've been . . . Now that you've shaved. I want us to be happy, Jane. The things you said last night . . . I don't want us to split up.'

'Give me time, Mat. I'm not sure what I want any more, just give me time.'

'OK, I'll see you this evening.'

Den would be round the minute he saw Mat leave, I was sure. My cunt shaved, my breasts thrashed, burning, I wasn't sure that I could endure a session of perverted sex. I'd make him wait, I decided, locking the back door and putting the latch up on the front door. He could rampage around knocking and ringing with his stiff cock in dire need of my orifices, and I'd make him wait. Could *I* wait for his stiff cock?

Climbing the stairs, I sat on my bed thinking about Mat, the dreadful things he'd put me through. Why had he done it? I wondered again. What had triggered his perversity? Since the day Den had brought the magazine round, Mat and I hadn't made love. He'd fucked me, spunked in my mouth, spermed up my bottom – but we'd not made love. Love had gone, evaporated into the ether without a trace.

Mat's jealousy had finally got the better of him, I reflected. His perverse games might have brought him sexual gratification for a while, but now the thought of me with another man riled him. I'd make sure that there were tell tale signs after Den's visits – his leather belt, a length of rope, anything to prove that he'd used and abused me yet again. Better still, if Mat were to come home and catch Den fucking me . . .

The idea appealed to me, but what was I trying to do? Did I want Mat to think that Den was still blackmailing me? Or to believe that I was having an affair with him? The dangerous game was taking new twists, new turns.

Chapter Eleven

As I was pouring a cup of tea, Den wandered into the kitchen from the hall with a carrier bag as if he owned the place. 'How the hell did you get in?' I gasped, suddenly remembering that I'd put the latch up.

'I have my ways,' he said, grinning at me as he placed the bag on the table. 'So, you've shaved your cunt.'

'How do you know that?' I asked as he realized his mistake. There was no way he could have known, other than hearing it from Mat.

'I . . . I saw you in the garden.'

'I haven't been in the garden.'

'The point is, I know that you've shaved your cunt. Show me.'

More sex, more abuse. But my desperation for sexual satisfaction was running higher than ever. I needed him. Mat was due home in about half an hour. Was there time to enjoy a session of crude sex? I wondered. Would I be better off without Mat? I'd be free – free to fuck.

'There,' I said, lifting my skirt up over my stomach and displaying my naked mound, my youthful pussy slit.

'Nice, very nice! It takes fifteen years off you. Now, this arrangement you talked about. You're going to be at my beck and call, you'll do everything I ask, when I ask. Do you understand?'

'Yes, I just don't want my mother seeing . . .'

'She won't discover the truth, not if you behave yourself.

If I phone and tell you to kneel by the hole in the fence, you'll do it immediately, without question. If I order you to come round to my place you'll be there within two minutes.'

'And if Mat happens to discover the truth?'

'He won't.'

'What if he comes home unexpectedly and . . .'

'I don't want him discovering our secret any more than you do. It'll be up to you to make sure we're safe.'

'How can I do that?'

'That's your problem. He'd better not find out because . . .'

'All along, you've threatened to tell him, and now you're terrified that he might find out. What's happened? What's changed?'

'Nothing . . . nothing's changed. OK, take your clothes off and come down the garden.'

'Mat's due home soon,' I mumbled, my juices oozing from my tightening vagina.

'As I said, that's your problem. You'd better make sure he doesn't catch us.'

'I can't make sure.'

'We'd better hurry up, then.'

So, he hadn't told Mat that I'd phoned, I reflected as I unbuttoned my blouse. Perhaps this was the time to have Mat catch us. I'd say that I'd been blackmailed, had no choice, had been forced into debased sex. Mat could hardly blame me for the debauchery! But no, the timing was wrong. I had to decide where I was going, what my long-term plan was before igniting the explosion.

'Right, let's go,' Den grinned, grabbing the bag and opening the back door as I stepped out of my skirt and slipped my blouse over my shoulders. 'Christ! What the hell have you done to your tits?'

'My lover, he . . . That's my business.'

'You look as if you've had them whipped.'

'I have.'

'Shaving your cunt, having your tits whipped . . . Quite a little tart, aren't you? OK, to the apple tree.'

Following him down the garden, I recalled the three penises fucking me, spunking into my orifices. I wanted them again, using me, violating my naked body. Perhaps I should tell Mat that I knew his game and suggest that they both share me, my body, my cunt. Den and Mat fucking me without threats, blackmail . . . My tormented mind was forever formulating insane plans.

As Den took the dog collar and chain from the bag, I thought he was going to force me to get on all fours again. But he fixed the collar round my wrists and slung the chain over a branch above my head. My arms above me, he secured the chain and ordered me to stand with my feet wide apart. Again, I was defenceless, at his mercy, but it was different this time. I craved crude sex! If trees could talk . . .

'I really do like your cunt,' he grinned, running his fingertips over my swollen love lips, up and down my open sex groove.

'No!' I gasped as he clipped clothes pegs to my sore nipples. 'Please, it hurts!'

'Good, that's what I like to hear from my sex slave. There's nothing like a little pain to discipline you.'

'Christ, take them off!' I cried as the pain seared through my swollen breasts.

'Far from take them off, I'm going to clip two more to your cunny flaps!' he chuckled. 'Unless you want more pain, you will obey your master at all times.'

Taking each outer lip between his finger and thumb, he attached the clothes pegs, squeezing my fleshy sex hillocks tightly between the wooden jaws. I didn't protest, there was no point. He had it firmly in his mind to abuse my naked body, and there was nothing I could do to stop him. The four pegs tightening, I grimaced as the strange combination of pain and pleasure coursed through my tethered body. Was this really what I wanted from my once dignified, feminine form? I believed it was.

'We'll start with a thrashing, just to wet your cunt,' he drooled, taking a leather strap from the bag and moving behind me. My eyes squeezed shut, my buttocks tensed, pressed together, I waited in anticipation. I wanted Mat to watch the abuse, the abuse of his once faithful and loving wife. Knowing that he'd been there the last time I was tethered to the tree had sent an unknown thrill up my spine, a quiver through my womb. Do any of us really know what we want? Did I? How could I make plans when I didn't know what I wanted?

'Here it comes!' Den chortled. The leather strap cracking loudly across my taut buttocks, I screamed, almost jumping out of my skin with the shock. 'And again!' he laughed, the strap striking me, transmitting stinging pain through my rigid globes. Three, four, five times the strap lashed me, my buttocks burning, my nipples hurting as my breasts bounced and the pegs tightened. On and on he thrashed me, the strap catching the backs of my thighs, neglecting not one inch of my creamy flesh.

After twenty or so lashes he halted the gruelling thrashing and stood before my naked body. 'And now for your cunt,' he grinned wickedly. My eyes closed, I thought he was going to fuck me, drive his solid penis deep into my vagina and spunk up me. 'Without pubes, your cunt looks just like a little bottom,' he laughed, removing the clothes pegs from my fleshy vaginal cushions. 'And girls' bottoms should be thrashed regularly!'

Grimacing, I tried to cry out, to plead for mercy as the strap lashed my vaginal lips, arresting my words of protest.

The leather flailing my protruding inner petals, never had I known such beautiful sensations of combined pain and satisfaction. My clitoris swelling, my cunt milk streaming from my open sex hole, I yearned for orgasm. I wanted Den inside me, fucking me, sperming me. My body had become an object of pleasure, its sole function to bring me perverted sexual gratification. Where was Jane?

'Fuck me,' I whimpered as the beautiful instrument of torture thrashed my burning pussy lips again and again. Ignoring my crude request, he continued the gruelling beating as I hung my head. My blonde hair cascading over my swollen breasts, I gazed at my nipples, the wooden pegs pinching my sensitive brown buds. My naked body, my temple, was desecrated and defiled beyond belief. What had I become?

As he halted the beating, I raised my head and gazed at him. An evil glint in his dark eyes, he removed the pegs from my nipples and squeezed my full breasts. 'So, you like having your tits thrashed?' he taunted. I said nothing as he raised the strap and lashed my breasts. With each deafening crack I jolted, my nipples standing painfully erect as if seeking their abuser. How much more could I endure? I wondered. How much longer could I wait for the release of orgasm?

After a dozen lashes he discarded the strap and knelt before my naked body. Was I now to be allowed my orgasm? I pondered as he parted my stinging love lips and tasted my flowing juices. His tongue driving deep into my cunt, I quivered, my clitoris pulsating, yearning attention.

Pressing on the pink flesh surrounding my sex button, I thought he was going to lick me to orgasm. 'No!' I screamed as he clipped a peg to my clitoris, pinching my sensitive pleasure nodule. 'Den, please!' He ignored me as he moved behind my naked body and yanked my burning buttocks wide apart. My clitoris swelling, throbbing, the exquisite sensations coursed through my quivering womb, transporting me to new heights of sexual ecstasy.

His bulbous knob between my buttocks, pressing against my delicate anal iris, I gasped as he tried to enter me there. 'God!' I breathed as his glans slipped past my sphincter muscles and drove deep into the heat of my bowels. Hanging from the chain, my body jolting as he grabbed my hips and began his anal fucking, the beautiful sensations driving me wild, I whimpered in my pleasure.

'Spunk me,' I whimpered in my sexual delirium as he repeatedly drove his knob into my rectal duct. My brown ring stretched around his thrusting shaft, his balls slapping between my thighs, I felt his knob rudely opening me with each ramming thrust. Again and again he forced his swelling glans deep into my tightening duct, taking me to my sexual heaven as the clothes peg pinched my pulsating clitoris. I was going to come, I knew, as my womb trembled and my cunt tightened. Gasping, I wondered how it would feel as my clitoris erupted in orgasm within the wooden jaws of the peg.

'Coming!' he cried, ramming his knob into me with such force that I thought I'd split open. His sperm gushing, lubricating our debased union, my own climax exploded within my throbbing pleasure nodule. The incredible sensations emanating from my abused clitoris transmitting deep into my pelvis, rippling through my trembling body, I thought I'd die of an overload of ecstasy as the exquisite pleasure peaked.

'Fuck me!' I pleaded in my obscenity as he rammed into my bottom-hole, filling my bowels with his jetting jism. 'Fuck my arse!' Somewhere in the distance, through the haze of my mind, I thought I heard a car – Mat's car. Was I dreaming? I wondered as my orgasm peaked again, gripping my naked body, shaking me to the core. I wanted Mat to see me, to witness the debauched act. I wanted him to see the pure sexual bliss depicted in my expression as another man fucked and spermed my arse.

'God, you're tight!' Den gasped as he withdrew his shaft, his swollen knob sliding out of my brimming anal duct. My own orgasm subsiding, I hung from the chain, my pinched clitoris sending ripples of pleasure deep into my contracting womb. Was the abuse over? I wondered as he removed the clothes peg, my clitoris ballooning in its freedom. Was Mat home?

Releasing the chain, Den grinned as I collapsed to the ground, sperm oozing from my brown hole, running between my stinging buttocks. My cunt lips crimson from the thrashing, my breasts a fire-red, I lay quivering on the grass, recovering from my incredible ordeal. My mind drifting, thoughts swirling, I knew I'd become an insatiable nymphomaniac. I wanted more sex, another thrashing, another anal fucking. I wanted Lisa.

'Get up and put your clothes on, bitch!' Den ordered me. I clambered to my feet and staggered across the lawn to the house. Almost falling into the kitchen, I hurriedly covered my abused body with my skirt and blouse as I heard the front door close. Den made his escape around the side of the house, leaving me to face Mat. Still trembling in the aftermath of my climax, my hair matted, dishevelled, I wondered what to say as he appeared in the doorway and stared at me.

'Are you OK?' he blurted out. 'What the hell's happened to you?'

'I've been running,' I managed to reply as I felt Den's sperm oozing from my inflamed anal tube and running down my legs.

'Running?'

'Running around the garden. Jogging to keep fit.'

'Has Den been here? I've been ringing his doorbell but he's not in.'

'No, he's not been here.'

'His car's in the drive. Are you sure he's not been round?'

'Of course I'm sure! It's not something I'd be unsure of, is it?'

'No, I suppose not.'

Stepping out of the back door to escape Mat, I noticed the leather strap lying on the grass beneath the apple tree. Perfect! I mused as Mat joined me. Now all hell would be let loose! Mat was quick to notice the evidence as he walked across the lawn. Picking the strap up, he turned and faced me. As he walked uncertainly towards me, I could see that he knew only too well what I'd been up to. What would he say? What *could* he say?

'What's this?' he demanded.

'I don't know, I haven't seen it before,' I replied innocently, sitting on a chair, the evening sun warming me.

'It's a leather strap.'

'Yes, I can see that.'

'What's it doing down the garden?'

'I have no idea, Mat. As I said, I haven't seen it before.'

Reclining in the chair, I discreetly tugged my skirt up and parted my thighs, revealing my roseate cunny lips, the evidence of my thrashing. My eyes half closed, I watched Mat through my lashes as he gazed at my abused cunt. He didn't bother to question me, knowing I'd come up with some excuse or other. Parting my legs a little further, I wondered whether he'd notice my sperm-wet inner thighs, my spunked bottom-hole.

'I'm going to see if Den's back,' he scowled, nervously running the belt through his hands as he scurried off. I didn't bother to hide by the fence and listen, I knew what the conversation, the argument, would be about. I felt pleased with myself. Things were going according to plan, whatever the plan was. The phone rang after ten minutes. Leaping to my feet, I dashed into the kitchen and grabbed the receiver, surprised to hear Den's deep voice.

'Kneel by the fence, bitch!' he ordered me.

'Isn't Mat with you?' I asked.

'He was, but he's gone down the road. He said something about looking at a computer. I want to spunk in your mouth.'

'He might come back any minute.'

'Remember our deal, whore! Kneel by the bloody fence – now!'

As he hung up, I realized that he must have admitted to Mat that he'd abused me again. Sure that Mat was still there as I left the house, I knew that the evil pair were back in business. But I had only myself to blame, I told myself. I'd started the whole thing off again. What could I do? So much for Mat's attempts to woo me back! Why had he changed his mind? Why hadn't he told Den to keep away from me until he'd won me back? Perhaps he was thinking that he might as well take what was on offer from the filly before she bolted through the stable door.

I had a choice, I knew – and I chose to enjoy my body, the crude sex, to the full. The thought of sucking Mat to orgasm through the fence, his sperm bathing my sweeping tongue, excited me, sent a thrill through my womb. I'd leave Mat when I was ready. For Lisa?

Whose cock was I to suck to orgasm? I wondered, kneeling by the hole in the fence. Hearing movements, I waited in anticipation, sure that I'd be able to identify their penises. The foreskin pulled right back, a swollen purple knob peeped through the hole, followed by a solid, veined shaft. It was Mat's cock, there was no mistaking it. The majestic purple crown pointing skywards, this was the penis I'd taken in marriage – in love.

'Suck it, bitch!' Den growled, fool that he was to think that I'd not know the difference between two cocks. Encompassing the purple globe within my hot mouth, I gently sucked. Now who was using whom? I reflected. I was using Mat to satisfy my thirst for sperm, he was using me to satisfy his craving for orgasm. We were all using each other.

Moving my head back and forth, the solid cock gliding in and out of my wet mouth, I heard muffled gasps coming from the other side of the fence. I was back at square one, but in control now. Knowledge is power, I reflected as I ran my tongue around Mat's silky-smooth glans. But what to do with that knowledge? Perhaps I could set Mat up with Lisa, discover him fucking her and throw him out. There was no rush.

Wondering whether I could take the entire length of Mat's cock into my hungry mouth, I moved my head forward. His knob gliding over my tongue, my lips taut around his broad shaft, I almost swallowed his twitching organ. Obviously appreciating my effort, he gasped, his cock swelling as I moved forward a little more. My nose pressed against the fence, I felt his knob pulsating in my throat, desperately close to orgasm.

His shaft twitching, swelling, his sperm gushing, he groaned in his pleasure as I moved my head back and sucked his throbbing glans. My cheeks filling, I moved forward again, taking him down my throat. His knob between my lips again, his spunk jetting over my snaking tongue, I brought out his seed, sustained his orgasm. I was an expert.

Would Den's cock slip through the hole after I'd finished Mat off? I wondered. Would I have to swallow another mouthful of sperm? I imagined sucking ten men to orgasm, taking one after the other into my thirsty mouth and drinking their spunk. The notion wet my cunt, swelled my clitoris. Ten cocks each taking my cunt in turn, spunking my cervix? The days of monogamy had gone, the days of love were long since past.

As I swallowed the last of Mat's sperm and slipped his shrinking cock out of my mouth, my clitoris craving orgasm, I wondered whether to allow him to catch me masturbating. My legs over the arms of the chair, my eyes closed, I'd massage my clitoris and ram a banana in and out of my cunt. On cue, he'd appear in the lounge doorway to gaze gobsmacked at the lewd scene. Would he hide behind the door and watch, or would he ask me what the hell I thought I was doing? I liked bananas.

Den didn't stick his cock through the hole as I'd hoped he would. Perhaps, after fucking my bottom, he wasn't ready to come again? Rising to my feet, I licked my sperm-wet lips and returned to the kitchen. Den might ring during the evening, order me to suck him off, call upon my services. Would Mat spy on me, watch me taking another man's penis into my mouth and swallow his sperm?

'Oh, there you are,' Mat smiled as he wandered through the back door. 'I popped down the road to see Dave about that computer. Has anything interesting happened?'

'Interesting? No, nothing's happened. By the way, Lisa and I aren't going on holiday together.'

'I'm pleased to hear it. The idea of you going away with a lesbian is . . .'

'That has nothing to do with it. I don't know what your problem is. You don't want Den coming round, you don't want me to see Lisa . . .'

'I don't mind if Den calls in for coffee. I was over-reacting earlier.'

'You change with the wind.'

'Talking of Den, he's having some people round for drinks this evening. He invited us but I have to go and see a client.'

'Will you be long?'

'A couple of hours, I suppose. Why don't you go to Den's and I'll join you later?'

'I might. I haven't cooked anything, so . . .'

'We can eat later. I'm going to take a shower and then see this damned client.'

'OK, I'll sit in the garden for a while.'

So, Den was having people round for drinks – for sex with me, more than likely! And Mat, predictably, had to go out. I could always ruin the evening by going out myself. But no, I wanted sex. How many people? I wondered as I stepped out onto the patio. Ten men? Women, perhaps? No doubt Den would ring me the minute his perverted friends arrived and Mat went out. My heart fluttering, my vaginal muscles tightening, I found myself looking forward to the evening, the beautiful sexual abuse.

Back at square one, I reflected again, wondering what I was doing with my life, my body. Far from having a concrete plan, I didn't even have a dream. Without a dream, a dream can't come true. Perhaps my dream was to offer my naked body to men and women for their sexual pleasure? For my own sexual pleasure.

Knowing that Mat would be the voyeur, I decided to play the part of sex slave to the full. I'd beg to be fucked, whipped, spunked. How would he feel, knowing that I was enjoying the perverted sex, begging for more? I might even murmur his name as I was being fucked, murmur comments about him being unable to fuck me properly, satisfy me. I was feeling wickeder by the minute.

'I'll see you later!' Mat called as he finally came downstairs. 'See you at Den's!'

'OK!' I replied, a quiver of excitement running through my womb as the time for crude sex grew closer.

After a shower I hung around in the lounge, looking out of the window, wondering when Den would ring me. I didn't have to wait long. Informing me, when I answered the phone, that I'd be entertaining several men and a couple of women, he ordered me to his house – his lair. Replacing the receiver, I lifted my skirt and gazed at my abused cunt, my crimson love lips, the opaque liquid oozing between my inner petals. 'You're going to be fucked and spermed,' I whispered with a smile, lowering my skirt and leaving the house.

The evening air still and warm, the birds fluttering in the avenue trees, I felt a presence with me as I walked up Den's path. The spirit of sex, of carnality. I'd given my body to the angel of sex, surrendered my very femininity in the name of lust. My cunt was the epitome, the essence of my being. I was now the devil's daughter.

'Ah, right on time!' Den grinned as he opened his front door. Ushering me through the hall into the dining room, he beamed triumphantly as I gazed at five naked young men, their huge penises standing erect, their balls hanging heavy, fully laden. They were in their late teens, fresh, masculine, powerful in youth, a carnal desire reflected in their bright eyes. There were no women. Perhaps they would come later – come in my mouth later. As the men surrounded me, removing my blouse and skirt, running their hands over my naked body, a quiver of desire ran up my spine.

Taken by strangers! I mused joyfully, my cunt wetter than ever. Watched by Mat, wherever he was hiding, fucked by five good-looking studs . . . This was my dream, I knew, as one man knelt before my naked body and licked my gaping sex slit. My lust juices flowing from my love hole as he peeled my inner lips apart, I closed my eyes. My nipples sucked into hot mouths, a tongue delving deep into my cunt, another licking the full length of my yawning buttock valley, teasing my anal rose, I was in my sexual heaven.

My buttocks held wide apart, the tongue tried to enter my private hole, probing, tantalizing, sending electrifying tingles up my spine. Fingers penetrating my moistening cunt, teeth sinking into my nipples, I felt dizzy with desire. Two fingers driving into my bottom-hole, opening my tight duct, I gasped and swayed on my sagging legs as the base sensations touched my very being. Never had I known such sexual bliss, such an agony of ecstasy.

Where was Mat hiding? I wondered as the fingers massaging my inner anal flesh slipped out of my bottom-hole. Was he watching, his penis stiff, yearning for orgasm? *I* yearned for orgasm. Fingers and tongues attending me, my nakedness, I *craved* orgasm. Was Mat jealous?

Hands cupped the roundness of my full buttocks, parting my globes. I felt a penis-head within my yawning crease, probing, seeking. I was to be arse-fucked, bowel-spunked – and I shuddered in my ecstasy. The penis knob pressed against my anal iris, pushing, twisting in its urgency to gain entry to my rectal sheath. My bottom bucked, my belly tightening as the glans penetrated me, absorbing the inner heat of my once secret duct.

I was ordered to kneel. The man behind me, his penis held tight within my gripping bottom, knelt with me. Two men stood before me as my anal canal spasmed, embracing the solid penile shaft. Their cocks swaying, their knobs pressed against my mouth, I took their shafts in my hands and engulfed their purple crowns. Two cocks, two bulbous knobs within the wet heat of my mouth, I imagined their spunk jetting simultaneously – a double mouth-fucking.

As I sucked, my eyes closed, someone slipped something into my aching cunt. A cucumber? I pondered as the cold dildo dilated me, its girth stretching my cunt wide open. In and out it glided, in rhythm with the penis fucking my bottom – up and down, in and out. The abuse thrilled me, sent tingles of sex running up my spine, through my distended pelvis.

My mouth bloated, my lips stretched tautly around the two knobs, I snaked my tongue over the silky globes, probing the sperm-slits, the rims of the helmets. Cupping the two pairs of heavy balls in my palms, breathing heavily through my nose, I had never known such beautiful crudity. Impatient for their bubbling sperm, their jetting spunk, I sucked the knobs deeper into my mouth, the shafts twitching expectantly.

Sperm suddenly gushed from the orgasming crowns, jetting simultaneously, bathing my seeking tongue, filling my already swollen cheeks. I heard gaspings from above, and then from behind as my anal abuser rammed his cock deep into my arse and loosed his spunk. Sucking, licking, swallowing, I shuddered as fingers massaged my clitoris and the huge dildo fucked my spasming cunt. My full breasts squeezed, my nipples pinched, I'd entered my blissful sexual kingdom.

Slipping the cocks out of my mouth, I grabbed the shafts and wanked them, the sperm jetting over my face, my protruding tongue, as my naked body jolted with the arse fucking and my heavenly orgasm peaked. My cunt heaved, spasming as the dildo rammed into me, and my bottom bucked, my sphincter muscles gripping the thrusting cock like a vice as the jism splattered my face, dripped from my lapping tongue.

As the cocks before my sperm-drenched face shrank, the men moved aside. Two more penises hovered before me, the foreskins retracted, the purple heads swollen, awaiting the heat of my mouth. The man behind me stilling his spent cock within my burning arse, I sucked the fresh penises into my sperm-filled mouth as my climax began to wane.

More sperm, I mused, tickling the heavy balls, taking the knobs as deep into my mouth as I could to the accompaniment of outrushings of breath. Five men, six including Den . . . I wanted ten, fifteen, twenty . . . Where were the women? Where were their well-juiced cunts? Where was Mat?

Sucking, mouthing, I left their balls to swing and wanked their shafts to bring out their sperm. My tongue snaking between the two knobs, I moved my head back and forth, delighting in the double mouth-fucking, praying for Mat to be close by, voyeuring in his perversity. Was I to be blindfolded? I wondered as I impatiently awaited the gushing of spunk. Before Mat emerged from his hide to abuse me, my eyes would be shielded, I knew.

The gasps above me now low moans of pleasure as the penis within my bottom slid out with an obscene sucking sound, I licked the knobs with a desperation, an urgency. The sperm finally came, bubbling and then jetting, squirting, pumping. My tongue drowning, my mouth overflowing, I swallowed again and again, relishing my crude act, delighting in my perversity.

The men rocked their hips, double-fucking me, spunking my spunk-thirsty mouth until they'd drained their swinging balls. Slipping the knobs out of my mouth, I lapped up the spilled spunk, sweeping my tongue over their sperm slits, swallowing their male come until they stepped back, their cocks shrinking, snaking over their huge balls.

Now what? I wondered as the dildo slipped out of my aching cunt and I was helped to my feet. The men lifting me onto the table, they laid me on my back, my arms outstretched, my buttocks over the edge of the table, my legs parted wide, my hairless cunt gaping. Placing my feet on two chairs, they tethered me with lengths of rope, securing me in the beautifully degrading position before leaving the room.

'You'll enjoy this,' Den grinned as five more young men filed into the room, their bodies naked, their penises huge, erect. Wondering how he'd rounded up so many studs as they gathered around the violin curves of my naked body, I closed my eyes as one stood between the chairs, between my parted thighs, his magnificent cock pointing skyward.

His knob between my gaping love lips, he drove into me, my tethered body jolting as his glans pressed against my cervix. Grabbing my hips, his heavy balls slapped my buttocks as he began his fucking, his knob repeatedly gliding along my tightening duct and battering my cervix. Fingers tweaked my nipples, yanked my fleshy cunny lips wide apart and massaged my erect clitoris.

Was this my dream come true? I wondered as my cunt spasmed, my lust milk coursing between my buttocks, mingling with the sperm oozing from my dilated bottom-hole. Men queuing up to fuck me, to sexually abuse me, this was Mat's doing. In his quest for perversity he'd brought me a nightmare – a nightmare which, melting into a dream, had become reality. Now I was lost to my dream.

As the man between my legs groaned in his pleasure, I felt his sperm gushing deep into my gripping cunt. My clitoris massaged to an incredible orgasm, I gasped as my perspiring body rocked and my cunt filled and overflowed. 'God, yes!' I cried as my orgasm shook me to the very core. *Watch me now, Mat!* I chuckled inwardly as I arched my back and tossed my head from side to side. *Watch me come in my dream come true!*

Ramming into me, the unknown man's balls slapping my tensed buttocks, he gasped his last gasp of sexual gratification, slowing his thrusting to a gentle, massaging pistoning.

Finally stilling his huge cock, he leaned over me, breathing deeply as he recovered from the illicit union, his male coming.

Sliding his penis out of my saturated sex sheath, he moved to one side as the next man stood between my twitching thighs. Lifting my head, I watched as his erect cock wavered over my inflamed sex slit, the purple head swollen, ballooning. Suddenly driving into me, my cunt yielding to his sheer girth, he grabbed my hips and began his fucking.

Resting my head on the table, I trembled as my nipples were sucked into hot mouths, my clitoris teased again by anonymous fingers. Gasping filled the room – gaspings of sex from our mouths as our genitals squelched in their adulterous fucking. Would I be turned and whipped after the men had pumped their spunk into my inflamed cunt? I yearned a whipping, craved the cane.

Gasping turned to groaning – groans of lust as the young man neared his goal. My cunt tightened, rhythmically gripping the thrusting cock, teasing the pistoning knob. 'Ah!' he finally cried as his sperm pumped, jetting from his slit, filling my vaginal cavern. On and on he thrust, driving his cockhead deep into my hot cunt until his balls had emptied and he collapsed over my shaking body.

Another man quickly entered me as the sated cock withdrew, his fresh knob squelching within my sperm-drenched vaginal cavern. The orgasmic cream oozed, flowed between my buttocks as my cunt squeezed, lovingly hugging the new cock. How much more could I take? I wondered as he withdrew and thrust into me again. How many more orgasms, how many more cocks, how much more spunk?

This was the third penis to penetrate my cunt, to slide into my abused vagina. Another two awaited, proud in their erectness, stiff in their yearning for my thirsty quim. Were more waiting outside? When was Mat going to use and abuse my adulterous body? *Adultery.* Group adultery, multiple adultery. It didn't matter how many men fucked and spermed me now. Twenty, thirty, forty – what was the difference?

No one spoke as the solid cock thrust in and out of my drenched cunt, taking me closer to yet another orgasm. There were no words, no need for words, I reflected hazily as my nipples were bitten, sucked and nibbled. No words – only the gasping and squelching and slapping of sex.

Again, I felt my vaginal sheath expand as the thrusting organ swelled, sperm jetting, pumping into my cunt, oozing from my bloated hole and bathing my anal rose, my arsehole. On and on he fucked me, draining his balls, pumping out his spunk as he gasped and groaned in his coming. Where were the women? I wanted their cunts, my mouth tongue-fucking their cunts as my cunt was cock-fucked and spermed. Ever lewder in my lewdness.

The pistoning cock finally slipping out of my inflamed pussy hole, I was left trembling, delirious with sex as I awaited yet another vaginal fucking. As my bonds were released and my naked body lifted off the table, I wondered what further delights lay in store for me. There were still two cocks waiting to fuck me, to sperm me. Were they eager for my bottom-hole, my mouth? Laying my trembling body on the floor as the other men filed into the room, their cocks revived, solid in arousal, they all stood around me.

Ten penises wavered over me, high above me. Where was Den? Didn't he want me? Where was Mat? As I looked up at the swinging balls, the erect penises, the men began wanking, rolling their foreskins back and forth over their glistening knobs. I cast my eyes over each penis in turn, watching the knobs appear and disappear as the men gasped in their wanking. I wanted them inside me, fucking me, sperming me. Why were they teasing me?

First one knob exploded in orgasm, and then another and another until all ten were spraying me with spunk. Landing on my naked skin with splatting noises, the sperm covered me, my thighs, my hairless mound, my breasts, my face, my hair. On and on the pearly-white liquid jetted from the swollen knobs until sperm was running in milky rivers over my curves and crevices.

Massaging the last of their spunk out of their slits, running their fingers and thumbs up their shafts to expel their cream, they finally moved away and lined up against the wall, forming a queue. The first man knelt over my head, his flaccid cock above my mouth as he rested his weight on his hands. I knew what to do as his balls swung and his glistening glans brushed against my lips. I needed no instruction.

Taking him into my mouth, I sucked his knob, eliciting the residue of his sperm. As he moved away, the second man took his place and I sucked and cleansed him. The third, the fourth, the fifth . . . All ten hung their cocks over my face to be licked clean, the last of their spunk sucked from their slits. My mouth salty, my holes bubbling with male come, I was exhausted – well and truly fucked.

As, finally, they left the room, I lay there quivering, drenched, dripping with sperm and the sweat of debased sex as Den stood above me. Was it his turn to fuck me now? I wondered as he grinned down at me. Was Mat still in hiding, watching the debauchery? Taking my hand, Den hauled me to my feet. I staggered on my weak legs as the sperm trickled over my quivering skin, oozed from my inflamed sex ducts.

'Until tomorrow,' he said indifferently, tossing my clothes at me.

'What about . . .'

'I'll fuck you tomorrow.'

'The women, you said there were women.'

'I lie sometimes.'

As I covered my sperm-sated body with my summer clothes, Den perched himself on the edge of the table and watched me. I couldn't understand why he'd not used and abused me, or where Mat had been hiding. Why lie about the women? To tease me? Perhaps they had something planned for later, I pondered as I buttoned my wet blouse and almost crawled from the room. It was just as well, I reflected – I couldn't have taken any more sex.

Leaving Den's house, the sun setting, I staggered home, wondering what to say to Mat should he be there, how to explain my sperm-soaked clothes. Physically depleted, I climbed the stairs to the bedroom, thanking God that he wasn't home. I couldn't have faced him, his lies, his questioning, his deceit. All I wanted was to slip beneath my quilt and hide from the world.

I was too exhausted to have a shower and cleanse my abused body, too tired to eat, even. Beneath my quilt, my skin sticky, starched with spunk, I closed my eyes, not caring what Mat would say when he got in beside me and discovered the dire state of my body. He'd presented me with a nightmare, and I'd turned it into a dream. My dream had come true.

Chapter Twelve

I woke the following morning to find myself alone in bed, my skin taut with dried sperm. Where was Mat? Sleepy-eyed, I squinted at the bedside clock – seven-thirty. Perhaps he was downstairs? Leaping out of bed, I dashed into the bathroom and took a shower, washing the spunk away, cleansing my aching sex ducts. The jetting water between my inflamed pussy lips exciting me, I wanted to come. *Later*, I promised myself.

Hurriedly slipping into a blouse and skirt, I bounded downstairs to the kitchen. 'Oh, there you are,' I smiled as he peered at me over his newspaper. My knickerless pussy was wetting, my clitoris calling.

'You'd left by the time I got to Den's last night,' he said, folding the paper. 'I stayed there until the early hours.'

'I was tired, exhausted – I couldn't wait for you any longer. Did you have a good time?'

'Yes, chatting and drinking – it was OK. They were a good crowd.'

'There were no women there,' I remarked, opening the back door. The sun was hot, I wanted the hoe.

'Lucky old you, surrounded by young men!' he laughed.

'Yes, lucky old me.'

In the garden, I breathed in the flower-scented morning air, wondering what the day would bring. Den had said that he'd fuck me tomorrow. Could I take another fucking? My body aching, my lust holes sore, I recalled the evening of unadulterated debauchery. Mat must have been watching me. What had he thought as I'd gasped and writhed in the grips of my orgasms, gulped sperm from geysering cock-heads? I'd been double mouth-fucked, arse-fucked, cunt-fucked. Lower and lower in my depravity, deeper and deeper into the bottomless pit of perverted sex. Had Mat watched the men wank over me, shower me with their perverse seed? My clitoris swelled as I pictured the young men, their heavy balls and huge penises. I wanted them again.

'What plans have you for today?' Mat asked as he joined me on the patio.

'Lisa's coming round for coffee,' I smiled. 'And Den.'

'He didn't mention it.'

'He doesn't know.'

'What do you mean?'

'I haven't asked him, yet.'

'Why ask him round?'

'To thank him for a wonderful evening. He entertained me, looked after me. The least I can do is invite him round for coffee.'

Walking across the lawn, I wanted to tell Mat that I knew everything, of his involvement, his wickedness. Pausing by the hoe, I pondered again on letting him catch me masturbating, fucking myself with the long plastic handle. My cunt tightened, my love lips swelling, my sex valley opening as I imagined the implement ramming into me. Mat would think me a tart – as if he didn't already!

But what were his long-term plans? To carry on with the debauchery, to continue watching me being fucked by other men? When he'd first come up with his evil plan, he must have thought about the future. What did he really want?

Ambling towards me, he stood next to me and smiled. 'We're OK, aren't we?' he asked.

'I still need time to think, Mat,' I replied. 'There are things about myself that I have to discover.'

'What things?'

'I don't know, not until I've discovered them.'

'We haven't made love for a while.'

'No, I've not been in the mood.'

'Have you been masturbating?'

'Have *you*?' I giggled.

'No, of course not. So, you had a good time last night?'

'Yes, it was fun. You were right when you said that I should get to know Den. I like him, and his friends.'

'It's a shame you left before I arrived.'

'I had to go, I was exhausted.'

'Why, what had you been doing?'

'Just having a good time. Look, I have something to do, Mat. You'd better get off to work.'

'What do you have to do?'

'Something . . . There's something I want to do.'

'OK, I'd better make a move. I'll see you this evening.'

'Yes, have a good day.'

He'd be back, I knew. My mysterious words would goad him to park the car down the road and come sneaking back to see what it was I had to do. Slipping my blouse off, I tugged my skirt down, the sun warming my naked body. Cupping my swollen breasts in my hands, I gently squeezed them, my nipples distending, standing proud, begging to be suckled. I liked my breasts, my nipples. I liked sucking them, having them whipped. They brought me immense pleasure.

My hand between my thighs, my fingertip tracing my swollen outer lips, running up and down my wet crack, I shuddered. My body, my temple – it was as if I'd been sleeping for a thousand years and had suddenly woken to discover my body, my cunt. I had Mat to thank for my awakening, I reflected. In his wickedness, he'd given me life. My clitoris summoned me.

Grabbing the hoe, I drove it into the earth, the handle about twelve inches from the ground, perfectly positioned to penetrate my yearning cunt as I knelt on all fours. Mat would peer at me from the house, watch me fucking the hoe, gasping in my obscenity. What would he think? He'd think me crude, earthy.

I gave him a few minutes to return before taking my position on my hands and knees, my buttocks jutting out, facing the house as I manoeuvred my hips and aligned the plastic handle with my open vaginal portal. Turning my head, I glimpsed Mat peering round the dining room curtain, his eyes wide as I moved back, the hoe slipping into my drenched sex sheath, entering my cunt.

More sex, more masturbating, more orgasms. What was I doing? I wondered as I rocked my naked body back and forth, abusing my cunt, fucking myself with the hoe. I suppose I wanted to show Mat how his wicked plan had changed me, transformed me into a nymphomaniac. He'd regret it, I vowed – every cock that had fucked me, every jet of spunk, every stroke of the cane, every lash of the leather strap. I wanted to tell him that I was bisexual, that I loved licking clitorises to orgasm, drinking the honeydew from young girls' cunts. The time would come when I'd reveal all.

Reaching between my parted thighs, I massaged my erect clitoris as I rocked my quivering frame back and forth. Knowing that Mat was watching me sent a thrill running through my contracting womb, and I masturbated like fury. 'Ah, yes!' I finally cried, as the sensations built. 'God, I'm coming!' My orgasm erupting within my pulsating clitoris, my cunt tightening around the thrusting plastic handle, I shuddered as waves of pure sexual ecstasy rolled through my trembling body.

On and on I massaged the pleasure from my insatiable clitoris until I collapsed to the ground, the hoe slipping out of my dripping cunt as I writhed on the grass in the aftermath of my self-abuse. The sun warmed me as I lay on my back, my thighs wide, exhibiting my well-juiced sex crack to Mat. I'd done it, taken another step down the road to complete and utter perversity. I felt wicked.

Glimpsing Mat out of the corner of my eye as I recovered, I clambered to my feet and clothed my perspiring body, veiling my swollen breasts, my dripping sex slit. What was he thinking? I wondered as I staggered across the lawn to the house. Was his cock stiff? Would he have a wank before sneaking off to work? Perhaps Den would order me to kneel before the hole in the fence, and have me suck Mat's knob to orgasm. I desperately wanted sperm.

Mat was lurking in the dining room as I slipped into the lounge and grabbed the phone, a wicked plan formulating in my devious mind. He'd listen, his eyes frowning, a thousand thoughts swirling around his tormented mind as he eavesdropped on my conversation.

'Den, it's me,' I trilled, the dialling tone purring in my ear. I was becoming a good actress, a good liar. 'Yes, it was a wonderful evening! No, he's gone to work. Listen, this photographic idea of yours – I've decided to do it. The photographer who works for the men's mag, when can I meet him? Yes, that's fine. Don't worry, I know what he wants! Yes, really dirty, hardcore porn! Yes, I've spoken to Lisa and she's all for it. Of course there'll be plenty of lesbian scenes – you know me! That's great! OK, I'll see you later.'

Now what was Mat thinking? I pondered as I replaced the receiver. I was becoming clever, well practised in the art of deception. Mat would confront Den and he'd deny all knowledge of a photo session, Lisa would say that she knew nothing about it . . . Suspicion, lies, deceit. I felt exhilarated, powerful, wicked!

Hearing movements, Mat slipping into the kitchen and out of the back door, I knew he was going straight round to Den's to have a go at him. Following at a safe distance, I hid behind the fence as he rang on the doorbell. 'Come in,' Den invited, much to my annoyance. From my hide, I'd not be able to hear their conversation, their argument. Stealing down the path, I noticed that Den's lounge window was open so I crept into his garden and hid behind a bush below the window.

'She didn't ring me,' Den was saying, surprise in his deep voice.

'I was there, hiding in the hall. I heard her talking to you about photographic work,' Mat whined. More trouble, more confusion.

'I'm telling you, she didn't phone me.'

'Look, when we started all this, the arrangement was that you only had sex with her when I was around to watch or join in.'

'Yes, and that's the way it's been.'

'She's had her fanny shaved, her tits whipped . . .'

'We've been through all that. I had nothing to do with it, Mat.'

'The plan was that we should have some damned good sex with her, that I watch you fucking her arse, and now . . .'

'And now what?'

'The plan's gone all wrong. She's going on about me and her, our relationship, wanting time to think. All that's happened is that she's drifted away from me.'

'If your plan's backfired on you, you can't blame me. The magazine was your idea, the hole in the fence was your idea, to bring Lisa in was your idea, the guys I know from the college – you asked me to invite them round. The whole thing was your idea, Mat.'

'Yes, I know. But I didn't think that Jane would enjoy it like that. Bloody hell, she was almost begging for it! And she was in the garden a while ago with the handle of the hoe up her cunt, frigging herself off like there was no tomorrow!'

'Bloody hell, she *has* been transformed!'

'You're telling me! I didn't think that she'd change like this! I thought . . . I don't know, I suppose I thought, if anything, it would spice up my sex life with her, that she'd be more demanding sexually. We haven't had sex, not properly, since all this started.'

'It's not my fault, Mat.'

'By the way, she hasn't got a lover.'

'How do you know that?'

'If she had, and he saw the weals, her shaved fanny . . . He'd want to know what the hell she'd been up to.'

'She told me that her lover shaved her and whipped her tits.'

'No, I don't believe that.'

'Going back to this phone call, maybe she rang someone else about photographic work.'

'No, she mentioned your name and said that she'd enjoyed last night. She was talking to you, Den – I know it.'

'She wasn't! Maybe she was pretending to talk to me.'

'She didn't know I was in the house, so why would she do that? Besides, she'd hardly talk about porn mags if she knew that I was there.'

'Well, I know nothing about it.'

'Look, let's cool it for a while, Den.'

'We did that before.'

'Yes, and you . . .'

'I told you, she rang me. She was really worried about her

mother seeing the video. She virtually asked me to blackmail her.'

'Do you know a photographer who works for a dirty mag?'

'No, of course I don't! I have no idea who she rang, but it wasn't me. And I'll tell you this, if we cool it, as you put it, she'll go elsewhere for sex.'

'What do you mean?'

'You said yourself that she's changed, that she was almost begging for it last night. If we cut the sex, she'll go elsewhere for it. And with her looks, she'll have no problem rounding up a few good-looking studs.'

'Christ, things couldn't be worse! She's gone off me, she craves perverted sex, she . . .'

'Let's carry on as we have been and see what happens.'

'All right. But I want to get to the bottom of this phone call.'

'I can't help you there. I wouldn't lie to you about it, there'd be no point.'

'No, I suppose not. So much for our ultimate goal!'

'That's what I was just thinking. There's still a chance that . . . Let's play it by ear.'

'OK, I'll see you this evening as planned.'

Sneaking back into my house, I dashed into the lounge just in time to see Mat slink off down the road to his car. Den couldn't ask me about the phone call because he'd reveal the fact that Mat had been hiding in the house. No one could question me. Mind games, games of sex, lies and deceit . . . But what was their ultimate goal? What was the blackmail and perverted sex leading up to? I had to find out. And I still had no idea who had sent the notes. Knowledge is power, I again reflected.

Knowing that they had an ultimate goal, I decided not to rock the boat too much. I'd carry on pretending to be fearful of my mother discovering my wanton behaviour and allow the perverted sex to continue. Intuition told me that their goal wasn't far away. Their ultimate aim, whatever it was, was looming.

Answering the phone, I knew instinctively that it was Den. I had to come up with more lies, something that would throw the cat among the pigeons and cause mayhem. An idea came to mind as he asked me whether I'd liked two knobs spunking in my mouth. I'd loved it!

'How's your cunt?' he chuckled. 'Well spunked, I'll bet!'

'What do you want?' I asked sulkily.

'I thought I'd ring to see how you are after the orgy.'

'I'm worn out.'

'I'm not surprised!'

'By the way, the men from the college – I'm going to meet one of them.'

'How do you know they're from the college?'

'He told me. You were probably too busy with the orgy to have noticed, but one of them asked me out.'

'Who? Which one?'

'I'm not telling you.'

'Which one, Jane?'

'That's my secret. I'm seeing him this evening.'

'Where?'

'I have to go, someone's at the door.'

Hanging up, I knew the first thing he'd do would be rush out into his garden to discover the identity of my phantom visitor. Then he'd ring Mat and tell him that I was meeting one of the studs that evening. I was right on both counts. Peering round the lounge curtain, I saw him surveying my house, and within ten minutes, Mat was on the phone.

'Jane . . . Er . . . This evening,' he began hesitantly. 'I thought we might go out together, to dinner or something.'

'I can't, I'm seeing Carole,' I replied. 'Another time, perhaps.'

'You're going out with Carole?'

'I spoke to her earlier, we're going out for a drink. I thought, as you're always round at Den's, I'd have an evening out.'

'I'm not always round at Den's.'

'Mat, you're always going to see him. Either that, or you're out with a client or down the road looking at a computer or . . .'

'Can't you put her off? I was looking forward to an evening alone with you.'

'I've been wanting an evening alone with you for ages. Several times, I've told you that I want us to have an evening together. But no, it's always Den this, Den that . . .'

'I know, but . . .'

'As I said, another time, perhaps.'

'What time are you meeting Carole?'

'Eight.'

'Where?'

'In the pub.'

'Which one?'

'Questions, questions! Anyone would think you suspect that I'm going off to meet some man or other!'

'Of course I don't! I just wanted to know which pub.'

'The Smugglers' Inn, by the private estate.'

'Yes, I know it. Oh well, another time, then.'

'That curry's still in the fridge. Heat some up when you get in.'

'Yes, I'll do that. I'll be back before you go, so . . .'

'I might leave early, have a walk before I meet her.'

'Oh, right. OK, I'll see you later.'

Replacing the receiver, I realized that I'd have to tell Carole of my plan in case Mat called her. Hopefully, she'd be able to meet me for a drink somewhere. Mat would obviously follow me, spy on me, so I'd have to leave before he came home. Knowing Mat, he'd probably come home early, and then I'd have to lose him. Later, he'd question me, and I'd say that we changed our minds and went to another pub. And so the lies and deceit would roll on!

'Carole, it's Jane,' I said as she answered the phone.

'Hi, how are you?'

'Fine. How about going out for a drink this evening?'

'Yes, I'd like that.'

'Shall we meet outside that pub in the High Street?'

'The Ship?'

'That's the one. About eight?'

'I'll be there. Actually, John's at a meeting this evening and I was wondering what to do.'

'Great, I'll see you at eight.'

The plan was coming together nicely, I reflected as I replaced the receiver. But I might have a job losing Mat. I'd have to head off in the direction of the Smugglers' Inn and then slip down a side street and make for The Ship. I'd do it, I knew!

Den didn't bother me again and I reckoned that he was trying to discover which of the young men had arranged to meet me. He'd be furious, contacting them and demanding to know who was going behind his back for sex with his slave. They'd all deny it, of course, leaving him pondering on which one was lying.

As the afternoon dragged on, my clitoris swollen in desire, my vaginal milk streaming down my inner thighs, I contemplated masturbating. But with the time nearing five, my clitoris would have to wait. Mat would soon be home, lurking, watching me, and I decided to dress in a microskirt and loose blouse. *Dress like a tart.* My thoughts whispered to me. Applying my make-up, crimping my long blonde hair, I looked great.

'Why dress up like that?' Mat asked as he wandered into the lounge and dumped his briefcase on the floor.

'I told you, I'm going out with Carole,' I smiled sweetly.

'You've never bothered to do yourself up like that when you've gone out with her in the past.'

'I might meet a handsome young man!' I giggled.

'What do you mean?'

'I was joking, Mat.'

'Are you leaving now?'

'No, not yct. How comc you'rc home early?'

'I had to call in on a client. Have you seen anything of Den today?'

'Yes, we sat in the garden. I really like him, he's such a nice man.'

'Nice?'

'He knows how to treat a woman.'

'What do you mean by that?'

'There's something about him that . . . Oh, I don't know.'

'What is there about him? Do you fancy him?'

'You and your suspicious mind, Mat! He's our neighbour, our friend, that's all. Can't I have a coffee with our neighbour without you thinking that I'm having an affair with him?'

'I wasn't thinking that at all.'

'I like having Den next door, I feel secure knowing that he's there. Anyway, no doubt you'll be seeing him this evening – as usual.'

'I've no reason to see him. I'll probably do a bit in the garden, seeing as you don't seem to bother any more.'

'I've been using the hoe.'

'I know . . . I mean, it doesn't look like it.'

As he answered the phone to one of his clients, I slipped out of the room, grabbing my bag and quietly closing the front door behind me. Praying that he wasn't looking out of the window, I made my escape and ran down the street. Turning as I reached the corner, I grinned. There was no sign of him.

After a long walk, I arrived at the pub early and sat at a corner table, sipping wine. Mat would have searched the house and garden, and no doubt be making his way to the Smuggler's Inn to check up on me. Den would probably join the search and . . .

'Hi!' a young man greeted me as he approached the table.

'Oh!' I gasped, immediately recognizing him as one of the college men.

'What are you doing here?'

'Er . . . Meeting a friend,' I stammered as he sat down.

'I'm Ian.'

'Ian, yes. Er . . . Jane.'

'Yes, I know. So, did you have a good time last night?'

'I . . . Look, my friend will be here in a minute. I don't want her to think . . .'

'I'll go when she arrives. I've never known a woman like you. I've read about these things, orgies and gang bangs, but I never thought I'd . . .'

'I don't want to talk about it,' I interrupted him, recalling his thick rod in my mouth, his sperm bathing my tongue.

'Any chance of seeing you some time?'

'No, I . . . I don't know. It's difficult.'

'Here, let me get you another drink,' he smiled, taking my empty glass.

'Thanks, medium white wine.'

As he headed off to the bar, I thought of the irony of the situation. I'd told Den that I was going to meet one of the men, and I'd met one! Perhaps it was meant to be, I reflected. Should I arrange to meet him? Obviously, it was my body he wanted, my cunt. It might be an idea to get to know him, keep him in reserve as a young stud.

'Medium white,' he smiled, placing my glass on the table as he sat down. 'So, tell me about yourself, how you and Den . . . Well, you know.'

'Don't you know the situation?'

'No, I don't.'

'What did Den say when he invited you round?'

'Just that he knew a horny . . . That he knew a woman who enjoyed group sex.'

'Was there someone else there, hiding, watching?'

'If there was, I didn't see him. Why would someone hide?'

'It doesn't matter. Do you know where I live?'

'I know nothing about you, other than your name.'

'Has Den arranged another evening?'

'He's going to let us know – he reckoned within a few days.'

'Give me your address and phone number and I'll be in touch.'

Taking a pen and paper from my bag, I imagined meeting Ian at his place and excluding Mat and Den from the orgy. Word was bound to get back to Den, and I'd win another round. I'd got Lisa on my side. Having the young men too, I'd be in a good position – for what, I didn't know.

'You'd better go,' I said, checking my watch as I stuffed Ian's credentials into my bag. 'I'll ring you. But don't tell Den anything about this.'

'If that's the way you want it.'

'It is. I don't want him knowing that we've met, OK?'

'OK. It's a shame you're not free this evening,' he smiled as he stood up, gazing at my shapely thighs. He didn't know that my cunt was knickerless, naked, hot and ready for sex.

'It is,' I reciprocated, licking my succulent red lips provocatively as I eyed the bulging crotch of his jeans. 'It's a great shame.'

As he walked over to the bar I felt my clitoris swell, my

intoxicating lust juices flowing between my hairless love lips. It *was* a shame that I wasn't free that evening, but there'd be plenty of other times for crude sex, I reflected. My heart fluttering, my stomach somersaulting, I pictured the men standing over my naked body, wanking their beautiful cocks, showering me with their sperm. Things were definitely looking up!

'Hi, Jane,' Carole smiled as she approached with her drink and sat down. 'How are you?'

'I'm fine, couldn't be better.'

'So, what have you been up to? Anything interesting?'

'No, not really. How about you?'

'No, just the same old thing day in, day out. I need something to spice my life up. Got any ideas?'

Carole was very attractive, and I certainly had ideas that could spice up her life no end. Again, I pondered on her cunt, licking her clitoris to orgasm – as only another woman knows how. *Dare I suggest it?* I wondered, admiring her lush nipples, clearly outlined by her tight lycra top. I could bring her the best orgasms she'd ever had. Would she like ten men wanking over her, sperming her naked body?

'I have one or two ideas,' I said mysteriously, sipping my wine.

'Oh?'

'Actually, I haven't.'

'I was saying to Mat just before I left that . . .'

'Mat?'

'Yes, he rang.'

'Why?'

'He said something about you leaving while he was on the phone. He didn't get a chance to ask you when you'd be home.'

'And he asked where we were meeting.'

'Yes, how do you know that?'

'Just a guess, you know how suspicious Mat is. I'll tell you what, let's finish our drinks and go to that new wine bar down the road.'

'OK, good idea.'

That little trick would sort Mat out, I mused as we left the pub. When I got home and he said that he'd been to The Ship and I hadn't been there, I'd guiltily stammer some explanation or other, leaving him believing that I really had met one of the college men for a session of rampant sex.

Finally arriving home at eleven-thirty, I found Mat pacing the lounge floor, anguish reflected in his accusing expression as I flopped onto the sofa. I was a little drunk and couldn't help giggling as he asked me whether I'd enjoyed going to the Smugglers' Inn with Carole.

'We had a great time!' I chuckled. 'We met in The Ship and . . . and I think I drank too much.'

'You met in The Ship?'

'Yes, we were going to the Smugglers' but changed our minds.'

'So you were in The Ship all evening.'

'No, we went to a wine bar. So, what have you been up to?'

'Which wine bar?'

'I don't know, that new one in the high street.'

'Did you meet anyone else?'

'Meet anyone else?'

'Did you bump into anyone you know?'

'No, why do you ask?'

'No reason.'

'What have you been doing?'

'Paperwork, a bit of gardening . . .'

'I thought I saw you in the High Street, but it couldn't have been you.'

'No, no – I've not left the house. Do you want some coffee?'

'No, I think I'll go up to bed. I've had an exhausting evening, I can tell you!'

'Exhausting?'

'Tiring. Right, I'm going up.'

'I'll be with you shortly.'

Beneath my quilt, I pondered on the day's events. More suspicion, trickery and lies. But I'd met Ian, and would ring him and arrange to meet. Perhaps I could meet him in the woods by the recreation ground? Sex beneath the trees, the birds twittering, fluttering above me as I writhed in orgasm. I'd come home dripping with sperm, my face sex-flushed, my cunt inflamed. Mat would run around in circles, question me, discuss the matter with Den, and drive himself crazy!

After Mat had gone to work the following morning, I went downstairs and found another note lying on the doormat. It concerned me screwing a young stud the night before, and I immediately knew that it was either from Mat or Den. Why bother with notes? Was it to rile me, worry me? What was the point?

I came up with an idea – I'd send notes to Mat telling him of my debauchery, my secret lovers, my clandestine sex romps. The notes would also threaten to tell me of his involvement in the plan, that he'd been the perpetrator. Lisa didn't know of Mat's involvement, so he'd know that it wasn't her. The students knew nothing about Mat. He'd be beside himself wondering who the hell knew his secret.

Writing the first note, I slipped it into an envelope and tossed it on the doormat before ringing Ian and arranging to meet him in the recreation ground that evening. He suggested that he bring his friends, and I readily agreed, my cunt wetting as I recalled their beautiful penises, the spunk jetting from their bulbous knobs. I was going to ring Lisa and ask her to join us in the woods for a night of sex, but changed my mind. I'd keep her for myself, I decided. Her curvaceous teenage body, her tight cunt fresh in youth, smooth, hairless – I'd keep her for myself.

I didn't realize the depths to which I'd fallen until I answered the front door to John. Wearing my ridiculously short microskirt and no panties, I invited him into the lounge. Seemingly not noticing my long legs, my shapely thighs, he began to question me about Carole, our outing the previous evening. His blue eyes frowning, I could see that something was wrong, that he suspected something. But what?

'We went to that new wine bar in the High Street,' I imparted as he seated himself uneasily on the sofa and brushed his blond hair away from his forehead. 'Didn't she tell you?'

'Yes, she did. Jane, the reason I'm here is because Mat rang me. He seemed to think that you'd not gone out with Carole last night.'

'That sounds like Mat!' I giggled, parting my thighs as I reclined in the armchair opposite him, my naked pussy slit blatantly bared. 'His suspicious mind will be the death of him!'

'You did meet Carole, then?' he asked, seeming not to notice my feminine wares.

'Yes, in The Ship – and then we went on to the wine bar.'

'She's been rather fidgety lately and, in view of Mat's phone call, I just wondered whether she'd gone to meet someone else.'

'No, no, not Carole. Between you and me, she did say that she needs something to spice her life up.'

'Yes, she's said the same thing to me. I suppose, with me

working all the time, she gets fed up being in the house alone.'

'I know the feeling!' I laughed, parting my thighs further.

'Well, I just thought I'd check with you,' he smiled, looking down and focusing on my sex crack. 'Er . . . I'd better be going.'

'You don't have to rush off, do you?' I demurred, a suggestive grin furling my lips, my eyes wide – bedroom eyes.

'Well, I . . . There's no rush.'

'Good.'

As we talked about his promotion, Mat's work, the weather, and every other mundane subject under the sun, I continued to exhibit my beautiful cunt. Averting his gaze every now and then, he was drawn back to my ripe but hairless lips, my gaping sex slit, like a magnet. All men were the same, I reflected, observing the bulge in his trousers. Given half the chance, a glimpse of a fanny, and they were eager for sex. Adultery didn't seem to bother men. It no longer bothered me!

'How's your sex life?' I asked, licking my lips enticingly as I unbuttoned my blouse.

'My sex life? Well, er . . .'

'Is Carole good in bed?'

'She . . .' His words tailed off as I opened my blouse, revealing my firm breasts, my erect nipples.

Standing before him, I tugged my skirt down, allowing it to fall around my ankles as I kicked my shoes off. He gazed open-mouthed, unable to believe his eyes, or his luck, as I moved closer to him and stood with my feet wide apart. Jutting my hips forward, my sex mound level with his face, I parted my cunny lips, exposing my drenched inner folds, my open sex hole.

'Well?' I grinned. 'What do you think?'

'Jane, I . . .'

'You don't have to say anything, I know what you think.'

'Why are you doing this?'

'Because you're an attractive male and I'm an attractive female, we'd be good together. Don't you fancy me?'

'Yes, of course, but . . .'

'I fancy you, John. Finger me, my cunt. Go on, allow yourself the pleasure – and bring me pleasure.'

Leaning forward, he parted my swollen love lips and drove a finger deep into my well-juiced cunt. Gasping, I bent my knees, my sex valley opening wide, my clitoris emerging from its hide. Slipping a second finger into my sex sheath, he licked the warm skin of my smooth stomach, his breath sending tingling sensations up my spine as he kissed the top of my open slit.

'Carole would never shave,' he murmured as I gripped his head.

'Does she allow you to fuck her arsehole?' I asked in my crudity.

'God, no!'

'You'd like to fuck my arsehole, wouldn't you?'

'Jane, you really are . . .'

'A dirty little bitch?'

'Well . . .'

'Go on, say it – say that I'm a dirty little bitch.'

'You're a dirty little bitch. Christ, I'd love to fuck your arse!'

'Come on, then!' I urged, pulling his fingers out of my cunt and turning round. Bending over with my feet apart, I offered him my bottom-hole, my anal rose. 'OK, fuck my arse!' I giggled. 'Spunk right up my arse!'

Standing behind me, he dropped his trousers and yanked my bottom cheeks wide apart. I shuddered as his fingers scooped my lust juices from my vaginal valley and lubricated my brown tissue. Looking up between my thighs, I could see his heavy balls swinging, brushing against my wet love lips as he pressed his purple plum against my secret portal.

I could feel my arsehole yielding, opening as his solid knob entered me. 'Yes!' I breathed, my tight ring gripping the rim of his helmet. 'All of it! I want all of it!' He held my lips and moved forward, his huge shaft gliding into my rectal tube, filling me, the crudeness of my adulterous act driving me wild. 'More!' I cried, imagining Carole walking in, discovering her husband's infidelity, his arse-fucking.

His balls finally pressing against my swollen love lips, my taut brown tissue gripping the broad base of his beautiful cock, he'd impaled me completely. Withdrawing until my anal ring hugged his swollen knob, he drove into me again, my pelvic cavity bloating as his shaft thrust into my arsehole. Again and again he propelled his cock deep into my bowels, gasping as the illicit coupling brought his climax nearer. His fingers exploring between my cunny lips, massaging my erect clitoris as he arse-fucked me, I wanted him to come, to feel his spunk gushing deep inside my rectal sheath.

'Coming!' he finally breathed, his shaft swelling, his knob exploding in orgasm. His massaging fingertips bringing out my climax, his balls slapping my pussy lips, he rammed his piston into my channel again and again. I could feel his sperm, jetting, filling me, lubricating the debased union as his swinging balls drained and my orgasm peaked. My sphincter muscles spasming, gripping his solid cock, he arse-fucked me until his sperm-flow ceased and he was done.

'God, Jane!' he murmured, sliding his spent cock out of my brimming bottom-hole. 'God, I've never met a woman like you!'

'I do seem to be different!' I giggled as I stood upright and turned to face him. 'You'll have to come again.'

'Yes, I will,' he smiled, buckling his belt. 'Look, I'd better go.'

'Now you've come, you can go.'

'I'll ring you.'

'You just have!' I laughed as he moved towards the door.

'I'd like to ring you every day!'

'You will, John. Now, off you go.'

As the front door closed, I pondered on my latest conquest, wondering about Carole. She was all right in her innocence, in her unknowing, I reflected. What she didn't know couldn't hurt her. I wanted to tell her. No, perhaps not! Looking around the room, my blouse and skirt strewn across the floor, I wondered when John would call again and arse-fuck me. He'd be back again and again for crude sex, I knew. I wanted to lick Carole's clitoris to orgasm. One day, maybe. One day.

'Not naked *again*?' Mat asked incredulously as he appeared in the lounge clutching the note I'd left on the doormat.

'Oh, Mat!'

'God, now what's your excuse?'

'I . . . I don't have an excuse, as you put it.'

'Explanation, then?'

'Explanation? Mat, we're man and wife, not employer and employee, not master and slave! Why do I have to have an excuse or explain why I'm naked in my own house?'

'Well, it's not normal.'

'Normal? I don't want to be normal, thank you. I'm quite happy being myself.'

'How many men continually come home to find their wives naked?'

'I have no idea. Anyway, I would imagine that most men would be delighted, not annoyed.'

'I passed John as I was driving up to the house. Has he been round?'

'Yes, he called in to see me.'

'What for?'

'Because he was passing.'

'I hope you weren't naked when he was here.'

'Of course I wasn't.'

'He was just passing? He must have wanted something, Jane.'

'Why? He's called in to see me before when he's been passing.'

'You've never told me.'

'You've never asked. I am allowed to have visitors, aren't I?'

'Well, yes, but . . .'

'Den calls round for coffee, as do Lisa and Carole. John pops in on the odd occasion to see me . . . What's your problem?'

'Nothing, nothing.'

'What are you doing home in the middle of the day?'

'I was passing.'

'Everyone seems to be passing.'

As Mat answered his mobile phone, I gathered my skirt and blouse and bounded upstairs to the bathroom. Locking the door, I stepped into the shower and washed my curvaceous body – my weapon. I ignored Mat as he hammered on the bathroom door and called out that he was going back to work. I wasn't interested in Mat. I had the evening – Ian's magnificent penis – to look forward to.

No one would know where I was or who I was with. Suspicion, confusion, anger, hatred, jealousy . . . Mat was seething with a lethal cocktail of painful emotions. He'd used and abused me, and now it was my turn! Had he read the note yet?

Chapter Thirteen

Lisa came round after lunch, her ebony tresses shining, her succulent red lips glossed, alluring. She was more attractive than ever, and I longed for her naked body, her youthful cunt gaping over my thirsty mouth. Was she wet? I wondered, leading her into the lounge. Was her clitoris ripe for sucking?

'Are you doing anything this evening?' she asked, plonking herself on the sofa, her red microskirt riding up her delicious thighs.

'I'm going out with a friend,' I replied as I stood before her, gazing at her breast buds pressing against her tight blouse.

'Anywhere nice?'

'I'm not sure where we're going yet.'

'That's a shame. I was hoping we could spend some time together.'

'There'll be other times, Lisa.'

'Yes, but . . . Oh, I don't know. Sitting in my flat night after night, I get bored. I don't suppose I could come along?'

'Er . . . I don't know.'

'I'd really like to go out somewhere.'

I gazed into the dark pools of her eyes. What could my intuition tell me? Wringing her hands, she seemed different, nervy, uneasy. She was obviously trying to wheedle her way in, but I wasn't sure why. Perhaps she was still in league with Den? No one knew that I was meeting Ian and his friends, but Den might have got at Lisa, dispatched her to discover my movements, my plans.

'We can spend some time together now,' I smiled.

'Yes, but it's the evenings . . . I get so bored and lonely. Who are you going out with?'

'No one you know.'

'I wouldn't be in the way, Jane. If you let me tag along I'll . . .'

'I don't know, let me think about it. Are you wearing panties?'

'No, I never wear them. Are you?'

'No, I'm not. Lisa, there's something I'd like to do. I have this fantasy where you're bending over the back of the armchair and . . . Well . . .'

'You are naughty!' she giggled. 'What happens when I'm over the chair?'

'You're tied down with rope, your pussy bulging between your lovely thighs. I lick you, finger you and make you come.'

'What else do you do to me?'

'Finger your bottom and your cunt at the same time. You writhe and cry out when you come and then I drink the delicious cream from your dripping pussy.'

'Go and get some rope!' she giggled, leaping to her feet and slipping her blouse off. 'Your fantasy is about to come true!'

My cunt starting to moisten in excited anticipation, I dashed into the kitchen. Rope – I didn't have any. *I should organize myself*, I reflected. A hiding place to keep rope, whips, handcuffs, Vaseline, candles . . . Recalling kicking some lengths of rope beneath the sofa when Mat had come home unexpectedly, I opened the fridge door. Taking a cucumber from the shelf, I cut it in half. 'That'll do nicely,' I breathed, my mind brimming with wicked thoughts.

Returning to the lounge to find Lisa's lithe, naked body over the back of the chair, her rounded buttocks projecting, her hairless labia swelling below the melons of her youthful bottom, I placed the two halves of cucumber on the floor and grabbed the rope from beneath the sofa.

'I feel really horny,' Lisa breathed as I tied the ropes to her wrists and ankles, securing her in the lewd position.

'So do I!' I giggled. 'You have a lovely cunt. If only you could see your love lips, your open crack, your pink inner flesh. Mmm, very alluring.'

'God, your words alone make me want to come! Talk dirty to me.'

'I'll tell you what I can see,' I murmured, kneeling behind her. 'Two perfectly formed cushions of hairless, fleshy lips. They're smooth, soft, unblemished. Nestling between them, your inner lips are wet, curled like the open petals of a pink flower. And between your inner lips I can just see the entrance to your vagina, your girl juice oozing from your cunt. Where your outer lips fuse, there's a small bridge of skin running up to the brown eye of your bottom-hole. At the other end of your crack, your clitoris is peeping at me, looking at me from beneath its little pink bonnet, begging to be licked.'

'What are you going to do to me, to my cunt?' she asked eagerly.

'I'm going to push my tongue into your cunt and taste your milk. But first, I'm going to push a cucumber into you, just to excite you, to wet you more.'

Taking the fruit from the floor, I pressed the cut-off end between her fleshy sex pads and gently twisted and pushed until it slipped deep into her tight sheath. Gasping, she wiggled her hips, her outer lips stretching tautly around the green shaft as I pushed it fully home. Taking the other half of the phallus, I pressed the thin end against her anal portal, pushing and twisting until the rounded end slipped into her tight hole.

'What's that?' she cried as the shaft slid into her rectal sheath, stretching her delicate brown tissue. 'Jane, take it out!'

'It's all right,' I chuckled. 'Just relax and enjoy it.'

'No, it's too big!'

'Of course it's not! There, it's almost in. You look lovely with both your holes forced open. You should see it!'

'Please, don't push it in any further!'

'Now the little bridge of skin between your holes has almost gone, the cucumbers virtually touching each other. Your pussy lips now form a perfect circle around the cucumber. You really do look beautiful.'

'God, it feels . . . it feels heavenly!'

'I knew you'd like it. OK, wait there while I go and get something.'

'What? What are you going to get?'

'You'll see.'

Scurrying into the garden, my lust juices coursing down my inner thighs, my clitoris crying out for my caressing fingers, I grabbed a thin bamboo cane from a flower border. In the kitchen, cleaning the mud off the cane, I felt a cloud of evil engulf me, as if I were possessed by the devil himself. Would Lisa enjoy the thrashing of her life? I mused, returning to the lounge. Whether she enjoyed it or not didn't matter – I knew *I* would! Was I the devil's daughter?

'What have you got?' she gasped as I stood behind the naked melons of her bottom and eased the cucumber deeper into her tight rectal duct.

'You'll see,' I breathed huskily, leaving an inch of the fruit protruding between her rounded buttocks, nestling in her anal crease.

Bringing the cane down with a loud crack, I chuckled as her naked body jolted, her bottom bucking to meet its instrument of torture. 'No!' she screamed as I brought the cane down again, lashing her pale orbs. 'Jane, please!' Again, I landed the cane squarely across her tensed melons, watching the thin, pink weals forming, fanning out across her quivering skin. 'Why are you doing this?' she screamed. Halting the thrashing, I ran my fingertips over her taut buttocks, moving down and caressing her open sex valley beneath the cucumber protruding from her bloated cunt.

'You're still in league with Den, aren't you?' I asked, rubbing her swollen clitoris.

'No, of course I'm not!' she sobbed.

'I'll thrash the truth out of you, Lisa. You might as well own up and save yourself from . . .'

'I am *not* in league with Den!'

'It seems odd that you want to know where I'm going this evening, who I'm going with. And odder still that you want to come along. I suppose your plan was to discover where I'm going, and who with, so that you could tell Den.'

'No! Why would I want to do that?'

'You tell me.'

'That wasn't my plan! I just wanted to be with you because . . . I've had nothing to do with Den since . . .'

'You're lying, Lisa. Lying young girls deserve a good thrashing.'

'Please, I'm not lying!'

'I'll cane your bottom until you tell the truth!'

Resuming the thrashing, I watched gleefully as her buttocks turned a fire-red. The glistening cucumber shooting out of her cunt like a bullet as her muscles tightened, I didn't stop, bringing the bamboo cane down again and again with deafening cracks. Ignoring her screamed protests, her pleas for mercy, I continued to lash her burning buttocks until my arm ached.

'You'll have some more in a minute,' I hissed, dropping the cane to the floor and rubbing my arm.

'Jane, please!' she sobbed. 'I'm not in league with Den!'

'Who was the man Den brought here?'

'I don't know. You've asked me before and I've told you, I know nothing about another man.'

'You don't seem to know much. Considering that you're Den's accomplice, you don't know much at all.'

'I am *not* his accomplice!'

'I really thought we had something together, Lisa. I thought that we might even end up together, living together as a couple.'

'That's what I wanted, too.'

'Then why ruin it?'

'I did *not* ruin it!'

I was a damned good liar, and so was Mat – but Lisa? She was too young, too inexperienced and naive to lie. But I had to be sure. I wasn't going to be taken in, to be made a fool of by the girl. Another twenty or so cracks of the cane across her scarlet buttocks, and I might believe her.

Retrieving the cane, I resumed the gruelling thrashing, landing one stinging blow after another across her bucking bottom orbs. She screamed and screamed, begged for me to stop, offered me anything and everything in return for her freedom – but I continued the beating until the cane snapped in two. The cucumber gliding out of her anal duct as her muscles spasmed, I focused on her inflamed holes, her sex milk streaming from her gaping cunt.

Kneeling behind the sobbing girl, I licked the full length of her yawning cunt slit, lapping up her flowing honeydew, drinking from her burning duct. The squelching and lapping sounds of lesbian lust filled the room. I wanted her tongue lapping between my swollen love lips, licking my pulsating clitoris. But there was plenty of time for her to reciprocate, I reflected.

Parting her outer sex lips, I pressed my mouth against the hot, pink flesh forming a cone around her open hole and sucked out her juices. Her sobs becoming whimpers of pleasure, I decided to take her to orgasm, to lick and mouth on her clitoris and allow her some satisfaction after her thrashing. But I might well thrash her again, should the fancy take me.

'That's nice!' she gasped as I parted her vaginal lips as wide as I could and sucked her swollen clitoris into my hot mouth. My nose almost up her cunt, I repeatedly swept my tongue over the sensitive tip of her pleasure button, taking her ever closer to her desperately needed release. 'Don't stop!' she gasped, her lust juices flowing in torrents from her sex duct, flooding my face.

Her orgasm finally erupting, her bottom bucking, her naked body shaking violently, she screamed out in her coming. Again and again I swept my tongue over her pulsating clitoris, sustaining her climax as her cunt milk spewed from her open hole and ran down my face in torrents. Her orgasmic juices spurting from her cunt like spunk jetting from a knob, never had I known such a copious flow of female come. As she cried out, her orgasm obviously peaking, I drove a finger deep into her tight bottom-hole, taking her higher to her sexual heaven. 'More, more!' she gasped as I pistoned my finger in and out of her spasming rectal sheath, her muscles gripping me like a vice. 'Don't stop!'

Repeatedly fingering her hot bottom-hole, I lapped at her throbbing clitoris until her trembling body began to calm. She was almost done, her orgasm gently relinquishing her sated body. Her climax finally over, I slid my mouth up to her open hole and sucked out her sex milk, swallowing her creamy offering as her body relaxed, leaving her serene.

'Nice?' I asked, slipping my finger out of her hot anal sheath.

'God, yes!' she breathed as I stood behind her, eyeing her crimson bottom cheeks, the spilled cunt milk streaming down her inner thighs. Another thrashing? I pondered. Or should I now have *her* attend *my* cunt, lick and suck *my* clitoris to orgasm?

Slipping into the kitchen, I took a large wooden spoon from the drawer – the nearest thing I had to a paddle. Thrashing her with the convex side of the spoon would ensure that her beautiful bottom melons would glow red, burn all over. Wickeder and wickeder! In the lounge, I gazed at her rounded bottom globes, the thin weals. Her fiery melons were asking for more, I knew.

'So, you say that you're not in league with Den?' I pursued.

'Of course I'm not.'

'I have to be sure, Lisa. Ally or adversary, friend or foe – I have to know.'

'I've told you, I'm a friend.'

'I'll know one way or the other within a few minutes.'

'What do you mean? How will you know?'

The first deafening slap of the spoon against her left buttock caused her to yelp like a dog. Again, she yelped and screamed as the spoon slapped her right globe. Repeatedly slapping each crimson globe in turn, I didn't give in to her cries and pleas for mercy. Her screams and beseechings only serving to drive me on, I continued the beating, delighting in my debauchery as every inch of her rounded melons glowed, burning like fire.

'Christ, Jane!' she screamed as I whacked the backs of her shapely thighs as hard as I could. 'Please, stop!'

'I'll carry on unless you tell me the truth,' I panted, halting the beating.

'I *have* told you the truth!' she sobbed.

'OK, I believe you now.'

'You should have believed me in the first place!' she returned as I released her trembling body and helped her to her feet.

'I had to be one hundred per cent sure.'

'God, my bum really hurts!'

'Here, come and rest on the sofa.'

'I don't think I'll ever be able to sit down again!' she moaned as she gingerly lowered her naked buttocks and reclined on the sofa, tears flooding down her flushed cheeks as she looked up at me. 'You're horrible!'

'And you're beautiful. Now, stop complaining and rest.'

As I grabbed the ropes and cucumbers, I wondered whether to allow Lisa to join me that evening. Would I mind sharing her, her beautiful cunt? I didn't know. Hiding the ropes in the kitchen drawer and tossing the cucumbers into the bin, I suddenly had an idea and dashed back into the lounge.

'Lisa, I want you to ring Den,' I said, placing the phone next to her.

'What for?'

'Tell him that you've been to see me and . . .'

'I haven't spoken to him for ages, Jane. I don't want to get involved in whatever it is you're doing.'

'You *are* involved, like it or not.'

'What about your husband?'

'Mat? What about him?'

'You said that we might live together, as a couple.'

'Oh, that. It's early days, Lisa. I have no plans, I don't know what to do about Mat, or Den.'

'Come and live with me.'

'No, I don't want to live in a flat. Look, ring Den and tell him that you want to join him again, join in with the blackmail and sex.'

'All right, but . . .'

'There are no buts. I reckon that he'll ask you to find out where I'm going this evening. Tell him that you'll get back to him after you've spoken to me. Dial one four one first, I don't want him to know that you rang from here.'

'OK.'

Eyeing her firm breasts, her succulent nipples as she rang Den, I pondered on my plan. If Lisa rang Den back later and told him that I was meeting one of the college men at a pub, he'd tell Mat and . . . and what? My crazy plans never seemed to go anywhere, apart from causing confusion.

'Den, it's Lisa,' the sex-kitten purred. 'Yes, I know. Look, I want to become involved again. I can change my mind, can't I? Yes, I do need money. Jane? What, this evening? OK, I'll ring her and find out. By the way, she asked about a man you took to her house. Who was it? Don't tell me, then. OK, I'll ring you back later.'

Replacing the receiver she looked up at me, a slight grin furling her full red lips. At least I was now sure that she knew nothing about Mat's involvement. 'He seemed to believe me,' she sighed. 'He wants me to find out what you're up to, where you're going and who with.'

'Good. We'll wait for ten minutes and then you can ring him back. Tell him that I'm going to meet the college men and . . .'

'Who are the college men?'

'It doesn't matter who they are. Tell him that I'm meeting them on the common, Broadridge Common, at eight o'clock.'

'OK, but I don't see the point.'

'Neither do I, yet. You'd better dress in case Mat makes one of his untimely appearances. I'll go and make some coffee.'

Filling the kettle, I felt that my plan, whatever it was, was coming together nicely. Lisa would tell Den where I was going, he'd tell Mat, and Mat would . . . Sadness enveloped me as I thought of Mat, the time before it had all begun. Why had he done it? Why had he treated me as a sex object, used and abused me, had me whipped and fucked by other men? Perhaps Lisa could discover his so-called ultimate goal.

Lisa – what the hell was I doing with her? She was like a little girl, needing mothering, looking after. There was an angelic innocence in her dark eyes, the way she pouted her full lips. Live together as a couple? She had no money, no job, and lived in a rented flat above a shop. What did the future hold for her? I wondered, pouring the coffee. Or for me, for that matter!

'Shall I ring him now?' she asked as she appeared in the kitchen doorway.

'Yes, I'll bring the coffee through,' I replied, pouring milk into the cups. 'Right, let's go.'

'Where are you really going this evening?' she asked as I followed her into the lounge, my eyes transfixed on her rounded buttocks billowing her short skirt.

'I'll tell you later. Ask Den what his ultimate goal is.'

'Ultimate goal?'

'Yes, ask him what this is all leading up to, what he hopes the blackmail will result in. Right, make the call, and don't forget to dial one four one first.'

Placing the cups on the coffee table as she sat on the sofa and grabbed the phone, I glimpsed her wet vaginal crack. The more I thought about her, the more I wanted her, but . . . Could I live with her? I pondered. Could we live as a couple? The notion intrigued me. She'd make a good partner, in bed as well as for company. My thoughts began whispering to me. Did I love her?

'Den, it's me,' she purred, breaking my reverie. 'Yes, I rang her. She's going to Broadridge Common at eight o'clock. To meet some college men, whoever they are. Yes, she believes that I'm her friend. Yes, I will. Den, where will this blackmail end, what's the point?'

She listened intently for a while, her dark eyes catching mine now and then as I sipped my coffee. Was Den spilling the beans? I wondered. Would he tell her about Mat? I doubted it very much. He'd not trust her, I was sure. As she said goodbye and hung up, I was beside myself with anticipation.

'Well?' I finally asked.

'The ultimate goal is to transform you into a nymphomaniac,' she declared.

'Why?'

'So that you want sex, group sex, lesbian sex, all the time. He reckons that the time will come when there'll be no need to blackmail you because you'll be willing to have sex with anyone and everyone, including the other man, whoever he might be.'

As she took her coffee from the table, I paced the floor, pondering on her words. So, Mat had come up with a plan to transform me, to heighten my libido to the extent that I'd perform lesbian shows for him, enjoy group sex with him, so that he and Den could both enjoy fucking me without having to blackmail me. The plan had certainly worked well, I had to admit!

How they intended to bring Mat into the games, I didn't know. Perhaps Mat was going to walk in and find Den fucking me, and I'd be in such a state of arousal that I wouldn't mind my husband joining in. Henceforth, there'd be no need for blackmail – I'd willingly participate with Den and Mat, and whoever else came along.

'You've done well, Lisa,' I smiled as she finished her coffee. 'What I want you to do now is go home. I'll ring you when I'm ready.'

'What about this evening?'

'You can't come with me. I have something very important to do and I can't have you with me.'

'But . . .'

'Trust me, Lisa. I'll ring you, don't worry.'

'If you say so,' she replied sullenly, depositing her cup on the table.

'I do say so. When you go, try not to let Den see you. Sneak out into the street, OK?'

'OK, I'll wait to hear from you.'

As she left the house and closed the front door, the phone rang. It was Mat, ringing to tell me that he had to see a client that evening. Obviously Den had called him and told him about the common, and they'd planned to meet there. While they were wandering aimlessly over the common, I'd be in the woods enjoying my studs. I'd arrive home late, sperm-drenched and exhausted. Mat would question me, his suspicious mind paining him as I poured out my lies. I was now the omnipotent!

Hanging up, I again pondered on the ultimate goal. Why had Mat wanted to change me from a loving wife into a perverted bisexual nymphomaniac? Because he was a man, I supposed. Making love wasn't good enough for him, he wanted to watch other men fuck me, other women lick my cunt, suck and lick my clitoris to orgasm. Knowledge might well be power, but what to do with that knowledge?

I spent the rest of the afternoon preparing for the evening, taking a shower, shaving the stubble from my vulval flesh, applying my make-up and dressing in my microskirt and white silk blouse. I really looked the part, I thought, gazing at myself in the full-length mirror. I really looked like a tart. I *was* a tart!

Mat arrived at six, asking me why I was dressed up to the nines, where I was going, who I was meeting. I gazed into his brown eyes, the hurt there, the regret, the failure. His incredibly wicked plan had backfired on him, leaving him wallowing in self-pity, suspicion, anger, jealousy.

'I'm meeting Lisa,' I lied. 'As you phoned and said that you're seeing a client, I thought I'd have an evening out with her.'

'Have you seen anything of Den?'

'Yes, he came round this afternoon.'

'He doesn't seem to be working very hard these days. He's always round here sitting in the garden with you and having coffee.'

'I wouldn't know anything about his work, he never mentions it.'

'John, Den, Lisa, Carole . . . You have quite a social life, don't you?'

'No, not really.'

'Who else calls in for coffee?'

'Aren't I allowed to have any friends?'

'Yes, but . . .'

'I'd better be going, Mat.'

'What time will you be home?'

'I really have no idea. It depends on . . . I'll see you when I see you, OK?'

'I suppose so,' he sighed. 'Have you given any more thought to us?'

'No, I still need time. I'll see you later.'

Leaving the house, I walked down the leafy avenue, the sun warming me, my mind swirling with thoughts of perverted sex. Mat and Den would be together by now, talking, discussing, planning . . . The ultimate goal? Perhaps I should allow Mat's plan to work, I pondered. A life of perverted sex, and a husband to support me. It might not be such a bad thing after all.

The evening sun warming me, I ambled across the grass towards the trees, wondering where Ian and his friends were. My juices seeping from my sex sheath as I thought of several young men taking me, using my naked body to satisfy their lust for debased sex, I sat on the grass by the woods and looked about me. A woman pushing a pram, children playing football, the world going about its business. Where were my studs?

'I didn't think you'd turn up,' Ian called as he emerged from the trees behind me. Rising to my feet, I turned to face him. His tight jeans caught my eye, the bulge of his crotch. Wearing a white T-shirt, his suntanned arms strong, his face grinning, he smiled. 'We've found a clearing in the woods,' he said. 'Follow me.'

I said nothing as he led me along the path, the path to sex. The cool air in the woods caressing my naked pussy, my wet sex crack, I wondered how many men were waiting for me, my cunt. Six, seven, eight . . . I wanted their sperm, their gushing sperm filling me, my mouth, my cunt, my arsehole.

'How many?' I finally ventured.

'There are six of us,' he replied, turning his head and flashing a smile at me. 'OK?'

'Yes, that's OK.'

There were four naked men standing in the clearing. I gazed longingly at their fully erect penises, their swollen purple knobs, their heavy balls. Where was the sixth? I wondered, greedy for as many cocks as I could lay my hands on, take into my cock-hungry mouth. Perhaps Ian had got it wrong and he was the fifth, not the sixth.

My stomach somersaulting as two young men unbuttoned my blouse and tugged my skirt down, I looked down at my breasts, my swollen melons, my succulent milk teats. My nipples throbbing, erect in arousal, I let out a sigh of pure lust as a finger ran up and down my yawning sex crack.

'She has a lovely cunt,' someone murmured as a finger slipped between my inner folds and snaked its way into my aching sex duct.

'And a beautiful arse,' another rejoined as my buttocks were squeezed and parted.

I felt alive with the sensations of sex as hands ran over my naked body, seeking my crevices, my mounds. The evening sun filtering through the trees, casting streaks of light across my firm breasts, I imagined going to the woods every day and giving my body to the young men, offering my cunt in the name of lust. I didn't need Mat, he was in my way. Without him, I'd be free – free to offer my naked body to other men. What price freedom?

To my great delight, a naked girl emerged from the bushes, her breasts firm in her youth, her love lips adorned with fine blonde curls. She'd obviously been hiding from me, waiting until I was naked and ready for sex before showing herself. As she moved towards me, I focused on her sweet sex crack, her pinken inner lips protruding seductively from her young slit. I wanted my tongue inside her beautiful cunt, tongue-loving her.

The finger embedded deep within my wetting vagina leaving my tight sheath, the men moved aside as the girl stood before me. Her long blonde hair cascading over her pretty face as she lowered her head and sucked my breast bud into her hot mouth, I breathed in her aroma, her female scent. I knew I was about to find my sexual paradise.

Five beautiful penises and an angelic young girl all to myself . . . This was my domain. How wonderful it would be to have Mat watching, I mused as the girl knelt before me and kissed my fleshy pussy lips, sucked each one into her hot mouth. But Mat had lost out, as had Den. Their wicked plan had more than backfired on them, leaving them alone while I enjoyed sex in the woods. Were they wanking?

'Lie on the ground, on your back,' Ian instructed me. As I obediently complied with my master's order, the soft grass tickling my naked flesh, the young girl knelt astride my head and buried her face between my thighs. Her tongue entering me as I gazed at her yawning sex valley, her open lust hole, I was about to pull her curvaceous body down and reciprocate when one of the men knelt behind her. His fully-erect penis hovering above me, his huge balls swinging, I watched as he slipped his purple glans between her swollen sex lips and drove his magnificent cock deep into her young cunt.

His balls brushing my forehead as he withdrew his penis and thrust into her again, I focused on his glistening shaft, her inner lips rolling along its veined surface. Never had I witnessed sex at such close quarters – a massive cock thrusting in and out of a beautiful cunt – and the sight sent a lascivious quiver through my womb. In and out of her fresh young cunt his shaft glided, solid, wet with her juices of lust, fucking her.

As the girl sucked my clitoris into her ravenous mouth, I arched my back, desperate to tongue her love nodule. Lowering her body, the top of her open sex crack pressing against my mouth, I knew exactly what she wanted. Her copious love milk dripping onto my face, I pushed my tongue out and licked her swollen clitoris as the huge penis drove in and out of her cunt. Would I have my cunt fucked as she licked my clitoris? I wondered, imagining the beautiful sensations. Her tongue driving deep into my cunt again, I knew that my turn would soon come.

The squelching sounds of sex resounding in my ears,

warm pussy milk dripping onto my face, I licked and sucked on the girl's clitoris as she parted my cunny lips and mouthed my throbbing pleasure bud. The young man's balls slapping my forehead as he quickened his fucking, I prayed for him to slip his cock out of her cunt when he came and spunk over my face, sperm my lapping tongue.

Gazing in awe at the stiff wet cock as it repeatedly emerged and drove back into the nameless girl's drenched vaginal duct, I felt the birth of my orgasm stirring within my contracting womb. My anal sphincter muscles spasming as my climax approached, I wanted a huge penis there, arse-fucking me, sperming into my bowels. I loved cocks, spunking knobs, swinging balls . . . I loved cunts, solid clitorises, the flowing honeydew of lust. I loved sex.

'Coming!' the man cried, his shaft swelling to an incredible size as my own orgasm erupted within my tongued clitoris. His bulbous knob leaving her vaginal opening every time he withdrew to thrust into her again, his spunk splattered my face, jetted over my lapping tongue. I licked and sucked as the girl writhed in her orgasm, delighting in my crudity. Her milk spewing from her inflamed cunt as the man's spunk jetted, I drank the aphrodisiacal blend of their orgasmic juices.

The pistoning cock finally stilling, embedded deep within the girl's sex sheath, I licked the sperm running down the heavy balls dangling above my face. My own climax subsiding, my clitoris sending the last ripples of orgasm through my quivering pelvis as the female tongue snaked around my swollen sex button, I relaxed at last.

The penis finally gliding out of the girl's sated vagina, I pressed my lips to the pink flesh surrounding her open hole and sucked, swallowing the young man's sperm. Moaning in her pleasure, she swivelled her hips, pressing her wet sex flesh hard against my mouth as I pushed my tongue out and entered her cunt. Reciprocating, her tongue driving deep into my drenched vaginal sheath, I shuddered. I wanted to come in her mouth again.

'That's enough,' a deep voice called. The girl moving aside, I looked up as the men stood around me, their balls heavy, their penises fully erect. Who was to enter me, and where? I wondered as I was instructed to position myself on all fours. My buttocks jutting out as I assumed the crude position, displaying my vaginal hillocks, my anal iris, I rested my head on the grass, awaiting my fate.

As I'd expected, a young man slid beneath my naked body and guided his knob between my vaginal lips. Driving his cock deep into my yearning cunt, he reached behind me and grabbed my buttocks, yanking my globes wide apart, exposing my anal entrance. As before, I was to have another cock up my arse, but would I also have one fucking my mouth?

A tongue licking my brown hole, lubricating my delicate tissue, I closed my eyes, desperate for a penis to enter me there, to stretch my tight duct wide open and fuck me. The men murmuring, whispering to each other, I knew they were deciding who should take me from behind, fuck my arse and spunk into my bowels. The cock stirring within my gripping vagina, I hoped the men would each fuck me, take it in turns to pump their torrid lust juices into my rectal duct.

As someone knelt behind me and pressed his bulbous knob against my wet anal rose, I lifted my head, looking for a penis to suck as my holes were fucked. Two men kneeling down, their huge shafts erect, they pressed their knobs together, offering me their purple crowns. Devouring them as the man behind me drove his cock into my anal duct, I sucked on the two beautiful plums. The male organs between my legs driven in to the hilt, I took the two knobs as far as I could into my mouth, my mind swirling with crude thoughts, my arousal soaring to frightening heights.

The quadruple fucking commencing, my body rocking as the four shafts drove in and out of my orifices, I shuddered as soft fingers gently massaged my clitoris. It was the girl, I knew, as she expertly masturbated me, sending electrifying sensations through my abused body. Squelching, sucking, slapping, gasping . . . The sounds of sex filled my ears as five people attended my feminine needs, fucking me, massaging my love spot, plummeting me to hitherto unimaginable depths of sexual depravity.

Gobbling on the two knobs as they exploded in orgasm, pumping sperm over my snaking tongue, I felt the cocks within my inflamed lust holes swell, the spunk jetting into my spasming ducts. My clitoris erupting in orgasm beneath the girl's massaging fingertips, I drank from the men's swollen plums, my entire body quivering with perverted sex. On and on the male organs thrust, deep into my cunt and my arse, filling me with spunk until I overflowed. Sperm running down my chin, oozing between my legs, I'd found my sexual utopia.

Delirious with sex, my body shaking violently, I could no longer rest my weight on my hands. The penises slipping out of my mouth, gliding out of my anal sheath as I collapsed on top of the man beneath me, I lay trembling in the aftermath of an orgasm so intense that I almost passed out. The only remaining cock slipping out of my cunt as I rolled to one side, I lay on my back, licking the remnants of sex from my lips.

My eyes closed, I listened to the movements around me, wondering what I was to endure next. *A whipping?* I speculated, hearing twigs cracking underfoot. Or would they now take it in turns to spunk up my sopping cunt? I wanted more men, more cocks, men standing over my naked body, wanking over me. I wanted as much crude sex as I could get!

Finally opening my eyes as I recovered from my beautiful ordeal, I looked about me. They'd gone, crept away, leaving me alone, desperate to come again. But there was always tomorrow evening, I consoled myself. And the following evening, and the following. Clambering to my feet, I dressed, covering my abused body, veiling my sperm-bubbling holes, and staggered out of the wood. The sun setting, I made my way home on my trembling legs, wondering what Mat had been up to. Wanking?

I arrived home to find Mat pacing the lounge floor. He looked tired, his expression pained as I smiled at him and flopped onto the sofa. My exhaustion was obvious, my body shattered from the quadruple fucking.

'You're late,' he murmured.

'Yes, we had a great time!' I laughed.

'Where did you go?'

'Everywhere. Lisa's become a good friend, we get on really well together.'

'What about her girlfriend?'

'Oh, she went off with someone else. That's one reason that I went out with Lisa this evening, she was down in the dumps. What have you been up to?'

'I saw my client and then watched TV.'

'How boring! Well, I'm going to bed.'

'Yes, yes, I'll be up later.'

Mat did his usual trick the minute I'd left the room. I stood on the stairs, spunk oozing from my abused sex ducts as I listened to him whining and complaining on the phone to Den. I was about to go up to bed and leave him to whinge when he mentioned the ultimate goal.

'Tomorrow,' he said. 'We'll do it tomorrow. Because we're running out of bloody time, Den. She wasn't on the common but I know that she went off somewhere with those mates of yours. I reckon that we're losing it. It won't be long before she takes off and leaves me – and then we'll have nothing. Right, I'll arrive at eleven o'clock, on the dot, and walk in to find you fucking her. Yes, that's a good idea, get Lisa round. OK, tied down, sex-crazed, begging for it – and I'll join in. If that happens, I'll say that I knew what was going on all along, and I didn't want to spoil her fun, I didn't want to lose her. The way she is now, I can't see that she'll say no! Great, I'll arrive at eleven sharp. We don't need luck! Until tomorrow.'

Now what? I wondered as I climbed the stairs to my bedroom. I had to decide, make my choice – either leave Mat, or go along with the perverted plan and allow them to achieve their ultimate goal. I'd have the security of a husband, the college men, Den and . . . and Lisa? Deciding to sleep on it, I stripped off and climbed into bed. My naked body sperm-laden yet again, I'd enjoyed the evening. But I only had until eleven the following morning to come to a decision. A decision that would mould the rest of my life. What life?

Chapter Fourteen

Only two hours to go. Mat had supposedly gone to work, Den was no doubt hovering in his house waiting to pounce – and I still hadn't come to a decision. Washed, dressed, ready for sex, I sat in the garden, reflecting, contemplating my choices.

If I sold the house, left Mat to live with Lisa, I'd have to endure a poky flat. No garden, no sunbathing naked – I didn't want that. If I allowed the ultimate goal to be achieved I'd have more than enough perverted sex, plus the security of a husband. The hindrance of a husband!

Mat had started the whole damned business – wrecked our lives, our plans. Ideally, the best way would be for him to leave. I'd have the house, Lisa, the college men, and Den – if I wanted him. But Mat would never leave, I knew.

Walking around the garden, my head aching, I tried to come up with an answer. If only I had more time! If I'd known of the ultimate goal earlier, known sooner that Mat had been the perpetrator of the wicked plan . . . Hindsight – about as useful as a man without a cock! More time? Yes, that's what I needed. If I made myself scarce for the day, escaped from Den and ruined the plan, I could delay the decision. I might even have the luxury of another twenty-four hours before deciding on my future – my fate.

Leaping into the house as the phone rang, I hesitated. Den? Perhaps it was Mat, checking up on me, making sure that I was at home, vulnerable. I didn't want to live like this, jumping whenever the phone or the doorbell rang. Finally snatching the receiver up, I was relieved to hear Lisa's husky tone.

'Den rang me,' she imparted with a hint of urgency. I pictured her succulent red lips, her pink tongue. I wanted her to suck my clitoris to orgasm. 'He told me to be at his place by ten-thirty.'

'Don't go,' I replied firmly. 'Stay at home and don't answer the door or the phone.'

'But . . .'

'Do as I say, Lisa. I'll ring you later.'

'If I'm not to answer the phone, then . . .'

'Don't answer the phone before midday, OK?'

'OK. What's going on?'

'I'll tell you later.'

'All right, I'll wait for you to ring.'

My cunt aching, my clitoris painfully swollen in arousal, I desperately needed sex. Mat was arriving at eleven, expecting me to be in full flight with Den and Lisa in the lounge. If I changed the venue at the last minute . . . A million thoughts gnawed at my tormented mind, like a physical pain. I couldn't think straight, decide what to do. Checking my watch every five minutes, I realized that I was becoming neurotic and finally rang Den.

'I was going to ring you,' he said, darkly menacing.

'Den, I need sex,' I breathed, softly, sexily.

'So do I! You really are a horny little tart, aren't you?'

'You've made me the way I am.'

'Look, I've one or two things to do . . . I'll be round about ten-thirty, OK?'

'No, don't come here. I'll come to your place.'

'Er . . . Well, I . . .'

'What's the matter?'

'Nothing, nothing's the matter. OK, be here at . . . at a quarter to eleven.'

'That's an odd time.'

'It fits in nicely with my plans, with my work.'

'Right, I'll be there.'

So far so good. Den would ring Mat and tell him about the new arrangement, and I'd change it at the last minute. But where to? Where the hell could I have sex with Den? With Mat lurking . . . I had to get rid of Mat. My insatiable clitoris screaming for attention, I had an idea. Scurrying round to Den's house, I rang the bell. He opened the door, his dark eyes frowning as he stared at me, wondering what I was doing there, what I wanted.

'You're too early,' he complained.

'It's never too early for sex,' I grinned salaciously.

'No, but . . .'

'If you don't want me, then I'll . . .'

'It's not that. Can't you come back later, as we'd arranged?'

'I might have to go out, I can't be sure that I'll be around later.'

'Look, it's rather awkward. I've made plans and . . .'

'As you're obviously not interested, I'll go and find someone else to satisfy me.'

'No, no. Er . . . Come in.'

Following him into his lounge, I realized that he might sneak off into another room and ring Mat. I was right. As I unbuttoned my blouse, he made some excuse or other to go to the kitchen. There was no way I was going to have Mat catch me with my knickers down! Grabbing Den, I licked my lips seductively and grinned at him.

'I want you now!' I said, massaging his crotch.

'I'll only be a minute. I'm just going to . . .'

'I can't wait a second, let alone a minute! Suck my

nipples, Den! Suck them hard!' I ordered him, slipping my blouse over my shoulders and jutting my swollen melons forward. Now who was in control?

His hot mouth closing over my breast bud, I gasped as he gently nibbled my sensitive teat. Tugging my skirt down as my cunt milk flowed in rivers down my inner thighs, I slipped my fingers between my ballooning love lips and massaged my erect clitoris. Letting out low moans of pleasure as the sensations ran through my quivering pelvis, I instructed Den to masturbate me, to finger-fuck me.

'You're a horny little bitch!' he chuckled as my elongated nipple slipped out of his mouth. 'Is this what you want?' he asked, his fingers driving deep into my wet cunt.

'God, yes!' I sighed as he stretched me open, massaging my inner flesh.

'You want my cock up your cunt, don't you?'

'Yes, and up my arsehole,' I whimpered, delighting in my dirty words, my crudity. 'I want your cock, your fingers, your tongue! Use me, Den! Really use me!'

Wailing my appreciation as he managed to slip more fingers into my tight cunt, I decided to have him believe that the ultimate goal was closer than ever. Perhaps it *was*, I reflected, imagining Mat's solid cock ramming deep into my arse while Den shafted my tight cunt. Would I enjoy licking Lisa's clitoris to orgasm as Mat fucked her kittenish pussy? I'd never watched Mat fuck another woman, perhaps it would turn me on. The ultimate goal – ultimate sex.

'If only Mat were as good as you!' I gasped as Den bit my nipple and thrust his fingers in and out of my steaming sex cauldron. 'It would be great to have the two of you fucking me at the same time, one up my arse and the other screwing my cunt. I'd like to suck both your knobs, drink your spunk as you both mouth-fuck me.'

My crude words obviously exciting Den, he slipped his

drenched fingers out of my sex sheath and knelt before me. Stretching my hairless love lips wide apart, he licked the entire length of my pink groove, his tongue repeatedly sweeping over my throbbing clitoris, sending electrifying sensations through my contracting womb. His hand groping between my parted thighs, I clung to his head as he drove a finger deep into my tight bottom-hole. Managing to slip two fingers into my cunt, he began his thrusting, pistoning my two sex ducts as he licked and sucked my clitoris.

'Coming!' I cried in my ecstasy as my vaginal muscles tightened and my arsehole gripped his finger. 'Suck me, finger me!' Grinding my vulval flesh into his face, forcing my pulsating clitoris into his wet mouth, I swayed on my sagging legs as my orgasm peaked. Whimpering in the agony of my sexual euphoria, my sexual delirium, I tossed my head back as he sustained my climax, fingering my lust holes, licking my clitoris, taking me to my sexual heaven.

Pinching my erect nipples to heighten my pleasure, my cunt milk spurting from my vagina, I rode the crest of my incredible climax until my legs juddered and I crumpled to the floor, drowning in my ecstasy. On my back, with Den's fingers embedded deep within my arse, my cunt, I writhed as the torturous sensations of sex began to fade.

'You enjoyed that, didn't you?' he chuckled as I gasped in the aftermath of my eruption. His fingers leaving my inflamed sheaths, he slipped his trousers off and knelt either side of my head. Leaning on his hands, his cock hovering over my mouth, his balls swinging, he lowered his body. 'Suck it,' he ordered me, his knob brushing my lips as he swivelled his hips.

Opening my mouth, I took his glans inside and ran my tongue around his silky crown. Rocking his hips, he fucked my mouth, his knob gliding over my snaking tongue, repeatedly driving to the back of my throat as he gasped in his pleasure. I wanted another cock fucking my yearning cunt, and another driving deep into my bowels. I wanted ten men wanking over me, their sperm splattering my naked body. In my ever-deepening thirst for debauchery, I craved crude sex as never before.

Mat would be on his way home soon, I thought abstractedly as Den continued to ram his knob in and out of my gobbling mouth. He'd lurk, waiting for the appointed hour, waiting to pounce and catch me in an adulterous act. Would he be stiff as he pictured me tied down with Den fucking me and Lisa grinding her gaping cunt into my mouth? Did he wank?

'Here it comes!' Den finally gasped, his knob swelling as his spunk jetted from his slit, bathing my snaking tongue. His balls jouncing, he repeatedly thrust into my mouth, pumping out his sperm, mouth-fucking me, using me for his perverse pleasure. I swallowed again and again as his sperm gushed from his throbbing knob, filling my cheeks. His heavy balls draining, he gasped and grunted as I gobbled and licked, sucked and swallowed, delirious in my debauchery.

His glistening cock leaving my mouth, hanging over my face, I lifted my head and lapped up the last of the opaque liquid as it bubbled from his slit. His organ shrinking, I wanked his shaft, desperate to restiffen him, to have him fuck my cunt. 'Come on!' I urged him. 'I want you up my cunt!' Breathing heavily, he moved to one side and lay on the floor, his deflated penis snaking over his huge balls.

'You'll have to give me a minute to recover,' he panted. 'I'll fuck you in a minute.'

'I wish Mat was here,' I murmured. 'I want you both fucking me.'

'God, you're insatiable!' he chuckled.

'It's your doing, Den. You woke my sleeping desires, my dormant craving.'

'And I've done a bloody good job! Would you really like Mat to join in?'

'Yes, I've thought about it often. Evenings of debauched sex. Two beautiful cocks thrusting into my holes, pumping spunk into me, two mouths to suck and lick me, hands all over my naked body. I've thought about it many times.'

'It could be arranged.'

'How?'

'Well, if Mat agrees . . .'

'Mat would never agree to sharing me!'

'You never know, Jane. You never know.'

I knew only too well! I reflected as he knelt between my splayed thighs, his cock reviving as he towered above my naked body. 'Fuck me like you've never fucked me before!' I gasped as he guided his knob between my swollen love lips and drove deep into my yearning cunt. 'Fuck me senseless, Den! Fuck me until my cunt's on fire!'

Driving his penis in and out of my beautiful cunt hole, he fucked me with a vengeance, my naked body gliding across the floor with each thrust. My hands between my parted thighs, I yanked my cunt lips wide open and massaged my ballooning clitoris, the incredible sensations driving me wild. 'Spunk!' I gasped. 'Spunk up my wet cunt!'

'I will!' he cried, his balls slapping my rounded buttocks, his swollen knob battering my cervix. 'I'll spunk up your cunt until you overflow!'

'I want to feel your sperm gushing into my cunt. Fuck me harder!'

His belly slapping mine, his cock ramming into me, jolting my naked body, he grimaced as his sperm jetted from his knob, splattering my cervix, lubricating our illicit fucking. On and on he thrust into me, filling me with his cream until my cunt bubbled and overflowed, our orgasmic milk mingling, running between my buttocks, irrigating my anal rose.

Massaging my orgasm from my pulsating clitoris as he continued his beautiful fucking, I wailed as my climax gripped me, my entire body trembling, my very being drifting in a pool of sex. I wanted more cocks, more sperm, as much dirty sex as I could get. Cunts, knobs, girl juice, sperm . . . I wanted to drown in crude sex.

'God, you're bloody good!' he gasped, his masculine body collapsing on top of me, his cock shrinking within my gripping sex duct. 'I could fuck you three times a day!'

'You will, Den – you will,' I breathed as my climax receded, leaving my trembling body temporarily satisfied.

As he rolled off me, I climbed to my feet, torrents of sperm and cunt milk streaming down my legs as I grabbed my blouse. Dressing, I thought again of Mat. He'd be checking his watch, waiting for the hour of revelation, the hour of the ultimate goal. What should I do? I wondered. Allow him to catch Den fucking me? Or should I go out and ruin their plan?

I thought it best to be alone in the house when Mat arrived. My devious mind devising a plan, I looked down at Den as he lay on the floor, his wet cock limp over his rolling balls. Den up my cunt and Mat up my arse?

'I wonder whether Mat would like to join in?' I murmured pensively.

'I'm sure he would!'

'I'll tell you what I'll do. I'll ring him, get him to come home, and I'll talk to him about it. If I broach the subject carefully, he might . . .'

'I reckon that he'd be only too willing!' Den grinned, leaping to his feet. 'Go home and ring him now.'

'OK. But you must leave this to me, Den. I don't want you butting in, trying to persuade him.'

'I wouldn't dream of it.'

'Don't go phoning him or anything, OK?'

'OK. Let me know . . .'

'When he comes home, if all goes according to plan, I'll ring you. We'll have an afternoon of sex.'

'Great!'

'Right, wish me luck,' I smiled, leaving the room.

So far so good, I mused as I walked up the path and opened the front door. But I still hadn't come to a decision, I reflected as I wandered into the lounge. Pacing the floor, my apprehension rising as the appointed hour drew closer, I knew that I had to calm down and compose myself. The outcome of my talk with Mat would change my life! I had to get my mind together and think straight.

Mat crept into the lounge at eleven o'clock, not a minute before, not a minute after. Looking around the room as I smiled at him, he frowned, holding his hand to his head in his puzzlement. His miserable plan in ruins, I almost felt sorry for him.

'What are you doing here?' I asked innocently.

'Er . . . I . . . Has anyone been to see you?'

'No, should they have done?'

'No, no. I just wondered, that was all. Have you seen Den today?'

'I haven't seen anyone, Mat.'

'Have you been out?'

'No, I've been here all the time. Why all these questions? What's the matter?'

'Nothing, nothing.'

He paced the floor, his head low, his expression pained. Loosening his tie, he stood by the window and gazed at the garden. He'd obviously psyched himself up for the moment, prepared, planned . . . And now? Nothing.

'Mat, sit down. I want to talk to you,' I said as he turned to face me.

'About us?'

'Yes, about us.'

Sinking into his armchair, he checked his watch nervously and asked me the right time. Was there ever a right time? Rechecking the disobedient hands, he looked pathetic, riddled with confusion. Poor Mat, his plan had gone so terribly wrong, and here he was now, anxiously waiting for me to talk about us, our future, our marriage. I remained standing, concerned to give the impression of authority, of power.

'Well?' he frowned.

'I . . . I know everything, Mat,' I began hesitantly.

'Everything about what?'

'About you. You were the perpetrator of the plan.'

'Plan? What plan?'

'The plan to blackmail me, to use me for debased sex and . . .'

'Jane, what *are* you talking about?' he asked, feigning puzzlement as he leapt to his feet. 'Blackmail? Debased sex?'

'You set me up – the magazine photographs, the cassette tape with my so-called confession . . . You framed me.'

'I really have no idea what you're talking about!' he protested.

Pacing the floor again, guilt mirrored in his brown eyes, he was obviously stunned. His hands visibly trembling as he loosened his tie a little more, I could hear his breathing quicken as his anxiety rose. The day had come, the moment of confrontation that I always knew would inevitably arrive.

I drew an intake of breath. 'Your ultimate goal was to

turn me into a nymphomaniac so that you could enjoy perverted sex with me, watch Den fuck me and watch me perform lesbian acts.'

'Watch Den fuck you? Jane, what's he been up to? I'll kill him if he's laid a finger on you!'

'He's done more than that, and you know it!'

'I don't know . . .'

'Seeing as you've been watching, you know exactly what he's done to me.'

What could he say? Rubbing his forehead, he obviously realized that there was no point in denying his involvement. I felt a mixture of sorrow and anger, pity and hatred. But now what? Now that I'd confronted him, what next? Should I allow him to achieve his Nirvana?

'Well, what have you got to say?' I asked.

'Jane, I . . . I don't know what to say.'

'You could try explaining why you did it, why you put me through hell.'

'Our sex life . . . I thought that . . .'

'Was our lovemaking no good? My cunt wasn't enough for you, is that it? You wanted to fuck my arsehole, didn't you?'

'Don't use that word.'

' "Don't use that word?" That's rich, coming from you!'

'I'm sorry. I suppose I thought that the sex would change you, make you more adventurous in bed.'

'It *has* changed me, Mat.'

'Yes, I know. I thought we'd be better together, sexually. I thought that, with Den and Lisa, we might discover new pleasures, bring some excitement into our sex lives. That was the plan.'

'And your plan worked very well. I enjoy lesbian sex, I enjoy having one man after another, several men at the same time. Oh yes, your plan worked all right.'

'So . . . You mean that . . .'

'I mean your plan worked, you achieved what you set out to achieve. I'm now a bisexual nymphomaniac.'

'Why tell me all this now?'

'Because I don't want to have to pretend any more. The so-called blackmail, the threats . . . I don't want to have to go on play-acting.'

'So, things are OK?'

'Things could never be better as far as I'm concerned.'

'That's great!'

His face glowing, I don't think he could believe his luck. But what was I doing? I'd still not come to a decision. Mat now thought that we were okay together, that we were going to enjoy group sex, naked romps with Den and Lisa. What did I want? I didn't know.

'You and Den put me through hell,' I said angrily.

'We went too far, I realize that,' he admitted, his head low again. 'It was supposed to be just Den and me, and then Lisa came on the scene and . . . Well, as I said, we went too far.'

'I'm glad that Lisa came on the scene. She's a lovely girl, we get on great together.'

'I know that!' he chuckled. 'So, you have no regrets?'

'I'm more than pleased by the way things have turned out. I'm a new woman, I enjoy sex to the full, and I wouldn't want to turn the clock back.'

'That's great, Jane! I'm sorry for all the things you had to endure, but I'm over the moon because it's all worked out so well.'

'So am I, Mat. So am I.'

As he answered his mobile phone, I wandered over to the window and looked out at the front garden. The weeds were prolific, the daisies spreading like wild-fire through the long grass. *Daisy chains. Chains of bondage*. When I was young

I'd masturbated in my bed, my fingers between my hairless lips massaging my ripe clitoris to orgasm. When I was young . . . I wanted to masturbate now, to bring myself off. The garden hoe? No, later.

'I've got to go to work,' Mat said, slipping his phone into his pocket. 'I've had so much time off recently that I'm going to be in trouble if I'm not careful. I wish I had more time, there's a lot to talk about.'

'Yes, there is.'

'How did you find out about the plan?'

'A shrewd guess, intuition. I put two and two together.'

'Oh, right. Shit, I'd better go. This evening . . . This evening we'll have some fun, celebrate our new way of life, our new beginning.'

'OK, I'll see you later.'

'I'll get some wine. I . . . I love you, Jane.'

Love? That was a rich one. He didn't know the meaning of the word! Did I? As he smugly left the room, I realized that I still had time to come to a decision. Again, I thought that the best thing that could happen would be for Mat to leave. Love? No, I felt no love for him, not after all he'd put me through. He wanted a dirty bitch who'd revel in perverted sex, not a loving wife. I'd become a dirty bitch, but I didn't want perverted sex with Mat. I didn't need him. And I didn't want to be anyone's loving wife.

I wandered aimlessly around the house. One hour, two . . . Mat would definitely have to go, I finally decided. But how? How could I get him to leave me? I couldn't envisage him walking away from me, his wife, his home – not for anything. But there had to be a way.

Answering the phone, I was pleased to hear Lisa. 'What's happening?' she asked excitedly. 'I thought you were going to ring me.'

'Yes, I was about to.'

'Den rang me.'

'I told you not to answer the phone, Lisa.'

'It was after midday, I thought it was you.'

'What did he say?'

'He said that he'd spoken to your husband and . . .'

'To my husband?'

'Yes, he said you're having an orgy this evening and he asked me to come.'

'I am *not* having an orgy! Sorry, I didn't mean to shout. Lisa, if I managed to get rid of my husband, would you come and live with me?'

'Yes, I'd love to!'

'Don't get too excited, I don't know whether I can get him out of the house yet. I'll ring you later, OK?'

'OK. Do your best, Jane. I'd really like to live with you.'

'Yes, I will. Just be patient.'

'I'll wait for you to ring.'

'All right.'

I sat on the sofa contemplating, listening to my whispering thoughts as I waited for the time to pass. My hand between my thighs, I massaged my erect clitoris, recalling the debauched sex, the spunking cocks. How to get rid of Mat? Would my thoughts tell me?

My orgasm suddenly erupting, shaking me to the core, I slipped two fingers into my drenched cunt as I massaged my clitoris faster. I didn't need Mat, I had my fingers, the hoe, the doorknob . . . But I needed Lisa, I knew, as I elicited my enveloping climax, frantically fingering my cunt, appeasing my engorged pleasure nodule.

Finally relaxing in the wake of my beautiful eruption, I sucked my fingers clean, savouring the exquisite blend of Den's sperm and my sex milk. I wanted Lisa there, her head between my thighs, her tongue between my love lips. I wanted my tongue up her cunt, both tongue-fucking each other, writhing in our electric sixty-nine lesbian sex-circuit. But there was plenty of time to enjoy her skittish delights.

'It's me!' Mat called excitedly on his arrival. Slamming the front door shut, he bustled into the lounge clutching a bottle of wine and a bunch of flowers. I smiled at him, wondering what to say. Out of the blue, a wicked idea held me as he placed the wine and flowers on the coffee table. My racing thoughts had finally whispered the answer. I now had my own ultimate goal.

'Mat, this plan of yours,' I began.

'Yes?'

'As I said earlier, it's worked.'

'You're telling me it's worked!' he beamed. 'I thought I'd invite Den round, and Lisa.'

'Wait a minute, I haven't finished. Do you really believe that I'd allow our neighbour, a virtual stranger, to use me as he did just because he threatened to show you some crummy men's magazine?'

'What do you mean?'

'A shoddy photograph of a girl exhibiting her cunt . . . Admittedly, there's a slight resemblance, but do you honestly think that I'd succumb to blackmail?'

'But you did.'

'Do you think that I'd suck men's cocks, drink their spunk, allow men to fuck my arse, my cunt, my mouth . . . Do you believe that I'd allow ten men to wank over me, shower me with spunk, just to save my marriage?'

'I don't understand, Jane.'

'No, of course you don't.'

'You did all that because you enjoyed it, you became turned on and . . . You loved every minute of it.'

'Your plan had one flaw in it, Mat. One fatal flaw.'

'A flaw?'

'The evening Den came round to dinner. I knew that you were going to pretend to go out for cigars.'

'How? There's no way you could have known.'

'Den told me.'

'What?'

'When you went to check the food and left us alone in the lounge, he told me.'

'Of course he didn't!'

'I've known everything from day one. From the day Den brought that magazine round, he's told me everything.'

'But . . . Why would he tell you? I don't believe it! The whole idea was to . . . There's no way he'd have said anything, Jane.'

'He told me that you were going to make out that you were going to look at a computer, and that I was to suck you off through the hole in the fence. He told me that you fucked my arse when I was tied up and blindfolded beneath the apple tree. He told me that you were going to fuck my arse when I was tied over the back of the armchair, that you were going to watch him shove a cucumber up my arse.'

'Why? Why did he tell you? I don't understand.'

'Do you know what your plan did?'

'Yes, of course. It changed you from a . . .'

'I'd been screwing Den since the day he moved in next door. All your plan did was allow us to have sex without having to worry about you catching us.'

'What? You were having an affair all along?'

'Yes, I was. Your pathetic plan was the best thing that could have happened. Den could come here and fuck me, I could go to his place for sex – and we didn't have to worry about you.'

'You're a bitch! And he's a fucking bastard!'

'And what are you? You're the biggest bastard of all! We laughed at you behind your back. We allowed you to watch us fucking on the odd occasion, even allowed you to join in, just to keep you happy. God, did we laugh at you! I'll tell you this – I was going to end the affair. It was a stupid mistake, succumbing to Den's charms, and I didn't want our marriage to end. The day Den came round with the magazine I was going to tell him that it was over, that I loved you and wanted only you. But because of your evil plan, I carried on screwing Den.'

'I've never known such an evil bitch as you! My God, I'm at work, and you're fucking our next-door neighbour behind my back? You dirty whore!'

'Yes, I am a dirty whore – and you're the one who made me what I am!'

'Since Den moved in, you were fucking him, sucking spunk from his cock?'

'I was doing far more than that while you were at work! He'd fucked my arse, my cunt, my mouth . . .'

'You two-timing bitch! Every day when I came in from work and kissed you, you'd been swallowing that bastard's spunk! When we made love, he'd been shoving his cock up your dirty cunt!'

'Funny how things turn out, isn't it?'

'I'm leaving you, Jane. Never have I known a cow like you! My plan was to bring us closer together, make our sex lives better and . . .'

'Bring us closer together? Other men fucking me, whipping me, a girl licking my cunt while I was forced to lick her cunt . . . *That's* bringing us closer together?'

'No wonder you were all for it! You were nothing but a filthy whore in the first place! I'm going up to pack!'

'Good!'

As he bounded upstairs and started banging around in the bedroom I gazed out of the window. I felt dreadful, but I'd done it – successfully disposed of Mat. If he asked Den about the affair, which I knew he wouldn't, Den would deny the whole thing. There'd be a massive row and Mat would probably punch Den in the face. Whatever happened, I didn't care – I was free at last. They could kill each other as far as I was concerned!

Ringing Lisa, I told her to pack her case and come over. She was over the moon, like an excited child at Christmas. She was a child at heart, I knew. But she'd be good company, and good in bed. What Carole would say about my live-in lesbian lover, I had no idea! Poor Carole, I'd taken her husband, his penis – his spunk. Still, all's fair in lust and sex.

I grinned as Mat lugged a suitcase downstairs and stomped through the hall. I watched him through the lounge window as he dumped the case in the boot of his car before going up to the bedroom for more of his things. It was a sad sight, but he deserved all that had come to him. Lugging another case downstairs, he burst into the lounge and opened the bureau.

'I've been stuffing thousands into our joint account for our future,' he growled, slipping our cheque book into his pocket. 'But you needn't think I'm giving you a bloody penny! You can starve for all I care! And you'll have to move out because I'm selling the house!'

'You're forgetting that my aunt left me this house. It's in my name,' I smiled.

'Bitch!'

'Oh, I forgot to tell you. I took all the money out of our account.'

'What? You fucking bitch!'

'Yes, I do believe I am. By the way, Lisa's moving in with me.'

'You're a fucking lesbian!'

'Yes, thanks to you, I am. I fuck, and I'm a lesbian.'

'You'll be sorry, you'll see! It won't be long before you'll be begging me to come back. You'll soon get fed up with the next-door bastard.'

'Oh, no. No, I'm not interested in Den any more. I have Lisa and my college friends. I don't want Den – or you.'

'I can't believe it, Jane. Having an affair with that bastard, ruining our marriage, our future . . . I really can't believe it!'

'I must admit that I had some difficulty believing that you'd set me up, that you got your perverted kicks by watching three men fuck my mouth, my cunt and my arsehole.'

'Listen to you, the way you're talking. You're nothing more than a common slut!'

'That's me! Den and I used to fuck in the garden, in our bed, in the lounge, over the kitchen table . . . I'll tell you what I liked most of all. I liked him fucking my arsehole – his beautiful cock spunking up my tight arse.'

'Dirty cow!'

'When you used to fuck me – I should say, attempt to fuck me – I used to pretend that you were Den. It was the only way I could come. When you used to lick my cunt and tell me how wet I was, it was Den's spunk that you were lapping up, not my cunt juice.'

'You disgust me!'

'From the day he moved in next door, the minute you went to work he'd come round and we'd enjoy sixty-nine on the lawn. He'd spunk in my mouth and I'd squirt my cunt milk into his. Then we'd fuck like there was no tomorrow.'

'You dirty, filthy, vile bitch!'

'Your plan gave us the opportunity to have all the sex we wanted.'

'Goodbye, Jane. And good riddance!'

'Goodbye, Mat. And thanks for all you've done!'

As the front door slammed shut, I breathed a sigh of relief. Watching Mat climb into his car and drive off, I wondered about the furniture, the rest of his belongings. Would he come back to collect his things? Would he want half the furniture? I didn't know, or care. I'd won, if there was a winner.

When Lisa turned up with her case, the first thing I ordered her to do was strip off. 'You'll be naked at all times,' I smiled, holding her shoulders. 'When we go out together, you'll wear only a gymslip and blouse. Oh, and white ankle socks. I'll buy the clothes tomorrow.'

'OK,' she smiled sweetly, unbuttoning her blouse.

'Take your case up to our bedroom and then join me in the garden.'

Wandering out onto the patio, I slipped my skirt and blouse off. My cunt oozing with Den's sperm, I decided to have Lisa cleanse me, suck and lick me clean. She'd become my sex slave, attend me, my feminine needs and desires. I wouldn't share her with the college men, not with anyone. She was mine, all mine.

'Hi!' Den grinned as he walked around the side of the house. 'God, you look horny! How did it go with Mat?'

'Mat's gone,' I replied, jutting my naked breasts forward.

'Gone?'

'For good, thank God. Lisa's moved in with me, she'll be down in a minute.'

'Christ, I didn't think . . .'

'No, neither did Mat. I'm entertaining my college friends this evening. Or, I should say, they'll be entertaining me.'

'God, you've moved fast.'

'What are you doing this evening, Den?'

'Well, nothing. I'd love to . . .'

'Ah, Lisa, there you are,' I smiled as she stepped out of

the back door, exhibiting her fresh, naked body. 'You look lovely.'

'Thanks.'

'God, you look beautiful!' Den gasped, eyeing her pert breasts, her hairless pussy swelling beneath the slight curve of her stomach. 'I can hardly believe my luck! Two naked beauties living next door to me!'

'It's a funny thing, luck,' I said softly.

'Yes, it is. So, what time . . .'

'What did you say you were doing this evening, Den?'

'Nothing, so . . .'

'Well, I hope there's something good on television. Poor old you, having to spend the evening alone.'

'But I thought . . .'

'Come on, Lisa, let's go inside.'

Leaving Den standing open-mouthed in the garden, I closed and locked the back door. *Two losers*, I reflected leading Lisa into the lounge. Sitting on the sofa with my thighs wide apart as the phone rang, I instructed her to lick me, to tongue-fuck my yearning cunt.

'Hallo,' I purred, pressing the receiver to my ear as her eager tongue entered me.

'It's me,' Mat hissed. 'I'm just ringing to say that . . .'

'Ah, ah! Yes!' I sighed. 'Sorry, Mat – Lisa's tonguing my cunt. What was it you wanted?'

'My God, you're a filthy bitch! You've changed beyond all . . .'

'Thanks to you, Mat, I *have* changed. Now, if you don't mind, I want to enjoy Lisa's intimate attention. Goodbye.'

Moaning my unrestrained pleasure, I lowered my gaze to my splayed thighs, to my glistening cuntal butterfly wings, spread to a vibrant shade of red. Lisa's predatory female tongue snaking the length and breadth of my open pupa, I knew there could be no turning back. Ensnared, laid bare, violated, the old Jane was gone forever. Quivering, preparing to soar as my sensitive soft core palpitated, I had metamorphosed into a creature unknown to me. And from my noisy summit I heard a distant whisper.

I am not what I once was, nor ever again will be.